Praise for beloved romance author Betty Neels

"Neels is especially good at painting her scenes with choice words, and this adds to the charm of the story."
—*USATODAY.com's Happy Ever After* blog on *Tulips for Augusta*

"Betty Neels surpasses herself with an excellent storyline, a hearty conflict and pleasing characters."
—*RT Book Reviews* on *The Right Kind of Girl*

"Once again Betty Neels delights readers with a sweet tale in which love conquers all."
—*RT Book Reviews* on *Fate Takes a Hand*

"One of the first Harlequin authors I remember reading. I was completely enthralled by the exotic locales... Her books will always be some of my favorites to re-read."
—*Goodreads* on *A Valentine for Daisy*

"I just love Betty Neels!... If you like a good old-fashioned romance...you can't go wrong with this author."
—*Goodreads* on *Caroline's Waterloo*

Romance readers around the world were sad to note the passing of **Betty Neels** in June 2001. Her career spanned thirty years, and she continued to write into her ninetieth year. To her millions of fans, Betty epitomized the romance writer, and yet she began writing almost by accident. She had retired from nursing, but her inquiring mind still sought stimulation. Her new career was born when she heard a lady in her local library bemoaning the lack of good romance novels. Betty's first book, *Sister Peters in Amsterdam*, was published in 1969, and she eventually completed 134 books. Her novels offer a reassuring warmth that was very much a part of her own personality. She was a wonderful writer, and she is greatly missed. Her spirit and genuine talent live on in all her stories.

BETTY NEELS

A Good Wife &
Britannia All at Sea

HHARLEQUIN® SPECIAL RELEASE

ISBN-13: 978-1-335-04513-3

A Good Wife & Britannia All at Sea

Copyright © 2019 by Harlequin Books S.A.

The publisher acknowledges the copyright holder of the individual works as follows:

A Good Wife
Copyright © 1999 by Betty Neels

Britannia All at Sea
Copyright © 1977 by Betty Neels

Recycling programs for this product may not exist in your area.

Printed in U.S.A.

CONTENTS

A GOOD WIFE

was half hidden by a small wood, the hills were close by and beyond them lay the quiet countryside. The church clock struck seven and she withdrew her head and set about getting dressed, then skimmed downstairs to the kitchen to make the early-morning tea.

The kitchen was large, with a lamentable lack of up-to-date equipment. There was a scrubbed wooden table ringed around by sturdy chairs, an old-fashioned gas cooker flanking a deep sink and a vast dresser along one wall. There was a shabby rug in front of the cooker and two Windsor chairs, in one of which there was a small tabby cat to whom Serena wished a good morning before she put on the kettle. The one concession to modernity was a cumbersome fridge which, more often than not, ran amok.

Serena left the kettle to boil and went to the front door to fetch the post. There was a small pile of letters in the post box, and just for a moment she pretended that they were all for her. They weren't, of course: bills, several legal-looking envelopes, a catalogue or two, and, just as she had expected, two birthday cards for herself. And no card from Gregory. But she hadn't really expected one from him; he had made it plain to her on several occasions that birthdays were scandalously overpriced and a waste of money. Gregory didn't believe in wasting money; her father and brothers approved of him for that reason. Serena wasn't sure of that, but she hoped in a vague way that when they married she would be able to change his frugal ways.

She went back to the kitchen and made the tea, offered milk to the cat and, as the clock struck the half hour, took a tray of tea up to her father's room.

This was a large, gloomy apartment with heavy old-fashioned furniture, closely curtained against the morning brightness. She tweaked one curtain aside as she crossed the room, the better to see the occupant in the vast bed.

Mr Lightfoot matched the room, gloomy and the epitome of a late-Victorian gentleman, whiskers and all. He sat up in bed, not speaking, and when Serena wished him good morning, he grunted a reply.

'A good morning for some,' he observed, 'but for those who suffer as I do, daylight is merely the solace after a sleepless night.'

Serena put the tray down and handed him his letters. That her father's snores shattered the peace of the house was something on which there was no point in remarking. She had long ago learned that the only way in which to live with him was to allow his words to flow over her head. She said now, 'It's my birthday, Father.'

He was opening his letters. 'Oh, yes? Why have the gas company sent me another bill? Gross carelessness.'

'Perhaps you didn't pay the first one?'

'Don't be ridiculous, Serena. I have always paid my bills promptly.'

'But it is possible to make a mistake,' said Serena, and took herself out of the room, wondering for the thousand and first time how her mother could have lived with such a tiresome man. She herself very often found life quite intolerable, living here with him, doing almost all of the housework, cooking and shopping and

looking after him. He had for some time now declared
that he was an invalid, and he led an invalid's life with
no concern for her.

Since Dr Bowring had said that there was nothing
wrong with him he had refused to see him again, declaring that he knew far better what was wrong with
him than any doctor. So he had devised his own treatment for his illness, having declared that he was suffering from a weak heart and congestion of the lungs.
He had over the years added lumbago to these, which
gave him every reason to take to his bed whenever he
wished to do so.

It hadn't been so bad when her mother had been
alive. They had had a housekeeper, and between the two
of them Serena and her mother had devised a routine
which had allowed them enough freedom; there had
been a certain amount of social life for them. Serena
had had her tennis parties and small dances at friends'
houses, and her mother had been able to play bridge
and enjoy coffee with her friends. Then her mother had
fallen ill and died without fuss or complaint, only asking Serena to look after her father. And, since Serena
had known that her mother had loved her despot of a
husband, she had promised that she would. That had
been five years ago…

Her life since then had altered dramatically: the
housekeeper had been dismissed; Serena, her father
had declared, was quite capable of running the house
with the help of a woman from the village who came
twice a week for a few hours. What else was there for
her to do? he'd wanted to know, when she had pointed

out that the house wasn't only large, it was devoid of any labour-saving devices. Sitting in his armchair by his bedroom window, wrapped in rugs, with a small table beside him bearing all the accepted aids to invalidism, he had dismissed her objections with a wave of the hand.

Since she had to account for every penny of the housekeeping allowance he gave her each month she'd had no chance to improve things. True, there was a washing machine, old now, and given to rather frightening eruptions and sinister clankings, and there was central heating in some of the rooms. But this was turned off at the end of March and not started again until October. Since the plumber from Yeovil came each half year and turned it on and off, there wasn't much she could do about that.

Serena, recognising the brick wall she was up against, had decided sensibly to make the best of things. After all, Gregory Pratt, a junior partner in the solicitors' firm in Sherborne, had hinted on several occasions that he was considering marrying her at some future date. She liked him well enough, although she had once or twice found herself stifling a yawn when he chose to entertain her with a resumé of his day's work, but she supposed that she would get used to that in time.

When he brought her flowers, and talked vaguely about their future together, she had to admit to herself that it would be nice to marry and have a home and her own children. She wasn't in love with Gregory, but she liked him, and although like any other girl she dreamed of being swept off her feet by some magnificent man, she thought it unlikely that it would happen to her.

Her mother, when she'd been alive, had told her that she was a *jolie laide*, but her father had always been at pains to tell her that she was downright plain, an opinion upheld by her brothers, so that she had come to think of herself as just that—a round face, with a small nose and a wide mouth, dominated by large brown eyes and straight light brown hair worn long, in a rather careless knot on top of her head. That her mouth curved sweetly and her eyes had thick curling lashes was something she thought little of, nor did she consider her shape, pleasingly plump, to be much of an asset. Since Gregory had never, as far as she could re-member, commented upon her appearance, there had been no one to make her think otherwise.

She went back to the kitchen and boiled an egg for her breakfast, and put her two cards on the mantelpiece. 'I am twenty-six, Puss,' she said, addressing the tabby cat, 'and since it is my birthday I shall do no house-work; I shall go for a walk—up Barrow Hill.'

She finished her breakfast, tidied the kitchen, put everything ready for lunch and went to get her father's breakfast tray.

He was reading his paper and didn't look up. 'I'll have a little ham for lunch, and a few slices of thin toast. My poor appetite gives me concern, Serena, although I cannot hope that you share that concern.'

'Well, you had a splendid breakfast,' Serena pointed out cheerfully. 'Egg, bacon, toast and marmalade, and coffee. And, of course, if you got up and had a walk that would give you an appetite.'

She gave him a kindly smile; he was an old tyrant, greedy and selfish, but her mother had asked her to look after him. Besides, she felt sorry for him, for he was missing so much from life. 'I'm going out for a walk,' she told him. 'It's a lovely morning…'

'A walk? And am I to be left alone in the house?'

'Well, when I go to the shops you're alone, aren't you? The phone is by the bed, and you can get up if you want and go downstairs for a change.'

She reached the door. 'I'll be back for coffee,' she told him.

She fetched a jacket—an elderly garment she kept for gardening—found stout shoes, put a handful of biscuits into a pocket and left the house. Barrow Hill looked nearer than it was, but it was still early. She turned away from the road leading down to the village, climbed a stile and took the footpath beside a field of winter wheat.

It was a gentle climb to start with, and she didn't hurry. The trees and hedges were in leaf, there were lambs bleating and birds singing and the sky was blue, a washed-out blue, dotted with small woolly clouds. She stopped to stare up at it; it was indeed a beautiful morning, and she was glad that she had rebelled against the routine of housework and cooking. No doubt her father would be coldly angry when she got back, but nothing he could say would spoil her pleasure now.

The last bit of Barrow Hill was quite steep, along a path bordered by thick undergrowth, but presently it

opened out onto rough ground covered in coarse grass
and strewn with rocks, offering a splendid view of the
surrounding countryside. It was a solitary spot, but she
saw that today she was going to have to share it with
someone else. A man was sitting very much at ease on
one of the larger rocks—the one, she noticed crossly,
which she considered her own.

He had turned round at the sound of her careful
progress through the stones and grass tufts, and now
he stood up. A very tall man, with immensely broad
shoulders, wearing casual tweeds. As she went towards
him she saw that he was a handsome man too, but past
his first youth. Nearer forty than thirty, she reflected
as she wished him good morning, casting a look at her
rock as she did so.

His 'Good morning,' was cheerful. 'Am I trespass-
ing on your rock?'

She was rather taken aback. 'Well, it's not my rock,
but whenever I come up here I sit on it.'

He smiled, and she found herself smiling back. He
had a nice smile and it was unexpected, for his features
were forbidding in repose—a powerful nose, heavy-
lidded blue eyes and a thin mouth above the decidedly
firm chin. Not a man to treat lightly, she thought.

She sat down without fuss on the rock, and he sat on
a tree stump some yards away. He said easily, 'I didn't
expect to find anyone here. It's quite a climb...'

'Not many people come up here for that reason, and,
of course, those living in the village mostly go to Yeovil
to work each day. In the summer sometimes people

come and picnic. Not often, though, for they can't bring a car near enough...'

'So you have it to yourself?'

She nodded. 'But I don't come as often as I would like to...'

'You work in Yeovil too?'

He asked the question so gently that she answered, 'Oh, no. I live at home.'

He glanced at her hands, lying idly in her lap. Small hands, roughened by work, not the hands of a lady of leisure. She caught his glance and said in a matter-of-fact way, 'I look after my father and run the house.'

'And you have escaped? Just for a while?'

'Well, yes. You see, it's my birthday...'

'Then I must wish you a very happy day.' When she didn't reply, he added, 'I expect you will be celebrating this evening? A party? Family?'

'No. My brothers and their families don't live very close to us.'

'Ah, well—but there is always the excitement of the postman, isn't there?'

She agreed so bleakly that he began to talk about the country around them; a gentle flow of conversation which soothed her, so that presently she was able to tell him some of the local history and point out the landmarks.

But a glance at her watch set her on her feet. 'I must go.' She smiled at him. 'I enjoyed talking to you. I do hope you will enjoy your stay here.'

He got up and wished her a pleasant goodbye, and

if she had half hoped that he would suggest going back to the village with her she was disappointed.

It had been pleasant, she reflected, going hurriedly back along the path. He had seemed like an old friend, and she suspected that she had talked too much. But that wouldn't matter; she wasn't likely to see him again. He had told her casually that he was a visitor. And now she came to think of it he hadn't sounded quite English...

She reached the house a little out of breath; her father had his coffee at eleven o'clock each morning and it was five minutes to the hour. She put the kettle on, still in her jacket, and ground the beans, then kicked off her shoes, smoothed her hair, laid a tray and, once more her quiet self, went up to her father's room.

He was sitting in his great armchair by the window, reading. He looked up as she went in. 'There you are. Gregory telephoned. He has a great deal of work. He hopes to see you at the weekend.'

'Did he wish me a happy birthday?' She put down the tray and waited hopefully.

'No. He is a busy man, Serena. I think that you sometimes forget that.' He picked up his book. 'I fancy an omelette for lunch.' He added reprovingly, 'My bed is not yet made; I shall probably need to rest after I have eaten.'

Serena went back downstairs, reminding herself that she had had a few hours of pure pleasure on Barrow Hill; it would be something to think about. She supposed that it was because it was her birthday that she had been so chatty with the stranger there. She blushed at the thought.

'Not that it matters,' she told Puss, offering the small beast sardines from the tin she had opened. 'He doesn't know me from Adam, and I don't know him, though I think he'd be rather a nice person to know. He'll have forgotten all about me...'

However, he hadn't. He walked back to Dr Bowring's house, thinking about her. He had known the doctor and his wife for many years—they had been medical students and she a nurse—creating an easy friendship which had lasted, despite the fact that he lived and worked in Holland. On his occasional visits to England he contrived to see them, although this was the first time he had visited them in Somerset. At lunch he told them of his walk up Barrow Hill.

'And I met a girl there—rather shabby clothes, round face, brown hair—very untidy, nice voice. Said she looked after her father but she'd escaped for an hour or two because it was her birthday.'

'Serena Lightfoot,' chorused his companions. 'A perfect darling,' said Mrs Bowring. 'Her father's the horridest old man I've ever met. Threw George out, didn't he, darling?'

The doctor nodded. 'He's perfectly fit, but has decided to be an invalid for the rest of his life. I'm not allowed in the house, but from what I can glean from the village gossip he spends his days sitting around or lying in bed, enjoying ill health. When his wife died he sacked the housekeeper, and now Serena runs the place with old Mrs Pike going there twice a week. No life for a girl.'

'So why doesn't she leave? She's old enough and wise enough, surely?'

'I've done my best to persuade her to get a job away from home—so has the rector—but it seems that she promised her mother that she would look after him. It's not all gloom and doom though. It's an open secret in the village that Gregory Pratt intends to marry her. He's a partner in a law firm in Sherborne. A prudent man, with an eye on Mr Lightfoot's not inconsiderable financial status and the house—both of which it is presumed he will leave to Serena. She has two brothers, both with incomes of their own and steady positions, but neither of them see much of her or their father, and have let it be known that they neither expect nor want anything when he dies.'

'So is Serena by way of being an heiress?'

'It seems so. Neither her father nor her brothers seem to have mentioned it to her, but I have heard that Gregory is aware of it.'

'So he would have told her, surely?'

'Oh, no. That might give her the idea that he only wants to marry her for her money and the house.'

The Dutchman raised heavy brows. 'And does he?'

'Of course. My dear Ivo! He's not in love with her, I feel sure, and I doubt very much if she is with him, but he's always very attentive if they should go out together, which isn't often, and I think she likes him well enough. She's a sensible girl; she knows she hasn't much in the way of looks, and very little chance of leaving home unless her father dies. Even then she has had little chance to go out into the world and meet people.'

'It's a shame,' said Mrs Bowring, 'for she's great fun and so kind and gentle; she must long for pretty clothes and a chance to meet people of her own age. You've no idea what a job it is to get her here for drinks or dinner. Her wretched father manages to feel ill at the last minute, or he telephones just as we're sitting down to dinner and demands her back home because he's dying.'

They began to talk of other things then, and Serena wasn't spoken of again. Two days later Mr van Doelen drove himself back to London and shortly after, back to Holland.

It was the following Saturday when Gregory called to see Serena, although after greeting her in a somewhat perfunctory fashion he went upstairs to see her father. A man who knew on which side his bread was buttered, and intending to have jam on it too, he lost no opportunity of keeping on good terms with Mr Lightfoot. He spent half an hour or so discussing the stockmarket, and listening with every appearance of serious attention to Mr Lightfoot's pithy remarks about the government, before going back downstairs to the sitting room to find Serena sitting on the floor, doing the *Telegraph* crossword puzzle.

He sat down in one of the old-fashioned armchairs. 'Would you not be more comfortable in a chair, Serena?'

'Do you suppose an etui is the same thing as a small workbag, Gregory?'

He frowned. 'Really, my dear, you ask the most stupid questions.'

'Well, they can't be all that stupid or they wouldn't be in a crossword puzzle.' She sat back on her heels and looked at him. 'You forgot my birthday.'

'Did I? After all, birthdays aren't important, not once one is adult.'

Serena pencilled in a word. Gregory was probably quite right; he so often was—and so tolerant. Her brothers had told her that he would be a good and kind husband. Sometimes, though, she wondered if she would have liked him to be a little more exciting. And why was it that everyone took it for granted that she would marry him?

She said now, 'I should have liked a card, and flowers—a great sheaf of roses in Cellophane tied with ribbon—and a very large bottle of perfume.'

Gregory laughed. 'You really must grow up, Serena. You must have been reading too many novels. You know my opinion about wasting money on meaningless rubbish...'

She pencilled in another word. 'Why should flowers and presents be meaningless rubbish when they are given to someone you love or want to please? Have you ever felt that you wanted to buy me something madly extravagant, Gregory?'

He lacked both imagination and a sense of humour, and besides, he had a high opinion of himself. He said seriously, 'No, I can't say that I have. What would be the point, my dear? If I were to give you a diamond necklace, or undies from Harrods, when would you have the occasion to wear them?'

'So when you buy me a present at Christmas you think first, Now, what can I buy Serena that she can find useful and use each day? Like that thing you gave me for shredding things which takes all day to clean?'

He refused to get annoyed. He gave her an indulgent smile. 'I think you must be exaggerating, Serena. How about a cup of tea? I can't stay long; I'm dining with the head of my department this evening.'

So she fetched the tea, and he told her of his week's work while he drank it and ate several slices of the cake she had baked. Since she had little to say, and that was sensible, he reflected that despite her lack of looks she would be a quite suitable wife for him; he didn't allow himself to dwell on the house and the comfortable inheritance she would have, and which would make her even more suitable.

He went back upstairs to say goodbye to Mr Lightfoot, and presently came down again to give her a peck on a cheek and tell her that he would do his utmost to come and see her the following weekend.

Serena shut the door behind him and gathered up the tea things. She reflected that Gregory wasn't just frugal, he was downright mean. Washing up, impervious to her father's voice demanding attention, she considered Gregory. She wasn't sure when it had first become apparent that he was interested in her. She had felt flattered and prepared to like him, for her life had been dull, and, after a while, her father had signified his approval of him. When her brothers had met him, they had assured her in no uncertain terms that Gregory would be a splendid husband, and she, with the prospect of a life of her own, had allowed herself to agree with them.

But now the years were slipping away, and Gregory, although he talked often enough of when they would marry, had never actually asked her to marry him. He had a steady job, too. Serena being Serena, honest and guileless and expecting everyone else to be the same—except for her father, of course—had never for one moment thought that Gregory was waiting for her father to die, at which point he would marry her and become the owner of the house and a nice little capital. He had no doubt that Serena would be only too glad to let him take over the house and invest her money for her. He didn't intend to be dishonest, she would have all she wanted within reason, but it would be his hand which held the strings of her moneybags.

Of course, Serena knew nothing of this... All the same doubts were beginning to seep into her head. Other thoughts seeped in, too, about the stranger she had talked to so freely on Barrow Hill. She had liked him; it had seemed to her that she had known him for a long time, that he was like an old, trusted friend. Nonsense, of course—but, nonsense or not, his memory stayed clearly in her head.

During the week her elder brother came. His visits were infrequent, although he lived in Yeovil, but, as he pointed out, he was a busy man with little leisure. At Christmas and on his father's birthday he came, with his wife and two children—duty visits no one enjoyed—and every month or so he came briefly. He was very like his father, and they didn't get on well, so the visits were brief. Serena, offering coffee or tea, was always questioned closely as to finances, warned to let him know if she should ever need him, but was never asked if she was happy or content with the life she led. And this visit was like all the others: brief and businesslike with no mention of herself.

Over a second cup of coffee she said, 'I should like a holiday, Henry.'

'A holiday? Whatever for? Really, Serena, you are sometimes quite lacking in sense. You have a pleasant life here; you have friends in the village and leisure. And who is to look after Father if you were to go away?'

'You could pay someone—or your wife Alice could come and stay. You said yourself that you have a splendid au pair who could look after the children.'

Henry's colour had heightened. 'Impossible. Alice has the house to run, and quite a busy social life. Really, Serena, I had no idea that you were so selfish.' He added, 'And the au pair is leaving.'

He went away then, wishing her an austere goodbye, leaving her to go upstairs and discover why her father was shouting for her.

A few days later her younger brother came. Matthew was a gentler version of his brother. He also didn't get on well with his father, but he was a dutiful son, tolerant of Mr Lightfoot's ill temper while at the same time paying no more than duty visits. He was accompanied by his wife, a forceful young woman who was scornful of Serena, whom she considered was hopelessly old-fashioned in her ideas. She came into the house declaring breezily that Serena was neglecting the garden, and did she know there was a tile loose on the porch roof?

'These things need attention,' she pointed out. 'It doesn't do to neglect a house, certainly not one as large as this one. I must say you're very lucky to live so splendidly.'

Serena let that pass, allowing her sister-in-law's voice to flow over her unlistening head while her brother went to see his father. It was while they were having tea that she said, 'Henry came the other day. I told him I wanted a holiday.'

Matthew choked on his cake. 'A holiday? Why, Serena?'

At least he sounded reasonably interested.

'This is a large house, there are six bedrooms, attics, a drawing room, dining room, sitting room, kitchen and two bathrooms. I am expected to keep them all clean and polished with the help of an elderly woman from the village who has rheumatism and can't bend. And there's the garden. I had a birthday a week or so ago—I'm twenty-six—and I think I'm entitled to a holiday.'

Matthew looked thoughtful, but it was his wife who spoke. 'My dear Serena, we would all like holidays, but one has one's duty. After all, you have only yourself and your father to care for, and uninterrupted days in which to arrange your tasks to please yourself.'

'But I don't please myself,' said Serena matter-of-factly. 'I have to please Father.'

Matthew said, 'Well, it does seem to me to be quite reasonable... You have spoken to Henry...?'

'Yes, he thinks it's a silly idea.'

Matthew was at heart a good man, but under his brother and his wife's thumbs. He said, 'Oh, well, in that case I don't think you should think any more about it, Serena.'

When Serena said nothing, he added, 'I dare say you see a good deal of Gregory?' Then he said, 'A steady young man. You could do worse, Serena.'

'Well, I dare say I could do better,' said Serena flippantly. 'Only I never meet any other men.'

She had a sudden memory of the man on Barrow Hill.

Gregory came at the weekend. She hadn't expected him and, since it was a wet, dreary day, had decided to turn out a kitchen cupboard. Her untidy appearance caused him to frown as he pecked her cheek.

'Must you look like a drudge on a Saturday morning?' he wanted to know. 'Surely that woman who comes to clean could do the work in the kitchen?'

Serena tucked back a strand of hair behind an ear. 'She comes twice a week for two hours. In a house this size it barely gives her time to do the kitchen and bathrooms and Hoover. I didn't expect you...'

'Obviously. I have brought you some flowers.'

He handed her daffodils wrapped in Cellophane with the air of a man conferring a diamond necklace.

Serena thanked him nicely and forebore from mentioning that there were daffodils running riot in the garden. It's the thought that counts, she reminded herself as she took off her pinny. 'I'll make some coffee. Father has had his.'

'I'll go and see him presently.' Gregory added carefully, 'Henry tells me that you want to go on holiday.'

She was filling the kettle. 'Yes. Don't you think I deserve one? Can you think of somewhere I might go? I might meet people and have fun?'

Gregory said severely, 'You are being facetious, Serena. I cannot see why you should need to go away. You have a lovely home here, with every comfort, and you can please yourself as to how you organise your days.'

She turned to look at him. He was quite serious, she decided, and if she had expected him to back her up she was to be disappointed.

'You make it sound as though I spend my days sitting in the drawing room doing nothing, but you must know that that isn't true.'

'My dear Serena, would you be happy doing that? You are a born housewife and a splendid housekeeper; you will make a good wife.' He smiled at her. 'And now how about that coffee?'

He went to see her father presently, and she began to get lunch ready. Her father had demanded devilled kidneys on toast and a glass of the claret he kept in the dining room sideboard under lock and key. If Gregory intended to stay for lunch, he would have to have scrambled eggs and soup. Perhaps he would take her out? Down to the pub in the village where one could get delicious pasties…

Wishful thinking. He came into the kitchen, saying importantly that he needed to go to the office.

'But it's Saturday…'

He gave her a tolerant look. 'Serena, I take my job

seriously; if it means a few hours' extra work even on a Saturday, I do not begrudge it. I will do my best to see you next Saturday.'

'Why not tomorrow?'

His hesitation was so slight that she didn't notice it. 'I promised mother that I would go and see her—sort out her affairs for her—she finds these things puzzling.'

His mother, reflected Serena, was one of the toughest old ladies she had ever encountered, perfectly capable of arranging her affairs to suit herself. But she said nothing; she was sure that Gregory was a good son.

On Sunday, with the half-hope that she might see the stranger again, she walked up to the top of Barrow Hill, but there was no one there. Moreover, the early-morning brightness had clouded over and it began to rain. She went back to roast the pheasant her father had fancied for his lunch, and then spent the afternoon with Puss, listening to the radio.

While she listened she thought about her future. She couldn't alter it for the moment, for she had given her word to her mother, but there was no reason why she shouldn't try and learn some skill, something she could do at home. She was handy with her needle, but she didn't think there was much future in that; maybe she could learn how to use a computer—it seemed that was vital for any job. There were courses she could take at home, but how to get hold of a computer?

Even if she found something, where would she get the money to pay for it? She had to account for every penny of the housekeeping money her father gave her each month, and when she had asked him for an allowance so that she might buy anything she needed for herself, he had told her to buy what she needed and have the bill sent to him. But to buy toothpaste and soap and expect the shopkeeper to send a bill for such a trivial purchase really wasn't possible, so she managed to add these items to the household bills from the village shop.

Since she hardly ever went out socially, she contrived to manage with her small wardrobe. She had on one occasion actually gone to Yeovil and bought a dress and had the bill sent to her father, but it had caused such an outcry that she had never done it since. She had never been sure if the heart attack he had assured her she had given him had been genuine or not, for he had refused to have the doctor. Instead he had lain in his bed, heaping reproaches on her head every time she had entered the room. By no means a meek girl, Serena had nonetheless felt forced to believe him.

Ten days later, on a bright May morning, Mr Perkins the family solicitor called. He was a nice old man, for when her mother had died, and he had been summoned by Mr Lightfoot, he had come upon Serena in the kitchen, crying her eyes out. He had patted her on the arm and told her not to be too unhappy.

'At least your father has provided for your future,' he had reassured her. 'You need never have that worry. I should not be telling you this, but it may help a little.'

She had thanked him and thought little of it at the time, but over the years she had come to assume that at least her future was secure.

Now Mr Perkins, older and greyer, was back again, and was closeted for a long time with her father. When he came downstairs at length he looked upset, refused the coffee she offered him and drove away with no more than a brief goodbye. He had remonstrated against Mr Lightfoot's new will, but to no avail.

Serena's brothers had mentioned her wish to have a holiday to their father. They had been well meaning, but Mr Lightfoot, incensed by what he deemed to be gross ingratitude and flightiness on the part of Serena, had, in a fit of quite uncalled for rage, altered his will.

Mr Perkins came with his clerk the next day and witnessed its signature, and on the following day Mr Lightfoot had a stroke.

Chapter 2

Mr Lightfoot's stroke was only to be expected; a petulant man, and a bully by nature, his intolerance had led him to believe that he was always right and everyone else either wrong or stupid. High blood pressure and an unhealthy lifestyle did nothing to help this, nor did his liking for rich food. He lay in his bed for long periods, imagining that he was suffering from some serious condition and being neglected by Serena, and now the last straw, as it were, was to be laid on the camel's back: he had ordered sweetbreads for his lunch, with a rich sauce, asparagus, and baby new potatoes, to be followed by a trifle.

Serena pointed out in her usual sensible manner that the sweetbreads would be just as tasty without the sauce, and wouldn't an egg custard be better than trifle? 'And

I shall have to go to the village—the butcher may not have sweetbreads. What else would you like?'

Mr Lightfoot sat up in bed, casting the newspaper from him. 'I've told you what I wish to eat. Are you so stupid that you cannot understand me?'

'Don't get excited, Father,' said Serena. 'Mrs Pike will be here presently, and I'll go to the village. She will bring your coffee...'

While she was in the village he refused the coffee, and then, when Mrs Pike was working in the kitchen, he went downstairs and unlocked the cupboard where he kept the whisky.

Serena, back home, bade Mrs Pike goodbye and set about getting her father's lunch. She did it reluctantly, for she considered that he ate the wrong food and was wasting his life in bed, or sitting in his chair doing nothing.

'A good walk in the fresh air,' said Serena, unwrapping the sweetbreads, 'and meeting friends, playing golf or something.' Only fresh air was contrary to Mr Lightfoot's ideas of healthy living and he had no friends now.

At exactly one o'clock she bore the tray up to his room. He was sitting up in bed, propped up on his pillows reading the *Financial Times*, but he cast the paper down as she went in.

'Well, bring the tray here, Serena. How very slow you are. Probably because you don't have enough to do. I must consider dismissing Mrs Pike. There isn't enough work for two strong women to do in this house.'

Serena set the tray on his knees. She said, in the colourless voice she used when she needed to show self-restraint, 'Mrs Pike is sixty and has rheumatism; she can't kneel or bend—you can hardly call her strong. Even if I'm strong, I have only one pair of hands. If you send her away it would mean that either I do no housework and look after you and cook, or do the housework and feed you sandwiches.'

He wasn't listening, but poking at the food on his plate with a fork.

'These aren't lamb's sweetbreads. I particularly told you that they are the only ones I am able to digest.'

'The butcher only had these...'

Mr Lightfoot raised his voice to a roar. 'You thoughtless girl. You are quite uncaring of my comfort and health.'

He picked up the plate and threw it across the room, and a second later had his stroke.

'Father,' said Serena urgently, and when he lay silently against his pillows she sped to the bed. Her father was a nasty colour and he was breathing noisily, his eyes closed. She took his pulse, settled his head more comfortably on a pillow and reached for the phone by the bed.

Dr Bowring, on the point of carving the half-leg of lamb his wife had set before him, put down the carving knife as the phone rang.

He addressed his wife and their guest in a vexed voice. 'This always happens just as we are about to have a meal. Sorry about this, Ivo.'

He went to answer the phone, and was back again within a minute.

'Serena Lightfoot. Her father has collapsed. He isn't my patient. He showed me the door a couple of years ago; doesn't believe in doctors, treats himself and has turned into a professional invalid. But I'll have to go…' He glanced at Ivo van Doelen. 'Like to come with me, Ivo? She's alone, and if he's fallen I'll need help.'

Serena, shocked though she was, didn't lose her head. She ran downstairs and opened the front door, and then went back to her father. She had little idea as to what to do for him, so she sat on the side of the bed and took one of his flaccid hands in hers and told him in a quiet voice that he wasn't to worry, that the doctor was coming, that he would be better presently; she had read somewhere or other that quite often someone who had had a stroke was able to hear, even if they were unable to speak…

The two men came quietly into the room and saw her sitting there. They saw the mess of asparagus, potatoes and sweetbreads, too, scattered on the floor. Dr Bowring said quietly, 'Hello, Serena. You don't mind that I have brought a friend—a medical man, too—with me? I wasn't sure if there would be any lifting to do.'

She nodded, and looked in a bewildered fashion at his companion. It was the man who had been on Barrow Hill. She got up from the bed to make way for the two men.

'Can you tell me what happened?'

She told him in a quiet voice, and added, 'You see,

he was angry because they weren't the sweetbreads he had told me to get. The butcher didn't have them.' She sighed. 'I annoyed him, and now he's really ill…'

'No, Serena, it has nothing to do with you. Your father, while I was allowed to attend to him, had a very high blood pressure; neglect of that condition made a stroke inevitable. You have no reason to reproach yourself. Perhaps you would like to make yourself a cup of tea; we shan't be long.'

So she went down to the kitchen, made a pot of tea and sat at the kitchen table drinking it, for there was nothing else for her to do until Dr Bowring came downstairs.

When he did he sat down at the table opposite her. 'You don't mind Mr van Doelen being here?'

She glanced at the big man, who was leaning against the dresser. 'No, no, of course not…'

'Your father has had a severe stroke. He is too ill for him to be moved to hospital, I'm afraid. In fact, my dear, I believe that he will not recover. I'll get the community nurse to come as soon as possible. If necessary she will stay the night. Presumably your brothers will come as soon as possible and see to things?'

'I'll telephone them. Thank you for coming, Dr Bowring.'

'I'll come in the morning, or sooner if you need me. If by any chance I'm on another case, will you allow Mr van Doelen to come in my place?'

She glanced at the big man, standing so quietly, saying nothing and yet somehow making her feel safe. 'No, of course I don't mind.'

'Then if I may use your phone to get Nurse Sims up here. Until she comes I'm sure Dr van Doelen will stay with you.'

'Oh, but I'll be all right.' She knew that it was a silly thing to say as soon as she had uttered the words, so she added, 'Thank you, that would be very kind.'

Dr Bowring went presently, and Mr van Doelen, with a reassuring murmur, went upstairs to her father's room. Presently Nurse Sims came, and he bade Serena a quiet goodbye after talking to Nurse Sims.

Serena had phoned her brothers; they would come as soon as possible, they had both told her. She sensed that they found her father's illness an inconvenience, but then illness never took convenience into account, did it? She set about getting a room ready for Nurse Sims, and getting the tea. She had gone upstairs to see her father, but he was still unconscious and she could see that he was very ill. Nurse Sims had drawn a comfortable chair up to the bed and was knitting placidly.

'There's nothing for me to do. It's just a question of waiting. Are your brothers coming?'

'As soon as possible, they said. Is there anything I can do?'

'No, Serena. Go and have a cup of tea. I'll have mine here, if you don't mind...'

Henry arrived first, and went at once to see his father, then accepted the cup of tea Serena offered him before going away to see Dr Bowring. He was closely followed by Matthew, who stayed with his father for some time and then came down to sit with Serena, not saying much until Henry returned.

Neither of them would be able to stay. Henry explained pompously that he had important work to do, and Matthew had his parochial duties. She was to telephone them immediately if their father's condition worsened. She would be companioned throughout the night by the nurse, and in the morning they would review the situation.

'It is impossible for Alice to come,' Henry pointed out. 'She has the children and the house to run.' And Matthew regretted that his wife Norah had the Mother's Union and various other parish duties to fulfill.

Serena bade them goodbye and went into the kitchen to see about supper. She wasn't upset; she hadn't expected either of them to offer any real help. They had left her to manage as best she could for years, and there was no reason to expect them to do otherwise now.

She got supper, relieved Nurse Sims while she ate hers, and then got ready for bed and went and sat with her father while Nurse Sims took a nap. Since there was nothing to be done for the moment, presently she went to her own bed.

She was in the kitchen making tea at six o'clock the next morning when Nurse Sims asked her to phone the doctor.

It was Mr Van Doelen who came quietly into the kitchen. 'Dr Bowring is out on a baby case. Shall I go up?'

Serena gave him a tired 'Hello.' She was both tired and very worried, her hair hanging down her back in a brown cloud, her face pale. She was wrapped in an elderly dressing gown and she had shivered a little in the early-morning air as he had opened the door. She led the way upstairs and stood quietly while he and Nurse Sims bent over her father. Presently he straightened up.

He said gently, 'Would you like to stay with your father? It won't be very long, I'm afraid.' When she nodded, he drew up a chair for her. 'I'll sit over here, if I may?' He moved to the other end of the room. 'I'm sure Nurse Sims would like a little rest?'

Mr Lightfoot died without regaining consciousness; Serena, sitting there holding his hand, bade him a silent farewell. He had never liked her, and she, although she had looked after him carefully, had long ago lost any affection she had had for him. All the same, she was sad...

Mr van Doelen eased her gently out of her chair. 'If you would fetch Nurse Sims? And perhaps telephone your brothers? And I'm sure we could all do with a cup of tea.'

He stayed until her brothers came, dealt with Henry's officious requests and questions, and then bade her a quiet goodbye. 'Dr Bowring will be along presently,' he told her, 'and I'm sure your brothers will see to everything.'

She saw him go with regret.

The next few days didn't seem quite real. Henry spent a good deal of time at the house, sorting out his father's papers, leaving her lists of things which had to be done.

'You'll need to be kept busy,' he told her, and indeed she was busy, for the writing of notes to her father's few friends, preparing for their arrival and the meal they would expect after the funeral fell to her lot, on top of the usual housekeeping and the extra meals Henry expected while he was there. Not that she minded; she was in a kind of limbo. Her dull life had come to an end but the future was as yet unknown.

At least, not quite unknown. Gregory had come to see her when he had heard the news and, while he didn't actually propose, he had let her see that he considered their future together was a foregone conclusion. And he had been kind, treating her rather as though she were an invalid, telling her that she had always been a dutiful daughter and now she would have her reward. She hadn't been listening, otherwise she might have wondered what he was talking about.

Not many people came to the funeral, and when the last of them had gone old Mr Perkins led the way into the drawing room. Henry and Matthew and their wives made themselves comfortable with the air of people expecting nothing but good news. Serena, who didn't expect anything, sat in the little armchair her mother had always used.

Mr Perkins cleaned his spectacles, cleared his throat and began to read. Mr Lightfoot had left modest sums to his sons, and from the affronted look with which this was received it was apparent that, despite the fact that they had expected nothing, they were disappointed.

'The house and its contents,' went on Mr Perkins in a dry-as-dust voice, 'are bequeathed to a charity, to be used as a home for those in need.' He coughed. 'To Serena, a sum of five hundred pounds has been left, and here I quote: "She is a strong and capable young woman, who is quite able to make her own way in the world without the aid of my money". I must add that I did my best to persuade your father to reconsider this will, but he was adamant.'

He went presently, after assuring them that he was at their service should he be needed, and taking Serena aside to tell her that he would see that she had a cheque as soon as possible. 'And if I can help in any way...'

She thanked him, kissing his elderly cheek. 'I'll be all right,' she assured him. 'I don't need to move out at once, do I?'

'No, no. It will be several weeks before the necessary paperwork can be done.'

'Oh, good. Time for me to make plans.' She smiled at him so cheerfully that he went away easier in his mind.

Serena went back to the drawing room. Her brothers were discussing their inheritance, weighing the pros and cons of investments, while their wives interrupted with suggestions that the money would be better spent on refurbishing their homes and wardrobes. They broke off their discussions when she joined them, and Henry said gravely that of course the money would be put to good use.

'I have heavy commitments,' he pointed out, 'and the children to educate.' That they were at state schools and not costing him a penny was neither here nor there. Serena could see that he was anxious to impress upon her that she couldn't expect any financial help from him.

It was Matthew who asked her what she intended to do. 'For I am surprised at Father leaving you so ill provided for. Perhaps we could—?'

His wife interrupted smoothly, 'Serena is bound to find a good job easily; such a practical and sensible girl, and only herself to worry about. I must admit that I—we are very relieved to have inherited something. It will be just enough to have central heating put in—the house is so damp...'

'I thought the Church Council, or whatever it is, paid for things like that,' said Serena.

Her sister-in-law went red. 'We might have to wait for months—years, even—while they decide to have it done.' She added sharply, 'Matthew's income is very small.'

Serena reflected that Matthew had a private income from a legacy both brothers had received from an old aunt years ago. Neither of them needed to worry about money, but there was no point in reminding them of that! She offered coffee and sandwiches and presently bade them goodbye. They would keep in touch, they told her as they drove away.

She cleared away the cups and saucers and plates, fed Puss and sat down to have a think about her future. She was a practical girl, and for the moment she put aside her own vague plans. They were to be allowed to take personal property and gifts before the house was handed over, and the house would need to be left in good order. She would need to get the cases and trunks down from the attic so that their possessions could be packed. There were bills to be paid, too, and people to notify. Only when that was done could she decide what she would do.

At the back of her mind, of course, was the reluctant

thought that Gregory might want to marry her. It was an easy solution for her future but, tempting though it was to have the rest of her life settled without effort on her part, she was doubtful. It was, of course, the sensible thing to do, but under her practical manner there was the hope, romantic and deeply buried, that one day she would meet a man who would love her as dearly as she would him. And that man *wasn't* Gregory.

She went to bed presently, with Puss for company, and since it had been a busy and rather sad day, she went immediately to sleep.

Gregory had been at the funeral, but he hadn't come to the house afterwards, pleading an appointment he had been unable to cancel. He would come, he had assured her, on the following evening.

'We have a great deal to talk about,' he had told her, smiling and looking at her with what she'd decided was a proprietary look.

She hadn't minded that, for yesterday she had been feeling in need of cherishing. Now, in the cold light of early morning, common sense took over. Gregory might not be the man of her dreams, but if he loved her she might in time learn to love him, too. She liked him, was even a little fond of him, but she had the wit to know that that was because she hadn't had the opportunity to meet other men…

She spent the day busily, dragging down cases and a trunk from the attics, clearing out her father's bedroom, and, after a sandwich and coffee, sitting down to write letters to those who had written and sent flowers. She had tea then, and changed into a sweater and skirt, did her hair and face and put a tray ready with coffee. She lighted a small fire in the sitting room, for the evening was chilly, and sat down to wait for Gregory.

He was late. His car wouldn't start, he explained, adding that he would soon be able to get a new one. He smiled as he said it, but Serena, pouring the coffee, didn't see that.

They talked for a little while about the funeral, until he put down his cup, saying, 'Well, Serena, there's no reason why we shouldn't get married as soon as we can arrange it. I'll move in here, of course. I've always liked this house. We can modernise it a little—perhaps another bathroom, have the central heating updated, have the rooms redecorated.' He smiled at her. 'We must use your money to its best advantage, and you can rely on me getting the best advice as to investing your capital…'

Serena had been pouring herself another cup of coffee. She put the pot down carefully. 'But this house isn't mine.' She sounded quite matter-of-fact about it. 'Father has left it to charity.'

Gregory said sharply, 'But he has left you a legacy? He was comfortably off, you know.'

'Five hundred pounds,' said Serena, still very matter-of-fact. 'The rest goes with the house.'

'But this is preposterous. You must contest the will. What about your brothers?' Gregory wasn't only surprised, he was angry. 'And how are you supposed to live? Something must be done about it at once.'

'I don't see why,' said Serena in a reasonable voice. 'If this is what Father wanted, why change it? Henry and Matthew are quite happy about it.' She paused. 'And if you're going to marry me, I don't need to worry, do I?'

Gregory went red. 'You must see that this alters all my plans, Serena. I'm an ambitious man and I need a secure background, a good living standard, a suitable house…'

'What you mean is that you need to marry a well-to-do girl. Not me.'

Gregory looked relieved. 'What a sensible girl you are, Serena. You understand me…'

Serena stood up. 'Oh, I do, Gregory, and nothing would make me marry you if you were the last man living. Now, will you go away? I don't want to see you again, and now I come to think about it, I wouldn't like to be married to you. Run along and find that rich girl!'

Gregory started towards her. 'Let us part…' he began.

'Oh, do go along,' said Serena.

After he had gone she went to the kitchen to get her supper—scrambled eggs on toast—and, since she felt that this was something of an occasion, she took the keys of the sideboard and chose a bottle of claret.

She ate at the kitchen table, with Puss at her feet enjoying a treat from a tin of sardines. And she drank two glasses of claret. She supposed that she would have been feeling unhappy and worried, but she was pleased to discover that all she felt was relief. She had five hundred pounds and the world before her in which to find the man of her dreams. She tossed back the last of the claret in her glass.

There was no need to look for him. She had already
found him, although she wasn't sure if a brief acquaintance with Dr van Doelen was sufficient to clinch the
matter. She thought not. Indeed, it was unlikely that
their paths would cross in the future. She would do
better to get herself a job and hope to meet a man as
like him as possible.

Nicely buoyed up, she by the claret and Puss by an
excess of sardines, they went upstairs to bed and slept
dreamlessly.

Henry came in the morning, telling her importantly
that he had taken a few hours off in order to look round
the house and claim anything to which he was entitled.
Which turned out to be quite a lot: the table silver, a
claret jug and three spirit bottles in a metal frame, and
the best part of a Spoke tea service which had belonged
to their mother, that Matthew would have no use for
nor would Serena, Henry pointed out.

'But I have no doubt that Matthew will be glad
to have the dinner service. Father bought it from
Selfridges, I believe, so anything which may break can
be replaced. There's the new coffee percolator, too;
I'll leave that for him. Where is the Wedgwood biscuit
barrel, Serena?'

'In the cupboard in the dining room, Henry. Shouldn't
you wait and see what Matthew wants—and what I
might want?'

'My dear girl, Matthew will want useful things
which he can use in his home. Remember that he is,
after all, living in a very small house, and has no social life worth mentioning.'

'But he will have when he gets a parish of his own...'

Henry ignored that. 'And you—you won't want to be lumbered with a number of useless things.'

'I don't know why you say that, Henry. You have no idea what I am going to do or where I'm going. You don't want to know, do you? Do you know that Gregory has jilted me? Or perhaps I should say he jilted my five hundred pounds.' She added bleakly, 'I thought he wanted to marry me, but all he wanted was this house and the money he thought Father would be sure to leave me.'

Henry looked uncomfortable. 'You must understand, Serena, that Gregory has his way to make in the world.'

'And what about me?'

'You're quite able to find a good job and do very well. You might even marry.'

Serena picked up a fairing from the side-table in the drawing room, where Henry was inspecting the contents of a china cabinet. The fairing was small, a man and woman holding hands, crudely done, yet charming. The kind of thing Henry and Matthew would find worthless. She would keep it for herself, a reminder of her home in happier days when her mother had been alive.

Henry bore away what he considered to be his; he had written a list of various other things, too. Serena hoped that Matthew wouldn't wait too long before making his own choice. Henry was obviously going to exert his rights as elder son.

Matthew came the next day, bringing his wife with him. The dinner service was packed up, as was an

early-morning teaset which hadn't been used since their
mother died. To these were added two bedspreads, a
quantity of bedlinen, the cushions from the drawing
room and, at the last moment, the rather ugly clock on
the mantelpiece.

'We shall probably be back,' said Matthew's wife
as they left.

'My turn,' said Serena to Puss, and went slowly from
room to room. She would take only small things that
would go in her case or the trunk: her mother's work-
box, family photographs, two china figurines to keep
the fairing company, a little watercolour of the house
her mother had painted. She tried to be sensible and
think of things which would be of use to her in the
future. The silver-framed travelling clock which had
stood on the table by her father's bed, writing paper
and pens, the cat basket from the attic—for of course
Puss would go with her.

But where would she go? Mr Perkins had told her
that she would be able to stay at the house for two or
three weeks. Tomorrow, she decided, she would go to
Yeovil and go to as many employment agencies as possible.

Without much success, as it turned out. She had no
qualifications, and she couldn't type, the computer was
a mystery to her, and the salesladies asked for had to
be experienced. She was told, kindly enough, to leave
her phone number, and that if anything suitable turned
up she would be notified.

But nothing turned up. The charity, anxious to take
possession, were kind enough to let her stay for an extra

week, and at the end of that week, still with no job in sight, Serena, Puss, her trunk and a large case, moved unwillingly into Henry's house.

Just as unwillingly she was welcomed there. There was room enough for her, for Henry lived in a large house on the outskirts of the town, but, while he wasn't slow to confide his generosity towards his sister to his colleagues, his wife made no bones in letting Serena see that she was a necessary evil. It was bad enough having her, her sister-in-law pointed out in the privacy of their bedroom, but to have to give house room to a cat as well...

As for Serena, she redoubled her efforts to find some sort of job. Housekeepers were in demand, and that was something she could do, but she wasn't going to part with Puss, and no one, it seemed, was prepared to accept a cat, especially when the applicant had no references from previous employers.

Between fruitless visits to Yeovil, she was given no chance to be idle. Her sister-in-law, a social climber by nature, quickly saw her opportunity to widen her social life, since Serena was so conveniently on hand to do the shopping and prepare meals. And when the children came home from school there was no reason, since she had nothing better to do, why she shouldn't give them their tea and keep an eye on them while they did their homework.

Serena, gritting her splendid teeth, accepted the role of unpaid domestic and put up with the childish rudeness of her nephew and niece and her brother's pompous charity. His wife's ill-concealed contempt was harder to bear, but since she was out a good deal Serena was almost able to ignore it.

She had been living with her brother for more than a week when one morning, as she was washing the breakfast dishes, alone in the house, there was a ring on the doorbell. She didn't stop to dry her hands; it was possibly the postman—probably with the answer to two more jobs she had applied for. Perhaps her luck had changed at last…

It wasn't the postman. It was Dr Bowring on the doorstep.

'I had to come to Yeovil,' he told her smilingly. 'I thought I'd just see how you were getting on.' He glanced at her wet hands and pinny. 'Is Mrs Lightfoot at home?'

'No, just me. Do come in. How nice to see you. If you don't mind coming into the kitchen, I'm sure no one will mind if I make coffee.'

He looked at her enquiringly. 'No job yet?'

'Well, no. You see, I must have Puss with me, and so far no one will have her…'

He followed her into the kitchen. 'What kind of job?'

'Housekeeper or companion. I can't do anything else.' She spoke lightly, but he noted her rather pale face and the shadows under her eyes.

He said bluntly, 'You're not happy here?'

She put the instant coffee into two mugs. 'Well, it's not really convenient for Henry to have me here, and they don't like Puss.' She smiled. 'But something will turn up.'

He stayed for a little while, vaguely troubled about

her, deciding silently that he would keep an eye open for a job which would suit her. It was obvious that she was unhappy, although she had made light of it.

He told his wife about her when he got back home.

'All we can do is keep our eyes open for a job for her,' said Mrs Bowring, 'and we shall have to go carefully; Serena is proud in the best sense, and she would hate to be pitied.'

Mr van Doelen had spent a busy day at one of the London hospitals; he was an orthopaedic surgeon of some repute and had come to assist at a complicated operation on a boy's shattered legs. It had been successful, and he was free to return to Holland that evening, but, leaving the hospital early that lovely summer evening, he decided against driving up to Harwich and instead picked up the car phone and dialled Dr Bowring.

Of course he was to come and spend the night—as many nights as he could spare. 'We'll wait dinner for you,' said Mrs Bowring. 'It's only four o'clock; you'll be with us in a couple of hours.'

Once free of the London suburbs, the traffic thinned and he sent the Bentley powering ahead. The countryside was bathed in sunshine, green and pleasant and exactly what he needed after hours in an operating theatre. And he need not return until the evening ferry on the following day; he had expected to be away for two days, but the operation had gone better than they had expected.

It would be good to see his friends again. He wondered idly how that girl whose father had died was getting on. She was probably married by now, to the man Mrs Bowring didn't like… Mr van Doelen had thought about her frequently, due, he considered, to the unusual circumstances of their meeting. He must remember to ask about her…

He was warmly welcomed, and Mrs Bowring went away to put the flowers he had brought into a vase while he and the doctor sat over a drink. They always found plenty to talk about and dinner was a leisurely meal. It wasn't until the men had washed up and they were all sitting in the drawing room that Mr van Doelen asked about Serena.

'You remember her?' asked Mrs Bowring. 'Such a dear girl; how that brother of hers could treat her so shabbily is beyond me.'

'Did she not intend to marry? You mentioned that…'

George Bowring explained. 'Her father left the house and almost all his money to a charity. Serena had a few weeks of leave before they took over—it's to be a home for the elderly and impoverished. He left the two sons quite adequate legacies, so I'm told, and five hundred pounds to Serena. With the observation that she was young enough and strong enough to look after herself.

'And if that wasn't bad enough, Gregory Pratt, who had let it be known that he intended to marry her, changed his mind as soon as he discovered that she hadn't inherited the house and the money. She's been trying to find work, but she refuses to abandon her cat and it's hard to find employment with no references and no skills except that of a housewife. She's living with

Henry, her elder brother, at Yeovil. I went to see her and I must say that I'm not at all happy about her. She said very little but I fancy she's having to work hard for her keep. Her sister-in-law doesn't like her overmuch, and of course Henry is a pompous ass.'

Mr van Doelen said slowly, 'It just so happens that I know of someone who is anxious to find a companion-governess for her daughter. It's the mother of the boy whom I operated on today. She plans to stay in London until the boy is fit to go home—six weeks or so. Her husband travels a good deal on business, and there is a daughter, thirteen or fourteen, living at home—Penn, near Beaconsfield, is it not? She goes to school there. There's a housekeeper and daily help, but it seems the girl is difficult to control and jealous of her brother. Would you give Miss Lightfoot a reference if they are interested? Would you like me to talk to Mrs Webster about it and see what she says? And would Miss Light-foot be prepared to take on the job?'

'I'm sure she would, provided that she can have her cat…'

'They are extremely anxious to get someone. I should imagine that Miss Lightfoot could take any ani-mal with her provided that she was suitable. Anyway, I'll see Mrs Webster about the boy tomorrow and let you know. It's a temporary post, but it would give her time to find her feet.'

He went back to London early the next day and, true to his promise, told Mrs Webster about Serena. 'I have met her,' he said. 'She seems a very sensible and level-

Chapter 3

Henry, looking up briefly as Serena put a plate of bacon and eggs before him, said, 'You'll see to the children's breakfast, will you, Serena? Alice will be down later.' He sorted through the post by his plate. 'There is a letter for you. Let us hope that it is an offer of work.'

'Let's hope it is,' agreed Serena pleasantly. She put the letter in her pocket and presently, boiling eggs for the children's breakfast, she had a look at it. The writing on the envelope was a firm and almost illegible scrawl, but there wasn't time to read the letter. It wasn't until Henry had gone and the children had been seen off to school that she sat down at the table, surrounded by breakfast debris, and opened the envelope.

The letter was short and businesslike; she read it through and then read it again. Mr van Doelen clearly had no time for the niceties of correspondence, but the facts were clear enough, and the one fact that Mrs Webster would be coming to see her that very morning with a view to engaging her as a companion for her daughter stood out like a flaming beacon. At ten o'clock, too. Serena looked at the clock; it was just after nine.

She got up, shut the door on the breakfast chaos, and went to her room, where she changed into a cotton dress, its blue rather faded but still a likely garment for a companion to wear. She powdered her nose, applied lipstick and brushed her hair into a neat coil, dusted off her sandals and went downstairs to put on the coffee pot and set a tray with cups and saucers. There had been no sound from Alice; hopefully she would sleep for another hour or two, though the doorbell might wake her.

Serena went into the hall and stood patiently by the door until, a few minutes before ten o'clock, a car stopped in front of the house.

Serena had the door open as Mrs Webster reached it. She was a tall, handsome woman, with a discontented face, expertly made up. She was well dressed, and looked as though she was used to having her own way. She paused on the porch. 'Miss Lightfoot? I'm Mrs Webster. You have been told that I would be coming to see you?'

'Yes, I had a letter. Please come in.'

Mrs Webster sat down in the drawing room and looked around her. 'I understand that you live with your brother? You have no ties? There would be no delay were I to engage you?'

'None at all, Mrs Webster. Would you like coffee?'

'Thank you. I left London quite early and I must return as soon as possible. Do you know that my son is in hospital?'

'Yes. Mr van Doelen has given me the brief facts. I'll fetch the coffee before we talk, shall I?'

Mrs Webster wasted no time. She drank her coffee quickly while she explained what she wanted. 'Heather is a wilful child, given to moods. My housekeeper is quite unable to cope with her, and I can't have her with me in London—in any case, she mustn't miss school. I shall want you to take complete charge of her until my son is able to come home. Six weeks or so, they say. My husband is away a great deal and I shall stay at a hotel so that I can visit Timothy each day. You won't have a great deal of free time, but I don't expect you to do any housework or cooking. Can you drive? Yes? There is a small car for you to use if you wish. I want you to come immediately—tomorrow, if possible. I'll send a car for you and you can go straight to Penn from here. You will be paid weekly.'

She mentioned a sum which sent Serena's spirits soaring.

'I'm offering you the post on trust; I have telephoned a Dr Bowring, who vouches for you, and, of course, Mr van Doelen's recommendation is really sufficient...'

But he hardly knows me, thought Serena, agreeing pleasantly to be ready to go to Penn on the following morning. She had no idea what the job would be like, but anything would be better than the grudging hospitality Henry and Alice were offering. Besides, she would be paid, and she could save every penny...

Mrs Webster, having got what she wanted, was disposed to be gracious. 'I'm told that you have a cat. I have no objection to you having it at Penn. I understand that you wouldn't consider going anywhere without it.' She prepared to leave. 'I shall probably see you from time to time.'

She got into her car and drove away, and Serena carried the coffee tray into the kitchen, where Puss sat uneasily in her basket. She spent her days there, aware that she was as unwelcome as Serena.

'Our luck's changed,' Serena told her. 'We're off tomorrow morning. I expect you'll be able to go where you like in the house and garden, Puss. It won't be for long, but if they like us, we'll be able to stay…'

She went upstairs to the box room, got her trunk and case and carried them into her bedroom. She hadn't unpacked everything in the trunk, and now she put it on the bed and lifted the lid. She was opening the suitcase when Alice came in, still in her dressing gown and half awake.

'What are you doing?' she demanded. 'Go and make me a cup of tea; I can't possibly get up until I've had something. I should have thought you would have come to see how I was…'

'Henry told me not to disturb you. And I'm packing—I'm going to a job tomorrow morning. I'm being fetched at nine o'clock.'

'A job? Where? Does Henry know, and why wasn't I told?'

'Henry doesn't know, and I only knew myself this morning, after he'd gone.'

'But who is to take your place? How can I manage on my own? You can't go, Serena.' She added angrily, 'How ungrateful can you be? Living here without it costing you a penny, treated like one of the family…'

'Well, I am one of the family,' Serena reminded her. 'But I can't say that I've been treated as such. I haven't much liked being a poor relation. I should have thought that you would have been glad to see the back of me.'

'I suppose I shall have to make my own tea.' Alice went away, banging the door behind her; Serena heard her squawk of rage when she opened the dining room door and saw the breakfast table.

She went downstairs presently and found Alice in the kitchen, sitting at the table. She had a pot of tea in front of her and a plate of toast.

'You'll have to clear the dining room and kitchen,' she told Serena.

'When you're dressed we'll do it together,' said Serena briskly, and she fetched a mug and poured herself some tea and sat down opposite her sister-in-law. 'You're glad I'm going, Alice,' she observed quietly. 'I've not been welcome here; you've made that very obvious.'

'I'll be glad to see the back of you and that cat of yours. If I had my way you'd be out of the door as soon as you've packed your things.'

Serena sighed. She had tried hard to like Alice and be grateful to Henry. She took her mug to the sink. 'I'll clean the vegetables,' she said. 'By the time you've dressed I'll be ready to help you with the dining room.'

They worked silently together, and when the last

plate was washed Alice threw the teacloth down by the sink. 'I'm going out to lunch. Give the children their tea when they come in.'

Serena finished her packing, made a cheese sandwich for her lunch and washed her hair, and all the time she wondered why Mr van Doelen had been the means of finding her a job, and how he had known she was in need of work. And that reminded her that she must let Dr Bowring know that she was leaving. He might not be home, but Mrs Bowring would tell him...

He was home, on the point of leaving for his surgery. When she told him he said worriedly, 'Oh, Lord, Ivo phoned me and asked me to tell you about this job—I clean forgot. I'm so sorry, Serena.'

'It doesn't matter. He wrote to me and Mrs Webster came to see me. I'm going in the morning. I'm very grateful to him, though how he knew that I wanted a job is beyond me.'

Dr Bowring said, 'I believe that I mentioned it last time I saw him. I must go, Serena. Write and let us know how things are...and good luck!'

Which was more than Henry wished her when he got home that evening. 'I am amazed,' he said, at his most pompous. 'After all we have done for you—the ingratitude...'

Serena said matter-of-factly, 'Don't be silly, Henry. You know as well as I do that you're glad to see the back of me. I know it means you'll have to pay for another au pair, but you can afford that, can't you?'

'I don't know what Matthew will have to say to this,' began Henry.

'Why, he'll be just as relieved as you are. Only he'll be pleased that I've got a job and can start living my own life.'

She was fetched in the morning by an elderly man in a cloth cap, driving an equally elderly car. He had a rugged, cheerful face, and explained that he was Mr Webster's gardener and handyman as he stowed her luggage in the boot. There was no one to see her go. Henry had bidden her an unforgiving goodbye when he'd left for work, the children were uncaring whether she was there or not and Alice was still in bed. Henry had made much of the fact that Alice was feeling very poorly and could scarcely lift her head off the pillow.

Serena got into the car beside the elderly man and didn't look back as he drove away.

His name, he told her, was Bob, and he'd been with the Websters for a number of years. 'Live in a cottage near the house with me wife. She cooks and house-keeps and that…there's a girl comes in each day to give an 'and.'

'It must be quite a big house,' said Serena, anxious to find out all she could before she got there.

'Middlin' big. Nice big garden. That your cat in the basket?'

'Yes. Mrs Webster said that I might have her with me. I hope your wife won't object?'

'Lor', no. Likes animals. Miss Heather'll be pleased. Always wanted a dog or cat, but Mrs Webster don't approve of them in the 'ouse.'

Serena said uneasily, 'But Puss isn't used to living out of doors. Mrs Webster had no objection when I asked her.'

He gave a chuckle. 'Don't you worry, miss. She were that anxious to find someone to stay with Miss Heather she'd 'ave put up with a herd of elephants. See, it's like this. Master Timothy's the apple of 'is mum's eye—'is dad's too, for that matter—and Miss Heather, well, she's difficult. 'Ad her nose put out of joint when the boy was born and no one has bothered to put it straight.'

'Poor child. Thank you for telling me; it will be a great help.' She longed to ask more questions about the Websters, but it seemed prudent not to do so. Instead she asked him to tell her something about Penn.

The house was on the edge of the village, a white-walled gentleman's residence of some size, with green-shuttered windows and a wrought-iron balcony, surrounded by a large and beautifully kept garden.

'What gorgeous flowers, and such a lovely lawn,' said Serena, which pleased Bob.

'Mrs Webster, she doesn't care much for gardens; let's me 'ave a free 'and.'

'Oh—and Mr Webster? Doesn't he like gardens either?'

They were standing by the car before the door, looking around them.

''E's hardly ever home. Come on in, miss; Maisie'll 'ave coffee ready.'

Maisie was small and stout and placid. She welcomed Serena warmly and led the way to the kitchen. 'If you don't mind having coffee with us, miss? Your room's ready, and I thought you might like to use the little sitting room—there's a door to the garden for your cat. When Mrs Webster's away we shut up the drawing room and the dining room.'

She pulled out a chair at the kitchen table and Serena sat down. The room was large and very well equipped; no expense had been spared and everything gleamed and shone. The coffee was delicious and hot and there were slices of home-made cake to go with it. The three of them sat comfortably talking until Maisie said, 'You'll want to see your room, miss. Bob's taken your things up, and you'll have plenty of time to settle in before Heather comes back from school. She's been eating with us, but now you're here she can have her meals with you in the sitting room.'

'Oh, but won't that give you a lot of extra work?'

'To tell you the truth, miss, me and Bob will like to be on our own.'

She led Serena, with Puss in her basket, up the staircase and along a corridor at the back of the house. The room was small, but nicely furnished, and there was a small balcony overlooking the garden.

'There's no reason why you shouldn't have your little cat up here, miss, there being a balcony.'

Serena thanked her and Maisie went away, saying that they would be downstairs when she was ready to come down.

The small sitting room which Serena and Heather were to use was plainly furnished and obviously not often used. A few flowers, thought Serena, and a cushion or two, a few books lying about and Puss sitting there and it would look cosier.

She was glad to see that the garden was enclosed by a high wall so that Puss could safely roam. Lunch would be at one o'clock, and until then she was free to explore the house and the garden. The house could come later, she decided, and went into the garden with a cautious Puss. It was beautifully kept, with trim lawns and weedless flowerbeds, and away from the house there was a small summer house beside a pool filled with goldfish. A very nice garden, she considered, but it didn't look as though anyone enjoyed it much; it was all too perfect. She found a swimming pool, too, tucked away behind a high hedge…

Called to have her lunch presently, she persuaded Maisie to let her share it with them in the kitchen. 'Because I know nothing about Heather—Mrs Webster was anxious to get back to her son and there was really no time. Is her school far from here? And does she have tea when she gets home? And when does she go to bed? And her friends? Do they come here sometimes?' She smiled. 'An awful lot of questions, I'm afraid.'

'Well, she's thirteen, and independent-like,' said Maisie. 'Likes her own way, too. Never has her friends here, spends a lot of time just mooning around. Got a telly of her own, and a radio…'

'She's lonely?'

'Yes, miss. Always has been. Wanted a dog or a cat, but Mrs Webster didn't want the bother.'

Serena was in the garden with Puss when Heather came home from school. She watched the girl coming towards her, a thin child, with untidy hair and a pale face, which one day would be pretty but which scowled now.

'Hello,' said Serena, ignoring the scowl. 'Shall we sit here for a bit, or do you want tea straight away?'

Heather stood in front of her, staring. 'I'll have my tea when I like.'

'Right, but don't shout, Heather, or you'll frighten Puss.'

And Puss, as if on cue, poked a furry head round a nearby bush.

'You've got a cat. Mother let you have a cat here? She said I couldn't have one; it would be a nuisance.' The scowl had gone.

'Well, perhaps when she finds out how good Puss is you might be allowed to have a cat of your own.'

Serena had sat down on the grass again, and Puss came to sit beside her.

'May I stroke her?'

'Of course, she loves to be cuddled and loved.'

'Mother actually said that she could be in the house?'

'Yes, but I think we won't allow her in the drawing room or dining room. Just the sitting room we are to use and my bedroom.'

'And my bedroom…?'

'Once she has got to know you, yes, I don't see why not.'

Heather said slowly, 'I dare say you're quite nice…'

'I hope so! Now, shall we go and have tea? And perhaps you'll tell me how you spend your days.' Serena picked up Puss and started towards the house, and after a moment Heather followed her.

She said airily, 'Oh, I have to go to school, of course, and you wouldn't be interested in what I do when I'm free—I've friends…tennis and swimming…and I've a bike.'

'Well, yes, of course you have friends…'

'You wouldn't want to do any of the things we do,' said Heather rudely.

'Oh, I don't know. I play tennis and I swim, and I've ridden a bike for years and years. I drive a car, too.' She smiled at the girl. 'Though I haven't got one of my own.'

'There's a Mini in the garage; Bob and Maisie use it. Perhaps you could borrow it. Not that I'd want to come with you.'

'No, no, of course not—you'd be bored stiff,' Serena said pleasantly.

She was just as pleasant during tea, ignoring Heather's deliberate bad manners, suggesting that she might like to give Puss a saucer of milk. 'Homework?' she asked presently, and was told that homework was something to be ignored as much as possible.

'Oh, a pity. I was going to suggest that when you had done it you might like to give Puss her supper and take her for a little walk in the garden—she likes someone with her.'

Heather eyed her. 'When Timothy is away at school and Mother and Father are away, Mother hires someone to come and stay here—I've hated them all, but probably you won't be too ghastly.'

Serena agreed placidly. Heather was an ill-behaved girl, but probably it wasn't her fault. It seemed to Serena that she was lonely, and only aggressive because she felt that no one loved her. Serena thought that there might be stormy days ahead, but they would be no worse than the years of living with her father and the week or two with Henry.

Mrs Webster telephoned quite late that evening, after Heather had gone to bed. She had rung, she told Serena, to make sure that she had arrived safely, and rang off without asking after Heather.

Serena decided that she didn't like her.

An opinion, if she did but know it, which Mr van Doelen shared with her. He had given Mrs Webster reassuring news of Timothy and was pointing out that there was no need for her to spend the day at the hospital. 'I am sure you will want to go home and see how things are there. You can phone to the hospital each day if you wish...'

'Certainly not, Mr van Doelen. I intend to stay in London, close to Timothy, until he is fit enough to be taken home. There's nothing for me to worry about at Penn. That girl you recommended is there to keep an eye on Heather. She seems to be capable, and reasonably well educated. Of course, one never knows with these young women, but I had to take a chance. Timothy is more important than anything else at the moment. As long as she doesn't go off with the silver!'

She laughed at her joke, but Mr van Doelen didn't so much as smile.

He said coldly, 'Miss Lightfoot is hardly likely to

do that, Mrs Webster, but of course you have only met her briefly, I believe.'

'You know her well?'

Mr van Doelen said coolly, 'I know her family and her friends, as well as Miss Lightfoot. I would not have recommended her to you if I had any doubts about her, Mrs Webster. You will not find anyone more suitable.'

Mrs Webster didn't say any more. Mr van Doelen looked just as usual, with his calm, rather austere good looks, but somehow she sensed that he was angry.

He was indeed angry. He had wanted to help Serena, but he suspected that he had merely helped her out of the frying pan into the fire!

He had been unable to forget her—something which he had found disturbing. His work filled most of his life, though he supposed that one day he would marry; perhaps a woman from his circle of friends. But he had felt no urgency to do so—until he had looked around and seen Serena coming towards him on Barrow Hill.

He had fallen in and out of love like any normal man, light-hearted affairs which had come and gone and been forgotten, but he had taken one look at Serena and known that he had met his true love at last. He had no doubt in his mind that he would make her his wife, but since, at the moment, there wasn't even the remotest possibility of that, he was content to wait. Opportunities to see her again seemed unlikely, but when she left Mrs Webster's employ he would make sure that he was there…

He bade Mrs Webster goodbye with a still austere politeness, and pressed the buzzer on his desk for his nurse to send in the next patient. He hoped that Serena would find life better now that she was away from her brother. He must find a way to go and see her...

Serena was finding life considerably better; Heather wasn't an easy child, and she objected to everything suggested to her—from the changing of a grubby frock to a clean one, the brushing of her hair, the cleaning of her fingernails, to getting up in the morning, getting to school on time and eating her meals. All the same, she had an Achilles' heel: Puss. She showed an unexpectedly tender regard for the little cat and gradually, after the first week or so, she began to show friendliness towards Serena.

She was cautious about it, though, and Serena did nothing to spoil things. She spent all Heather's free time with her, for she never evinced a wish to ask her friends from school to come to the house. Bit by bit she began to respond to Serena's matter-of-fact manner—a game of tennis, swimming in the pool together, visits to Penn to spend her pocket money. And Serena was able to give Mrs Webster an honest report when that lady telephoned.

Not that Mrs Webster was particularly interested in Heather. She supposed, she had said in her rather loud, aggressive voice, that the girl was behaving herself, and Serena was to be firm with her. As to Serena herself, Mrs Webster made no enquiries as to her comfort, or if she had settled down, and there was no mention of any free time...

Serena didn't mind. She had enough leisure, for beyond seeing to her own and Heather's rooms, helping to clear the dishes and arranging the flowers she was free for several hours while the child was at school. She spent some of them going into Penn to shop for Maisie and, when Bob was amenable, helping him in the garden. But when Heather was home there was no leisure; there was homework to be dealt with—no easy matter since the child avoided doing it whenever she had the chance—and the long evenings had to be filled with tennis or clock golf, and sometimes just sitting in the garden, talking.

The mornings were the worst, though, for Heather lay in bed until the last minute and then refused breakfast, mislaid her schoolbooks and thought up a dozen reasons why she should not go to school that day. Serena wasn't easily beaten.

When Mrs Webster rang one day Serena listened while she was told every detail of Timothy's progress, and when his mother said, 'You have nothing to report, I dare say,' she uttered the speech she had rehearsed so carefully.

'Heather is behaving splendidly, Mrs Webster. I'm sure that she misses you all, but she never grumbles. Of course, she is lonely without her family, and I wondered if you would allow her to have something to love. She is very fond of my cat, and loves to look after her. Would you allow her to have a cat of her own? She would delight in looking after it and feeding it, and it would give her a sense of responsibility.'

'A cat? I have never allowed her to have a pet...'

'She is old enough to look after it herself.'

'Well, I suppose she can have a cat if she wants one—she's such a difficult child, not like Timothy. But if it becomes a nuisance it will have to go.' Mrs Webster added sharply, 'I shall hold you responsible, Miss Lightfoot.'

That evening Heather was particularly tiresome, dawdling over her tea, declaring that she couldn't do her homework since she had the wrong books with her, and then going into the garden to look for strawberries—something she knew she shouldn't do until Bob said that they were ready.

Serena, fetching her indoors for her supper, forebore from scolding her, but as they ate their supper she said, 'I talked to your mother on the phone this morning. It's a pity you're so cross because I had some news for you.'

Heather said rudely, 'All about Timothy, I suppose—spoilt brat. You can keep your news to yourself.'

'Well, I could, but I won't. I asked your mother if you might have a cat of your own, and she said that you could…'

'A cat! I can have a cat? I don't believe you…'

Serena said calmly, 'I thought we might go on Saturday to the Cat Shelter in Penn and you could choose one.'

'You mean that?' Heather got up and flew round the table and flung her arms around Serena. 'My own cat? And he can live in the house with me?!'

'Well, I told your mother that you would train him so well that by the time she came home she would hardly know that he was in the house.'

'You did? You'll help me? Timothy won't be coming home yet, will he? Did mother say?'

'No, but I was told six weeks when I came here, so there is still plenty of time.'

They went to choose a cat on Saturday, and came back with a small thin tabby found abandoned on a bypass. About a year old, they thought, and timid. Heather put her into the cat basket Serena had bought and carried her home. 'I shall call her Tabitha,' she told Serena.

And, to Serena's great surprise, Heather kissed her awkwardly on a cheek.

It was astonishing what Tabitha's arrival to join the household did—Heather changed from a rebellious and ill-mannered child almost overnight. True, she still had bouts of sulky disobedience and sudden flashes of bad temper, but even they grew less. She had discovered that there was something she could love and who would love her in return. And Tabitha did just that. She was a gentle little creature, quickly learning what she might and might not do, accompanying Heather to bed and waiting for her when she got back from school; moreover, she was on excellent terms with Puss.

Watching Heather play with the little creature in the garden, Serena hoped that Mrs Webster would realise that her daughter needed as much attention and affection as she gave her son.

She would miss Heather, reflected Serena. She had grown fond of the child, despite their initial difficulties. And very soon now she would no longer be needed. Mrs Webster had hinted that Timothy's progress was so good that he would be allowed home soon.

Serena counted her wages and thought about the future. Armed with a reference from Mrs Webster, she had a better chance of getting another job. There were dozens of advertisements in the *Lady* magazine for similar work. But there was the question of where she would go while she found something. It might have to be Henry again, for if she stayed in Penn her money would be swallowed up in no time, however cheaply she lived. She might find more opportunities in London. She worried about it a good deal, which was a pity, since kindly Fate had decided to stick her oar in...

Mr van Doelen, over in London on a brief visit to bring into practice his deep knowledge of broken bones, had spent the morning mending, with delicate fingers, a very small boy's shattered body, the result of falling out of a third-floor window. By some miracle there was no head damage, and his painstaking surgery was likely to be successful. But it had been hard work, and he was tired by the time he was ready to leave the hospital, only to find Mrs Webster, lying in wait for him as he reached the entrance beside her.

'I heard you were over here. I hope you aren't going again without seeing Timothy, Mr van Doelen?'

'My intention is to see him in the morning, Mrs Webster. Shall we say ten o'clock?'

'Very well. Mr Gould, who's been looking after him, thinks he's well enough to go home...'

'Splendid. We'll discuss that tomorrow, shall we? Now if you'll forgive me...'

He went out to his car, reflecting that if Timothy were to go home Serena would leave…

He was back at the hospital early the next morning; the small boy was doing well in Intensive Care. Mr van Doelen stayed there for some time, then made his way to his office in the orthopaedic block. Mrs Webster was already there.

He bade her a civil good morning, suggested that she stayed where she was while he and Mr Gould examined Timothy, and went to see the boy. There was no reason why he shouldn't go home; the boy was in plaster and learning to use crutches. Mr van Doelen gave it as his opinion that he could leave hospital within the next few days.

Mrs Webster said sharply, 'I shall make arrangements immediately. Of course he must have a nurse—I know of a good agency—she can go to Penn with us. There will be no need for the girl who's looking after Heather to stay. She can leave at once. I'll phone her today and she can pack her things…'

Mr van Doelen said smoothly, 'If I might suggest that you allow her to stay until the nurse is installed? Some help may be required getting the boy settled in. If you arrange for Timothy to go home in two days' time, I will still be here. I will drive over and make sure that everything is as it should be.'

Behind his quiet voice there was the ring of authority, and Mrs Webster found herself agreeing.

Serena knew that the six weeks of her job were running out, but she hadn't expected Mrs Webster's phone

call. She was to be ready to leave in two days' time, and
would she fetch Maisie to the phone so that she might
give her instructions?

'You will help the nurse when she comes with us,'
said Mrs Webster. 'No doubt she will need another
pair of hands to make Timothy comfortable, and then
you can go.'

'I'll fetch Maisie,' said Serena, and, that done, went
into the garden where the two cats were lying together
asleep. It had all been rather sudden; she had counted
on a week's notice, during which time she might possibly have gone to London, found cheap lodgings and
looked for a job—any job… There was nothing for it
now but to ask Henry if she might go back there until
she found work. And that wasn't the worst. She had to
tell Heather…

The child had grown fond of Serena in a guarded
way, and she was certainly happier. Besides, she had
one or two friends now, encouraged by Serena to come
to tea and see the cats. She broke the news as they had
their tea, and Heather burst into a storm of tears.

'It'll be beastly,' she sobbed. 'Can't you stay?'

'Well, no,' said Serena, 'but there's a nurse coming with your brother, and I dare say she'll be very
nice and like Tabitha, and you have your friends from
school. I'll have a word with her when she gets here,
and if you make her your friend, you'll find everything
will be all right.'

'Where will you go?'

'Oh, I have a brother. I shall stay with him for a

while. But if you like I'll write to you. Will you write to me?'

'Yes, and perhaps you could come and see me and Tabitha?'

'I'd like that. You'll have to take extra care of her; she will miss Puss.'

Serena was packed and ready to leave, and prayed that the nurse would be a nice girl. She heaved a sigh of relief when she saw her, for she was young and jolly with a kind face and a ready laugh. But she was competent, too, urging Mrs Webster to go into the drawing room and have coffee while they got Timothy to his room.

'He'll be up and about in no time,' she told Serena. 'My name is Maggie—what's yours? Can I come to your room while I give you a resumé?'

'It's your room now,' said Serena, leading the way, and explaining about Heather and Tabitha. 'She's a nice child, but no one has bothered with her. If you could stand between her and her mother? She has this little cat now, and she sees more of her friends at school. I've let them come to tea…'

'I'll keep an eye on her. When do you leave?'

'Now.'

But when they went back to Timothy's room it was just in time to see Mrs Webster and Mr van Doelen come in. Maggie became all at once very professional, and Serena slipped away and found Heather in the hall.

'They let me come home; I wanted to say goodbye to you. Where's Tabitha?'

'In the kitchen, and the nurse is awfully nice—her name's Maggie; she will be your friend...'

Mrs Webster and Mr van Doelen came into the hall then, and Mrs Webster said, 'Ready to leave, Miss Lightfoot? Heather, you have come to see Timothy, of course. You may go to his room; Nurse is there.'

'You'll write?' Heather flung her arms round Serena.

'Yes, I promise. Remember what I told you.'

Mrs Webster shook hands with Mr van Doelen and then stared at him as he picked up Serena's case and Puss's basket.

He said coolly, 'Are you ready, Serena?' And then, 'I'm giving Miss Lightfoot a lift. Mr Gould will be in touch if you have any worries, Mrs Webster.'

He took Serena's arm and led her out to the car. He popped her into it, put her case in the boot, Puss on the back seat, and got in beside her.

Serena found her voice. 'This isn't...you're very kind...if you would stop at the station...'

'Hush,' said Mr van Doelen in a soothing voice. 'Where had you intended to go?'

'Well, it was all rather sudden, so I'm going back to Henry while I find another job.' She added urgently, 'There's the station.'

'So it is. Unless you're anxious to go back and live with your brother we'll go up to town. I have one or two things to see to, but I'll see you this evening and we'll have a talk.'

Serena said, 'What about? Really, there is nothing for us to talk about. I'm grateful for the lift, but I'll be

Chapter 4

Mr Van Doelen had spoken in very decisive tones. Serena, still gathering her wits together, gave up asking questions for the moment. Possibly Mr van Doelen knew of some respectable person who let lodgings, and there was no denying the fact that she might have a much better chance of finding work with London on her doorstep than if she had gone to Henry. She began calculating the cost of bed and breakfast—and would it be quicker if she went to an agency? But that meant paying a fee...

Mr van Doelen glanced at her frowning profile and left her in peace to worry until they were threading their way through the outskirts of London.

'I'm taking you to my old nanny,' he told her. 'She lives in a small house in Chelsea.' He didn't say that he lived there, too. In fact, it was his house; a mews cottage, his pied-a-terre when he was in London.

'Oh, she won't mind? She does bed and breakfast?'

'Oh, yes,' said Mr van Doelen, omitting to mention that he was the one who had the bed and breakfast. He was aware that he was risking Serena's trust, but there had been no time to think of anything else. He had swept aside the idea of her returning to her brother's house and, although she was a sensible girl, she would have found it difficult to find anywhere to live at a moment's notice. Besides, she obviously had very little money. It was a calculated risk, but one he was prepared to take.

When he stopped the car in a narrow lane behind a terrace of houses, Serena looked carefully around. It wasn't at all the kind of street she had expected. He opened her door and invited her to get out, and she stood for a moment, not speaking; the houses were small, but elegant, with bay trees at their doors and pristine paintwork.

'Come along,' said Mr van Doelen in a no nonsense voice, 'and meet Nanny.'

He unlocked the door of the nearby cottage and urged her into its tiny hall.

'Oh, is this a mews cottage?' asked Serena doubtfully. It was certainly small enough, but it had all the elegance of a smart townhouse.

Before Mr van Doelen could answer her a door opened and an elderly woman came to meet them. She was tall and thin, with a very straight back, a sharp nose in a narrow face and dark eyes. Her hair was almost white, worn in an old-fashioned bun, and when she smiled her whole face lit up.

'Nanny,' said Mr van Doelen, 'I've brought a young lady to stay for a day or two. Serena Lightfoot. Serena, this is Miss Glover.'

Serena offered a hand, aware that she was being inspected, and waited for someone to say something. This didn't look like a bed and breakfast place; it was far too elegant. She turned an enquiring look on Mr van Doelen, who ignored it, merely inviting her to take off her jacket. 'And I'm sure you'll be glad of a cup of coffee. I'll fetch your case and Puss.'

Serena looked at Miss Glover; she appeared quite unsurprised by his remark. Serena said, 'I don't understand…'

'No, no, of course you don't. Now go with Nanny like a good girl—we will talk presently.'

He went back to the car and Serena followed Miss Glover into the living room, which was low-ceilinged, with windows at both ends and a fireplace opposite the door. It was furnished cosily, with easy chairs and a vast sofa, a scattering of small tables, a drum table under one window and a bow-fronted cabinet holding porcelain and silver against a wall.

'Just you sit down,' said Nanny, in a surprisingly gentle voice. 'A nice cup of coffee's just what you need, and a biscuit or two. Ivo will be back in a minute— you'll be needing to talk, no doubt.'

'Indeed we need to talk,' said Serena crisply. 'I trust he will explain.'

Nanny said gently, 'You may depend on that. A man to listen to is Mr Ivo.'

He came into the room a moment later with Puss in her basket. And Puss, that most placid of little animals, went at once and climbed into Serena's lap.

'You must explain,' said Serena.

'It's quite simple.' He had gone to sit in a chair opposite her. 'Mrs Webster told me that you were to leave as soon as Timothy went home, and as I had arranged to see him to his arrival there it seemed sense to offer you a lift. You didn't wish to go to your brother, and you had had no time to make any arrangements, had you? This seems to be the solution. You can't go traipsing around London looking for a room or a job at a moment's notice. Nanny will be glad of your company for a few days while you find your feet.'

'Is this house yours?'

'Yes. I need somewhere to live when I'm in England, and Nanny needs a home. It suits us both. But if you don't wish to stay here I'll drive you to wherever you want to go. Friends, perhaps?'

'I haven't any friends in London. I'll be glad to stay just for the night, if Miss Glover won't mind. I'm sure I can find somewhere and start looking for a job tomorrow.'

He agreed so casually that she felt, for no reason at all, vaguely put out.

Nanny came with the coffee then, observing comfortably that it would be a pleasure to have someone to stay for a while, and presently Mr van Doelen got up to go. He kissed Nanny's elderly cheek, remarking that he would see her shortly, a wish which he didn't repeat to Serena, merely hoping that she would find a job to her liking without too much trouble and offering her hospitality for as long as necessary.

The house seemed empty when he had gone, and Nanny said, 'He works too hard. Here, there and everywhere from one year's end to the other. He'll be back in Leiden operating in the morning, as cool as a cucumber and nothing but a few hours' sleep on the ferry.'

'He's going back to Holland this evening?'

Serena tried to sound casually interested. He might have told her, she thought, but there again there was no reason why he should. He had done her a good turn; he would have done the same for anyone—all the same, she felt hurt. She would leave in the morning, having no wish to be beholden to him. Indeed, she wished strongly that she had never accepted his offer to stay with Nanny. Upon reflection, she conceded that, since she hadn't known of his plans until they were actually at the door, she hadn't had the opportunity to do so. Her thoughts were interrupted by Nanny's voice.

'What kind of work are you looking for, child?'

Serena improvised wildly. 'Oh, I've always wanted to work in a shop—you see, I've lived for years with just my father, in a small village, and met very few people. It would be so nice to be among people.'

'And your little cat?'

'I think she'll settle down quite happily as long as she is with me.'

'Mr Ivo will want you to stay here until you've found

somewhere to live. Have you any money, my dear? London is expensive.'

'My father left me some money, and I have saved my wages while I was at Mrs Webster's house. I have more than enough.'

Miss Glover nodded. 'Good. You don't mind me asking? But I believe you're new to London.'

'Well, yes. I don't plan to stay here, but it is probably the best place to find work. I mean, there's more choice, isn't there?'

'Very likely. Now I'm going to take you to your room and then get our lunch. You have no idea how pleasant it is to have company, Serena.'

After lunch Miss Glover allowed Serena to help with the washing up, and then led the way back to the sitting room.

'Have you known Mr Ivo long?' she asked.

Serena shook her head. 'I really don't know him at all.' She went on to explain how they had met, gently egged on by Miss Glover. Presently that lady said, 'I have some photo albums you might like to see…'

Mr van Doelen as a baby in his pram with Nanny, sitting on his first pony, riding his first bike, in school uniform… Serena turned the pages of his faithfully recorded youth and reached for more formal photos of him in his cap and gown, receiving some award or other from some dignitary, and then several photos cut from newspapers, in some of which he was with pretty girls.

Nanny took the book from her. 'I've a book of cuttings from the papers, too. Famous, he is, but he's never been one to blow his own trumpet.'

'You must be proud of him,' said Serena.

'That I am. Now I'm going to make a pot of tea. If you're going job-hunting tomorrow I'd better find that bus timetable for you; you'll need it. But don't go doing too much; you're to stay here until you've found something to your liking. There's plenty of big department stores not too far away; you'd best try your luck with them first.'

Serena, in bed later, tried to sort out her plans. Everything had happened so quickly that she needed a good think. It was a pity that her sensible thoughts should be disrupted by the image of Mr van Doelen, very clear in her mind. She wondered what he would do when he got to Holland. Did he go home to a wife and children? Where was his home? And when would he return to England?

'I should like to see him again,' she told Puss, curled up on her feet, 'and thank him properly.'

She set off with high hopes in the morning, armed with a list of shops which might offer employment and the bus timetable, but as the day progressed she realised that finding work wasn't easy. And until she had a job she couldn't look for a room.

Miss Glover, over the nourishing meal she provided that evening, assured her that she would find something before long. 'And until you do, you are more than welcome to stay here, my dear. Now, tomorrow, why don't you go further afield?' She mentioned several big stores in the less fashionable shopping streets.

So Serena set off again in the morning, once more optimistic. And once more she was to be disappointed.

She told herself not to worry; something would turn up; there must be work in such a vast city for the inexperienced. This time, armed with a newspaper's 'jobs vacant' page, she began on the restaurants. It seemed that others had had the same idea. Either the jobs had been filled or she was asked what experience she had had...

She stopped for coffee and a sandwich, then began the long walk back to the businesses of Oxford Street, and it was on her way that her luck changed.

The supermarket was vast, brightly lighted and crowded, and in one of its windows there was a placard. Shelf-fillers were wanted, it seemed; early-morning and evening work, enquire within.

Serena enquired. The manager looked up as she went into his office. 'Shelf-filler? Strong, are you? Willing to work late in the evening as well as early mornings. Any experience?'

Serena said, no, she didn't. 'But I'm strong, and I don't mind working early and late.' She added, 'I've references...'

He glanced through Dr Bowring's letter and Mrs Webster's brief note with raised eyebrows. 'This isn't quite your cup of tea,' he said.

'No, but I need work, any kind of work.'

'OK. Start day after tomorrow. Live close by?'

'No. I shall look for a room.'

'Better try Mrs Keane, number ten Smith Street, round the corner from here. Several of our girls are there. Clean and as cheap as you'll get round here. You'll be paid weekly.'

He mentioned her wages—hardly generous, but she supposed fair enough.

She thanked him and went in search of Mrs Keane.

The house was one in a row of redbrick villas, shabby, but the curtains were clean. Serena rang the bell and was admitted by a harassed woman who said at once, 'I don't buy anything at the door...'

'The manager of the supermarket told me to come here and ask if you had a room to let?'

'Oh, he did, did he? As a matter of fact, I have. Upstairs back bedroom, or there's the basement. A bit dark, but there's a door into the garden.'

'If I might see it?'

Serena was led down the basement steps and through the door below street level. The room was dark, and smelled vaguely damp, but there was a door into the neglected garden at the back of the house. There was a small out-of-date gas fire, two gas rings on a shelf in a corner, and a sink beside it. The furniture was sparse— a divan bed against one wall, a couple of elderly chairs, a table under the window and a curtained-off corner, presumably for clothes. It was hardly ideal, but the rent, when she asked, was affordable and it would do until she found something better.

'You can use the bathroom on the first floor,' said Mrs Keane. 'Twenty-five pence and don't stay longer than twenty minutes.' She eyed Serena. 'On your own, are you?'

'Yes. But I have a cat...'

Mrs Keane shrugged. 'S'all right, so long as it doesn't come into the house.'

Serena paid a week's rent and began her journey back to Mr van Doelen's house. Neither her job nor her room were ideal, but at least she would be independent. She could start looking for a better job and find another place to live...

A truthful girl, she found it hard to bend the truth to Nanny. She had got a job, she told her, in a large store.

'Not serving at one of those tills?' asked Nanny sternly.

'No, no. It has nothing to do with the customers,' said Serena, which was true enough. 'And the manager kindly told me of someone living quite close by who lets rooms. I've a nice room opening onto the garden.'

'Hot water, I hope, and heating, and proper cooking facilities?'

'Oh, yes,' said Serena, 'all that.' That was true, too, for there was hot water if she boiled a kettle, and two gas rings.

'And when are you starting this job?' asked Nanny sharply.

'The day after tomorrow. I thought I'd go tomorrow to Mrs Keane's to settle in and be ready to start work the next morning. Miss Glover, you have been so kind to me and Puss, and I'm very grateful. I hope one day I shall be able to repay you for your kindness.'

Miss Glover said something which sounded like 'pish' or 'tush'. 'I'm sorry you are going, child. I'm sure Mr Ivo will want to know that you are settled in a good job with a future. You must write to me.'

Serena said that she would. And she meant it. Only she wouldn't give her address...!

She was going to miss the comfort of the little house, unobtrusively filled with understated luxury. She was going to miss Miss Glover, too, and most of all she was going to miss the chance of seeing Mr van Doelen again.

She packed her bag once more and set off in the taxi Nanny had insisted that Mr van Doelen had said she was to have, with Puss and her meagre wardrobe once more packed.

Now, at the last minute, she had fearful doubts; supposing she was sacked before she had had the time to save some money? Supposing Mrs Keane gave her notice and she had nowhere to go? It would have been so easy to have stayed in the delightful little house with Nanny.

'You're a faint-hearted fool,' Serena muttered. 'This is a chance to be independent.'

The room looked depressing, but that was because the windows hadn't been opened for some time, she told herself. The door into the garden hadn't been opened for a long time either; there was a key in the rusty lock, and she turned it and went into the garden with Puss under one arm.

It was covered in weeds, but she was relieved to see that there were no broken bottles or empty tins lying around, and the fences were high. At least Puss could roam if she so wished.

There was a cupboard in the room housing a broom and a bucket. The place needed a good clean, Serena decided. Besides, if she had something to do she wouldn't have time to think about anything else… She put Puss back in her basket, locked the door and went shopping.

She came back presently, laden with scouring powder and furniture polish, soap, dishcloths, teatowels and bath towels, a kettle and a saucepan and cutlery. Even bought from the local household store they had made a hole in her money, and there was still food…

She went out again, this time to the supermarket, and laid out more money prudently on groceries, and then went back to make a pot of tea in her new teapot and eat bread and cheese for her lunch while Puss toyed with a snack.

By the late afternoon Serena had swept and scrubbed and polished so that the room had lost its shabby air, and with her few photos and small ornaments arranged round it, and a cheap vase of flowers on the table, it looked much more like a home. Pleased with her efforts, Serena found her way up the steps and into the house, and thence to the bathroom for her twenty-five pence worth of hot water. But first she scrubbed the bath, trying not to think of the luxurious bathroom she had used in Mr van Doelen's house.

The first few days of work in the supermarket were a nightmare. Serena had plenty of good sense, but the work was mind-numbing; endless unpacking of tins and packets and jars, setting them in rows on the shelves, trying to remember what went where. And it all had to be done at speed. The mornings weren't so bad, but the evening shift! There were just a few of them in the vast empty place, something she disliked, and she dreaded walking back to her room. She wasn't a nervous girl, but at night the streets took on a sinister gloom, and there were always groups of youths with nothing better to do, roaming around. But beggars can't be choosers, she reminded herself, and her pay packet at the end of the first week was more than welcome.

After another week or two, after she had bought a few cushions, a colourful tablecloth and new curtains, the room took on a more cheerful look. Besides, she had food in the cupboard by the sink now, and Puss didn't have to go short... I have much to be thankful for, Serena told herself.

After the first few weeks, she wrote to Miss Glover. She gave no address, and described her job and her room in glowing terms, not exactly fibbing but embellishing the truth. It was a letter which should set Nanny's mind at rest, she decided, popping it into the nearest letterbox. She had the unbidden thought that it would set Mr van Doelen's mind at rest, too, only she was afraid that he hadn't given her a second thought.

In this she was mistaken. He had returned to London for a brief visit some weeks after she had left, and before Nanny had received her letter. He had listened to Nanny's rather worried account of Serena's departure, and although he had told her not to worry, that Serena was a young woman quite able to take care of herself, he was himself worried.

He had to admit that he had thought about her a good deal. Until he had met her his work had been the predominant thing in his life. He would marry, he had told himself, in due course, if and when he met a woman he could love. But the years had passed and there had been no sign of her—until Serena. And now she had disappeared. He had been a fool to think that she would stay with Nanny, that it would take her some time to find work...

He went back to Holland to his clinics and operating and patients, and it was another three weeks before he returned to his little house and Nanny. She handed the letter to him this time, and he read it carefully and then studied the postmark.

'Not a very pleasant part of London,' he observed. 'But at least we know roughly where she is.' He frowned down at Serena's polite missive. 'She may have posted it quite near where she is living or working. If I could find out the exact area—the post office should be able to help.'

'I should never have let her go,' said Nanny.

'Don't blame yourself, Nanny. You could not have stopped her, whatever you said; she is a grown woman, and a sensible one. She must have known what she wanted to do.'

'But you'll find her?'

He smiled at her. 'I shall do my best, Nanny. I can spare a few days; I haven't a great deal to do at the hospital this time.'

It took time and patience to discover someone at the post office headquarters who could help him.

That particular area of London wasn't large. He rummaged around in his study and found a street map of London, and carefully ringed the district. The following day, his clinic over, he drove through the city to the busy crowded streets and rows of small shops, so near the elegant shopping centres and quiet streets of town houses and yet so different in lifestyle. He wasn't sure what he was looking for. Probably, he thought ruefully, he would have to visit every shop in order to find Serena. There were few clues in her letter, but she had told Nanny that she was working in a large store.

Mr van Doelen began his patient search along the main shopping street, crowded by late shoppers and people going home after a long day. It took time; enquiries meant waiting while someone went to find someone else who might know, ending up with the manager with a list of employees. Each time he drew a blank. It was after nine o'clock by now. He was tired and hungry, and even the smaller shops were shut. Tomorrow, he promised himself, and turned down a side street so that he could reverse the car.

He would have overlooked the supermarket, since it was off the main street, but it was brightly lighted still. He got out of the car and tried one of the big glass doors. They were locked, so he went round the side of the building, along a narrow alley, at the end of which there were a couple of men loading trolleys from a small van. The door was open, and Mr van Doelen, bidding them a cheerful good evening, went through it.

It was a very large building, with wide aisles between the towering shelves of food. There were people in the aisles, replacing out-of-date groceries with fresh tins and packets, and halfway down the third aisle he saw Serena. She was on her knees, the better to arrange the lowest rung of tinned peas, and she was unaware of his approach, her mind on her work—she still wasn't as quick as the others.

He stood for a moment watching her, knowing that now that he had found her again he had no intention of losing her.

When he was close to her he said, 'Hello, Serena.'

She turned her head and he saw the instant delight on her face, so rapidly wiped away that he thought he had imagined it.

She got to her feet. 'Mr van Doelen—how ever did you get here? And should you be here? I mean, we are closed.'

'I walked in and no one stopped me. Why did you run away, Serena?'

She flushed. 'I didn't run away. I told you that I would find work...'

'But you didn't say where. Did you forget to put the address on your letter to Nanny?'

'No, I didn't forget,' she said seriously. 'How did you know that I was here?'

'A process of elimination. When do you finish work, Serena?'

She glanced at her watch. 'In half an hour.'

He nodded. 'I'll be back...'

Serena, loading apricots onto a top shelf, tried to keep her mind on her work. There were a great many tins, and they had to be in position before the place shut down for the night. She couldn't deny that she was overjoyed to see Mr van Doelen, but she must make it quite clear to him that meeting him again would make no difference to her life.

The last tin was in place just as the lights were lowered and everyone got ready to leave. Serena took off her nylon apron, went to the cloakroom for her jacket and made for the entrance opening onto the alley. To get away before Mr van Doelen came looking for her seemed important to Serena, although he might have changed his mind and already gone home.

He was waiting for her by the door. 'Ah, I was afraid that you might have escaped me,' he said briskly. 'I've seen the manager—a most sympathetic man. Considering the circumstances, you can leave as of now...'

Serena gaped at him. 'I can what? But this is my job. No one said that I was going to be sacked. What have I done? Why didn't someone tell me?'

They were out in the alley now, with everyone streaming past on their way home.

Mr van Doelen took her arm. 'You live nearby? Shall we go there and I'll explain.'

'No,' said Serena. 'We won't go anywhere. I don't know why you're here, Mr van Doelen, but just go away. I'm going home.'

'Yes, a good idea. We can talk there.'

'What about?'

He didn't answer, only took her arm and shoved her tidily into the car. 'Where do we go?' he said mildly, and she, her wits gathering wool, gave him the address.

He didn't say anything as she led the way down the steps and unlocked her door. He stretched an arm and switched on the light, and when they were inside, he shut the door behind him. When he still didn't speak, she said, 'I'm very comfortable here, and Puss has the garden...'

Puss came to meet them, pausing only a moment to rub herself against Serena's legs before making for Mr van Doelen with every appearance of pleasure. Serena turned to look at him.

'I don't know what you want to say, but if you'd say it and go—I don't want to seem inhospitable, but I go to work at half past seven in the morning.'

'Not any more, Serena.' He pulled out a chair. 'Shall we sit down? I want to talk to you.'

She sat down, and he drew up the other chair and sat down too, looking perfectly at home in the shabby room, stroking Puss, who had climbed without loss of time onto his knee.

'I had the devil of a job finding you,' said Mr van Doelen mildly, and reflected that he was about to embark on a future full of uncertainty. Somehow he would find ways and means to make Serena his wife—indeed, he already had a very good idea how to set about that— but would his love be sufficient for both of them? She was no young girl with a head full of romantic nonsense. He wasn't sure that she even liked him... Perhaps he should adopt a friendly, businesslike approach...

'First of all, will you give me an honest answer? Are you happy here, and does the job satisfy you?'

'It's a start, and I have to start somewhere.'

'You haven't answered my question.'

'Well, it isn't quite what I had hoped for.' She saw

that he was still waiting. 'No, I'm not happy, but I shan't stay here for ever, you know. There are other jobs.'

'You are wondering why I have been searching for you. We don't know each other, do we, Serena? And yet I feel that we could be friends, enjoy each other's company. I have for some time now considered taking a wife, someone who feels, as I do, that companionship and genuine liking for each other are of more importance than the romantic aspect. I have fallen in and out of love several times, but never once have I wished to marry. But a wife is necessary for a man in my profession. Someone to deal with the social side of life, entertain my guests, accompany me on necessary trips abroad. Above all, someone who will allow me to get on with my work and not make too many calls upon my time. In fact, a business arrangement.'

He had spoken quietly, his eyes on her face. 'I believe that we might deal very comfortably together. I need a wife and you need a future. Will you marry me, Serena?'

She said slowly, 'Supposing I fell in love with someone? Suppose you fell in love with another woman? You may not have met her yet...'

'I am thirty-seven, Serena. I have had ample time in which to meet a girl I wished to marry—the risk is slight. And you?'

'Me? Well, I've haven't met many men. You can't count Gregory, can you? I mean, he wasn't marrying me for love.' She sighed. 'I'm not sure that I believe in love.'

'But you do believe in liking, in friendship, in sharing your life with someone who shares your interests and enjoys your company?'

She said slowly, 'Yes, I do believe in that. And I do like you. I don't know anything about you, but I liked you when we first met. Sometimes one meets someone and one feels at home with them at once—like old friends…'

'Indeed, and that is how I feel with you, Serena. Comfortable.'

He smiled at her then, and she smiled back, feeling, for the first time in weeks, secure.

'Will you come back to my house and Nanny now?' he asked.

'I've just paid the rent—in advance, you know…'

'I'll go to see the landlady while you pack your things.'

He got up and put Puss down gently.

Serena said, 'Am I doing the right thing? Allowing you to arrange everything. I wish I had someone to advise me.'

'Try me,' said Mr van Doelen. 'Start packing, there's a dear girl. I have to return to Holland tomorrow, and we must discuss plans.' At her questioning look, he added, 'Our wedding.'

'I haven't said…' began Serena, but he had already gone.

She started to pack at once, and Puss got into her basket and waited patiently. She had been moved around quite a lot lately, and this basement room had been worse than the house at Yeovil. Her whiskers twitched at the memory of the dainty morsels Nanny had provided in her warm, comfortable kitchen. She hoped that she would be going back there.

Serena, her suitcase open half-filled on the divan, had stopped her packing and gone to stand by the window overlooking the dismal little garden. It must have been the surprise at seeing Mr van Doelen again which had caused her to lose her wits. Of course she wouldn't marry him. Of all the preposterous ideas. She would go to the supermarket in the morning and ask for her job back and explain to Mrs Keane that it had all been a mistake…

Mr van Doelen had come back. He saw the half-packed case and said cheerfully, 'Having second thoughts?'

'Second thoughts?' said Serena peevishly. 'How can I possibly think? I don't know whether I'm coming or going.'

He crossed the room and began to pack the small pile of clothes into the case. 'You're coming with me and we're going to be married.' He added in a soothing voice, 'A business arrangement between friends.'

He folded a dress carefully. 'Is there anything else to go in this case?'

She collected up the few photographs, one or two small figurines she had brought from home and her dressing gown, hanging behind the curtained-off corner of the room. She was suddenly tired; she would go with Mr van Doelen, and after a night's sleep she would be herself again, refuse his proposal in a few well-measured words, and go in search of another job. She put the last odds and ends into her case and got her jacket, closed Puss's basket and then told him gently that she was ready to go.

'But please understand that this is just for tonight.'

'No, no, dear girl. Let us be quite clear about it. I have asked you to marry me, and if you have any sense in your head you will accept me. I promise you I shan't think that you're marrying me for my money. I have offered you a bargain. If you will keep your side of it, I shall keep mine. I really do need a wife, and you are so exactly what I had in mind. Now come along. I don't know about you, but I need my supper.'

He gave her a friendly smile. 'If you take Puss, I'll bring the luggage.'

Chapter 5

M r Van Doelen didn't utter a word as he drove back to Chelsea. Only as they went into the little house he called cheerfully, 'Here we are, Nanny, and we're all three famished.'

Miss Glover came to meet them. 'Supper in ten minutes, and something tasty for Puss.'

She smiled at Serena and said, 'Your room's ready, love. Just you run up and tidy yourself while Ivo brings in your things.'

Serena, speechless, not knowing what to say, did as she was told. When she went downstairs again, Nanny called from the kitchen.

'I'm here, Serena.'

The kitchen was cosy, immaculate, and if there were any labour-saving devices in it they were successfully hidden behind the rows of copper saucepans, the small Aga, the old-fashioned wood dresser and the Windsor chairs round the table, covered by a white cloth and set for three persons.

Mr van Doelen was there, leaning against the dresser, eating a hunk of bread, and Puss was already before the Aga, her small nose buried in a saucer of food. He put the bread down and poured Serena a drink—a dry sherry.

'Just to whet your appetite,' he told her cheerfully, and came and sat down opposite her. They had *coq au vin* and the talk was cheerful, just as though Serena hadn't left. If the talk was mainly between Mr van Doelen and Nanny they didn't remark about it, including Serena in their conversation and not seeming to notice her brief, shy replies.

The *coq au vin* was followed by Queen of Puddings, and when that had been eaten Mr van Doelen said, 'Off to bed with you, Serena; you're asleep on your feet. I'll be here in the morning.'

She summoned her sleepy wits. 'We must talk… I'm not sure—you took me by surprise.'

He said gravely, 'You will be better able to do that after a good night's sleep, Serena.'

He got up and opened the door for her. She wished them goodnight, and with Puss eagerly anticipating a comfortable bed upon which to sleep she went upstairs, to lie in the bath wondering if she had become crazy and what she was going to do about it. She got into bed presently, and fell asleep at once.

She woke early, her sensible self once again, determined to tell Mr van Doelen that, grateful to him though she was for his kindness, she wished to find another job and lodgings as quickly as possible.

She dressed and went downstairs, treading softly, for the house was quiet and it was still early. Not too early for Mr van Doelen. He put his head round a door in the hall, wished her good morning and invited her to go in.

'A lovely morning,' he observed blandly. 'Nanny will have heard you and will bring us tea. Such a pleasant habit, this early-morning cup. It isn't the general rule in Holland!'

Serena, intent on explaining just why she intended to leave after breakfast, found herself agreeing very politely as Miss Glover came in with a tray and two mugs of tea, the sugar bowl and a plate of biscuits.

'Good morning, Serena,' she said briskly. 'Breakfast in half an hour or so.'

She swept out again and Mr van Doelen asked, 'Sugar?'

Mr van Doelen sat back in his chair behind his desk, the mug in his hand, very much at ease, and Serena, not at all at ease, sipped her tea and looked around her.

It was a small room, its walls lined with books, the desk a splendid example of a George II partner's desk. It was loaded down with papers, a pile of medical journals, and a computer and a stack of what she supposed were patients' notes half hiding the telephone, but the room didn't lack comfort. The carpeted floor was soft underfoot, there were some charming flower paintings between the bookshelves, and the small window had white muslin curtains. There was a small old-fashioned fireplace, too. She imagined that in the winter there would be a brisk fire burning in it...

'You wanted to talk?' said Mr van Doelen in an encouraging voice.

'Yes, well, I did—I mean, I do,' said Serena, wishing she was anywhere but where she was at the moment, but, since that wasn't possible, there was nothing for it but to do as he suggested.

'Last night,' she began, 'you took me by surprise. If I'd stopped to think I would never have let you go off like that and get me the sack and give up my room. And all that nonsense about getting married...!'

'I never talk nonsense,' said Mr van Doelen gravely.

She wasn't looking at him. She said sharply, 'Of course you did. You could marry anyone you wished to; that's the advantage of being a man. Don't tell me that you don't have any number of lady-friends.'

He hid a smile. 'Any number,' he agreed equably, 'but never once has it crossed my mind that I wished to marry any one of them.'

'You were joking...'

'I don't joke either,' he told her.

At a loss for words, Serena said, 'Well, then...' Since she could see that wouldn't end the conversation she added, 'That nonsense about getting married.'

Mr van Doelen settled himself more comfortably in his chair. 'Now, shall we start again? I think I made myself clear yesterday evening. If you remember, I told you that I need a wife and you need a future. We get on well together, and that is essential in marriage, do you not agree? Neither of us are in our first youth...'

'I'm twenty-six,' said Serena with a snap.

'Yes, yes. Still quite young, but you have reached years of discretion, have you not? Unlike Gregory, I do not profess my love for you, and there are many such as he around. You are, if you will forgive me for saying so, rather a green girl. I, on the other hand, like you, I enjoy your company, I am sure that we would have a pleasant and undemanding life together and I would do everything in my power to give you a happy life. So if I ask you to marry me once again, Serena, will you say yes? I promise you you won't regret it.'

'You don't think that I would marry just to have a home and no worries?'

'No, I don't think that.'

He looked untroubled and gave her a friendly, reassuring smile.

Serena said slowly, 'It's a bit unusual, isn't it? But if you're sure you only want that kind of a wife, then, yes, I'll marry you.'

He got up and came round the desk to her chair and took her hand, and for a moment she thought he was going to kiss her. She was disappointed when he didn't.

'We will shake hands on that,' he said cheerfully. 'Shall we have breakfast and discuss our plans?'

'I haven't any plans,' said Serena rather bleakly, and looked for a moment so forlorn that he bent to kiss her cheek.

'We'll see about that,' he told her briskly.

'You would like to marry here?' he asked her over their bacon and eggs. 'You wish your brother to marry us?'

'Matthew? No, I don't think so. He's fond of me,

but I don't think he would understand. If it had been Gregory… You see, Gregory expected to marry me; Matthew and Henry both knew him.' She frowned. 'It's difficult to explain…'

'Then don't. I think I understand. Shall we have a very quiet wedding here and return to Holland immediately afterwards?'

She nodded. 'That would be best. There's no one who would be interested, although I dare say your family would want to know?' She buttered some toast and added marmalade. 'I don't know where you live.'

'In a small village near the Hague. I have two married sisters, my father died last year, and my mother lives in Friesland.'

He passed his cup for more coffee. 'I shall tell them when I get back home tomorrow. Our engagement will be announced in the *Haagsche Post* and either *The Times* or the *Telegraph* here.'

She looked surprised. 'Oh, will anyone want to know here?'

He smiled a little. 'I have friends and colleagues here as well as in Holland. I expect you would like to tell your brothers. Invite them if you would like to. I think we might have the Bowrings up for the wedding, don't you?'

'Yes, I'd like that.'

'If you like the idea, a friend of mind could marry us. I'll see about a special licence and we could marry at St Faith's; it's a charming little church in the next street.'

Serena agreed, reflecting how pleasant it was to have someone arranging everything with such ease while at the same time making sure that she was agreeable to what was suggested. After years of her father's bullying and Henry's dictatorial ways it was bliss.

'Not a big wedding,' she said. 'I mean, just ordinary clothes…'

He hid a smile. 'Of course. We shall go over to Holland the same evening, so there won't be much time to dress up. I'm sure you'll look pretty in whatever you choose to wear.' Then he asked, 'Have you enough money to get something suitable for the occasion?'

'Yes, I've Father's five hundred pounds…'

'Then spend every penny of it.'

He watched her face. It held the same enraptured expression as a small girl offered the fairy on top of the Christmas tree. He had seen that look before; he had two sisters.

'I've got my wages from Mrs Webster, too…'

'Spend those as well.'

'It's quite a lot of money.'

'I am well able to provide for you, Serena.' He said that in a quiet voice which stopped her saying anything further about the matter.

When they had finished breakfast he said, 'I'll be half an hour or so phoning. Then will you come with me and we will choose a ring?' He paused as he went through the door. 'Would you be willing to marry me when I next return to London? I've several appointments here; when I've dealt with them I shall need to go back home for a time.' When she nodded, he added, 'And do phone your brothers if you would like to.' He smiled. 'If I'm hustling you, say so, Serena, but there isn't any reason for us to wait, is there?'

'No, no, of course not. I'll phone Henry and Matthew and be ready for you in half an hour.'

She phoned Matthew first. He had never bothered much with her, but at least he had never bullied her. He was surprised, but she had expected that. Still he wished her well in a cautious way and called Norah to the phone.

'Quick work,' said Norah. 'I always knew you were a deep one. Getting married so soon, too.' Her voice held a wealth of malice. 'Well, don't expect us to come to the wedding...'

'We hadn't intended inviting you,' said Serena.

Henry made no bones about his disapproval. 'The very idea!' he told her. 'Going off like that and marrying the first man you meet. A foreigner, too. Well, don't expect any help from me if things go wrong.'

'Well, I've never expected help from you, Henry, and nothing is going to go wrong. I'm going to live in Holland for most of the time—that should be a great relief to you!'

'I'm your elder brother,' said Henry at his most pompous. 'I consider myself responsible for your well-being.'

'Rubbish,' said Serena cheerfully. 'Aren't you forgetting that I shall have a husband to look after me?

'Of all the nonsense,' said Serena, putting down the receiver and turning round to see Mr van Doelen smiling in the doorway.

'And that I can promise I shall do, Serena—look after you. Were your brothers disapproving?'

'Yes, but then they have never really approved of me, if you see what I mean, so it really doesn't matter.'

'I've dealt with the special licence and my friend will be delighted to marry us. Now get a jacket and we'll go shopping.'

He took her to a famous jeweller's and they sat in a discreet alcove while they looked at rings together. 'I really don't know,' said Serena. 'I'm not a jewellery person, am I?'

'No, but I think that sapphires would suit you.'

'You choose,' said Serena, rather overcome by the display set before them by the discreet salesman.

It was a choice she would have made herself; she had been held back by doubts as to the price—a splendid stone set in rose diamonds—but apparently Mr van Doelen wasn't bothered about that. He chose it without hesitation, and without asking its cost. Either he was so deeply in love that money didn't matter any more or he was so rich that the price was of no account. Serena was sure that it was the second of these. It fitted; he slipped it onto her finger and the salesman smiled, not only because he had made a good sale but because he was a sentimental man and believed in true love.

Over coffee presently, Mr van Doelen said, 'I'll get the wedding rings now I know your size. Have you any preference?'

'No, just plain gold.' She admired the sapphire sparkling on her finger. 'This is a very beautiful ring. Thank you, Ivo.'

'I had a word with my bank. If you run out of money, apply to the manager. I'll leave the phone number on my desk. He will want to see you, of course, but there should be no problem.'

'Thank you, but I'm sure I've enough.' She hesitated. 'Shall I need a lot of clothes in Holland? I mean, do you go out a lot? Could I wait and buy things when I get there?'

'A very good idea. We shall go out from time to time. I have friends and family—aunts and uncles and so on—and social occasions to do with the hospitals where I work. But you don't need to worry about that at the moment.'

Serena finished her coffee. As far as she could see she had nothing to worry about at all.

They spent the rest of the day together, the best of friends. It was strange, reflected Serena, that they hardly knew each other and yet they felt so completely at ease together.

When he left that evening she felt bereft. He had bidden her goodbye quite casually, his kiss on her cheek so light and brief that she wasn't sure if she had imagined it. When he had gone she told herself not to get silly and sentimental, and she got out pen and paper and made a list of what she intended to buy. Five hundred pounds seemed a fortune, but from what she had seen in the shop windows it wouldn't go far. She had her wages still; she had meant to keep those against some future emergency, but now she could use at least some of them.

The list grew and she had to start again, crossing out

quite a few of the things she would have liked to have bought but which weren't actually necessary. Tomorrow she would go to the shops, not necessarily to buy but just to spy out the land, as it were.

Nanny joined her presently, sitting up very straight in her chair, knitting. She didn't speak for quite a while, but Serena found her presence comforting. Like sitting with your granny, she reflected, someone who didn't talk much, just was there. She added a couple more items to her list, and then crossed them out. She must stick to basics...

'Mr Ivo likes blue,' said Nanny. 'That soft blue like hyacinths. He likes pink too—rose-pink I suppose you would call it. Men like pink...'

'So shall I wear pink or blue for our wedding, Miss Glover?'

'Call me Nanny. Well, it's not for me to say, dear, but blue looks nice, doesn't it? Perhaps you could find a pink dress as well.'

'I thought I'd look for a dress and jacket, something I can wear later on...'

Nanny nodded. 'Very sensible. One of those little jackets. You've a nice shape; you don't need frills and flounces to fill you out.'

The business of buying new clothes suddenly became fun, with Nanny giving snippets of advice. 'You're a sensible girl; you'll know one good outfit is worth more than three cheap ones. Men notice these things.'

Which Serena took to mean that Ivo noticed them.

She set off the next morning, Nanny's voice ringing in her ears telling her that she was to stop and have lunch or she would be too tired. 'For you won't find all you want in a day,' she said. 'There'll be a nice tea ready for you when you get back. Go carefully!'

Serena thought how nice it was to have someone who actually minded what she was doing and where she was going. She hadn't felt as happy or as light-hearted for a long time.

By the end of the afternoon she was glad to get back to Nanny and a splendid tea. She hadn't bought anything. 'I saw quite a few things I liked, but I don't want to get anything until I've found an outfit,' she explained.

'Very sensible,' said Nanny, 'and you have time enough. Why not try some of the small dress shops? When Mr Ivo's sisters are over here on a visit they go to a boutique off Regent Street. I don't remember the name off hand, but I'll see if I can find a bill; they always leave the bills with me...'

So Serena set out again in the morning, full of hope. A hope which was to be fulfilled this time. It was nothing short of a miracle that the soft blue dress and jacket in the boutique's window fit her exactly. It was expensive, but she had been prepared for that, and there was still enough money to buy undies and a pretty dressing gown and slippers. She returned triumphant and tried the dress on under Nanny's sharp eye.

'Just right!' said Nanny. 'And such a pretty colour. Now, what else do you mean to buy?'

It took several days to find shoes and a hat for the wedding, as well as a jersey dress, plain and undateable, in a pleasing shade of russet. And then there was just enough over for a skirt and blouses…

Satisfied with her purchases, Serena packed her new wardrobe, hung her bridal outfit in the closet, gave Nanny a hand round the little house and took herself off for long walks in one or other of the parks. Ivo phoned; short, businesslike calls for only a few minutes. Was she well? Her brothers hadn't come to see her? She was happy with Nanny? She replied suitably to these questions and forebore from chatting since he showed no desire to linger once she had replied. He was busy, she told herself, and she thought that he wasn't a man to waste words.

Strangely enough, she had no doubts now. Their marriage was uncomplicated by romance, and she had no longings or fits of jealousy or uncertainties about the future. They would deal comfortably with each other.

Mr van Doelen walked into his house a few evenings later and Serena, winding wool for Nanny, dropped the ball and jumped to her feet.

'Oh, you're back. You didn't phone… Why didn't you?'

'Hello, Serena, Nanny. How very domestic you look.'

Nanny put down her knitting. 'You'll want a meal,' she said placidly. 'About half an hour? You had a good trip?'

'Yes, and I'm famished.'

Serena picked up the wool and sat down again. It seemed that Ivo came and went without fuss; she should have held her tongue. It must have sounded to him that she was critical of him for not phoning. She felt a fool. She must remember for the future.

Mr van Doelen went to his study with his bag and then came back and sat down in a chair from where he could watch her.

'You haven't been bored?' he wanted to know.

'No, no, not at all. I had shopping to do, and I've explored the parks, and the Reverend Thomas called to see me. He's nice.'

She couldn't think of anything to say then. Oh, for a witty tongue and facile conversation, reflected Serena. She wound the wool as though it was a matter of urgency, not looking at him.

He leaned forward and took it from her. He would have liked to have taken her in his arms and kissed her, but their rather fragile relationship might have been shattered. 'No doubts?' he asked her gently.

'No, of course not. But what about you? You must see how dull I am? That's because I never had anyone to talk to except Father. Won't you find me dull, too?'

'You aren't dull; you're restful. To come home to someone who doesn't start chattering the moment I get there is something I am looking forward to, Serena.'

She looked at him then. 'Really? I should have thought that after a day with patients and operating and wards, you would want a little light relief.'

'That, too, but at the right time.'

'Well, I'll remember that,' said Serena as Nanny came back to say that his supper was ready.

'Come and sit with me while I eat?' said Mr van Doelen. 'I want to know how soon you will marry me.'

At the table he told her that he was intending to be in London for three or four days, no longer. 'We could marry in the late afternoon of my last day and drive to Harwich for the evening ferry. It's a quick crossing by catamaran; we can be home in the late evening.'

'That sounds very sensible,' said Serena, doing her best to sound matter-of-fact. Suddenly the future was crowding in on her. 'The Reverend Thomas won't mind short notice?'

'I've already phoned him. He suggested three o'clock. We can come back here for tea, just us and Nanny and Reverend Thomas and his wife. We'll need to leave soon after.'

'Will you be here before then?'

'I doubt it. I hope to leave the hospital some time after two o'clock, but it may be later. You will wait here with Nanny, will you?'

'Yes.'

It was all rather businesslike, as though he was making an appointment with his dentist. It was disconcerting when Ivo said, 'I am afraid it is all rather rushed, but since we are to have a quiet wedding I believe you understand. I am committed to a good deal of work for the next month or so, and there seems no point in you staying here with Nanny until I'm clear of that!' He smiled a little. 'I promise you you won't be lonely. I have English friends who will be delighted to meet you.'

After supper he told her kindly to go to bed. 'I have some work to do, and I must leave early in the morning, but I should be home in time for us to have tea.'

That was the pattern of the next three days, and on the fourth day they were to marry...

Of course he had already left the house when she went down to breakfast. She had it with Nanny, obediently eating a boiled egg she didn't want and crumbling toast onto her plate. Now that their wedding day had dawned her usual sensible self was engulfed in doubts. Not that she thought for one moment of backing out of it; it was just the last hesitation, like the pause before diving into deep water.

Beside her vague doubts, she knew deep down that their marriage would be a success; they liked each other and enjoyed the same things and neither of them demanded anything from the other. It would be a calm, secure partnership. As if to squash any doubts she might have had, there was a letter from Dr Bowring to tell her that he and his wife would be at the church and how sure they were that she and Ivo would be happy together.

She went for a walk after breakfast, and then, mindful of Nanny's reminder that she had a long journey before her that evening, ate the dainty little lunch the dear soul had prepared. They ate it together in the kitchen and then went, together still, to Nanny's room so that Serena could help her decide which hat to wear.

And by then, it was time to dress.

The blue outfit looked all right; the new shoes were comfortable and the small-brimmed hat with its satin bow sat elegantly on her light brown hair. She took a last look at herself in the pier glass, caught up the light

coat she had had the foresight to buy, and went downstairs to wait for Ivo.

Nanny was in the kitchen, and when Serena poked
her nose round the door she was told to go and sit in
the drawing room. 'And take care not to get untidy,'
said Miss Glover at her most nanny-ish. 'You look very
nice.'

Which from Nanny was high praise indeed. Serena
hoped that Ivo would agree. Regardless of any damage,
she picked up Puss, sitting beside her.

She sat rather primly on a little balloon-backed chair
and tried not to look at the clock. If Ivo didn't come
soon they would be late for their wedding.

He came a few minutes later; she heard his key in
the lock and his quiet footfall in the hall and in a moment he was in the doorway.

'Oh, very nice,' he said, and smiled so that she felt
almost pretty. 'I'll be with you in ten minutes or so.'

And he was, in a beautifully tailored grey suit and
a silvery silk tie. He took Puss off her lap and Serena
got up as he said cheerfully, 'Shall we go?'

She couldn't think of anything to say as he drove the
brief distance to the church and helped her out of the
car. It was a small old church at the end of a quiet street.
There was no one about; Nanny had gone ahead, and
Serena supposed that the Bowrings were already inside.
They went inside together and in the porch Ivo handed
her a nosegay laid waiting on a bench. Roses and little
lilies, green leaves and sprigs of sweet-smelling stocks.

'We are going to be happy together,' he told her,

then took her arm and walked with her down the aisle to where the Reverend Thomas was waiting.

The Bowrings were there, and Nanny and Mrs Thomas, turning their heads to smile at them, and there were flowers—a feast of white and pink roses and trailing stephanotis. The afternoon sun shone through the stained glass windows above the altar and the air was fragrant and warm. Serena was aware of all this as she stood beside Ivo; she was aware, too, of feeling happy. Without any doubts as to the future she made her responses in a soft, clear voice and presently they walked back up the aisle, a married couple now, and got into the car and drove back to the little mews cottage where they were joined by the others.

Nanny, still in her wedding hat, served tea: tiny cucumber sandwiches, miniature scones, fairy cakes and a wedding cake which she had made herself. The talk was cheerful—of the wedding, and promises of a visit to Holland later on and how soon Ivo would be returning to London.

Before long it was time to leave. Puss was tucked into her basket, the cases were put into the car, and farewells said. Serena, in her coat now, her wedding hat sharing the back seat with Puss's basket, got into the car and turned to wave as Ivo drove away, suppressing a sudden small panic that she had burnt her boats and there was no going back.

Ivo said quietly, 'There is still time for you to change your mind, Serena...'

The panic melted before his calm voice. 'No, I don't

want to do that. You said that we are going to be happy together and I believe you.'

It took a while to cross London, but presently, with the suburbs thinning to fields and trees, he sent the car forging ahead.

'We'll have a meal on board,' he told her. 'It's a short drive from the Hoek but you may be tired by then, although there will be a light meal for us when we get home.'

'Did you have time for lunch?' she asked.

'No. Coffee and a sandwich. And you?'

'Well, I had time, but I wasn't hungry!'

'We'll make up for that on board. Are you comfortable?'

They found plenty to talk about. Theirs might be a marriage without love, but they were completely at ease with each other; it was as though they had known each other all their lives. Serena heaved a small sigh of content, and Mr van Doelen, glancing at her composed face, allowed himself to indulge in a brief daydream.

The crossing was calm, and they had a meal on board while Ivo patiently answered her questions about his home and his work. A small village, he told her, only a mile or so from Den Haag, and a house his family had lived in for many years. As for his work, he had beds in the principal hospitals in Den Haag, but he lectured at Leiden Medical School and had beds there too, and not only that, he had consultations in other countries as well as being an honorary consultant in London.

'I am a busy man,' he told her, 'but I'm sure you

won't be lonely, and when it's possible there's no reason why you shouldn't come with me.'

She assured him that she would like that. 'But you will be sure and let me know if I get things wrong, won't you?'

'Of course. But I don't think that is likely to happen. All my friends speak English…'

'Oh, but I'd like to learn to speak Dutch as quickly as possible. Perhaps I could have lessons?'

'A good idea.' He glanced at his watch. 'We shall be landing very shortly.'

It all looked a bit like England, except for the traffic driving on what she considered to be the wrong side of the road. When he observed that she might enjoy driving herself, she said uncertainly, 'Oh, I don't know—I might forget…'

'Not very likely with everyone else driving as they should. We shall be home very soon now.'

She was a little tired now, as well as hungry, and over and above this she had a sudden feeling of panic. She said rather faintly, 'I'm sure you must be glad to be home,' and heard the uncertainty in her voice.

'Oh, I am, and glad to have you with me.' He dropped a hand on her knee and said, 'Our home, Serena, and I shall do my best to make you happy in it.'

He was driving around the outskirts of Den Haag now and presently turned off into a side-road which in turn opened into a quiet country lane. All at once there were flat green fields and a canal running alongside it. It was dark now, and they had left all signs of the city behind them.

'This is a quiet corner which seems to have been overlooked,' said Ivo. 'It is delightfully peaceful, and so close to Den Haag. I must get you a car as soon as possible.'

'I could bike,' said Serena, and then wondered if a well-known surgeon's wife would be too grand to cycle.

It seemed not, for he said at once, 'Of course you can. Everyone here cycles.'

They had passed a couple of farms standing back from the road, and now there were trees on either side, and in a moment a cluster of small houses round a church.

'The village—we're just round the corner.'

Serena had very little idea what to expect; Ivo had been vague and she had pictured a comfortable villa, substantial and rather dull. But as he turned into a short drive between brick pillars she saw that she was mistaken. The house was brick, faced with stone, with a handsome door reached by double steps, its windows large with elaborate pediments. It wasn't a villa. She studied its handsome façade with faint misgiving. This was a country house, a gentleman's residence of some size.

He had stopped before the front door and she said rather sharply, 'You could have told me...'

He said mildly, 'I hope you won't dislike it. It is home to me. I hope it will be home to you, too.'

He got out of the car and opened her door and helped her out.

'It's a lovely house. I—I was—surprised.'

He took her arm. 'Come indoors and meet everyone.'

Chapter 6

The person who opened the door was short and stout, white-haired and dignified. Mr van Doelen clapped this dignified person on the back and then shook his head. 'Wim, it's good to see you.'

He had spoken in Dutch; now he turned to Serena. 'Wim looks after the house for me, Serena. He's been in the family for ever. His wife, Elly, is the cook and housekeeper.'

Serena offered a hand and Wim shook it carefully. 'Welcome, *mevrouw*.' He waved an arm and led the way from the vestibule into a broad hallway. There were several people there and he led her from one to the other; Mr van Doelen spoke again in his own language. Whatever it was he said, they smiled and shook hands with Serena in turn. There was Elly, as rotund as

Wim, with a round smiling face, a thin, tall woman—
Nel, and a short, stout girl—Lien. Also an old man—
the gardener, explained Mr van Doelen—Domus, and
a leggy youth beside him, Cor.

They all looked pleased to see her, reflected Serena,
but she hadn't expected them. She gave Ivo a reproach-
ful look which he ignored.

'Elly will take you to your room,' said Mr van
Doelen. 'There will be supper in ten minutes or so.'
Serena was led away to where a staircase curved its
way up at the end of the hall. It led to a gallery with
several doors, one of which Elly opened with a flour-
ish. The room beyond was large, with a four-poster bed
facing the two windows. There was a mahogany table
between the windows with a silver gilt mirror, flanked
by slender silver candlesticks, the bedside tables were
mahogany too, each with its porcelain lamp, and there
was a chaise longue upholstered in a pleasingly vague
patterned brocade; the same brocade draped the windows and formed the bedspread. A very grand room,
Serena thought, but a delight in which to sleep. She
took a quick look at the adjoining bathroom and opened
a door at its other end: another bedroom, rather austere but very comfortable. Well, really, thought Serena,
going back to peer at herself in the mirror and poke at
her hair, Ivo might have told her that he was so grand.

She went back downstairs and found him in the hall.

'In here,' he said, and opened a door and ushered
her into a panelled room with long windows overlooking the garden at the back of the house. He said, 'Be-

fore we have supper will you come and meet Casper and Trotter?'

She went with him to the window he had opened and two dogs came racing in: a golden Labrador and a small greyhound. They circled Mr van Doelen, beaming up at him, and he said, 'Here is Serena. Come and say hello.'

Serena bent down to fondle them. 'Oh, they're lovely. Which is which?' And when he told her she asked, 'Why did you call her Trotter? I mean a greyhound…'

'She was discarded as being of no use for racing. The man who threw her out told me that she was only fit to trot! She's elderly, and loves long walks, and Casper loves her dearly.'

It was obvious that Ivo loved her, too—and Casper. 'I hope they'll like me,' said Serena. 'I never had a dog; Father didn't like them. Would they go for walks with me?'

'Of course. We'll take them tomorrow afternoon and give you some idea of the country round us. I have to go to the hospital in the morning but I should be back for lunch; we can go after that. Now let us have supper—I'm famished.'

'So am I.'

They sat at one end of the long oval table with its gleaming silver and glass. There was a low bowl of flowers at its centre. It looked like a bridal bouquet, but she was too shy to say so. It was Ivo who observed, 'I see that Wim has produced a fitting floral tribute to the occasion. I expect Elly has thought up something equally bridal for us to eat.'

Certainly it was a meal to grace the occasion. Globe artichokes with a truffle dressing, grilled salmon with potato straws, and to crown these baked Alaska. And, of course, champagne.

Serena was hungry, and she did full justice to Elly's cooking. It was late now, but the food and drink had given her a new lease of life. To sit over their coffee talking seemed a splendid idea—only one Ivo didn't share. He said kindly, 'You must be tired; do go to bed. Have you everything you want?'

Serena said politely, 'Yes, thank you. At what time is breakfast?'

'Oh, eight o'clock, but I shall be gone before then. Ask Wim for anything you want. I'll see you at lunch.'

Serena got up from the table and he went to open the door for her. And as she passed him he put a hand on her shoulder.

'Sleep well, my dear. Tomorrow we shall have time to talk. I'll take you round the house and answer all your questions.' He bent and kissed her, a light kiss but at least a kiss... 'You were a beautiful bride,' he told her.

No one had ever called her beautiful before. She said soberly, 'And I'll be a good wife, Ivo.'

She slept soundly in her lovely room, to be awakened by Lien with early-morning tea. When she had showered and dressed and gone down the stairs there was Wim, waiting to escort her to a small room behind the drawing room where her breakfast was laid at a small table by a window. Casper and Trotter were there, too, to take up their places each side of her chair, looking expectant. She wasn't sure if they were allowed to be fed at the table, but since there was no one to see they shared her toast...

When she had finished she wandered into the hall, and Wim appeared silently to tell her in his basic English that she might like to walk in the garden with the dogs or go to the drawing room where he had laid out the English newspapers. There would be coffee at half past ten, he added, and lunch at half past twelve when Mr van Doelen would be back home.

Serena thanked him, feeling rather like a visitor no one quite knew what to do with, and went into the garden. A very large garden, she was to discover, stretching away in all directions and bounded by a high brick wall. She explored it thoroughly, with the dogs trotting to and fro, and she admired what she saw. Velvety lawns, herbaceous borders, a rose garden and flagged paths between lavender hedges. And, separated by another brick wall, a kitchen garden, filled with orderly rows of vegetables. There were fruit trees too, and stooping over a bed of lettuce was old Domus. He straightened up when he saw her and she wished him good morning, wishing she could talk to him. She must learn to speak Dutch as quickly as possible...

She went back into the house presently, and had her coffee and glanced through the papers, but she soon got up, feeling restless, and went into the hall and began opening doors. The drawing room, the dining room, the little room where she had had breakfast. That left two more doors as well as the baize door leading to the kitchen quarters. Ivo's study. She didn't go in, only stood at the door looking at the great desk and the chair behind it, the shelves of books, the powerful reading lamp. This was where he would come to work, she supposed, undeterred by the household's activities. She closed the door and crossed the hall to the last door. The library. Its windows overlooked the side of the house and the walls were lined with books.

She walked slowly, looking at titles, Dutch, German, French and, thankfully, plenty of English. And not only medical tomes, but a fine assortment of the English classics and a dozen or more modern bestsellers. There were magazines on one of the library tables, and comfortable chairs in which to sit and read them. Of one thing she was certain: she would never be bored; a lovely old house, a magnificent garden, the dogs and the friendly people who lived there... And Puss, of course, already placidly at home.

She perched on the library steps, studying the spines of the books above her, and was there when Ivo came in.

She put the weighty volume she was holding back in its place and got off the steps. She said a little breathlessly, 'You don't mind? It's such a beautiful library.'

He crossed the room. 'Of course I don't mind; it is your library, too. You like books and reading?'

'Yes, but I've never had much spare time. Have you had a busy morning?'

'Yes, and I shall be busy for a week or two. But I intend to find the time to take you round the hospital; everyone is anxious to meet you.'

'Oh—you mean the medical staff and the nurses?'

'Yes, and their wives and husbands. But it will be

just the medical staff to start with. In three or four days' time, if you would like that.' He added, 'Perhaps you would like to go shopping? You could go in with me tomorrow morning and you can have the day to yourself.'

She thought of the few pounds she had in her purse. He was suggesting in the nicest possible way that she needed the kind of clothes his wife would be expected to wear.

He watched her telltale face, and added in a matter-of-fact way, 'I've an account at several of the bigger shops, and I'll let you have an advance on your allowance.'

He strolled across the room towards the door. 'Shall we have lunch? Then we'll go for a walk with the dogs. Time enough to show you round the house after tea.'

Serena hadn't moved. 'I haven't any money of my own, you know that, but I don't like taking your money, Ivo.'

He leaned against the door he was holding open. He said in a level voice, 'You are my wife, Serena. You will share everything I possess; you will buy all the clothes you want and anything else you fancy.' He smiled then. 'I'm proud to have you as my wife and I want you to know that. And let us have no more nonsense about money. Buy what you like and send me the bills.'

'Oh, well,' said Serena, 'put like that it seems very sensible. Thank you, Ivo.'

They lunched together, talking about this and that in the comfortable manner of old friends, and presently took Casper and Trotter for a walk. They went through the village and Serena tried not to mind being stared at. She was, she supposed, a bit of an event in the quiet little place. They stopped to speak to several people, who beamed at her and shook hands and laughed a great deal with Ivo. But once clear of the village he took her down a narrow lane with flat meadows on either side. There were the black and white cows she'd expected to see, and farms, widely spaced, with their great barns and a few sheltering trees.

'Is all Holland like this?' she wanted to know.

'No, by no means. Limburg, in the south, is quite hilly, and in the north there is more space. Lakes, too. I go there in the summer and sail. I've a small farm in Friesland—a few sheep and cows, hens and ducks and geese. Will you like that?'

'Oh, yes, but I like your house here. It's old, isn't it? It feels like home...'

He took her arm. 'It is home, Serena. Our home.'

He whistled to the dogs and they turned back, going through the village again where they were stopped by even more people.

Serena, shaking hands and smiling and murmuring, hoped that they approved of her.

They drove into Den Haag early the next day, and Ivo parked the car and walked her round the shopping streets, pointing out where she could have coffee and lunch, showing her how she could get to the hospital if she needed to.

'But you should be all right,' he told her casually, 'I should be ready by four o'clock. Just tell the porter who you are and they'll tell me that you're there.' He gave her a quick look. 'You'll be all right on your own?'

Serena, her purse stuffed with notes, assured him that she would.

The arcade opposite the big departmental store looked promising. She went along its length, looking in all the windows—boutiques, jewellers, smart cafés, magnificent china and glass. She retraced her steps and paused at a boutique halfway down the arcade. There was a dress in the window, its accompanying jacket thrown carelessly over a little gilt chair. Honey-coloured, a silk and wool mixture. Very plain and simply cut— 'And very expensive,' muttered Serena, opening the door.

It was a perfect fit. She paid its outrageous price from the roll of notes in her purse and went off in search of shoes. Which naturally led to the obligatory purchase of tights. She stopped for coffee then, before going into De Bijnkorf in search of undies and something to wear at home. Prudently making sure that Ivo's account could be used by her, she went from one department to the other: simple dresses, skirts, tops, blouses, cardigans. She stopped for lunch then, since there was a restaurant there, and then went out into the street again. She had acquired a splendid wardrobe, although it was by no means complete. She needed a raincoat, and what about something for the evening? Ivo had said that he had friends. Presumably they would be asked out to dinner.

She began another round of the shops, not sure what she was looking for.

It stared her in the face from a shop window in another arcade. Pale pink silk and chiffon, simple, relying

on the cut and the delicate colour. Its modest neckline
and long tight sleeves were just right for dinner out or
an evening with any of Ivo's friends. She bought it,
and went in search of high-heeled strappy sandals...

And, after that, 'Enough's enough,' said Serena, and
went to one of the smart cafés for a cup of tea. She
would take a taxi to the hospital, she decided. She was
drinking her second cup when Ivo sat down opposite
to her at the little table.

'I finished early,' he told her, 'and decided to come
and give you a hand with your parcels.' He glanced at
the pile on the floor. 'You have had a successful day?'

'Oh, very, thank you. Would you like tea?'

'It's coming. Are you going to have one of these
cakes?'

'I've already had one...'

'Then have another while I drink my tea. You found
shopping easy? No language problems?'

'No, none at all.' She selected a mouthwatering con-
fection of chocolate and whipped cream. 'Have you
had a busy day?'

'Yes.'

She waited for him to say more, and when he didn't
she said, 'I'm not just inquisitive; I'm really interested.'

He gave her a thoughtful look. 'Yes? Then I shall
get into the habit of boring you each evening with my
day's work.'

'I shall like that.' She finished her cake and they
went together to where he had parked the car and drove
back home, silent now, but it was the pleasant, compan-
ionable silence of old friends or a long-married couple.

And that was what Ivo wanted, reflected Serena with a pang of sadness. But she had no reason to feel sad, she told herself, for he seemed content…

For the next few days she saw very little of him, for he spent them in Leiden and Utrecht, operating. He got home in the early evening, looking tired, so that she forebore from questioning him, but sat quietly with the wool and needles she had bought in Den Haag, intent on knitting a sweater for his Christmas present. True, that was some way off, but she was a slow knitter and the pattern was complicated.

She was rewarded one evening.

'You are a very restful woman, Serena. I find myself thinking of you sitting there with your knitting when I'm confronted by an over-large clinic and you act upon me like a tranquilliser. I shall be back here in a couple of days. We will go round the hospital together so that you can meet everyone. You're not bored? I've had to leave you alone…'

'I couldn't possibly be bored. Trotter and Casper take me for long walks, and I go to the kitchen each morning and Elly and I talk—about food and so on, with Wim helping out. I know quite a number of Dutch words already.'

'You shall have lessons. I'll arrange that for you. So, will you come with me on Friday morning?'

'With pleasure. I've been longing to wear the dress I bought.'

He raised his eyebrows. 'Only one? We must remedy that!'

'Oh, I bought some skirts and tops, and another dress or two. I'm wearing one of them.'

'And very nice, too,' said Mr van Doelen quickly; he hadn't noticed the dress, he saw only Serena's face and her large dark eyes. As far as he was concerned she could be wearing a sack. He made a mental note to be more observant in the future.

When she joined him at the breakfast table on Friday morning he got up to pull out her chair and kiss her on her cheek. 'You look delightful,' he told her, and meant it. The simple dress suited her, and the pleasure of wearing it had added a sparkle to her eyes and pink to her cheeks.

'Will it do?' she asked anxiously. 'There's a jacket to go with it...'

'It's just exactly right.' He must buy her a brooch, he thought, and some pearls—and there was that diamond necklace of his mother's...

He took her straight to the consultants' room behind the vast entrance, and just for a moment she panicked as he opened the door. The room appeared full of well-dressed men, all staring at her. But the moment was over. A tall grey-haired man and a small woman with a sweet face were smiling at her...

'The hospital *directeur*,' said Ivo, 'and his wife. Duert and Christina ter Brandt—my wife, Serena.'

'I've been dying to meet you,' said Mevrouw ter Brandt, 'well, we all have—I wanted to come and see you, but Duert said I must wait until you had settled in.'

Duert ter Brandt smiled at her and shook hands. 'We are delighted that Ivo has married at last and we hope you will both be very happy. I'm sure you will soon have many friends.'

And after that she was led from one person to the next, smiling and murmuring politely and forgetting names as fast as she was told them. When the last introduction had been made they went from group to group while they drank coffee and ate little biscuits, and presently Serena found herself without Ivo, smiling at a man younger than the rest, who took her coffee cup from her and, standing in front of her, screened her from the others.

'I'm sorry, I've forgotten your name,' said Serena.

'Dirk—you don't need to know the rest of it. How is it that Ivo found you first? I've been looking for a girl like you all my life…'

He was being familiar, decided Serena, and wasn't sure if she liked that. But it was rather fun to be chatted up—no one had ever done it before… She decided to ignore his remark and asked, 'Are you a doctor or a surgeon?'

'Doctor; I couldn't aspire to the surgical heights of your husband.' And, at her surprised look, 'Only joking—he's brilliant. Are you going to be happy here in Den Haag?'

'Yes, of course. And we don't live in Den Haag; our home is in the country.'

'May I come and see you there?'

'I'm sure we'll both be delighted, but not just yet.'

She glanced round and caught Mevrouw ter Brandt's eye. 'I must speak to Mevrouw ter Brandt.' She gave him a nod and a smile and crossed the room.

'You must come to tea—and call me Christina; I'm years older than you, but we're both married to Dutch medical men so we have a lot in common.' Christina smiled a little. 'What did you think of Dirk Veldt? A great one for the ladies. Come to tea on Monday; get Ivo to bring you. You must meet the children. I've three— a girl and two boys.'

'I'd like that very much, thank you.'

Serena felt an arm on her shoulders and Christina laughed. 'Ivo, I've invited Serena to tea on Monday. Will you bring her? Come early—it is your clinic afternoon, isn't it?'

'Two o'clock not too early? May I collect her around five o'clock?'

They said goodbye then, and Duert ter Brandt shook hands once again and said kindly, 'You must both come to dinner soon.' He clapped Ivo on the shoulder. 'You're a lucky man, Ivo.'

He kissed Serena, and Christina gave her a hug. 'Are you going round the hospital? We won't keep you, then; it will take the rest of the morning.'

Which it did. But, since Serena was interested in everything she saw, that didn't matter. Ivo took her home to lunch and then went back to work. 'But I'm free tomorrow,' he told her. 'We'll drive up to the farm.'

It was a cool, crisp morning when they left soon after breakfast the next day. He took the road through Alkmaar and across the great *dijk*, and once in Friesland turned away from the main road toward Sneek. There were lakes on all sides, and large farmhouses backed by vast barns, and the roads were mostly brick and narrow. Presently they reached a scattering of houses, too small for a village, and a mile or so further on Ivo turned in through an open gateway and stopped before a farmhouse standing back from the road.

A tall, thick-set man came round the corner of the house, calling a welcome, thumping Ivo on his shoulder and then shaking hands with Serena, and a moment later he was joined by a woman, almost as tall as he. 'Abe and Sien,' said Ivo, 'who run the farm for me.'

They all went indoors then, to drink coffee and eat little sugary biscuits, with Ivo patiently translating the conversation to Serena. It was all about sheep and cows and poultry, and presently she was taken to see the livestock before going back to the kitchen to sit at the table and eat sausage and red cabbage and delicious floury potatoes. And although she couldn't understand a word Abe and Sien were saying, Serena enjoyed every moment of it.

She was shown over the farmhouse next. It was a comfortable dwelling: a large living room, well furnished—although it was obvious that the kitchen was the hub of the house—and upstairs the bedrooms were large and airy.

'We can come up here for a weekend and go sailing if you like,' said Ivo, and Serena could think of nothing nicer. Although she had to admit that she had no idea of how to handle a boat.

'I shall enjoy teaching you,' said Ivo.

A lovely day, thought Serena as they drove home.

They went to church on Sunday, took the dogs for a walk, with Puss tucked under Serena's arm, and spent the evening pottering around the garden. After dinner, in the library, Ivo showed her the books she was most likely to enjoy.

A truly perfect day, and her visit to Christina to look forward to tomorrow. It was as she was going up to bed that Ivo came to the bottom of the staircase to ask, 'What did you think of Dirk Veldt?'

'He seemed a very pleasant man. Very good-looking too. Is he married?'

'No. Don't get too friendly with him, Serena.'

Surprise kept her silent for a moment then she said, 'Well, I'm not likely to see him, am I?'

She was on the point of adding that she was old enough to choose her own friends, but she thought better of it, for Ivo had sounded like a man who expected to be listened to and obeyed. And, after all, they had been married with old-fashioned vows, and one of them had been to love, honour and obey. Well, she honoured him, even if she didn't love him, so she would obey him—up to a point!

She said sweetly, 'Very well, Ivo. Goodnight.'

The ter Brandts lived in a large house in a quiet, tree-lined avenue in Scheveningen. As Serena and Ivo mounted the steps to its imposing front door it was opened by an elderly white-haired man, rather stout. Ivo shook his hand. 'Serena, this is Corvinus, who looks after Duert and Christina so well.'

A remark which Corvinus received with a dignified inclination of the head before leading them from the vestibule into the hall, just as Christina flung open a door and came to meet them.

'Oh, good, you're here. Ivo, must you go away at once, or can you stay for a while?'

He bent to kiss her cheek. 'Don't tempt me, Christina, I've a clinic in ten minutes or so. May I collect Serena around five o'clock?'

'And stay for a drink. Duert should be home by then.'

He turned to go, dropping a light kiss on Serena's cheek as he went.

A brotherly peck, reflected Christina. I wonder why?

She said cheerfully, 'Come into the sitting room. It's rather untidy but I'm sorting things for a jumble sale and the children's puppy and my cats have made it worse.'

It was a lovely room nevertheless, and splendidly furnished, although the vast sofa was covered by a variety of odds and ends and the big rent table under the window was piled with boxes. There was a puppy asleep in a basket and two cats curled up on one of the chairs.

It was obvious that Christina had been sitting on the floor, cutting something from a paper pattern. 'Corvinus doesn't approve of me making the room untidy; I have to clear everything up before Duert comes home—not that he would mind.' She smiled as she spoke and added for no reason at all, 'We've been married for seventeen years.'

Serena got down on the floor with her hostess. It was delightful to find someone so friendly and unselfconscious. She said, 'May I help?'

'Would you? That bag of wools—if you'd sort them out? Some of them are in a fearful tangle. You must come to the jumble sale. I've got a stall and I'll need help. It's on Thursday afternoon.'

'I'd love to, but I don't speak Dutch...'

'That won't matter as long as you can handle the money. You'll be the star attraction; we were so delighted when we saw your engagement in the *Haagsche Post*. Ivo's far too nice not to be married, and I'm so glad it's you.'

Christina rummaged in her workbasket. 'Now, tell me all about yourself.'

'Well, I'm not a bit exciting, I'm afraid. I lived at home looking after my father until he died—that's when I met Ivo. At least, we met out walking and talked a bit, although I didn't know who he was...'

Christina made a small encouraging sound and Serena found herself telling her about her brothers and her difficult father. She had to talk about Ivo, too, of course, but she glossed over her stay in London, merely saying that they had decided to marry quietly since Ivo had had to return to Holland.

'Very sensible,' said her hostess comfortably. 'I'm sure you will be happy here. You'll be swamped with invitations to dine and have coffee with all the wives, but they're all nice women; you'll like them. Gossipy, of course, but you can take that with a pinch of salt. They've been marrying Ivo off for some years...'

And then Corvinus came in, tut-tutting at the state of the room. Tea, he told his mistress, would be served in the garden room, if the ladies cared to go there very shortly.

Christina said something to him in Dutch to make him smile and added, 'We may have ten minutes to finish what we are doing.' When he had gone she said, 'He's been with Duert for years. When I first came here to work at the hospital it was he who met me at Schipol, and he's been my friend ever since.'

Serena finished sorting the wools, put them tidily in a box, and went with her new friend out of the room and across the hall to a much smaller room, very cosy, its window overlooking the garden. And here they had their tea.

'English afternoon tea,' said Christina with a twinkle, 'and in the winter Duert has crumpets sent from Fortnum and Mason.' She added simply, 'He spoils me...'

Serena felt a sudden pang of envy—to be so loved... The thought was followed immediately by the heartening one that Ivo might not love her but his liking had been deep enough to make him want her for his wife.

They lingered over tea, and they were still there when the two men came in together. Duert bent to kiss his wife and smiled at Serena. 'You found enough to talk about?' he asked.

Ivo had come to stand beside her chair, stooping to kiss her cheek.

'Indeed we did,' said his wife. 'Serena must come again and meet the children. She's going to help me at the jumble sale...'

'A nerve-shattering event for all but the most strong-minded women!' They all laughed as Duert said it.

They went soon after that; Ivo had to return to the hospital to check a patient's condition.

'But you'll come to dinner soon,' said Christina. 'We'll have a few people in to meet you. Serena must get to know everyone as quickly as possible.'

'You enjoyed your afternoon?' asked Ivo as they drove back to the hospital.

'Very much. I didn't know that Christina had been a nurse here.'

'Yes, but she and Duert met in London. I dare say she will tell you about it.' He didn't say more, and there was no chance to ask him since they had arrived at the hospital.

Ivo parked the car near the entrance, assured her that he would be a mere five minutes or so, and went into the hospital. The main door was glass, and she could see him walk the length of the entrance hall and then start up the staircase at its end.

It was comfortable and warm in the car, and she was content to stay there and mull over her pleasant afternoon, but she rounded herself presently and glanced at her watch. The five minutes was already fifteen...

She looked through the doors and watched several people passing to and fro, but there was no sign of Ivo. Several more minutes had passed before she saw him, walking slowly from the staircase. There was a woman with him—too far off to see her clearly—but she looked young, talking animatedly, and Ivo, his head bent, was listening. They slowed their walk and stood near the door so that Serena had a better view. The woman *was* young and pretty, and well dressed, and she had a hand on Ivo's arm.

Serena was surprised at the sudden rage which shook her, made worse when Ivo put a hand on the woman's shoulder. They had all the appearance of old, familiar friends, laughing together. Serena had the urge to jump from the car and remind Ivo that she was his wife. Then common sense took over. Ivo had friends whom he had probably known long before he'd met her, and she had no business to mind about that. It would be different if she loved him...

She looked away from the door. That was the trouble, of course. She did love him! She had never fallen in love before—you couldn't count Gregory—and she had had no idea. She drew a long, calming breath and took another look at the door. They were saying good-bye—no formal handshake—and Ivo was walking out towards the car.

Chapter 7

Ivo got into the car beside her.

'Sorry I was longer than I expected.' He gave her a brief, smiling glance and she waited for him to tell her about the girl. Only he didn't. Serena swallowed back the words she longed to utter; this was something she must sort out for herself, a complication she hadn't even thought of. And if she had discovered that she had fallen in love with Ivo before they had married, would she still have married him? Common sense said no, but her heart said yes. This was something she would have to learn to live with. She would have to fill her life with other interests, leaving Ivo free while at the same time fulfilling her wifely duties. And she might as well start straight away...

'Your patient was all right?' she asked. And when he

nodded added, 'You don't mind if I help at the jumble sale? Christina thinks it would be a good way of meeting a few of her friends.'

'I agree. Get to know as many people as you can, my dear, then when I'm away you won't be lonely.' He sounded casual. 'I'm going to Madrid—there is a case there I've been asked to operate upon. I won't take you with me for I shall be too busy.'

She kept her voice pleasantly interested. 'When do you go?'

'On Thursday.'

They were home by now, and the rest of the evening was spent pleasantly enough, walking the dogs and having a leisurely dinner. But as they left the table Ivo said, 'I've a good deal of work to do. I'd better say goodnight, Serena.'

So she sat for a while with Puss for company and her knitting to keep her fingers occupied. Her head was occupied too, but not with knitting.

Ivo was to take an afternoon flight to Madrid but first, he explained, he would have to go to the hospital. So Serena ate a solitary lunch on Thursday after bidding him a cheerful goodbye.

'I'm not sure when I'll be back,' he'd told her, 'but I'll phone.'

She hadn't been able to resist asking, 'A few days? Weeks?'

He'd smiled down at her. 'Days.'

She had nodded and smiled brightly, longing to say that she would miss him.

Wim was to drive her to the ter Brandts' house after

lunch, and because she felt unhappy, despite all her good resolutions, she decided to go earlier than was necessary. Wim could set her down in Den Haag and she could get the wool she needed for the sweater and take a tram to Scheveningen. The dogs had had their walk in the morning, so she bade Puss goodbye, got into Wim's little Fiat and was driven into the shopping streets. There was still plenty of time before she needed to be at the ter Brandts' house, and almost without thinking, she turned her steps to the hospital. Ivo would be gone, but just to look at the place would make him seem nearer...

She was idling along, close to the hospital now, when Ivo's car swept past her. And sitting beside him was the girl. She was talking animatedly but Ivo was looking ahead, which was a good thing otherwise he might have seen Serena's astonished face.

She stood stock-still, not quite believing her eyes. A woman with a pushchair and several small children rather pointedly nudged her out of the way and she turned on her heel and walked back the way she had come. She wanted to go home, to go into the garden and sit quietly and think, but there was the jumble sale. She stopped a taxi and got to the ter Brandts' house only a few minutes later.

Christina, coming to meet her as Corvinus admitted her, took one look at her face and said briskly, 'Good, you're on time. I hope you've come prepared for hard work. Did Ivo get away in time to catch his plane?'

She bustled around, carrying on a conversation which needed no replies, for she could see that Serena was in no state to chat. Had she and Ivo quarrelled?

she wondered. The girl looked as though she could burst into tears. Christina wisely forbore from asking, but hurried Serena out to her car and drove to the hall where the sale was to be held.

Mercifully there was so much to do when they got there, and she was introduced to so many people that Serena had no time to think, and when the doors were finally closed Christina drove her back and gave her tea before getting into the car once more and taking her back home, all the while chatting quietly about nothing much, relieved to see the colour come back into Serena's cheeks. She didn't stop.

'I must get back home; Duert likes me to be there when he comes back. He mulls over his day with me. I expect Ivo does the same?'

Serena conjured up a small smile. 'Oh, yes, he does.' But she sounded so forlorn that Christina just stopped herself in time from asking what was wrong.

Back home later that evening, with the children in their rooms, she looked across at Duert, sitting in his chair, reading the paper.

'There's something wrong,' she told him. 'Serena isn't happy—in fact she was on the point of tears. Do you suppose they've quarrelled?'

Duert put down his paper. 'My darling, it is perfectly natural for couples to quarrel, and they are neither of them young and foolish.'

He smiled at her and she smiled back, sure of his love and of her love for him. She said, 'We're happy, aren't we?'

'Blissfully so, dear heart, and so will they be, but give them time.'

* * *

Serena ate a solitary dinner, took the dogs and Puss into the garden and went early to bed, explaining to Wim that she had a bad headache.

'More like she's missing the master,' he told Elly. 'Pity she couldn't have gone with him.'

'He wouldn't take her to Madrid—all those foreigners.' She sighed sentimentally. 'Missing him, of course, and he'll be glad to get back home to her.'

Serena didn't sleep much. She did her best to be sensible; she must not let imagination run away with her. Perhaps the girl was one of his assistants, or a special nurse to look after his patient. She had been very well dressed for a nurse, and she hadn't looked like one. Ivo would phone her in the morning and she would ask in a casual manner. No, she couldn't, because he would know that she had seen them together.

Her mind in knots, Serena's imagination became more and more vivid as the night advanced. It was almost daybreak when at length she dozed off.

She took the dogs out directly after breakfast, intent on being in the house if Ivo should ring, but there was no phone call; she pottered in the garden, never far from the house, but although various of the ladies whom she had met at the jumble sale phoned, with invitations to coffee or tea, there was nothing from Ivo. 'He's been too busy,' she told Puss, and, since there was nothing better to do, took the dogs for another walk.

He didn't phone the next morning either, so that by lunch time she was not only desperately unhappy, she was in a fine rage. Just because they weren't madly in love with each other—well, he wasn't anyway, she amended—that didn't mean to say he could forget her the moment he left home.

She pecked at her lunch and went to the library to look for a book. It was while she was there that Wim came to tell her that she had a visitor.

'Dr Veldt, *mevrouw*,' said Wim, 'in the drawing room.'

Serena put down her book. 'Doesn't he want to see my husband, Wim? Perhaps he doesn't know that he's away. I suppose I'd better go.'

Dirk Veldt was standing looking out of the window, but he turned as she went into the room.

'I thought that you might be lonely now that Ivo is away,' he said, and crossed the room to take her hand. 'Too bad of him to leave his bride so soon after the wedding.'

Serena said calmly, 'Good afternoon, Dr Veldt. I'm not in the least lonely, although it is kind of you to ask.'

'I thought you might like to drive into the country? The real country.' He sneered a little. 'The Veluwe is beautiful at this time of the year.'

'It's a famous beauty spot, isn't it? But, no, thank you.'

She hadn't asked him to sit down, and waited quietly for him to leave. He was an attractive man, and amusing, but she wasn't sure if she liked him.

He smiled. 'Oh, well, there was no harm in asking. Perhaps another time—Ivo goes away quite frequently, you know. Madrid this time, wasn't it? Some VIP, I suppose, with a broken leg. Still, he'll have Rachel to keep him company.' He smiled widely at her.

She met his gaze with an answering smile. 'Yes, it's a good thing that he has,' said Serena, with what she hoped was just the right amount of casual interest. 'I'm sorry that I can't ask you to stay for tea…'

It was just as well that he left then, otherwise she might have burst into tears. He was a mischief-maker, with nothing better to do than stir up trouble, she told herself. All the same, he had sewn the seeds of doubt in her mind.

She must forget his sly remarks, she told herself. If she hadn't fallen in love with Ivo she supposed they wouldn't have mattered, but now it was hard to banish them. She went back into the library, determined to ignore them, but when at last Ivo telephoned that evening she found it hard to talk to him. In reply to his questions as to how she had spent her days she gave stilted answers, and she didn't tell him of Dirk's visit, only enquired as to his work.

'I hope to be home in a couple of days. You aren't lonely?'

'No, no. There's so much to do—the dogs, you know—and—and…' She was stuck. 'Do you want to speak to Wim?'

His voice sounded suddenly cool. 'Yes, please. Goodnight, Serena.'

She went to see Christina in the morning; there was to be coffee, and there would be several wives there whose husbands were colleagues of Ivo. She dressed carefully, anxious to make a good impression, and did her face and hair with a good deal more attention than she usually paid them. She must remember that she was a happy bride...

There were two or three wives of her own age, one or two slightly older women, and an elderly lady with an air of great importance. The *burgermeester's* wife. Serena was being circulated from one group to the next, and soon she found herself sitting on one of the sofas beside her and submitted to the questions put to her.

'You should be happy,' pronounced her companion. 'Ivo is a most successful surgeon, and not only in Holland. A charming man too. He has had many opportunities to marry.' She smiled—a rather mean smile, Serena thought. 'And he ignores some of the most eligible young women in his own country and marries you. Men are so unpredictable.'

Serena wondered if she was being deliberately rude or whether she was just tactless. She said, 'Yes, they are, aren't they? But he chose me...'

'Yes, one wonders... Have you met Rachel Vinke? Now there is a beautiful and very clever girl. I had always thought that she and Ivo would marry...'

'Probably Ivo found her too beautiful and clever,' said Serena in a sweet voice. Her companion gave her a sharp look, and then looked away from Serena's cool, calm gaze. 'And I must go and speak to Christina,' said Serena, 'and go home. The dogs need their walk.'

She offered a hand and crossed the room to where Christina was talking to two younger women, and presently, when the *burgermeester's* wife had gone, one of them asked, 'Was she cross-examining you, Serena? Don't let her worry you. She can be very unkind.'

Serena made some laughing rejoinder and said that she must go home, and went round the room saying goodbye and accepting invitations to coffee and tea and dinner parties.

It was as Christina accompanied her to the door that she said, 'Is there something wrong, Serena? Someone's been gossiping. Don't listen to it. Have you heard from Ivo?'

'Yes, he'll be home in a day or two.'

Ivo had phoned while she had been at Christina's house. He would be home on the following evening, said Wim, looking pleased.

Serena spent a restless day, which seemed endless. The *burgermeester's* wife's snide remarks refused to go away, so that she went a dozen times to a mirror to confirm her fears that she was hopelessly plain—and this Rachel was beautiful and clever, she had said. Could she be the girl she had seen Ivo with? Serena did her hair again, renewed her make-up, and took the dogs and Puss for a quite unnecessary walk.

She changed her dress after tea. Pink jersey silk— Nanny had said that Ivo liked pink. She did her hair once again and went and sat in the drawing room, the dogs at her feet, Puss curled up beside her, her knitting on her lap.

Ivo, coming quietly into the room, paused at the door. While he had been away he had thought of her constantly, and here she was, exactly as he had pictured her, sitting there, tranquil, a delight to the eye...

The next moment she had seen him, and got to her feet.

'Ivo, how nice to have you home again. Was it a success?'

He bent to kiss her cheek. 'Yes, I'm glad to say. How delightful it is to come home and find you sitting there with your knitting.'

He bent to fondle the dogs. 'Have you enjoyed your days?'

'Yes, thank you.' She gave him an account of her activities. 'And I've been in the garden with Domus; he let me help him plant out the winter pansies.'

'He did?' Ivo smiled. 'How did you manage that? He won't allow anyone to touch a blade of grass.'

'I expect it's because we can't understand a word we say to each other!'

He laughed then. 'Dinner in half an hour? I'll go and change...'

She asked questions about Madrid, and the hospital there, and the operation he had performed, and he answered her readily. But he had nothing to say about the girl who had been with him.

Serena sat wrestling with her knitting and wondered how she could find out. She could, of course, ask him, but supposing his answer was unsatisfactory? It would be best to do nothing about it. She was probably making a mountain out of a molehill.

He didn't look as if he were keeping anything from her, sitting there, reading his post. She had put some invitations addressed to them both in with the pile of letters and he read them out.

'They're all from friends of mine. I see Duert and Christina have asked us for Saturday—there will be others there, of course.'

'What should I wear?'

'Something pink; you look nice in the dress you are wearing. I shall be free tomorrow afternoon; shall we go and look for something?'

'Oh, yes, please. And there's an invitation to a reception. Will that mean a long dress?'

'Oh, yes. We might see a dress we like tomorrow. Have you had any invitations to coffee, and tea parties?'

'Yes, quite a few. I went to Christina's yesterday and met several of the wives we saw at the hospital. And the *burgermeester's* wife…'

'Who no doubt peppered you with questions…?'

'Indeed she did, and a great deal of gossip. I don't think she liked me overmuch.'

He had picked up another letter and said carelessly, 'She doesn't like anyone, my dear.'

Going shopping with Ivo was much more exciting than being on her own. For one thing, she didn't need to ask the price of anything, and, for another, he was interested in what she bought. They found a deep pink dress in a silk crêpe and, since the evenings were getting chilly, a marabou stole to go over it, and while they were about it he suggested matching sandals. Serena, who would have called a halt at the dress, was enchanted. After a leisurely search around the boutiques they found a dress just right for the reception.

The blue-green of a summer sea, its bodice embroidered, its taffeta skirt wide, rustling deliciously—and sandals to match, insisted Ivo, and swept her away to tea and cakes.

'Thank you, Ivo,' said Serena, choosing a rich cream cake. 'I can wear them to all the parties we will be going to. I mean, they're quite suitable for the winter.'

'My dear girl, you will need several more frocks before then. We must get some sort of a cloak for the evening too. I'm due back at the London hospital in a couple of weeks' time; would you like to come with me?'

'Yes, please. I'd like to see Nanny again, and your nice house…'

'Our nice house, Serena.'

It had been a lovely afternoon, she reflected later, watching him drive away. A private patient, he had told her, and she wasn't to wait dinner for him. He still wasn't home when she went to bed.

He was at the table when she went down to breakfast. She wished him good morning and told him not to get up, and slipped into a chair opposite him. His own good morning was absent-minded, but since he was reading his post that seemed reasonable enough to her.

She was completely taken by surprise when he said quietly, 'Dirk Veldt came to see you while I was away. Why didn't you tell me?'

He looked as calm as usual, but she had a nasty feeling that he was angry. 'Well, I really don't know, Ivo. I mean, it wasn't important. He thought I might have been lonely with you away and came to ask me to go with him for a drive in his car. I didn't want to go and I told him so. He was only here for fifteen minutes or so. I didn't invite him to stay.'

'And it was so unimportant that you didn't think to tell me of it?'

She said matter-of-factly, 'That's right. There was nothing secret about it, you know.' She added coolly, 'Husbands and wives shouldn't have secrets.' And then went slowly red, for she had a secret, hadn't she? Loving him and not saying so.

Ivo watched the telltale colour. 'I have no intention to censor your friendships, Serena. There was no reason why you shouldn't have gone for a drive with Veldt; he's an amusing companion, so I've been told.'

'I don't want to be amused,' said Serena tartly. 'Are we quarrelling?'

He laughed. 'No, no. We're both far too sensible to do that. What do you intend to do today?'

'I've been asked to have coffee with someone called Mevrouw Kasper... She's rather nice.'

'Yes, Kasper's one of the anaesthetists, a sound man. They've four children—all boys.'

'Oh, then we shall find plenty to talk about.' She buttered toast. 'Will you be home for lunch?'

'No, but in time for tea, I hope, and a long, peaceful evening.'

Mevrouw Kasper lived in Wassenaar, a leafy, wealthy suburb of Den Haag—a modern house, but not aggressively so, and roomy, with a fair-sized garden.

'We moved here,' explained Moira Kasper, pouring coffee, 'because of the boys. We needed more space.'

She laughed. 'Wait till you start a family…not that that should trouble you. Ivo's house is pretty big, isn't it, and the grounds are vast.' She saw Serena's pink cheeks and added, 'Sorry, it's none of my business. How do you like living in Holland?'

'Very much, though I haven't seen a lot of it yet. We went to Friesland, to Ivo's farm there. I hope we can go again soon.'

'Perhaps now that he's married he'll take more time off—he's a glutton for work. What are you wearing to the ter Brandts' on Saturday?'

Serena enjoyed the dinner party. She knew almost everyone there, and they stood about gossiping in the ter Brandts' drawing room, drinking sherry and eating the tidbits which the three children offered. And at dinner she sat between Dr Kasper and an elderly rotund man who was quite a famous pathologist. He had a dry sense of humour, and Dr Kasper an endless fund of funny stories, so that she was happily entertained. Dirk Veldt was there, but at the other end of the table, and beyond saying hello before dinner she hadn't spoken to him. Although later, as they sat over coffee in the drawing room, he came and sat beside her for a few minutes, making polite conversation before drifting away again. Serena, aware that Ivo was watching her, made no attempt to delay him.

The pattern of her days settled into a quiet round of small chores around the house: the flowers, discussing the meals with Elly—a laborious and sometimes hilarious task, helping Domus when he was in a good mood and didn't mind her being there, taking the dogs for their walks, playing with Puss, writing longer letters to Nanny and shorter notes to her brothers, who never replied. I'm a lady of leisure if ever there was one, reflected Serena, enjoying every minute of each day, so different from her days looking after her father.

And each evening there was the joy of seeing Ivo come home, and to sit and listen while he told her about his day. She understood perhaps half of what he told her, but she stored up his remarks and spent time in the library, where she buried her head in the medical tomes there. She had started Dutch lessons, too, going in to Den Haag twice a week with Ivo in the morning and spending an hour or more with a fierce little woman who worked her hard and was ruthless about homework not properly done.

And she had a busy social life now, and not all idleness, for there were various charities she had been asked to join. Life, decided Serena, was a pleasure—although not perfect. It would never be that unless Ivo discovered that he loved her, but loving him coloured her days.

The reception was to be a grand affair, and everyone she knew was going. There was a lot of talk about dresses and hairstyles, and a rumour that royalty might put in an appearance.

'I'm just a bit nervous,' she confessed to Ivo.

'No need. You will look delightful in that gown—which reminds me...'

He went out of the room and came back with two leather cases. 'The family pearls, yours now, and these

earrings.' A double row of pearls with a diamond clasp
and pearl earrings surrounded with diamonds.

'My goodness,' said Serena, 'they're heirlooms?'

'Yes.' He took another case from a pocket. 'And this
is a very late wedding present, Serena.' He opened the
case and took out a bracelet, a delicate affair of diamonds and pearls, and fastened it onto her wrist.

'It's beautiful, Ivo,' said Serena, 'thank you.' And
she kissed him. And felt him draw back. She swallowed, hurt; she must be more careful, and remember
that they were friends and nothing more...

Dressed for the reception, taking a last look at herself in the pier glass, she knew that she looked almost
pretty. Nothing would improve her face, of course, but
her eyes were bright with excitement, her hair, in its
usual simple style, had gone up well, and the dress was
perfection. And, to crown everything else, the pearls
and earrings and bracelet gave her an air of opulence.
'I look like a successful man's wife,' she told herself,
and went downstairs to where Ivo was waiting for her.

He watched her coming carefully into the room and
thought that he had never seen anyone so beautiful.
He said, 'You look charming. I'm very proud of my
wife, Serena.'

'Thank you—and I'm proud of you—tails do something for a man. No wonder the *burgermeester's* wife
told me that you could have had any one of the beautiful and talented young women in Den Haag.'

She laughed as she spoke, and he laughed with her.
'You will see some splendid uniforms tonight. They
will probably outshine the women.'

The great hall was already crowded when they arrived. They were received by the *burgermeester* and his wife—she in purple velvet cut too tight for her ample proportions. She eyed Serena up and down before observing that she had never been able to wear that particular shade of blue-green herself, adding, 'You know many of the people here; it should be an enjoyable evening.'

Serena thanked her prettily and was swept onto the floor by Ivo. He was a good dancer, if conventional, but she was glad of that for she had had little chance to dance when she had been living at home. When the dance ended they were joined by friends and she was swept away by Duert. And after that she never lacked partners.

Her dress, she was pleased to see, was as pretty as any in the room, and that knowledge gave her an added sparkle. She was enjoying herself, and when Ivo claimed her for the supper dance she lifted a happy face to his. 'Such a lovely evening,' she told him.

Soon to be spoilt.

Leaving the supper room presently, they came face to face with the *burgermeester* and his wife, and with them was a young woman. Serena recognised her at once—she had been with Ivo at the hospital and in his car. And now, having a closer look, she could see that she was strikingly beautiful, with almost black hair and large dark eyes. She was dressed in black, something slinky and soft, showing off her splendid figure.

And Ivo had stopped, so that Serena had to stop, too.

'You must meet,' said the *burgermeester's* wife. 'Ivo must have mentioned Rachel to you, Serena—such old friends.' She smiled maliciously. 'Serena, this is Rachel Vinke. Serena is Ivo's wife.'

She watched them both with sharp eyes and Serena offered a hand, somehow managing to keep a smile on her face. 'How nice to meet you,' she said, and was pleased to hear how friendly she sounded.

Rachel shook hands, murmured something conventional and turned to Ivo.

'Ivo, we must talk; there is a great deal I have to say to you.'

She flashed a smiling look at Serena. 'You do not mind? A personal matter, you understand?' She turned back to Ivo. 'Tomorrow, perhaps? If I come to the hospital?' She frowned. 'No, of course it will be Sunday…'

'Why not come to lunch?' asked Serena, surprised at the words which had popped out of her mouth before she could stop them. She had been mad to utter them, but at least she had seen the disconcerted look on the *burgermeester's* lady's face. When she glanced at Ivo there was no way of knowing if he was pleased or not; he looked exactly the same as always: calm and remote and pleasant.

'That would be ideal,' said Rachel. 'We will then have the leisure to talk, you and I?'

Ivo's voice was giving nothing away; he agreed with just the right amount of interest expected of him, and after a few minutes' talk they separated.

Serena, not sure what was to happen next, said quickly, 'I'm going to tidy myself before the dancing starts again,' and whisked herself away. She wasn't certain, but she had the feeling that Ivo was angry.

And so he might well be, she thought angrily, pinning her already tidy hair, springing a surprise like that on her just when she was enjoying herself. Well, he couldn't say that she was interfering in his life like a possessive wife. They were friends and nothing more, weren't they? She whirled herself back to the ballroom, and the first thing she saw was Ivo with Rachel. She was looking up at him as they danced, and talking… The second was Dirk Veldt, who swung her onto the floor before she had the chance to speak.

'I was beginning to think that I would never get the chance to dance with you,' he told her, 'but I see Ivo is engrossed with Rachel Vinke. You've met her? She's beautiful, isn't she? Personally I prefer your type of beauty, Serena. You look gorgeous tonight.'

She didn't believe that, of course, but it was welcoming to her unhappy ears. He was holding her too tightly, but she didn't care. If Ivo could go dancing off with this Rachel who seemed to know him so well, she had every right to dance with Dirk. And what did they want to talk about? Something that necessitated her coming to lunch….

'You're not listening to a word I'm saying,' said Dirk, bending his head to speak softly into her ear.

She wasn't, but as Ivo and Rachel were close enough to see them, Serena gave Dirk a brilliant smile.

The dancing went on for some time. She had partners for all the dances, and two more with Dirk, but at last it was the final dance and Ivo claimed her. They danced in silence, and when it finally ended they made their way back out of the ballroom, stopping to speak to friends as they went.

Ivo said, 'I will wait here while you get your coat.' He spoke pleasantly, but his eyes were cold. She had made him angry and she told herself that she was glad of it. If he wanted to quarrel she was quite willing...

In the car, beside him, she said defiantly, 'What a delightful evening. I did enjoy it. Didn't you, Ivo?' She added daringly, 'Meeting so many people too.'

He gave a grunt and didn't speak again until they were home. In the hall, Serena yawned. 'There's coffee on the Aga if you want some, Ivo. I think I'll go straight to bed.' She turned as she reached the staircase. 'Goodnight Ivo.'

He was standing in the hall, looking at her. 'You danced a good deal with Veldt.' He spoke very quietly.

'Yes.' It seemed prudent to start climbing the staircase. 'He's a good dancer and great fun...'

'Were you paying me back in my own coin, Serena?' he asked blandly.

'As a matter of fact I was. What's sauce for the goose is sauce for the gander.'

The look on his face didn't exactly frighten her, but it sent her running up to her room at a fine rate.

By the morning's light she regretted every word she had said. Never mind that he had hurt her so that she actually ached with unhappiness. When they had married they had struck a bargain; she had known exactly what he had wanted and she had agreed to it—a calm partnership with no pretence of love, only friendship and liking and a comfortable knowing that they got on well together. And now she had shattered that.

She got up and dressed and went down to breakfast, and found him standing by the open door. The dogs were in the garden and Puss was sitting by his feet.

He turned to wish her a genial good morning and she said at once, 'Oh, don't be nice, Ivo. I'm sorry—I shouldn't have said what I did last night. If you want to be angry I'll deserve every word of it. And I only danced with Dirk Veldt to annoy you...'

He turned from the door as the dogs came in. 'My dear, Serena, why should I be angry? You may dance with whom you choose and say what you wish.'

'Yes, that's all very well, but that isn't what we agreed, is it? We were to have a friendly marriage and not—not interfere. And you have every right to see your friends. She's very beautiful...'

'Ah,' said Ivo, in such a strange voice that she looked at him again.

'You believe that I am enjoying the resumption of a love affair?' he went on bitingly. 'We have been married a matter of a few weeks, Serena. If that is what you think of me then perhaps we should confine our feelings to the friendship to which you so often allude and avoid looking too closely at each other's lives.'

'Oh, Ivo,' said Serena miserably.

'Shall we have breakfast? It's a splendid morning for a walk, and you can tell me what you thought of the reception.'

Chapter 8

It was still early when they started out with the dogs, and Serena, anxious to make amends, said, 'We mustn't be too long. I don't know at what time Juffrouw Vinke is coming. I told Elly there would be a guest for lunch—it's duckling and cherry sauce, but there's one of Elly's raised pies in case she doesn't like duckling. And Domus let me have some strawberries from the greenhouse.'

She fell silent, aware that she was babbling, and Ivo said, 'Rachel is married. I said I would fetch her around noon. How are you getting on with your Dutch lessons?'

It was a gentle snub; she had deserved it, she supposed. 'Very well, I think, though the grammar is puzzling and I quite often miss out on the verbs—I mean, having to tack them onto the end of a sentence, one tends to overlook them.'

'Well, you will have a short respite soon. I'm due at the hospital in London in just over a week. I have to go to Leeds too, but you will be happy with Nanny?'

'Oh, yes, it will be lovely to see her again. I must find something to take her.' She glanced at her watch. 'Shouldn't we be turning back? If you're going to fetch Mevrouw Vinke…'

He took her arm as they retraced their steps. 'You are anxious to meet Rachel again? I don't imagine that you have much in common.'

'We're both women,' said Serena, and heard his rumble of laughter.

Waiting for Ivo to come with their guest, Serena wandered around the drawing room, peering in the mirror beneath the windows, poking at her hair, putting on more lipstick and then rubbing it off again. A waste of time, she told herself. She had no hope of competing with someone as beautiful as Rachel.

She told herself how right she had been as she went to welcome Rachel as she got out of the car—in white from head to toe. The simplicity of her dress owed its art to couture, and made Serena's straw-coloured linen two-piece insignificant. And her make-up was faultless…

Serena, very aware of her own shortcomings, greeted her with the social smile she had learnt, to cover her true feelings.

'Such a lovely day,' she observed. 'Do come in. What can we get you to drink?'

They had their drinks sitting by the window over-looking the ornamental pool at the back of the house, and Serena made small talk and didn't look at Ivo. He was, as he always was, a perfect host, and it was impossible to tell from his manner whether Rachel was just a friend or someone much nearer than that. And over lunch Serena had to admit to herself that she quite liked Rachel; she was amusing and a good talker, and she had a warm and ready smile. And she was attractive...

As they finished their coffee, Rachel said, 'And now I must talk to you, Ivo. Serena does not mind?'

'Not a bit.' Serena summoned the smile again. 'I'll take the dogs for a run. You'll stay for tea?'

'I would have liked that, but I have a plane to catch...'

She watched them go to Ivo's study and whistled to the dogs. How long would they be? she wondered. And then set off at a brisk pace, trying to forget about them. But she was back in the house an hour later, sitting in the drawing room, her ears stretched to hear the study door open.

They came into the drawing room presently; Ivo's face showed no more than its usual calm, and Rachel was smiling widely.

'That is all settled,' she told Serena. 'And now I must go back to my dear Jan. He will be so relieved that everything is settled. I don't know what we would have done without Ivo's help, first to put together his broken arms and legs and then to deal with all this tiresome lawsuit. But now at last it is—how do you say?—plain sailing.'

But not for Serena, of course. She asked, 'Your husband—he has been hurt in an accident?'

'Ivo did not tell you? A car crash—not his fault. He has broken both his legs and both his arms. Can you imagine anything more terrible? And Ivo has put him together again. We knew he would, and he came to Madrid at once when I came to ask him—he and Jan are old friends, you see. And then he has arranged everything with Jan's solicitors—it is to go to court, you see. Today I brought the last of the papers for Ivo to see and sign.'

She flashed Serena a brilliant smile. 'It is so like Ivo to do all this and say nothing.'

She kissed Serena warmly. 'When Jan is well again you must both come and stay with us. And now I must go, but I am glad that I have met you. You are just as Ivo described you.'

Ivo had been standing at the window with his back to them. Now he turned round to say, 'We had better leave, Rachel, we're cutting it fine.'

He looked at Serena then. 'I should be back before dinner.'

He touched her shoulder as they went out, but he didn't kiss her.

By the time he returned Serena was in a bad temper. He had deliberately misled her; there had been no reason why he couldn't have explained about Rachel. Perhaps he had found it amusing. She ground her splendid teeth and tossed back a glass of sherry that she didn't want.

The moment he came through the door she rounded

on him, made reckless by a second glass of sherry and a strong sense of grievance.

'You could have told me.' Her voice was shrill, so she paused and started again. 'About Rachel. It was beastly of you to let me think the things I did.'

'And what did you think, Serena? Or shall we ignore your regrettable thoughts? And I didn't tell you for the simple reason that you had already drawn your own conclusions.'

He had crossed the room and come to stand before her, and suddenly gave a chuckle. 'You've been at the sherry…'

Which was just too much for her. 'I hate you,' said Serena in a choked voice, and raced out of the room and upstairs, where she banged her bedroom door shut, flung herself on the bed and burst into tears.

Ivo stood for a while, looking at nothing and deep in thought. He had the look of a man who had made a delightful discovery. Presently he went to his dinner, requesting Wim to make sure that *mevrouw* should have a supper tray taken to her bedroom.

'She has a severe headache,' he told his elderly retainer, who went to the kitchen and told Elly that he was willing to bet his week's wages on the master and missus being not on speaking terms for the moment.

'It'll blow over,' said Elly. 'Look at the times you and me have had words, and here we are after I don't know how many years.'

Wim took the supper tray from her and kissed her plump cheek. 'Forty next year,' he told her, and trod carefully upstairs to tap on Serena's door.

It was perhaps not very romantic to be hungry when one's heart was breaking, but Serena polished off the contents of the tray and then, since there was nothing else to do and she had no intention of going back to the drawing room, lay in a hot bath until she was as pink as a lobster and went to bed. Where, rather to her surprise, she fell asleep at once.

The thought of facing Ivo across the breakfast table was daunting, but she wasn't a coward, and dressed in a patterned skirt and a cashmere top, she went downstairs.

Ivo came in from the garden as she reached the breakfast table. His good morning was friendly, as was his enquiry as to her headache. 'You slept well?'

'Like a log,' said Serena, 'and I didn't have a headache, only a bad temper!'

He passed her the toast. 'One of the things I like about you, my dear, is your honesty, so perhaps you will set my mind at rest about something you said. That you hated me...'

He was staring at her across the table, not smiling, but not angry either.

'No, I don't hate you,' she said. 'I'm sorry I said that, but I was cross.'

He smiled at her. 'So you were...'

'Are you never cross, Ivo? I mean wanting to shout at someone?'

'Not cross, but angry. Yes, I can be angry, but self-control is something one learns quite quickly in the medical profession. I'll be home for lunch and I have to visit an old patient in the afternoon. Would you like to come with me?'

'Oh, yes, I would. In Den Haag?'

'No—an old lady who lives in Leiden.' He was sitting back in his chair and Puss jumped onto his knees, ignoring the dogs at his feet. He looked the picture of a happily married man. Something which he confidently expected to be, given the patience to wait for Serena to discover that she was a happily married woman...

They were back on their old friendly footing, thought Serena, happily going to the kitchen to discuss the day's meals with Elly.

Her Dutch was improving. She knew the names of their foods now, and could add a few words to them, and Elly never smiled at her accent or her mistakes so that her morning visit was a pleasure. And, that settled, she took the dogs for their walk and went back presently to write a letter to Nanny with Puss curled on her lap.

It was a short drive to Leiden—ten miles or so—and since they were on the motorway there wasn't much to see, but when they reached Leiden Serena found plenty to look at and admire. When Ivo stopped in a narrow street beside a canal, with a row of small gabled houses facing it, she exclaimed with delight. The houses were indeed old, leaning against each other, each gable different. They presented a pristine appearance, with shining paintwork and gleaming windows.

She crossed the cobbles with Ivo and stood beside him as he banged the heavy doorknocker, which was opened almost immediately by a stout woman with screwed up grey hair and very bright blue eyes. She broke into speech when she saw Ivo, shook hands with them both and ushered them inside.

The hall was tiny, with a steep, narrow staircase facing the door and a half-open door to one side. The room beyond was small and crowded with furniture, and every flat surface was covered by photo frames and china ornaments. And sitting in the middle of it was a very small old lady, dressed severely in black. She had a round face and small dark eyes, a little beaky nose and white hair, piled high.

Ivo went to kiss her cheek and then introduced Serena, who shook a hand as thin and light as a bird's claw and murmured a greeting in her careful Dutch. The old lady looked her up and down and had a great deal to say to Ivo. Whatever it was made him laugh, and he drew a chair forward for Serena. 'Mevrouw Boldt says you are as pretty as a picture, Serena. You will not mind if we speak Dutch? I must ask her questions about her health. She worked for my mother years ago, and had an accident recently and broke her leg and hip. I just need to check them.'

So Serena sat quietly, listening to Ivo's quiet voice, watching his calm face, wondering if he would ever love her. And presently the woman who had admitted them came in with a tea tray. The china cups and saucers were very small, and the tea was weak, without milk or sugar, but there was a plate of little sugary biscuits. Serena sipped her tea, making it last, and nibbled a biscuit. She had a nasty feeling that there wouldn't be second cups and she was right.

Ivo had finished his talk with Mevrouw Boldt, and the conversation became general, with Serena's faltering Dutch smoothly helped out by Ivo, who translated the old lady's questions to her and popped in the right word when Serena got stuck with her replies. But the old lady seemed to like her, and when they got up to go she was invited to kiss the paper-thin cheek.

'You are to come with me again,' said Ivo, bidding the woman who had admitted them goodbye.

In the car he said, 'Mevrouw Boldt is over eighty, but she lives in the manner of her youth and has no intention of changing her ways. She was with my parents for more than fifty years and retired here with her husband, who was our gardener. Until she fell and broke a hip a year or so ago she was very active.'

'So you keep an eye on her?'

'Yes. You liked her little house?'

'It's charming—rather a lot of furniture and ornaments...'

'Her possessions, much treasured.'

'Do you visit her often?'

'As often as I can. You'll come with me again?'

'Yes, please. And perhaps by then my Dutch will be better.'

'You do very well, Serena.' He turned to smile at her and she smiled back, just for the moment happy.

They went to England soon after that, and although Serena was glad to be seeing Nanny once more, she hated leaving the dogs and Puss; she hated leaving the lovely old house too, and her friends.

A Good Wife

'The change will do you good,' said Christina, 'and you can do some shopping for me.'

Ivo took the car, since he had to go to Leeds as well as London, and they crossed from the Hoek and then drove from Harwich.

It was nice to be in England again, reflected Serena, though at the same time she wished that they were back in Holland. But Nanny's welcome was so warm that she forgot that for the moment. The little mews cottage offered a cosy welcome, and London could look delightful on a fine day.

Ivo went at once to the hospital, leaving her to gossip with Nanny and unpack, and she didn't see him again until the evening. Over dinner he told her that he would be at the hospital all day. 'Have you any plans?' he wanted to know. 'I'm sorry to leave you on the first day...'

'I'm going shopping,' said Serena, 'for Christina and for me. Do you want anything?'

'No, thanks. I'll try and get tickets for the theatre. What would you like to see?'

They decided on a musical. 'And we might have a night out after I get back from Leeds.'

She realised after the first day that she wasn't going to see much of him. It wasn't just his operating lists at the hospital, there were clinics, and on several evenings meetings with his colleagues. But at least she saw him at breakfast, and for dinner in the evening. And they had their evening at the theatre. When she had been living at home no one had taken her to the theatre—indeed, no one had taken her anywhere. The visit to the theatre was a treat, and she enjoyed it with the whole-hearted delight of a child. Ivo, watching her rapt face, saw almost nothing of the show.

It was on the next day that he went to Leeds. He would be gone for three days, he told her, dropping a light kiss on her cheek, getting into his car and driving away.

Serena smiled and waved, and then went up to her room and had a good cry. She wasn't sure why she cried, but she felt better for it, and after mopping her face and putting on fresh make-up she went in search of Nanny. They would go shopping, she insisted. She needed several things, and surely Nanny, too, had things to buy?

And Nanny, taking a look at Serena's pink nose, agreed immediately.

They spent most of the day at Harrods, where Nanny expressed astonishment at the prevailing fashions and then spent happy hours in the food hall. Serena bought sweets for Christina's children, and a very beautiful scarf for Christina, and then searched for suitable gifts to take to Wim and Elly and the rest of the staff. And for old Domus she found a lavender bush, small enough to go in the car.

They went back home, tired but pleased with their efforts, and for her part Serena was glad that one day away from Ivo was already nearly over.

She and Nanny were in the kitchen when he came home. Nanny was making cakes and Serena was sitting on the kitchen table, running a finger round the remains of the cake mixture in the bowl. She was sampling it from one finger when he walked in.

She was off the table and running to meet him when she remembered that he might not like such a display of delight. She came to a halt before him and changed the happy grin on her face to one of friendly surprise.

'Ivo, how nice you're back. Did you have a good trip? Do you want a meal? Tea won't be for another hour, but we can get you a meal straight away.'

Ivo didn't kiss her because he wasn't sure if he could trust himself to stop at a peck on her cheek. He said in his quiet voice, 'Hello, Serena—Nanny. I'll wait for tea; I had a meal before I left. I must do some phoning and catch up on my post; I'll join you in an hour.'

He smiled at them and went out of the kitchen, then crossed the hall to his study and shut the door.

And that's how it will always be, reflected Serena unhappily, doors shut in my face, however gently. She helped Nanny tidy the kitchen and then went to the drawing room. A good thing she had brought her knitting with her; she plunged into it now, glad it was complicated, and that it needed her concentration and the counting of stitches.

So when Ivo came into the room there she was, sitting, to all intents and purposes, perfectly composed, looking up at him with the kind of smile a long-married wife might give her husband.

Ivo sat down opposite to her, studying her ordinary face and neat head of hair. She was, he considered, not only pretty—very pretty—she was the epitome of what every wife should be. She might not have loved him when they married, but from time to time—in the kitchen just now, he reflected—her behaviour made him hope that in time she would love him. He must have patience, he reflected, let her find her feet in this new life she was leading.

'Did you go shopping?' he asked.

'Yes, with Nanny. We had a lovely day, drooling round the Harrods food hall.' She added, 'And I bought two dresses—they were so pretty—and I'm sure I'll have a chance to wear them later on.'

'Before then. Would you like to dine out tomorrow evening? And I thought we might go dancing on Saturday night.' He smiled at her. 'A chance to wear those frocks.'

He took her to the Ritz, where, in one of the new dresses, she dined off jellied lobster, spinach and walnut salad, rump of lamb and a dessert of fruit, cream and ice cream which beggared description. Over coffee Serena said happily, 'This is a heavenly place. Do you come here often?'

Ivo smiled. 'No, only on very special occasions.'

'Oh, is this a special occasion?'

'I think we should make it one, don't you?'

She wasn't sure if he was serious or not. She looked out of the window to the park beyond and then, struck by a sudden thought said, 'Is it your birthday? I ought to know when it is, oughtn't I? If it is...'

'No, no, don't worry. We shall be going back home in two days' time. I've a meeting tomorrow evening, but we might go to Claridge's on the following evening. Would you like that?'

Serena beamed at him across the table. 'Oh, yes, I would. Is it as splendid as this?'

'Just about. Are you tired?'

'Tired? Heavens, no… But you've had a busy day, haven't you? It's been lovely, but I'm ready to go home if you would like that.'

'No, no. I'm not in the least tired. I wondered if you would like to walk. We'll take the car as far as the Embankment.'

It was a lovely night: moon and stars and cold enough for her to pull her soft coat around her shoulders. And the Embankment was the best possible place to be, she decided, with the lights reflected on the Thames and the hundreds of lights from the city's windows. They strolled arm-in-arm, not always talking, but happy in their silences. Serena's head was empty of thoughts; it was filled with content. This could go on for ever, she reflected, only of course it wouldn't! But just for the moment life was perfect.

They went back to the car later, and drove home and sat in the kitchen drinking the coffee Nanny had left on the Aga. And when she got up to go to bed, Serena kissed Ivo's cheek shyly, not sure if he minded that.

'It was a lovely evening, thank you, Ivo. And I look forward to going to Claridge's. Do you have to leave early in the morning?'

'Yes. I've a list at eight o'clock, but I should be home for tea.'

He stood looking down at her, waiting for her to go through the door he was holding open for her. The perfume she wore was faint but fragrant, and he dropped a quick kiss on the top of her neat head of hair as she passed him, so light that she didn't feel it.

She did the shopping for Nanny in the morning, and after they had had their lunch together took herself for a brisk walk. Ivo would be home for tea and they would have their evening together. She smiled widely at the thought so that passers-by stared at her happy face.

It was while they were having their tea that she remembered that he had a meeting that evening.

'When would you like dinner?' she wanted to know.

'Did I forget to tell you? I'm sorry, I'm dining with some of the committee members before the meeting starts.' He glanced at his watch. 'I'd better go and change.'

'I expect you'll be back late?'

'Probably.' He saw her downcast face. 'Don't wait up, my dear, I'll see you at breakfast.'

She bade him goodbye cheerfully enough; she had heaps of things to do, she assured him, and she must start sorting out things ready to pack.

Ivo nodded absently, his mind already on the meeting ahead.

But he made up for his absence by taking her to Claridge's, as he had promised. As sumptuous a restaurant as the Ritz, Serena decided. There wasn't a pin to choose between them, and the food was just as delicious. And to crown the evening's pleasure they danced into the small hours. When at length she got to bed she was too sleepy to think sensibly, but it had been another evening to remember for life.

Serena was sorry to say goodbye to Nanny, although,

as Ivo pointed out, it was only a matter of a few hours'
journey for her to return whenever she wanted to.

'You'll be coming again?'

'Certainly, in a couple of months' time. I may come
over for brief visits—spend one night, perhaps.'

He gave Nanny a hug, popped Serena into the car
and drove off. On the way to Harwich he asked, 'Did
you phone your brothers? Would you like to visit them?
Now that we are married and settled down they may
feel differently about us.'

Serena thought that even if Ivo had settled down
she hadn't. She peeped at his calm profile. 'I phoned
them, but they were still annoyed; I don't think I'd better visit them yet.'

Henry had been nasty, as only Henry could be, and
Matthew had talked to her as though she had disgraced
the whole family. She said, 'Gregory has married. She's
the daughter of the Mayor of Yeovil. He must be glad
he gave me up!'

Ivo's hand came down on her knees. 'I'm the one
who is glad,' he told her.

The crossing was smooth, and they were back home
in time to eat the light supper Wim had ready for them.
Ivo would be going to the hospital in the morning, so
he excused himself with the plea of letters to read,
phone calls to make and the dogs to take for a walk.
Serena, mindful of her wish to be the perfect wife, bade
him goodnight and went up to her lovely room with
Puss and unpacked and bathed and got into bed. She
was lonely. She supposed that loving someone and not
being able to tell them that made for loneliness. She

lay awake for a long time, until she heard Ivo come to bed well past midnight.

Life had settled down into its quiet pattern again.

She went to see Christina the next day, handed over the things she had bought for her, agreed to sell flags for a charity, to help at a bazaar in aid of orphans and attend a concert in which Christina's children were appearing, and then on an impulse she took a tram to Scheveningen, where she walked along the promenade until she was tired. There were plenty of people and a great many children playing on the sands. She took the tram back in a while, and went back home to eat her solitary lunch and take the dogs for a walk.

When Ivo got home after tea she was in the drawing room, knitting the second sleeve of the sweater. She was rather tired of it by now, and probably Ivo wouldn't like it. She decided that she would start on a set of tapestry covers for the dining room chairs. The work of a lifetime...

Several days later she went into Den Haag, collected her flags and collecting box and went to her allotted pitch outside a bookshop, which pleased her since she could from time to time study all the latest editions in its windows. The street was a busy one, and she rattled her box with a will, smiling at the passers-by whether they stopped or not. She was enjoying herself; it was a fine winter's morning and she liked the bustle around her, and later on she would meet Christina for lunch and compare notes...

The morning was well advanced when Dirk Veldt stopped in front of her.

'Serena, how delightful to see you, and what a marvellous excuse to stop and chat while you sell me one of these flags.'

She offered him a flag. 'Shouldn't you be working at the hospital?'

'A man must eat; I'm taking a long lunch hour.' He gave her a charming smile. 'Will you share it with me? There's a little restaurant near here where they serve the most delicious sole baked in cream...'

'No, thank you, Dirk. I'm here for another hour and then I'm lunching with Christina ter Brandt. You haven't given me any money for your flag.'

He shrugged, and fished in his pocket for a note. 'I shan't give up. You must be exciting under that matter-of-fact manner.'

'Well, you're wrong, and do go away. Enjoy that sole. Perhaps you'll find a pretty girl you can share it with.'

She smiled at him, wishing that he would go. And Ivo, driving to his consulting rooms, saw the smile. The rage which engulfed him needed all his self-control to subdue.

It was late afternoon when he got home and Serena, very satisfied with her efforts, was in the drawing room, the tea tray beside her.

She looked up as he went in, gave him a smiling greeting and asked if he would like tea. 'It's a bit late,' she explained, 'but I had lunch with Christina and we sat talking. I sold all my flags too.'

Ivo sat down, refused her offer of tea, and enquired idly if she had enjoyed herself.

'Yes, I did, and people were very generous.' She

went rather pink. 'Dirk Veldt bought a flag from me. He wanted me to have lunch with him.'

And Ivo sighed with relief—she had told him of her own free will...

'And why didn't you? He's an amusing companion, I should imagine.'

The pink deepened. 'I thought I liked him when I met him. I mean, I didn't know anyone, and he came and talked to me and made me feel that I was someone—if you see what I mean? You see, Ivo, I never had much of a social life, and I know I'm a plain Jane but he made me feel pretty. But now I have friends, and I go to committee meetings and bazaars and things like that. I've found my feet.' She stopped to think. 'And now I know that I don't like him. We're bound to meet, aren't we? But he doesn't have to be a friend.'

Ivo listened to this with deep satisfaction. His Serena had indeed found her feet; she was happy and busy and she was liked by everyone who met her. And he had glimpsed the look of delight on her face when he had come into the room. Perhaps now was the right time...

'Serena...'

The phone stopped him. He picked it up and she listened to his quiet voice saying little. She knew enough Dutch now to understand that it was urgent, and when he put the phone down and told her that he must return to the hospital for an emergency operation, she said, 'Hard luck, Ivo. We'll wait dinner for you. It's something that'll keep. I hope it's successful, whatever you will have to do.'

She smiled at him as he paused by her chair to kiss

her cheek, and she wondered what it was that he had been going to say to her.

He phoned from the hospital later on that evening; he would be late home. Would she ask Elly to leave something on the Aga for him? He would see her at breakfast.

She knew better than to waste his time asking questions. In the morning at breakfast he might tell her about it. It pleased her that he was getting into the habit of describing his work to her, and she still spent hours in the library looking up the long words that he used so that she could look intelligent.

She wrote letters after dinner, a long, newsy one to Nanny and dutiful ones to her brothers, and by the time she had finished it was almost eleven o'clock. She went upstairs to bed and then, suddenly making up her mind, went down the stairs again in her dressing gown to find Wim. She would stay up, she told him. He was to go to bed after he had locked up. Ivo had his key, and once he was home he would bolt the door after him.

Wim demurred. The master would probably be very late, he told her, and she would lose her sleep. But she persuaded him at last, and he went round securing the doors and windows, settling the dogs in their baskets and turning out all but the lights in the hall and the kitchen.

'For that's where I shall sit,' declared Serena. 'I can read Elly's cookbooks and keep an eye on whatever it is that she has left on the Aga.'

The kitchen was warm and quiet. The *stoelklok* by the dresser tick-tocked with soothing monotony, the dogs snored gently and Puss had curled up on her lap. It was a very cosy room, despite its size; it smelled of baking and coffee, mingled with a whiff of something tasty keeping warm in the oven. Serena sat contentedly, patiently waiting. She wasn't sleepy, and Ivo might like to mull over his work at the hospital.

She had been there for an hour or more when he came in, to stop short in the doorway as he saw her.

She put Puss down gently and got out of her chair. 'I wasn't sleepy, so I thought I'd wait for you. There's something in the oven, and coffee. Did things go well?'

He came slowly into the room. 'Yes, as far as we can tell at the moment. There was no need for you to wait up, Serena.'

'But you must eat something...'

'I had something at the hospital. Go to bed, my dear. I must just go to the study to check something, and then I shall go up myself...'

He was holding the door open for her. It was obvious that he didn't want her company. She summoned a smile. 'Well, the coffee's hot if you should change your mind,' she told him cheerfully. 'Goodnight, Ivo.'

That had been a mistake, she told herself, taking no notice of the tears trickling down her cheeks. She must remember never to do that again.

Chapter 9

It seemed to Serena that Ivo was avoiding her. Unless he had been called away early they breakfasted together, and either dined at home or with friends. They walked the dogs, went to an occasional theatre, but although he was a pleasant and thoughtful companion she sensed a reserve in his manner, and never once did he talk about them. She decided that no woman could feel less married than she did, and that something must be done about it. There was always some reason why he had to go to his study after dinner, or return to the hospital until the late evening. And of course when they dined with friends they had no chance to talk…

The plain unhappy fact was that he didn't enjoy her company. And yet when they had married he had made it very clear that he liked her well enough to marry her.

Rachel was no longer a threat, but perhaps there was someone else? He was a man any girl would want to attract... She squashed the thought as unworthy. Perhaps there was something about her which annoyed him? And the best way to find out would be to ask him.

She chose to do it one evening when, after half an hour or so together in the drawing room after dinner, Ivo put down the newspaper he was reading.

'I've some notes to look through...'

'Before you go there's something I want to ask you,' said Serena, and now that she had got the words out she wished that she hadn't spoken, because the look he gave her was suddenly intent.

'Yes?'

She must have been mistaken about the look; his voice was as mild as milk. She put down her knitting and met his look.

'There's something not right,' she began. 'Have I done something which has annoyed you? Am I too dull? Perhaps I don't behave as I should when we go out, or wear the wrong clothes. Whatever it is I wish you would tell me and I'll put it right.' She added in a voice which had become a little sharp, 'I think you are avoiding me. Oh, not just being with me, I mean when we're together you're remote.' She sighed. 'I'm not explaining very well, am I?' And when he didn't speak she added carefully, 'I don't want to intrude on your life. That was partly why you married me, wasn't it? To be a friend and a companion but not a real wife. And I thought it was working out very well.'

'Tell me, Serena, are you quite content with our marriage?'

He showed no signs of anger, only interest.

Serena longed to shout No at him. How could she be content when she loved him so much? Faced with the years ahead and never being allowed to tell him. Instead she said, 'Yes, I am,' and went rather red because she didn't lie easily.

Ivo got out of his chair and stood in front of her chair, towering over her so that she had to crane her neck to look at him.

He was smiling. 'Well, I'm not...' And the phone rang.

Ivo van Doelen wasn't a man who swore habitually, but now he let out a robust Dutch oath which fortunately Serena didn't understand, but his voice was quiet as he answered it, listened, replied briefly. He said, 'I must go at once,' and was out of the room before she could open her mouth.

She would wait up for him, she decided. He might be back within an hour or so. Now that she had broken the ice they could talk—at least she could do the talking. She wasn't sure if he had been listening, for all he had done was ask if she were content...

But when the *stoelklok* chimed eleven she gave up the idea; he would be too tired to listen, too tired to talk. She went up to bed; perhaps in the morning she would try again...

But she saw at once when she went down to breakfast that it was out of the question. Ivo was as immaculate as always, but there were tired lines in his face.

'Did you get any sleep?' she asked him, after wishing him a good morning.

'A couple of hours. I didn't disturb you when I came in?'

He was his usual friendly self, passing her the toast, commenting on the weather.

'No. Have you a busy day? You couldn't take a few hours off?'

'I'm afraid not. I've a clinic this morning, and I'm operating at Leiden this afternoon.'

He gathered up his post and got up from the table. 'I should be home around teatime.'

He laid a hand on her shoulder as he passed by her chair. 'Enjoy your day.'

Which of course she didn't; she worried until she had a headache.

A few hours in the garden with Domus made her feel better. They still didn't understand what the other was saying, but somehow they managed to work together, she undertaking the humbler tasks of weeding and thinning seedlings while he did complicated jobs such as grafting and pruning. She felt so much better that she went indoors and spent a long time learning her next lesson for her visit to her teacher on the following day. And when Christina phoned to ask her if she and Ivo were going to the *burgermeester's* dinner party she was so bright and chatty that Christina put down the phone wondering why Serena sounded so unlike herself.

Ivo thought the same thing when he got home. Serena, usually so quiet and restful, talked non-stop, barely giving him time to answer or make any comment, and although she asked him about his day, she gave him no chance to answer. Any ideas he had had about a serious talk he rejected, for Serena was clearly not in the mood.

And so it was for the next few days; Serena was hiding behind a barrier of small talk. She was friendly, made sure that his house was run exactly as he wished, was a charming hostess when he brought colleagues back with him one afternoon but the barrier was there, as intractable as barbed wire.

They just couldn't go on like it, of course; he would be free on the following weekend and he would tell her that it was impossible to go on as they were. His hope that she might learn to love him was fading fast, but he would tell her that he loved her, even if it meant that she would want to end their marriage. That she was unhappy about it seemed evident to him. It was such a pity that each time they had been on the point of talking about it they had been interrupted.

But nothing of their disquiet showed when they reached the *burgermeester's* house; they appeared to be exactly what they were: a newly married couple and very happy. Only Christina saw the dark circles under Serena's eyes and Ivo's bland expression which concealed his true feelings.

'There's something wrong,' she told Duert as they were getting ready to go to bed. 'I have a feeling in my bones...'

'Well, don't try and find out, my darling, it might make matters worse. Allow Fate to settle the matter in her own way; she always does.'

And he was right.

Several days passed, and Serena wondered uneasily if she would get a chance to talk to Ivo. He was busier than ever, it seemed, sometimes away overnight, often late home in the evening. He was invariably pleasant, enquiring after her days, her Dutch lessons, whether she had heard from Nanny…but there was never time to do more than give him a quick answer.

He was going to Luxembourg in the morning, he told her one evening. To operate on one of its leading citizens. 'Nothing too serious. If all goes well I should be home late in the evening, or at least the following morning. I'll phone you as soon as I know.'

He had gone with a quick peck on her cheek and a wish that she would have a pleasant day.

He phoned in the early evening. He would have to stay longer than he had expected. He would be home some time during the following evening.

Serena went to bed early, which was silly because she didn't sleep until early morning, and woke wondering how to fill the empty day stretching endlessly until Ivo should be home again. She would go to the sea, she decided, and got up to an early breakfast, took the dogs for their walk and went home to find a message from Christina. Would she go to the new day centre that had been opened in Den Haag? A project to keep young people with nothing to do off the streets. There was to be a free meal at midday, and they were short of helpers.

Serena agreed at once, and went in search of Wim.

She explained that she would be out for most of the day and asked him to drive her to the centre.

Wim didn't approve. The centre was in a poor quarter of the city; he wasn't sure if the master would approve either.

'There will be several ladies there, Wim,' Serena assured him, 'and I'll be back around teatime.'

She had to agree with him about the shabbiness of the centre's surroundings: mean streets with small houses, many of them with their windows boarded up.

Wim tut-tutted with disapproval. 'There are illegal immigrants here from all over Europe. They bring many children with them and there is not always any work.'

He was reassured to see several ladies going to and fro inside the centre, and Serena said briskly, 'You see, Wim, there are any number of us here. And I'll get a lift back.'

She was given an apron the moment she put her face round the door, and the *burgermeester's* wife—in charge, of course—directed her to one of the long counters set up in the main room. And no sooner was Serena behind it when the doors were opened and people poured in. A medley of humanity, not just the young people she had expected, but the old, and mothers with young children. She poured soup and handed bread and mugs of coffee, hoping she was doing the right thing, for there was no chance of talking to any of the other helpers.

It was a seemingly unending stream, and she was quite sure that several of the younger ones came back for second helpings. And while the food held out, why not? she asked herself. When the *burgermeester's* wife came round to make sure that everyone was doing things the right way, and told her that on no account must she allow anyone to have more than one helping, Serena replied with suitable meekness and doled out more soup to a very large and hungry-looking man who undoubtedly needed it.

The lady helpers were supposed to leave their positions in turn, in order to refresh themselves with coffee in a back room, but somehow Serena didn't manage to get there. The food and soup were beginning to run out and the afternoon was well advanced. The crowd was thinning, although there were still a great many young mothers with babies and toddlers.

After this, the opening day, marked by the free lunch, the centre would cater only for schoolchildren and teenagers, and the old people and small children would stand no chance. Serena scraped out the soup to the last drop and handed out the last of the bread. The coffee had long since gone.

The ladies began to collect up their things, ready to go home, telling each other that their efforts had been very successful while they ushered the last of the lingerers out of the door. Volunteers would come in the morning and clear up and prepare the centre for the evening. Now everything could be safely left.

Serena, offered a lift by one of the helpers who lived outside the city, looked around her. It worried her house-proud notions to leave the place scattered with used mugs and crumbs and spilled soup, but since there

were people coming to clear up…she started for the
door with the last few ladies. They had almost reached
it when Serena stopped.

Up against a wall in the shadows there was a bundle,
but somehow it didn't look like an ordinary bundle. She
went nearer to have a look and saw a child, little more
than a toddler, dark-skinned, with black curly hair and
very dirty. He was sound asleep.

All but one of the ladies had gone through the door;
the one who had offered her a lift came to join her.

'We can't leave him here,' said Serena urgently.
'Surely his mother will miss him and come back? He's
not Dutch, is he?'

'No, Bosnian, I should think; there were a lot of Bosnian women here, most of them with babies or toddlers.
Shall I phone the police? I'll call in at Christina's and
phone from there.'

She eyed Serena uncertainly. 'You wouldn't mind
waiting here with him? I can't stop—the children…'

'Of course. As long as Christina knows where I am
and will come pick me up later. I'm sure the mother
will return soon.'

'Then I'll go. Will you lock the door?'

'No, otherwise if she comes she may think there is
no one here.'

It was quiet once her companion had gone. Serena
went and looked at the child, still sleeping. She looked
round for a chair and found a wooden one in the room
at the back of the building. She took it back and set it
up against a wall facing the door, picked up the sleeping child and sat down. The chair was hard and the

child was surprisingly heavy, but she told herself it wouldn't be for long.

The minutes ticked away half an hour, an hour, and there was no sign of the mother, and presently the little boy woke up. He began to cry at once, bellowing his fright in a language Serena couldn't understand. Certainly not Dutch; if he was Bosnian then this wasn't her lucky day. For want of a better idea she spoke to him in English, which didn't help matters, although he stopped crying for a time while she sang all the nursery rhymes she could remember. And there was not a crumb to eat or a drop of drink, other than the water which dripped from the solitary tap in the bare little kitchen. And when she tried to put him down so that she could fetch some he roared and screamed so much that she gave up the idea.

'The police will be here soon,' she assured him, and hoped that they wouldn't be long.

But the lady who had promised to go to Christina's and phone from there had found her away from home and, rather than explain to Corvinus, had driven on home. In the small flurry of finding one of her children had cut her knee, she had forgotten all about the matter, a fact of which Serena was unaware—and a good thing too!

Another hour passed. The child slept again and she turned over in her mind what was best to be done. There was little noise from the street outside; she had tried calling but no one had answered, and she hesitated to roam the streets, knocking on doors to be confronted by people who would probably not understand a word she said. They might even think that she had kidnapped the boy. It was a silly situation, she reflected, but surely the police would come, and if Christina had been told she would come too. She decided that she would wait for another hour and then try to find someone to help her. It would be difficult, for she would have the boy with her and he wasn't a passive child.

He awoke then, and burst into tears once again, wetted himself, and then was sick all over her skirt...

Mr van Doelen, home from Luxembourg, wandered into his drawing room and found it empty. He turned to look enquiringly at Wim, who had hurried after him.

'*Mevrouw* went this morning to help at that new centre for young people. I drove her there, and it's not in a decent part of the city either. I didn't like leaving her, but she said she'd get one of her friends there to drive her back. Teatime she said. But she ought to be home by now.'

'Probably having tea with someone, Wim.'

'Oh, no, *mijnheer*, she would never be away from home if she knew you were coming.'

'I'll phone around and see where she is.'

It wasn't until he had rung several of Serena's friends and been told that she had certainly been at the centre and as far as they knew had left when they did that he began to worry. And Christina wasn't home. She had been the first person that he had phoned; now he phoned again. She had just returned. 'Wait while I ask if anyone has left a message,' she told him.

She was back very quickly. 'Anna opened the door

to Mevrouw Slotte—she was helping at the centre—
she said she had a message for me but couldn't stop
to tell Corvinus. I'm going to ring her now. I'll phone
you back...'

Ivo curbed his fierce impatience. It was several minutes before Christina rang. 'The silly woman—says
she forgot. Serena found a small child just as they were
leaving—the others had gone on ahead. It was asleep
and Serena said she would stop until the mother came
for him. Mevrouw Slotte said she would call here and
let me know, and also tell the police. She forgot all
about it when she got home—some small domestic cri-
sis, she said.'

'Thanks, Christina. I'll phone the police and go there
immediately.'

'I'll phone the police; you go and fetch her. There are
too many undesirables living around there...'

Ivo was out of his house, shouting to Wim as he
went, and driving to Den Haag as though the devil
were at his heels. But as he went through the door at
the centre to all appearances he was his usual, calm,
unhurried self.

He saw Serena at once, of course, sitting with the
child, sleeping again, on her lap, and saw her face light
up with joy and heard her voice, a bit squeaky with
emotion. He crossed the floor, lifted her and the boy
out of the chair and sat down, holding them both close.

For a moment he didn't say anything, but he kissed
her instead.

'Oh, Ivo,' said Serena, and kissed him back. Then
added, 'He's been sick all over my dress and he's...'

'Trifling matters, my darling. You're all right? You weren't afraid?'

'Not at first. I was just beginning to get scared, only you came. You called me darling; did you mean to?'

'Of course I meant to. I've been wanting to call you darling since the moment I set eyes on you—' He broke off as two police officers came in.

Ivo put Serena carefully back on the chair and picked up the boy, and she sat there, strangely content, smelling dreadful, listening to him explaining to the men. Presently he handed over the child to one of the officers and came with the other to where she was sitting. The officer understood English, and Ivo filled in gaps when Serena got stuck, and presently the police left.

'We are going home,' said Ivo. 'I'll lock the door and let Christina have the key.' He held out a hand. 'Come, my love.'

She looked down at her ruined dress. 'The car— I'm filthy...'

'Take it off.'

No sooner said than done. He cast the garment into a corner and took her hand without appearing to look at her, and he had her into his coat, out of the place and into the car before she could utter. Somehow it seemed quite a normal thing to be sitting there in a flimsy slip under his coat while he drove first to Christina, with the key, and then home.

Wim, opening the door, took one look and retired discreetly to the kitchen. 'They won't be wanting their dinner just yet,' he told Elly.

Serena made for the staircase, but Mr van Doelen

was too quick for her. She was held tight in his arms, her face grubby, her hair a disaster, in a slip that would never be the same again.

'Did I ever tell you that you are beautiful?' asked Ivo, 'And that I love you to distraction?'

'No,' said Serena, 'you didn't, but you can tell me now. No, wait until I've had a bath and got into clean clothes.'

He sighed. 'I've waited so long I suppose that I can wait a few minutes longer.'

She leaned up to kiss him. 'I love you too, you know.' She studied his face. 'Shall we be happy ever after now?'

His kiss gave her the answer she wanted.

* * * * *

BRITANNIA ALL AT SEA

Chapter 1

The sluice room at the end of Men's Surgical at St Jude's Hospital was deplorably out of date; built in Victorian times, it was always damp and chilly, its white-tiled walls and heavy earthenware sinks doing nothing to alleviate its dismal appearance. The plumbing was complicated and noisy and the bedpan washer made a peculiar clanging noise, but because some time in the distant future the hospital was to be re-sited and become a modern showpiece with every conceivable mod con the architect and Hospital Committee could think of, the antediluvian conditions which at present existed were overlooked—not by the nursing staff, of course, who had to cope with them and voiced their complaints, singly and in groups, round the clock. And a lot of good it did them, for no one listened.

But the occupants of the sluice room weren't aware of its shortcomings; the younger, smaller girl was crying her eyes out by the sink and her companion, a tall, splendidly built girl, was deep in thought, her large brown eyes gazing unseeingly at the conglomeration of pipes on the wall before her. She waited patiently until the crying had eased a little before speaking.

'Don't cry any more, Dora…' She had a soft, unhurried voice. 'I'll see Sister the moment the round's over—I'll not have you take the blame for something Delia has done—and knows she's done, too. I know you don't like telling on anyone and if Sister hadn't been in such a fuss about the round, she might have listened. Of course, it would happen on this very morning just when everything had to be just so for this wretched professor, but you're not in the least to blame, so dry your eyes, go down the back stairs and have your coffee and tidy up that face. I'll think of something to tell Sister if she wants to know where you are. She won't though, not while Mr Hyde and this tiresome old gent are here.'

She leaned across and switched off the bedpan washer so that there was more or less silence save for the gurgling of the pipes. But not quite silence; a faint noise behind her caused her to turn her head and look behind her. There was someone standing in the doorway, watching her, a very large man with grizzled hair and pale blue eyes, his undoubtedly handsome features marred by a look of annoyance.

'Lost?' she asked him kindly. 'Everyone makes the mistake of coming up these stairs, but I'm afraid you're out of luck; you won't be able to go into the ward until the round's over and that will be at least an hour. Look, Nurse is going down to her coffee—if you go with her, she'll show you the front stairs. There's a waiting room on the landing—I'll let you know the minute they've gone. Have you come to see someone special?'

He regarded her frowningly. 'Yes. Er—Staff Nurse, I presume?'

'That's right. Sister will know about you, I expect. Now if you run along…'

Perhaps it wasn't the best way of putting it, she thought; one didn't tell giants of six feet something and broad with it to run along, but he had no need to look so unsmiling, she had done the best she could to help him. She nodded to the little nurse, who gave a final sniff and managed a very small smile. 'There's a good girl,' said her champion, and put a hand to her cap to make sure that it sat straight on her crown of dark hair as she made for the door. The man didn't move, so she was forced to stop.

'What is your name?' he asked.

'My name?' She was vaguely surprised at the question, but if telling him was going to make him go the quicker, then she might as well do so.

'Smith—Britannia Smith.' She smiled fleetingly and he stood aside. 'Goodbye. Nurse Watts, make sure that this gentleman gets the right stairs, won't you?'

She watched him shrug his shoulders and follow the little nurse down the stairs before she went back into the ward.

It was as old-fashioned as the sluice, with a row of beds on either side and because it was take-in week, three beds down the middle as well. Britannia sped up its length to where Sister Mack, the Surgical Registrar, the surgical houseman, a worried bunch of medical students attached to Mr Hyde's firm, the lady Social Worker, and the senior physiotherapist had grouped themselves, awaiting the great man. The group dissolved and then reformed with Mr Hyde as its hub as she reached them, in time to hear his measured tones voice the opinion that Professor Luitingh van Thien should be joining them at any moment. 'I take it that everything is in readiness, Sister?' he asked, with no idea of it being otherwise.

Sister Mack shot a lightning glance at Britannia, who shook her head. She had been on a swift foray to see if anything could be done to recover at least some of the specimens and while doing so had discovered poor Dora. Sister Mack looked thunderous, but as Britannia saw that look several times a day, she could ignore it and turned her intention instead to the third-year nurse, Delia Marsh, standing there like an innocent angel, she thought indignantly, letting a timid creature like Dora take the blame. She gave the girl a cool thoughtful look and was glad to see that she had her worried; her pretty mouth curved just a little downwards in sympathy for Dora and then rounded itself into a surprised O, while consternation and horror showed plain on her lovely face.

The group had increased by one; the man who had been in the sluice—standing behind everyone else, just inside the ward doors, surveying her down his arrogant nose with the hint of a sardonic smile. Sister

Mack looked round then, and if Britannia hadn't been so taken up with her own feelings, she might have been amused at that lady's reaction, for her somewhat hatchet features broke into the ingratiating smile which Sister Mack reserved for those of importance, and there was no getting away from the fact that the man looked important, although not consciously so, Britannia had to concede him that. The party regrouped itself once more, this time with Mr Hyde and his companion wandering off in the direction of the first bed with Sister Mack hard on their heels. Britannia gave a soundless chuckle at the imperious wave she gave to the rest of them to keep at a respectable distance. After all, they rarely saw anyone quite as exquisite on the ward, and Sister Mack considered that she should have the lion's share of him. And that suited Britannia; with any luck she would be able to avoid having to speak to either Mr Hyde or the visitor; she was merely there as Sister's right hand, to pass forms, offer notes and whisper in Sister's ear any titbit of information she might have overlooked.

She wished she wasn't such a tall girl, for she stood out in the group, and she sighed with relief when the Registrar, edging his way along to join his chief by the bedside, paused beside her. 'And what hit you?' he wanted to know. 'Our professor looks the type to turn any girl's head and here's our gorgeous Britannia all goggle-eyed at the sight of him—anyone would think he had a squint and big ears!'

Britannia spoke earnestly in a thread of a whisper. 'Fred, he was in the sluice just now—he'd come up the staircase and I sent him all the way back and told him to come up the front stairs and wait until the round was over...'

Fred gave a snort of laughter which he turned into a fit of coughing as the two consultants turned round with an impatient: 'Come along, Fred—' from Mr Hyde. The visiting professor said nothing, only raked Britannia with a leisurely look from half-closed eyes. She wondered uneasily if he had heard what she had said and then, obedient to an urgent signal from Sister Mack, slipped behind her and bent her head to receive whatever it was her superior wished to say. 'Nurse Watts—where is she, Staff Nurse? I have not yet told Mr Hyde about the specimens.' She shuddered strongly. 'When I do so, I wish Nurse to be here so that she may admit her carelessness.'

Britannia bit back all the things she would have liked to have said; Sister Mack had been nursing for a good many years now, but apparently she still hadn't learnt that junior nurses could be admonished for their errors in the privacy of Sister's office, but in public they were to be protected, covered up for, backed up...

'I sent her for coffee,' she said with calm.

'You what...? Staff Nurse Smith, sometimes you take too much upon yourself! Why?'

'She didn't do it.'

Sister Mack went a pale puce. 'Of course she did it—anyway, she didn't say a word when I accused her.'

'That's why, Sister—she was too frightened to.'

Sister Mack eyed Britannia with dislike. 'We will discuss this later.' Her expression changed to one of smiling efficiency as she became aware that the two consultants had finished their low-voiced conversation and were looking at them both.

The patient in the first bed was a double inguinal hernia and nicely on the mend—a few minutes' chat sufficed to allay his dark suspicions that Mr Hyde had removed most of his insides without telling him, and they moved to the second bed; a young man who had been in a motor crash and had ruptured his liver; Mr Hyde had removed most of the offending organ, since it was no longer of any use, and his patient was making a slow recovery—too slow, explained Mr Hyde to his colleague. The two of them muttered and mumbled together and finally Mr Hyde enquired: 'The specimen from this lad, Sister? Both I and Professor Luitingh van Thien wish to examine it—the blood-clotting time is of great importance...' He meandered on for a few moments while Sister Mack's complexion took a turn for the worse and Britannia prayed that Dora wouldn't come tearing back too soon. The nasty silence was broken by the visiting professor. A nice voice, Britannia considered, even though it had a pronounced drawl: 'I understand that the specimens are not available.'

She shot him a look of dislike; if he was going to sneak on poor Dora in front of everyone, she for her part would never forgive him—an absurd resolve; consultant surgeons were unlikely to be affected by the feelings of a mere staff nurse. But he wasn't going to sneak. Sister Mack, interrupting him willy-nilly, declared furiously: 'The nurse responsible isn't here; my staff nurse has seen fit to send her to coffee...'

His cold eyes held Britannia's warm brown ones for a moment and then settled on a point a little above Sister Mack's shoulder. 'I have it on good authority that Nurse Watts wasn't responsible for the error,' he pointed out in a silky voice. 'I suggest that the matter be looked into and dealt with after the round.' He turned to Mr Hyde. 'I'm sure you will forgive me for saying this, but I happen to have been personally involved...'

Mr Hyde, not very quick to catch on, observed gamely: 'Oh, certainly, my dear chap. We can make do with the notes.' His eyes suddenly lighted on Britannia. 'You know who did it?' he asked. And when she said 'Yes, sir,' he went on, 'And of course, you don't intend to tell me.'

She smiled at him. 'That's right, sir.'

He nodded. 'I like loyalty. I daresay you can get fresh specimens, Sister?'

Sister Mack, quite subdued, muttered something or other and Britannia took the opportunity of putting the next case papers into her hands. The quicker the round got back into its old routine, the better. She looked up and found the professor's eye on her once more and this time, because she was so relieved that he had held his tongue, and at the same time stood up for little Dora, she essayed a smile. His eyes became, if anything, even colder, his fine mouth remained in an unrelenting straight line; he didn't like her. She removed her own smile rapidly and frowned instead.

The next patient, fortunately, was an irascible old gentleman who had a great deal to say for himself, and as the professor's face was a new one and he looked important, he was able to air his opinion of hospitals, doctors, the nursing staff and the Health Service in general, at some length. Mr Hyde, who had heard it all before, listened with veiled impatience and said 'Yes, yes,' at intervals, not wishing to offend the old man who had, after all, been something important in the War Office in his heyday, but the professor heard him out with great courtesy, even giving the right answers and making suitable comments from time to time so that when at last the diatribe came to an end, the speaker added a corollary to the effect that the professor was a man of sense and might do worse than join the hospital staff. Whereupon Mr Hyde pointed out that his colleague was only paying them a brief visit on his way to Edinburgh and had work enough in his own country. 'A distinguished member of our profession,' he added generously.

'A foreigner,' remarked his patient with a touch of asperity, and then added kindly: 'But his English is excellent.'

The professor thanked him gravely, expressed the wish that he would soon be on his feet again, and with Mr Hyde beside him, wandered on to the next bed. The round was uneventful for the next half a dozen beds; it was when they reached the young man in the corner bed as they started on the second side that interest quickened. He was a very ill young man, admitted only a few days previously, and it became apparent that this was the patient in whom the professor was interested— indeed, intended to operate upon that very afternoon. 'Hydatid cysts,' explained Mr Hyde to his audience, 'diagnosed by means of Casoni's intradermal test—the local and general reaction are very marked.' He signed to Britannia to turn back the bed-clothes and began to examine the patient while he murmured learnedly about rupture, peritonitis and severe anaphylaxis. The professor agreed, nodding his handsome head and adding a few telling words of his own, then said at length: 'We are unable to establish eosinophilia, but the X-rays confirm the cysts, I take it?'

Britannia, on the alert, produced the films with all the aplomb of a first-class conjuror getting a rabbit from a hat and obligingly held them up for viewing while the surgeons, this time with the registrar in attendance, peered and commented. 'Yes, well,' observed the professor at length, 'should you feel that I could help in any way…'

Mr Hyde took him up smartly: 'This afternoon?' He turned to include Sister Mack. 'Could that be arranged, Sister? Shall we say half past two in main theatre? He will go to ICU from theatre and I shall want a responsible nurse to look after him here.' His eye lighted upon Britannia. 'Staff Nurse Smith, perhaps.'

Which would mean that Britannia would have to forgo her evening off duty and, worse, Sister Mack would have to stay on and do her Staff Nurse's work. 'Certainly, sir,' said Britannia, not looking at her superior. She had been going out with Doctor Ross, the Medical Registrar, and now she would have to explain. David was impatient of interference with his wishes; he had booked two seats for the latest musical and the forgoing of a pleasant evening was going to put him out—perhaps a good thing, she decided; he had become a little possessive just lately…

The round rambled on, with frequent pauses while Mr Hyde and his companion murmured, occasionally drawing Sister Mack into their discussion and asking Fred for his opinion, invariably pausing too to say a few appropriate words to the occupants of the beds. At the last bed, Britannia nodded to the ward orderly, peering at them through the glass window of the door; it would never do for the coffee tray in Sister's office not to be there and ready. Not everyone had coffee, of course, only Sister Mack and the consultants and Fred; no one else was considered eligible. Britannia, used to Sister Mack's little ways, despatched the houseman and the students to the kitchen for refreshment and retired to the linen cupboard where Bridget, the ward maid, would have put a tray for her. But before she went she beckoned Delia Marsh to her.

'Before you go to coffee,' she said without heat, 'you will find Dora and apologise, and when you have had your coffee you will report to Sister and tell her that the error was yours, not hers. And I advise you not to do anything like that again. You're in your third year and you should know better.' She nodded dismissal. 'Dora will be back from her coffee, tidying beds.'

The linen cupboard was cosily warm and the frosted glass of its narrow window shut out the grey November morning. Britannia made herself comfortable on a laundry basket and poured her coffee. Bridget was one of the many people in the hospital who liked her; the coffee was hot and milky and two biscuits had been sneaked out of Sister's tin. Britannia munched and swallowed and thought in a vague way about Professor Luitingh van Thien; an ill-tempered man, and arrogant, she considered, then looked up in astonishment as he opened the door and walked in. And over and above that, she discovered with an almighty shock, the man she wished to marry; she had been in and out of love quite a few times, as any healthy-minded girl of twenty-four or so would, but never had she felt like this. Nevertheless, all she said in a mild voice was: 'You should have knocked, Professor.'

The cold eyes studied hers. 'Why?'

She said with some asperity: 'Manners.'

His thick dark brows rose, and then: 'But I have none,' and he went on deliberately, 'I am getting on for forty, unmarried, rich and something of a hermit; I need please no one.'

'How very sad,' observed Britannia with sincerity. 'Did you want something?'

The lids drooped over his eyes. 'Yes. I also wish to ask you a question. Why Britannia?'

She took a sip of her cooling coffee and stared at him over the mug's rim. 'My parents decided that with a name like Smith they should—should compensate me.'

He broke into such a roar of laughter that she exclaimed: 'Oh, hush, do—if Sister hears you she'll be in to see…'

His brows rose again. 'Chance acquaintances over a cup of coffee?'

'Put like that it sounds very respectable, but it

wouldn't do, you know. Visiting professors and staff nurses don't meet in linen cupboards.'

'You flatter yourself, Miss Smith. I cannot recall inviting you to meet me.'

She took another sip of coffee. 'Very prickly,' she observed, 'but I quite see why. There's no need for you to stay,' she added kindly, 'I've answered your question.' He looked so surprised that she went on: 'I'm sure that no one speaks to you like that, but it won't harm you, you know.'

He smiled, and she wasn't sure if she liked the smile. 'I stand corrected, don't I?' He put a large square hand on the door. 'And talking of manners, you didn't offer me coffee, Miss Smith.'

'You've just had it,' she pointed out, and added: 'sir.'

'Yes. A cup of vilely brewed liquid, curdled by Sister Mack's conversation. What an unkind woman!' He eyed the almost empty coffee pot as he spoke and Britannia said with real sympathy:

'The kitchen maid makes super coffee—I always have it alone on round days. I enjoyed mine.'

He opened the door. 'Heartless girl,' he remarked coldly, and went out.

Britannia poured herself the last of the coffee. She had forgotten to apologise for sending him out of the sluice, but her whole mind had been absorbed by her sudden uprush of feeling when he had come in so unexpectedly. She frowned, worrying that she would never have the chance to do so now—she wasn't likely to see him again, at least not to speak to. 'And that's negative

thinking, my girl,' she admonished herself out loud. 'If
you want to see him again, you must work at it.'

A heartening piece of advice, which she knew quite
well was quite hollow. The professor wasn't the kind
of man to be chased, even if the girl chasing him had
made up her mind to marry him. She sighed; probably
she would have to rely on Fate, and that lady was noto-
riously unpredictable. She picked up her tray and bore it
back to the kitchen, then crossed the landing to Sister's
office. The door stood half open; everyone had gone,
Mr Hyde, his firm and his handsome colleague. She
might as well get Dora's unfortunate little episode dealt
with at once. Undeterred by Sister's cross voice bidding
her to go in, she opened the door wider and entered.

Fate at least allowed her to see him again, although
the circumstances might have been more propitious;
it was quite late in the afternoon when the patient returned to the ward and by then Sister Mack, never the
sunniest of persons, was in a quite nasty mood. She
had an evening's work before her and instead of being
refreshed by a free afternoon, she had been hard at it
doing dressings, medicine rounds and writing the be-
ginnings of the day report, while Britannia, as she put
it, had been idling in theatre. Britannia hadn't been
idling at all, but she knew better than to protest. She
had rushed back to the ward while the patient was in
the Recovery Room and broken the news to her superior that ICU was up to its neck with a bad car crash
and the patient would be coming straight back to his
own bed. So she was engrossed in a variety of urgent
tasks to do with the well-being of the patient when Mr

Hyde and the professor arrived at the bedside. They were still in their theatre gear; shapeless white smocks and trousers; the professor, being the size he was, looking as though he might burst every seam although his dignity remained unimpaired. He barely nodded at Britannia before bending over the young man. She handed Mr Hyde the observation sheets she had been keeping, answered his questions with brief clarity, and stood silently until the two men had made their examination. Everything was just as it should be, they told her, she was to continue the treatment which had been ordered—and what, she was asked, were the arrangements for the night?

'There will be a special on at nine o'clock, sir,' said Britannia, and thought longingly of that hour, still some time ahead—tea, and her shoes off and her feet up...

It was disconcerting to her when the professor asked: 'You have been off duty?' because unless he was blind and deaf, which he wasn't, he would have seen her and heard her during the course of the afternoon; indeed, he had stared at her in theatre so intently that she had felt twelve feet tall and outsize to boot.

She handed Mr Hyde her pen so that he could add something to his notes and said composedly: 'No. I can make it up later in the week.'

'No tea?' And when she shook her head: 'A paragon among nurses, Miss Britannia Smith. Let us hope that you will get your just reward.' His voice was bland and the smile she didn't like was back again. She wondered what his real smile was like and wished lovingly that he wasn't quite so difficult. She said a little severely:

'You have no need to turn me into a martyr, Professor. I shall do very well.'

The two surgeons went presently; the professor's casual nod seemed positively churlish compared with Mr Hyde's courteous thanks and genial good evening. Britannia, fiddling expertly with tubes, mused sadly on her day. Surely when one met the man of one's dreams, it should be the happiest day of one's life? If that were so, then hers had fallen sadly short of that.

Sister went to supper at seven o'clock, leaving a student nurse in charge of the ward with the remark that Staff Nurse Smith was there and able to cope with anything which might turn up; she was still bad-tempered at the loss of her off-duty, and the fact that Britannia couldn't leave her patient didn't seem to have struck her, nor did it strike her that Britannia might like her supper too, for when she returned from her meal she finished the report, gave it to the night staff when they came on, and pausing only long enough to tell Britannia that she was worn out with her day's work, hurried off duty. The special wasn't coming on duty for another hour; Britannia, dealing with the dozens of necessary chores for her patient, hardly noticed where that hour went. Fred had been down earlier, he came again now, expressed his satisfaction as to the patient's condition, told Britannia with the casual concern of an old friend that her hair was coming down, and went away.

She still had no time to have done anything to her hair when she at last got off duty. Men's Surgical was on the first floor and she wandered down the staircase to the front hall, listening vaguely to the subdued sounds around her; the faint tinkle of china as the junior night nurses collected up bedtime drinks, the sudden distant wail of some small creature up on the children's unit above her, the creak of trolleys and the muffled to-ing and fro-ing of the night staff. She yawned hugely, gained the last stair and turned, her eyes on the ground, to go down the narrow passage which would take her to the Nurses' Home. She was brought up short by something large and solid—Professor Luitingh van Thien.

'Put on that cloak,' he advised her in a no-nonsense voice. 'We are going out.'

Britannia, aware of the intense pleasure of seeing him again, opened her mouth, closed it and then opened it again to say: 'I can't—my hair!'

He gave her a considered look. 'A mess. Why do women always worry about their hair? No one is going to look at you.'

She was forced to agree silently and with regret; not that she minded about that but because he didn't consider her worth looking at.

He had taken her hospital cape from her arm and flung it around her shoulders.

'And you have no need to look like that; you are a handsome creature who can manage very well without elaborate hairstyles or other such nonsense.'

She was torn between pleasure at being called a handsome creature—even though it put her strongly in mind of some outsized horse—and annoyance at his casual dismissal of her appearance. 'I don't think I want to go out,' she told him calmly.

'Tea? Hot buttered toast? Sandwiches? Are you not famished?'

Her mouth watered, but: 'I can make myself a pot of tea…'

She could have saved her breath; she was swept across the hall and out into the cold November night and walked briskly down a back lane or two and into Ned's Café, a small, brightly lit place much frequented by the hospital staff in need of a hasty snack or cup of coffee.

Britannia, seated willy-nilly at a small plastic table in the middle of the crowded place, put up a hand to tuck in her hair. 'How did you know about this place?' she enquired, and thought how like a man to choose to sit where everyone could see them, and her with her hair streaming around her head like a witch.

'The Surgical Registrar was kind enough to tell me.'

'Oh—haven't you had your supper either?'

His fine mouth twitched at its corners. 'Er—no.' He lifted a finger and Ned came over, his cheerful, round face beaming.

''Ullo, Staff—'ad a bad day? and I bet they didn't give yer time to eat. What's it ter be? A nice bacon sandwich or a nice bit o' cheese on toast? And a pot of tea?'

Britannia's nose twitched with anticipation. 'Oh, Ned, I'd love a bacon sandwich—and tea, please.'

They both glanced at the professor, who said at once: 'A generous supply of bacon sandwiches, please, and the cheese on toast sounds nice—we'll have that too— and the tea, of course.'

The tea was hot and strong, the bacon sandwiches delicious. Britannia sank her splendid teeth into one of them before asking: 'Why are you buying me my supper, Professor? It's very kind of you, of course, you have no idea how hungry I am—but I'm surprised. You see, I sent you all the way back to the ward this morning, didn't I, and I haven't apologised for it yet. I'm sorry, really I am—if you had said who you were...' She eyed him thoughtfully. 'I expect people mostly know who you are...'

Her companion smiled faintly. 'Mostly.' He watched her with interest as she daintily wolfed her sandwich. 'When did you last eat, Miss Smith?'

She licked a finger. 'Well, I should have gone to second dinner, but Sister was a little late and we had this emergency in... I had coffee on the ward, though, and some rice pudding left over from the patients' dinner.'

The professor looked revolted. 'No wonder you are hungry!' He pushed the plate towards her. 'It is nice to see a girl with such a splendid appetite.'

Britannia flushed faintly; she wasn't plump, but she was a tall girl and magnificently built. Despite the flush, she gave him a clear, unselfconscious look. 'There's a lot of me,' she pointed out.

Her companion drank his tea with the air of a man who was doing his duty and helped himself to one of the fast disappearing sandwiches. 'You are engaged to be married?' he asked coolly.

'Me? Whatever gave you that idea? No, I'm not.'

'You surprise me. In love, perhaps?'

She flicked a crumb away with the tip of her tongue.

For someone who had known her for a very short time, his question struck her as inquisitive to say the least. All the same, it didn't enter her head to tell him anything but the truth. 'Yes,' she said briefly, and wondered just what he would say if she told him it was himself.

The toasted cheese had arrived. She poured more tea for them both and sampled the cheese, then paused with her fork half way to her mouth because the professor was looking so very severe. 'It is, of course, only to be expected,' he observed in a nasty smooth voice. 'I suppose I am expected to say what a lucky man he is.'

Britannia munched her cheese; love him she might, but he really was quite disagreeable. 'You aren't expected to say anything,' she pointed out kindly, 'why should you? We hardly know each other and shan't see each other again, so I can't see that it could possibly matter to you. Have another piece of toast before I eat it all.'

The professor curled his lip. 'Thank you, no.' He sat back with his arms folded against his great chest. 'And as to seeing each other again, the unlikelihood of that is something for which I am deeply thankful. I find you far too ready with that sharp tongue of yours.'

Britannia choked on a piece of toast. It was mortifying that the professor should have to get out of his chair and pat her on the back while she spluttered and whooped, but on the other hand it concealed her feelings very satisfactorily. As soon as she could speak she said in a reasonable voice: 'But it is entirely your own fault that you brought me here, you know, unless

it was that you wanted to convince yourself of my—
my sharp voice.'

She got up suddenly, pulled her cloak around her,
thanked him for her supper and made for the door. She
was quick on her feet and through it before the professor had a chance to do anything about it—besides, he
had to pay the bill. There were several short cuts to
the hospital, down small dark alleys which normally
she wouldn't have chosen to walk down after dark,
but she didn't think about that. She gained the hospital and her room in record time, got ready for bed
and then sat down to think. She very much doubted
if she would see the professor again, and if she did it
would be on the ward where their conversation, if any,
would be of the patients. And he had presumably only
come for that one case. The thing to do would be to
erase him from her mind, something she was loath to
do. One didn't meet a man one wanted to marry every
day of the week and when one did, the last thing one
wanted to do was to forget him. He could have been
tired of course, but more probably just a bad-tempered
man, given to odd whims. She couldn't for the life of
her recall any consultants who had taken staff nurses
out for tea and sandwiches at nine o'clock at night, but
he looked the kind of man who was accustomed to do
as he pleased without anyone attempting to stop him.
She got into bed, punched up her pillows and continued to muse, this time on the probability of him being
engaged; he wasn't a young man, and surely he would
have an attachment of some sort. But if he hadn't...

She lay down and closed her eyes; somehow or other she intended to meet him again and some time in the future, marry him. She slept soundly on her resolution.

Chapter 2

The professor came to the ward twice the next day; during the morning when Britannia was scrubbed and doing a lengthy dressing behind screens, so that all she could hear was his deep voice at the other end of the ward. And in the afternoon when he came again, she was at tea.

Sister Mack, giving her the report before she went off duty in the evening, mentioned that he would be leaving for Edinburgh the following day and then returning to Holland. 'A charming man,' she observed, 'although he never quite explained how it was he knew about those tests...' She shot a look at Britannia as she spoke, and Britannia looked placidly back and said nothing at all.

She went about her evening duties rather morosely.

She had had no plans concerning the professor, except that she had hoped that if and when they met again something would happen; she had no idea what, but she was a romantic girl as well as a determined one, and without being vain she was aware that she was worth looking at. Of course, it would have been easier if she had been small and blonde and helpless; men, so her brothers frequently told her, liked their women fragile. She looked down at her own splendid person and wished she could be something like Alice and become miraculously fairylike. And David Ross hadn't helped; he had grumbled about his spoilt evening without once showing any sympathy for her own disappointment. They had met as she was on her way to dinner and he had spoken quite sharply, just as though she had done it deliberately, and when she had pointed out reasonably enough that if he wanted to grumble at someone it should have been Mr Hyde, he had shrugged his shoulders and bade her a cool goodbye.

She had had no deep feelings about David, but before the professor had loomed so largely over her world, she had begun to think that given time she might have got around to the idea of marrying him later on. But she was sure that she would never want to do that—indeed, she didn't want to marry anyone else but Professor Luitingh van Thien. She stopped writing the Kardex for a moment and wrote Britannia Luitingh van Thien on the blotting paper; it looked, to say the least, very imposing.

* * *

She went home for her days off at the end of the week; she managed to travel down to Dorset at least once a month and although the month wasn't quite up, she felt the urge to talk to her parents. Accordingly she telephoned her mother, packed an overnight bag and caught the evening train, sleeping peacefully until the train came to a brief halt at Moreton station, a small, isolated place, some way from the village of that name and several miles from Dorchester and Wareham. It was cold and dark and Britannia was the only passenger to alight on to the ill-lit platform, but her father was there, passing the time of day with Mr Tims, porter, station-master and ticket collector rolled into one. They both greeted her with pleasure and after an animated discussion about Mrs Tims' nasty back and Mr Tims' bunions, they parted, Mr Tims to return to his stuffy little cubbyhole and await the next train and Britannia and Mr Smith to the car outside; an elderly Morris Oxford decidedly vintage and Mr Smith's pride and joy. They accomplished the short journey home without haste, because the country road was winding and very dark and the Oxford couldn't be expected to hurry anyway, and their conversation was casual and undemanding. But once through the front door of the small Georgian cottage which was Britannia's home, they were pounced upon by her mother, a tall older replica of herself who rattled off a succession of questions without waiting for any of them to be answered. Britannia, quite used to this, kissed her parent with deep affection, told her that she looked smashing and remarked on the delicious aroma coming from the kitchen.

'You're famished,' said Mrs Smith immediately. 'I was only saying to your father this evening that you never get proper meals in that hospital.' She started kitchenwards. 'Take off your coat, darling, supper's ready.' She added to no one in particular: 'It will be a blessing when you marry, Britannia.'

Which could mean anything or nothing, thought her daughter as she went upstairs to the small room which had been hers since she was a very small girl. When her brothers had left home her mother had suggested that she might like to move into either of the two bigger rooms they had occupied, but she had chosen to remain in the little room over the porch. She flung her coat down on to the bed now, then went downstairs again without bothering to look in the looking glass; supper for the moment was far more important than her appearance. It was after that satisfying meal, eaten in the cheerful rather shabby dining room opposite the sitting room, when her parents were seated on each side of the fire and she was kneeling before it giving it a good poke, that she paused to look over her shoulder and say: 'I've met the man I want to marry, my dears.'

Her father lifted his eyes from the seed catalogue he was studying and gave her a searching look and her mother cast down her knitting and said encouragingly: 'Yes, dear? Do we know him?'

'No.'

'He's asked you to marry him?'

'No.' Britannia sounded matter-of-fact. 'Nor is he

likely to. He's a professor of surgery, one of the best—
very good-looking, ill-tempered, arrogant and rich. He
didn't like me overmuch. We—we don't come from the
same background.'

Her father, longing to get back to his seeds, said
vaguely: 'Not at all suitable, I gather.'

It was her mother who asked: 'How old is he, darling? And is he short or tall, fat or thin?'

'It doesn't matter what he looks like if he's unsuitable,' her father pointed out sensibly.

'Quite unsuitable,' agreed Britannia. 'He's in his late
thirties, I understand, and he's very large indeed. He's
Dutch and he went back to Holland a few days ago.'

'Do we know anyone in Holland?' queried her
mother.

Britannia threw her parent a grateful look for taking
her seriously. 'No—at least, one of the staff nurses—
Joan Stevens, remember her, you met her at the prize-
giving—she has a Dutch godmother and she's going
over there to stay with her for a couple of weeks very
soon. It's a small country,' she added thoughtfully.

'Very. Joan's a good friend of yours?' Her father
had left his catalogue to join in the conversation again.

'Oh, yes, Father. We were in the same set, you know,
we've known each other for years. She did suggest that
I might like to go with her this time.'

'And of course you said yes.'

Britannia nodded and laid the poker down. 'Am I
being silly? You see, it was like a sign, if you see what
I mean…'

Her parents nodded in complete understanding.

'You've always known what you have wanted,' observed her father, and, 'Have you plenty of pretty clothes?' asked her mother.

She said that yes, she had, and added earnestly: 'I had to do something about it. I'm not sure what, but Joan asking me to go with her seemed like a sign...'

'He'll be a lucky man,' remarked her father, 'if he gets you—though I should have put that the other way round, shouldn't I?' He added: 'It's a pity he's rich—it tends to spoil people.'

His daughter considered this. 'Not him, I think—I fancy he takes it for granted.'

'How did you meet?' her mother wanted to know.

'I sent him packing out of the sluice on Men's Surgical. I didn't know who he was, but he shouldn't have been there, anyway.'

'Hardly a romantic background.' Mr Smith's voice was dry.

'No—well...' Britannia sounded uncertain, for only a moment. 'Don't say a word to Ted or Nick, will you?'

'Of course not, dear,' promised her mother comfortably. 'Anyway, they're neither of them coming home for weeks. Such dear boys,' she continued, 'and good brothers to you, too, even though they tease.' She picked up her knitting again. 'What's his name?'

'Professor Luitingh van Thien. He's not married, but I daresay he's engaged or got a girlfriend.'

'Quite suitable,' commented her mother, and shot her husband a smug look. 'And one doesn't know, probably he's a misogynist.'

Her husband and daughter surveyed her with deep affection. 'In that case,' declared Mr Smith, 'he won't be suitable at all.'

The first thing Britannia did when she got back to St Jude's was to go in search of her friend. She found her in the pantry, making tea after her day's work, and said without preamble: 'Joan, you asked me if I'd like to go to Holland with you—well, I would, very much.'

Joan warmed the pot carefully. 'Super! The Veskes are dears but a trifle elderly, if you know what I mean. I'm a bit active for them, that's why they suggested that I should bring someone with me. Could you manage two weeks?'

Britannia nodded. 'Mack will be furious, but I haven't had leave for ages—she asked me to change with her, so she owes me a favour. When do you plan to go?'

'Ten days.' They had gone back to Joan's room and were sipping their tea. 'Can you manage that?' And when Britannia nodded again: 'Can you ride?'

'Yes—nothing too mettlesome, though.'

'And cycle? Good. I daresay the weather will be foul, but who cares? We can borrow the car if we want, too. Hoenderloo is fairly central and we could travel round a bit.'

Holland was small, thought Britannia, they would be able to visit a great many places, there was always the chance that she might meet the professor... 'Won't your godmother mind? I mean if we go off all day?'

'Not a bit of it, as long as we're home for dinner in the evening—they like to play cards in the evening—besides, we can always take her with us. She's pretty hot on a bike too.'

'Thick clothes?' asked Britannia.

'And a mac. Not much chance of dressing up, ducky, though I always pop in something pretty just in case Prince Charming should rear his handsome head.' Joan poured more tea. 'And talking of him, what happened to that splendid type who came to operate on that liver case of yours? I saw him in theatre for a minute or two and he quite turned me on.'

'He went back to Holland.' Britannia made her voice nicely vague. 'He made a good job of that liver, too.'

Her friend gave her a considered look. 'Britannia, are you up to something?'

'Me? What could I be up to?'

'Well, you haven't been out with Ross lately, and you were seen wining and dining in Ned's Café.'

'Cheese on toast and a pot of tea,' said Britannia in a very ordinary voice. 'Neither of us had had any food for ages and we happened to meet—he was very rude,' she added.

'So much for Prince Charming,' declared Joan comfortably. 'Oh, well, let's hope he turns up for both of us before we're too long in the tooth.'

It wasn't easy to persuade Sister Mack that she could manage very nicely without her staff nurse for a fortnight, but Britannia's mind had been made up; she was going to Holland, childishly certain that she would meet the professor again. What she would say to him when she did, she had no idea—that could be thought about later. Once having wrung her superior's reluctant consent, she clinched the matter at the office, telephoned her parents and began on the important task of overhauling her wardrobe.

Joan had said something warm and sensible; she had a Scottish tweed suit she had providentially bought only a few weeks previously, a rich brown, the colour of peat, into which had been woven all the autumn colours of the Scottish Highlands. She bought a handful of sweaters to go with it, decided that her last year's brown tweed coat would have to do, added a small stitched velvet hat which could be pulled on at any angle and still look smart, and then a modicum of slacks and thick pullovers before concentrating on the important question of something pretty. For of course when she and the professor did meet, she would be wearing something eye-catching and chic... To be on the safe side, she bought two new dresses, one long, with a sweeping skirt and a plainly cut bodice. It had long sleeves demurely cuffed and its soft pink, she felt sure, would enchant even the cold eye of the professor. The other dress was short; a dark green wool, elegant and simple and in its way, equally eye-catching.

The two girls left for their holiday on a cold grey day which threatened drizzle, and indeed when they arrived at Schiphol it was raining, a cold, freezing rain which made them glad that they had worn raincoats and tied scarves over their heads. Mijnheer Veske was waiting for them, a tall, quiet man whose English was excellent and whose welcome was sincere. He stowed them

into his Citroën and throughout the sixty-mile journey
kept up a running commentary on the country they
were passing through, but as he travelled fast and the
greater part of the journey was a motorway, Britannia
at least got a little muddled, but just before Apeldoorn
he left the motorway, to take a quiet country road winding through the Veluwe to Hoenderloo, a small town
composed largely of charming little villas surrounded
by gardens, which even in the winter were a pleasure
to the eye. But they didn't stop here, but took a narrow
country road lined with tall trees and well wooded on
either side, their density broken here and there by gated
lanes or imposing pillars guarding well-kept drives.

Presently Mijnheer Veske turned the car into one of
the lanes, its gate invitingly opened on to a short grav-
elled drive leading to a fair-sized house. It was elabo-
rately built, with a great many little turrets and tiled
eyebrows over its upstairs windows, and small iron
balconies dotted here and there. But it looked welcoming, and indeed when the front door was flung open,
their welcome was everything they could have wished
for; Mevrouw Veske was waiting for them in the hall,
a short, stout lady with carefully coiffured hair, a massive bosom and a round cheerful face. She embraced
them in turn, declared herself to be enchanted to entertain her goddaughter's friend, outlined a few of the
activities arranged for their entertainment and swept
them into a large and cosily furnished sitting room,
barely giving them time to shed their outdoor things.
The room was warm and a tea tray stood ready; very

soon they were all sitting round talking away on the very best of terms.

Presently the two girls were taken upstairs to their rooms, pleasant apartments overlooking the now bare garden at the back and the woods beyond, and left to unpack. Britannia, happily arranging her clothes in a vast, old-fashioned wardrobe, decided that she was going to enjoy herself. It would of course be marvellous if she were to meet the professor, but during their drive from Schiphol she had come to the conclusion that she had been a little mad to imagine that she might find him again. Holland might be small, but not as small as all that. She changed into the new green dress, piled her hair into a great bun above her neck, did her face and went along to see if Joan was ready to go down.

The evening had been very pleasant, she decided, lying in her warm bed some hours later. Dinner had been a substantial meal, taken in a rather sombre dining room and served by a hefty young girl who looked at them rather as though they had arrived from outer space and giggled a good deal. Berthe, explained Mevrouw Veske, was learning to be a general help in the house and doing her best. There was an older woman, it seemed, with the astonishing name of Juffrouw Naakdgeboren, who was away at a family wedding. 'Very important they are, too,' explained their kindly hostess, 'in the country at least it's a very gay affair.' She smiled at them both. 'That's something you have to look forward to, isn't it?'

Britannia had smiled back, agreeing fervently if silently, though whether the professor would fit into a gay affair was something she very much doubted. And really, she reminded herself crossly, she must stop behaving as though she were going to marry him; it was one thing to make plans and hope, quite another to take it for granted. She had the feeling that the professor wouldn't take kindly to being taken for granted.

It was raining when they got up the next morning, but since they were on holiday they had no intention of letting the weather spoil their days. They put on raincoats again, muffled themselves in scarves, thick gloves and high boots and accompanied Mijnheer Veske to the garage, where there was quite a selection of bicycles. Britannia, mounting her rather elderly machine dubiously, almost fell off again because she hadn't realised that its brakes were operated by putting the pedals into reverse, but after a rather hilarious start they pedalled off, down the drive and out into the lane, to take the cycle path running beside the road. Hoenderloo was their destination, and once there they intended to have coffee, buy stamps and have a look round its shops before going back for lunch. Their surroundings, even on a bleak November morning, were pleasant; the bare trees lining the lane formed an arch over their heads, and the woods behind them held every sort of tree.

'Estates,' explained Joan. 'Some of them are quite small, some of them are vast. There are some lovely places tucked away behind these trees, I can tell you, but we shan't get much chance to see many of them—Mevrouw Veske visits here and there, but only the smaller villas. There's a gateway along here, look—something or other rampant on brick pillars and the drive curving away so that we can't see anything at all. It's a castle or moated house or some such thing, I asked Mevrouw Veske last time I was here.'

Britannia was balancing precariously with an eye to the brakes. 'Does anyone live there?' she asked.

'Oh, yes, but I haven't a clue who it is.'

They spent a happy hour or so in Hoenderloo, pottering in and out of its small shops, managing, on the whole, to make themselves understood very well, before having coffee and apple cake and cycling back again. They went with Mevrouw Veske to Apeldoorn in the afternoon, their hostess driving a small Fiat with a good deal of dash and verve and a splendid disregard of speed limits. She took them on a tour of the city's streets, wide and tree-lined and, she assured them, in the summer a mass of colour, and then bustled them back to the town's centre to give them tea and rich cream cakes and drive them home again. They played cards after dinner and went quite late to bed, and on the following day the same pleasant pattern was followed, only this time the girls cycled to the Kroller-Muller-museum to stare at the van Gogh paintings there, and after lunch Mevrouw Veske took them by car again to Loenen so that they might see the Castle ter Horst, and in the evening they played lighthearted bridge. Britannia, who didn't much care for cards, was glad that neither her host nor her hostess took the game seriously.

It was raining the next morning and Mevrouw Veske was regretfully forced to postpone her plan to take them to Arnhem for the day, so they settled down to writing postcards and then tossed to see who should go to Hoenderloo and post them. Britannia lost and ten minutes later, rather glad of the little outing, she wheeled her bike out of the garage and set off in the wind and the pouring rain. She had reached the gate and was about to turn on to the cycle path when she saw something in the road, small and black and fluttering. A bird, and hurt. She cast the bike down and ran across to pick it up, the wind tearing the scarf from her head so that her hair, tied back loosely, was instantly wet, flapping round her face and getting in her eyes. It was because of that that she didn't hear or see the approaching car, a magnificent Rolls-Royce Camargue, its sober grey coachwork gleaming in the downpour. It stopped within a foot of Britannia and she looked over her shoulder to see Professor Luitingh van Thien get out. She had the bird in her hand and said without preamble: 'I think its wing is broken—what shall I do?'

'Fool,' said the professor with icy forcefulness, 'darting into the road in that thoughtless fashion. I might have squashed you flat, or worse, gone into a skid and damaged the car.' He held out a hand. 'Give me that bird.'

She handed it over, for once unable to think of anything to say. So dreams did come true, after all, but he hardly seemed in the mood to share her pleasure in the fact. She stood, the rain washing over her in a relentless curtain, while he examined the small creature with gentle hands. 'I'll take it with me,' he said finally, and nodded briefly before getting back into his car. Britannia, made of stuff worthy of her name, followed him.

'Do you live near here?' she asked.

'Yes.' He gave her a cold look which froze the words hovering on her tongue, and drove away.

She stood in the road and watched him go. 'I must be mad,' she cried to the sodden landscape around her. 'He's the nastiest man I've ever set eyes on!' She went back to collect her bike and got on to it and rode off towards Hoenderloo. 'But he took the bird,' she reminded herself, 'and he could have wrung its neck.'

She was almost there and the rain had miraculously ceased when he passed her again, going the other way, and a few moments later had turned and slid to a halt beside her so that she felt bound to get off her bicycle.

'The bird's wing has been set; it will be cared for until it is fit to fly again.' He spoke unsmilingly, but she didn't notice that, she looked at him with delight.

'Isn't it incredible?' she declared. 'I mean, meeting like this after the sluice at St Jude's and now you here, almost next door, as it were.'

He looked down his splendid nose. 'I can see nothing incredible about it,' he said repressively. 'It is a coincidence, Britannia, they occur from time to time.'

He could call it that if he liked. She thought secretly of good fairies and kindly Fate and smiled widely. 'Well, you don't need to be so cross about it. I've never met such a prickly man. Have you been crossed in love or something?'

The ferocious expression which passed over the professor's handsome features might have daunted anyone of lesser spirit than hers. 'You abominable girl!' he ground out savagely. 'I have never met anyone like you…'

Britannia lifted a hand to tuck back a wet strand of hair. 'What you need,' she told him kindly, 'is a wife and a family.'

His mouth quivered momentarily. 'Why?'

She answered him seriously. 'Well, you would have them to look after and care for and love, and they'd love you and bring you your slippers in the evening, and…'

His voice was a well-controlled explosion. 'For God's sake, girl,' he roared, 'be quiet! Of all the sickly sentimental ideas…!'

Two tears welled up in Britannia's fine eyes and rolled slowly down her cheeks. The professor muttered strongly in his own language, and with the air of a man goaded beyond endurance, got out of his car.

'Why are you crying? I suppose that you will tell me that it's my fault.'

Britannia gave a sniff, wiped her eyes on a delicate scrap of white lawn and then blew her nose. 'No, of course it's not your fault, because you can't help it, can you? It's just very sad that you should think of a wife and children as being nothing more than s-sickly s-sentiment.' Two more tears spilled over and she wiped them away impatiently as a child would, with the back of her hand.

The professor was standing very close to her. When he spoke it was with surprising gentleness. 'I didn't mean that. I was angry.'

She said in a woeful voice, 'But you're always losing your temper—every time we meet you rage and roar at me.'

'I neither rage nor roar, Britannia. Possibly I am a

little ill-tempered at times.' The gentleness had a decidedly chilly edge to it now.

'Oh, yes, you do,' she answered him with spirit. 'You terrify me.' She peeped at him, to see him frowning.

'I cannot believe that you are terrified of anyone or anything, certainly not of me. Try that on some other man, my dear girl, I'm not a fool.'

She sighed. 'Well, no—I was afraid you wouldn't believe me.'

He looked at her with cold interest. 'And were the tears a try-out too?'

She shook her head slowly; she might have met him again, just as she had dreamed that she might, but it hadn't done much good. She said quietly: 'Thank you very much for taking care of the bird,' and got on to her bike and wobbled off at a great rate, leaving him standing there.

She tried very hard not to think of him during the rest of the day, but lying in bed was a different matter; she went over their meetings, not forgetting a word or a look, and came to the conclusion that he still didn't like her. She was on the point of sleep when she remembered with real regret that she had hardly looked her best; surely, if she had been wearing the new pink dress, he would have behaved differently? Men, her mother had always said, were susceptible to pink. Britannia sighed and slept.

Chapter 3

It seemed that Britannia was never to discover the professor's taste regarding pink-clad females, but that was a small price to pay in the face of the frequency of their meetings. For she met him again the very next afternoon. Joan, laid low with a headache, had decided to stay indoors and Mevrouw Veske had an appointment with her dentist. Britannia, restless and urged by her friend to take advantage of the unexpectedly pleasant day, donned slacks, pulled on two sweaters, tied a scarf under her chin and went to fetch her bicycle. There was miles of open country around her; she chose a right-hand turn at the crossroads and pedalled down it, feeling a good deal more cheerful while she plotted ways and means—most of them quite unsuitable—of meeting the professor again. An unnecessary exercise as it turned out, for seeing a picturesque pond among the trees on the other side of the road she decided to cross over and get a better view. She was almost there when the professor's magnificent car swept round the curve ahead and stopped within a foot or so of her.

She jumped off her machine, quite undisturbed by the sight of his furious face thrust through the open window, and his biting: 'This is becoming quite ridiculous—you're not fit to ride a bicycle!'

Britannia, a girl of common sense, nonetheless realised that her fairy godmother, kind Fate or just plain good luck were giving her another chance. The sight of the professor glowering from the opened window of his stupendous car sent a most pleasing sensation through her, although her pretty face remained calm. She said: 'Hullo,' and got no reply; the professor was swallowing rage. When he did at length speak, his voice was cold and nasty.

'You were on the wrong side of the road. I might have killed you.'

She stooped to pick up her bicycle, observing that it had a puncture in the back tyre which seemed of no great importance at the moment; it was much more important to get him into a good mood. She said reasonably: 'I'm a foreigner, so you have to make allowances, you know. You aren't very nice about it; after all, we have met before.'

The blue eyes studied her in undisguised rage. 'Indeed we have, but I see no reason to express pleasure at seeing you again. I advise you to travel on the correct side of the road and use the cycle path where there is one.' He added morosely: 'You're not fit to be out on your own.'

Britannia took his criticism in good part. 'You can come with me if you like,' she invited. 'I daresay some healthy exercise would do you good; there's nothing like fresh air to blow away bad temper.' She smiled at him kindly and waited for him to speak, and when he didn't she went on: 'Oh, well, perhaps you can't cycle any more…'

The professor's voice, usually deep and measured, took on an unexpected volume. 'You are an atrocious girl. How you got here and why is no concern of mine, but I will not be plagued by you.'

She looked meek. 'I don't mean to plague you. My back tyre's punctured.'

'Mend it or walk home!' he bellowed, and left her standing there.

'He drives much too fast,' remarked Britannia to the quiet road. 'And how do I mend a puncture with nothing?'

She turned her machine and started to walk, doing sums as she went. She had been cycling for almost an hour—not hurrying—so she must have come at least ten miles. She would be late for lunch, she might even be late for tea. She had passed through a village some way back, but as she had no money and no one there would know or understand her, it wouldn't be of much use to stop there. She had been walking for twenty min-utes or so when an elderly man on a bicycle passed her, stopped, and with the minimum of speech and fuss, got out his repair kit. He had almost finished the job when the professor, coming the other way, slid his car to a halt beside them.

Britannia gave him a warm smile. 'There, I knew you weren't as nasty as you pretended you were!'

He surveyed her unsmilingly. 'Get in,' he said evenly. 'The bike can be fetched later.'

She shook her head at him. 'Oh, I couldn't do that; this gentleman stopped to help me and I wouldn't be so ungrateful as to leave him now.' She shook her pretty head at him again. 'You really must get out of the habit of expecting people to do what you want whether they wish to or not. This kind man hasn't shouted at me, nor did he leave me to mend a puncture all alone in a strange land, which I couldn't have done anyway because I had nothing to do it with.'

She paused to see the effect of this speech. The professor's splendid features appeared to be carved in disapproving stone, his eyes pale and hard. She sighed. 'Oh, well…it was kind of you to come back. Thank you.' She had no chance to say more, for he had gone, driving much too fast again.

She very nearly told Joan about it when she got back, but really there didn't seem much point; beyond meeting the professor again, nothing had happened; he still disliked her, indeed, even more so, she thought. There was the possibility that she might not see him again. She paused in the brushing of her mane of hair to reflect that whether he liked her or no, they had met again—she could have stayed her whole two weeks in Holland and not seen hair nor hide of him; she tended to regard that as some sort of sign. Before she got into bed she sat down and wrote to her mother and father; after all, she had told them about him in the first place, they had a right to know that her sudden whim to go to Holland had borne fruit. Rather sour fruit, she conceded.

But not as sour as all that; she was on her way down to breakfast the following morning when Berthe came running upstairs to meet her. She pointed downwards, giggling, and then pointed at Britannia, who instantly thought of all the awful things which could have happened to either Mijnheer or Mevrouw Veske and rushed past her and down the stairs at a great rate.

'I had no idea that you were so eager to see me again,' said the professor. 'Should I be flattered?'

He was standing in the hall, in his car coat with his gloves in his hand, and gave her the distinct impression that he was impatient to be gone.

'No,' said Britannia, 'you shouldn't—I thought something awful had happened to the Veskes. What are you doing here? Is someone ill?'

The professor's lip twitched faintly. 'Cut down to size,' he murmured. 'I called to see you.'

Britannia's incurable optimism bubbled up under her angora sweater, but she checked it with a firm metaphorical hand and asked: 'Why?'

'I owe you an apology for my behaviour yesterday. I offer it now.'

'Well, that's handsome of you, Professor, I'll accept it. I expect you were worrying about something and felt irritable.'

'You concern yourself a little too much about my

feelings, Miss Smith. Perhaps it would be better if you
were to attend to your own affairs.'

She had annoyed him again. The optimism burst
its bubble and she said quietly: 'I'm sure you're right.
Thank you for coming—I expect you want to go…'

He gave her a long look and went to the door without a word, but before he could open it she had nipped
across the hall to stand beside him. 'I'm only here for
a fortnight,' she told him, and then, unable to resist the
question: 'Do you really live near here?'

'Yes. Goodbye, Britannia.'

So that was that. She went into breakfast and made
lighthearted rejoinders to the questions fired at her, and
presently they all began talking about their plans for
the day and the professor was forgotten.

They spent the next day or so sightseeing; Mevrouw
Veske was a splendid hostess. They drove to Arnhem
and spent several hours in the Open-Air Museum, ab-
sorbing Holland's national culture through centuries
through its farms, windmills, houses from every prov-
ince and medieval crafts, and were taken to lunch at the
Haarhuis, where Britannia ate eel, so deliciously dis-
guised that she had no idea what it was until her hostess
told her. They spent the afternoon looking at the shops
and buying a few trifles to take home, and arrived back
at the villa exhausted but very content with their day.

The next day was Saturday and Mijnheer Veske had
offered to take the two girls riding. The weather had
turned cold and bright and he knew the charming country around them like the back of his hand. Britannia,
a rather wary horsewoman, found that she was enjoy-

ing herself immensely; her mount was a calm beast who made no effort to play tricks but was content to trot along after the other two, so that Britannia relaxed presently and looked around her. There were woods on either side of them, with here and there a small estate between the trees. Mijnheer Veske, who had lived there all his life, found nothing out of the ordinary about it, but she longed to explore away from the lanes; the glimpses of the houses she saw fired her imagination, and just as they were about to return home she caught a glimpse of a really splendid house, its gables tantalisingly half hidden by the trees surrounding it. There was a narrow lane running round the walls of the grounds, too. It was on the tip of her tongue to ask her host if they might ride a little way along so that she might see more of it, but it was already eleven o'clock and she knew that the Veskes lunched at midday. She made herself a promise that before she went back to England she would either cycle or ride that way and see it for herself.

They all went to church the next morning, driving to Hoenderloo in the Citroën. Britannia couldn't help but wonder if the service would be of any benefit to herself and Joan, but it had been taken for granted that they would accompany the Veskes, and it would be an experience.

The church was red brick, built in the jelly-mould style with whitewashed walls and plain glass windows. It was lofty and spacious and on the cold side, but Britannia forgot all about that in her interest in following the service. It seemed one stood up when one would kneel at home, and sat down when one would stand, but the hymns, surprisingly, had the same tunes even though the words were incomprehensible. They were sung rather slowly too, so that she had the chance to try out some of the verses, much to Joan's amusement. It was as the sermon began that she saw the professor, sitting in the front of the church and to her right, and he wasn't alone. Beside him was a fair-haired girl with a beanpole figure draped in the height of fashion. Britannia, sitting between her host and hostess, wondered about her. She was undeniably beautiful if one liked glossy magazine types. She glanced down at her own nicely rounded person and sighed to be slim and golden-haired. There was only one tiny crumb of comfort; the professor didn't look at his companion once; his arrogant profile was lifted towards the *dominee*, thundering away at the congregation from under his sounding-board.

And presently, as the congregation left the church, the professor and his companion passed the Veskes' pew. He acknowledged their greeting pleasantly, smiled nicely at Joan and then wiped the smile off his face as he bent his cold eyes on Britannia, who so far forgot herself as to wrinkle her nose at him and turn down the corners of her pretty mouth in an unladylike grimace. If he wanted war, he should have it!

A belligerent decision which was made to look silly, for as they rose from Sunday lunch the professor arrived at the front door to enquire for her, and when she went into the sitting room where the giggling Berthe had shown him, it was to find him nattily attired in tweeds and an anorak, with the bland invitation to go cycling with him.

'Me?' asked Britannia, much astonished.

He opened his eyes wide in exaggerated surprise. 'Certainly you. I was under the impression that you had asked me to accompany you—healthy exercise, you said, and the certainty that fresh air would be good for my temper.'

She eyed him with astonishment. 'And you've actually got a bike? You want to go cycling? With me?'

'Yes.'

She beamed at him; the fairies were very much on her side after all. 'Give me two minutes,' she begged him.

It took her rather less than that to pull another sweater over her skirt, wind a scarf round her neck and tie a scarf round her hair, and another minute to explain to Mevrouw Veske, who looked pleased if surprised. 'Well, at least one of us has found Prince Charming,' observed Joan.

'Stuff!' retorted Britannia. 'He's only doing it because he thinks I'm a fool on a bike.'

'Well, you are, ducky,' said Joan cheerfully. 'I expect he'll teach you the rules of the road.'

But he didn't; they cycled amiably enough along the route she had chosen and when he asked why she particularly wanted to go that way she told him about the house she had glimpsed and hadn't had time to see. 'It looked exciting, like things do look when you can't see them properly—just the gables between the trees and a lovely park.' She turned to look at him and wobbled alarmingly so that he put out a hand to steady her handlebars. 'I still don't know where you live, you know, and I quite understand that you don't want me to know, though I can't think why, but you must have a house somewhere within cycling distance; you'll know who the house belongs to, I expect. There's a little lane running round the park walls. Do you suppose the owner would mind very much if we went down it and looked over the wall?'

She was so intent on riding her bicycle in a manner to win his approval that she didn't see the professor's expression. Astonishment, amusement and then sheer delight passed over his features, but none of these were apparent in his voice. 'I believe it is possible to cycle right round the grounds—there should be a better view of the house. Why are you so interested?'

'Well, it sounds silly, but I had a funny feeling when I saw it first—as though it meant something to me.' She glanced at him and found him smiling and went on defensively, 'All right, so it's silly—I'm not even in my own country and I don't know anyone here except the Veskes—and you. Perhaps it's derelict.'

Her companion looked shocked. 'No—someone lives in it.'

'Oh, you know them?'

'Yes.'

They had passed the crossroads and were in the narrow lane curving between the trees with the professor leading the way.

'What I like about you,' observed Britannia, 'is the terseness of your answers.'

He slowed a little so that she could catch up with him. 'I had no idea that there was anything you liked about me,' he said suavely.

Which annoyed her so much that she forgot about the brakes and back-pedalled so that he had to put a steadying hand on her arm. 'Now, now,' he chided her in a patient, superior voice which annoyed her even more.

But she couldn't remain vexed for long; the air was cold and exhilarating and the countryside charming, and had she not got just what she had wished for most? The professor's company...

'It's down here,' she said eagerly, 'if we go along here and look to the left...'

'There will be a better view further on,' observed the professor matter-of-factly.

'Why are you laughing?' asked Britannia.

'My dear good girl, I am not even smiling.'

'Inside you—something's amusing you...'

He shot her a quick look. 'I can see that I shall have to be very careful of my behaviour when we are together,' he said smoothly. 'Since you asked, I was remembering something which amused me.'

She let that pass, although it was nice, she reflected, that the professor could be amused... 'There!' she exclaimed, and back-pedalled to a halt. 'That's the place. It must be sheer heaven in the summer—all those copper beeches and that row of limes. I wonder what the garden is like.'

'Probably if we go on a little further we could see it,' suggested her companion. He was right; the house came into view, typically Dutch, of mellow red brick, tall chimney pots among the gables, its large windows shining in the pale sunshine. It was too far off to see as much as she wanted, but she could glimpse a paved walk all round the house, outbuildings at the side of a formal garden laid out before its massive front.

'I hope whoever lives there loves it,' remarked Britannia. 'Do you suppose it belongs to some old family? Perhaps it had to be sold to pay death duties and now there's someone living there who can't tell Biedermeier from mid-Victorian Rococo...'

'What a vivid imagination you have! And do you really know the difference between Rococo and Biedermeier?' He wasn't looking at her but staring across the countryside towards the distant house.

'Yes, I think so. You see, my father is an antique dealer and I always went with him to sales and auctions. I didn't mean to boast.'

'You admire antique furniture? Which is your favourite period?'

Britannia had got off her bike and was leaning against the low wall. 'Oh, yes. Early Regency and Gothic.'

He asked casually, 'Have you been inside any of the houses round here?'

She shook her head. 'No, and I don't expect to. I only came to keep Joan company—she's the Veskes' goddaughter.' She got on her bike again. 'Can we get all the way round, or do we go back the way we came?'

The professor smiled faintly. 'You wish to return? We can go on. Do you intend visiting any of the hospitals while you are here?'

'I'd like to, but one can't just present oneself and say look, I'm a nurse, can I look round. Mijnheer Veske might be able to give me an introduction, but Joan isn't keen, anyway.'

They were side by side, pedalling into the chilly wind. 'I should be glad to arrange a visit for you,' said the professor surprisingly. 'Arnhem—I go there twice a week. I will call for you and bring you back after my teaching round.'

Britannia eyed him with surprise. 'Would you really? Why are you being so nice? I thought you couldn't bear the sight of me.'

His voice was smooth. 'Shall we say that the fresh air and exercise which you recommended have had their good effect?'

He didn't go into the house with her but bade her a casual goodbye without saying another word about her visit to the hospital. Probably he had regretted his words, decided Britannia as she went to her room to tidy herself before presenting herself in the sitting room for tea.

There were visitors; an elderly couple, their daughter and a son, home from some far-flung spot on long leave. Britannia was made instantly aware of the interesting fact that he and Joan were getting on remarkably well and being a true friend, engaged the daughter in a conversation which lasted until the visitors got up to leave.

Their car had barely disappeared down the drive when Joan told her happily: 'We're going out tomorrow. Britannia, do you mind? I mean, if you're left on your own. He's only got another week...'

'Plenty of time,' comforted Britannia. 'Besides, it was an instant thing, wasn't it? Flashing lights and sunbeams and things, it stuck out a mile.' She added: 'Prince Charming, love?'

Joan looked smug and hopeful and apprehensive all at the same time. 'Oh, yes. Oh, Britannia, you've no idea how it feels!'

In which she was wrong, of course.

Britannia, happily, did not have long to wait before the professor paid her another visit, although visit was hardly the right word. He drove up some time after breakfast, asked to see her, and when she presented herself, enquired of her coolly if she was ready to go to Arnhem with him. She felt a surge of pleasure, for Joan was committed for the whole day with Dirk de Jonge and Mevrouw Veske had asked her a little anxiously what she was going to do with herself until lunchtime; all the same she said sedately: 'How kind, but I didn't know that you had asked me to come with you today. It's not very convenient...'

He stood bareheaded in the hall, watching her. 'May I ask what you intended doing today?' His voice was very bland.

'Nothing,' said Britannia before she could stop herself, and then waited for him to make some nasty remark. But he didn't, he said quite mildly: 'In that case I should be glad to take you to Arnhem. I think you will find the hospital interesting. You have, after all, nearly a week here, have you not, and if your friend is going to spend it exclusively with de Jonge you will have to seek your own amusement, will you not?'

'Do you know him? I thought he looked nice…'

'Yes, I know him, and if by nice you mean unmarried, able to support a wife and anxious to marry your friend, then yes, he is nice.'

'You have no need to talk like that. You must live close by…?'

His brief 'Yes,' didn't help at all. Britannia sighed. 'I'll fetch my coat.'

Mevrouw Veske gave her a roguish look when she disclosed her plans for the day. 'Very nice, dear, I'm sure you'll enjoy yourself, and in such good company too.' She wore the pleased expression that older ladies wore when they scented romance with a capital R, and Britannia, incurably honest, made haste to explain that she was merely being given a lift to the hospital and a return lift when it was convenient to the professor. Rather a waste of time, for Mevrouw Veske, accompanying her to the hall to bid the professor good morning, wished them both a pleasant day together, with an arch look which wasn't lost on him, for the moment they were in the car he remarked silkily:

'Your hostess seems to be under the impression that we are to spend the day in each other's company. I hope that you don't think the same.'

'No,' said Britannia sweetly, and seethed silently as she said it, 'I don't—but you know what happily married women are like, they want to see everyone else happily married; such an absurd notion in our case that I see no point in wasting breath on it.'

'Why absurd?' he asked blandly.

Britannia settled down comfortably in her seat.

'Well,' she explained carefully, 'we're in—incompatible, aren't we? Different backgrounds and interests and…and…'

'Ages?' he queried.

'Lord, no—what has age got to do with it? That was a very pretty girl in church with you.'

'Yes.'

'Does she live close by, too?'

'Yes.'

Britannia turned to look at him. 'I wonder why you offered me a lift? Certainly not for the conversation.'

He said blandly: 'I thought I had explained about the fresh air and exercise…'

'Oh, pooh. I shall hold my tongue, since you like it that way.'

He ignored this. 'When you get to the hospital you will be put in the care of a surgical Sister who speaks excellent English. She will take you to any wards you wish to see. I shall be a couple of hours—you will be warned when I am ready to leave.'

'Who looks after you?' asked Britannia.

'I have an excellent housekeeper.'

'She must be a devoted one too if you fire orders at her in the same way as you're firing them at me. You know, I don't think I want to go to Arnhem after all. Would you stop, please? I'll go for a walk instead.'

He laughed aloud. 'We have come almost six miles and this isn't a main road, nor are there any villages—you may have noticed that we are passing the Air Force field. You could walk back the way we have come or continue on to Arnhem. It will be a long…' He broke off and slowed the car's quiet rush. There was a woman standing in the middle of the road, waving her arms and shouting. As the professor brought the car to a halt she ran towards it, still shouting and crying too, and he got out without more ado to catch her by the shoulders and say something firmly to her. Britannia had got out as well, for plainly there was something very wrong. The woman was pointing now, towards a very small, rather tumbledown cottage half hidden in the trees, and the professor started towards it, the woman tugging at his sleeve. 'A child taken ill,' he said briefly, and Britannia went too; after all, she was a nurse and there might be something she could do.

The child was on the floor of the small room, crowded with furniture, into which they went. A little girl, whose small face was already blue and who had no trace of breath. The professor went down on his knees, asking brief, curt questions of the hysterical mother, then turned to Britannia.

'Sit down,' he commanded her. 'Take the child on your knees and flex her head. There's a pebble impacted in her larynx, so her mother says.'

He waited a few seconds while Britannia did as she was bid and then swept an exploratory finger into the child's mouth. 'Have you a Biro pen with you?' he asked, and took a penknife from his pocket.

She didn't say more than she had to, for talk at that time was wasting precious seconds. 'My bag—outside pocket.'

She watched while he found the pen, pulled it apart

and handed her the plastic casing; a makeshift trachy tube indeed, but better than nothing.

'Hold the child's head back, give me the tube when I say so,' said the professor, and opened his knife. 'This may just work,' he observed. It took seconds and with the improvised tube in place the little girl's face began to take on a faint pink as air reached her lungs once more. But the professor wasted no time in contemplating his handiwork. 'Get into the car,' he said, and took the child from Britannia's knee and followed her as she ran back to the Rolls. 'Hold her steady on your knee and hold the tube exactly as it is now. I'm going to drive to the hospital.'

Britannia paled a little, but her 'yes,' was said in a steady enough voice and the professor, acknowledging it with a grunt, went back for the mother, and when she was in the car, still crying and hysterical, picked up the telephone she had noticed beside his seat. He spoke briefly, bent over the child for a moment, got into his seat and drove off smoothly. He drove very fast too; Britannia, her hand locked on the frail plastic tube, sent up a stream of incoherent prayers, mingled with heartfelt thanks that Arnhem couldn't be very far away now. And at the professor's speed, it wasn't. The city's pleasant outskirts enclosed them, gave way to busy streets and in no time at all, the forecourt of a hospital.

His few terse words into the telephone had borne fruit. Two white-coated young doctors, a rather fierce-looking Sister and her attendant satellite were waiting for them. In no time at all the professor was out of the car, round its elegant bonnet and bending over the child through Britannia's open door, with the two young men squeezed in on her other side and the Sister right behind the professor, a covered tray in her hands. He used the instruments on it with lightning speed; the plastic Biro case was eased out and a tracheotomy tube inserted and its tapes neatly tied. The professor muttered and the two doctors immediately started the sucker they had brought with them; after a few moments the child's face began to look almost normal again while the trachy tube made reassuring whistling noises with each breath. The professor spoke again and lifted the child off Britannia's knee; seconds later she was alone, stretching her cramped back and legs and watching the small urgent procession of trolley, professor and his assistants disappearing into the hospital.

It was almost an hour before anyone came—a porter, who eyed her with some surprise as he got into the driver's seat beside her. She bade him a quite inadequate hullo and hoped that he could speak English. He could after a fashion, but his 'In garage' hardly reassured her.

With the British belief that if she spoke enough he would understand her, Britannia asked: 'Will the professor be long?' and then when she saw how hopeless it was, managed a: '*De Professor komt?*'

He shook his head, thought deeply and came out with: 'Long time.'

He had forgotten her, of course. She smiled at the man, got out of the car and watched it being driven away, round to the back of the hospital. She could go and enquire, she supposed; ask someone where the professor was and how long he would be, but she fancied that he wouldn't take kindly to being disturbed at his work. She walked slowly out of the hospital gates and started towards the main streets of the town they had gone through. Sooner or later she would see a policeman who would tell her where she could get a bus.

It took a little while, for the streets confused her and there seemed to be no policemen at all, but she found one at last, got him to understand what she wanted and set off once more, her head whirling with lengthy instructions as to how and where to get a bus for Hoenderloo, so it was some time later when she boarded the vehicle and wedged herself thankfully between a stout woman and a very thin old man. There would be a mile or so to walk from the bus stop and the afternoon was closing in rapidly, reminding her that she had had no lunch, but she cheered herself up with the thought of the cosy sitting room at the villa and the plentiful dinner Mevrouw Veske set before her guests each evening.

The bus made slow progress, stopping apparently wherever it was most convenient for its passengers to alight, but it reached her stop at last, and she got out quickly, the only passenger to do so, anxious to get back to the villa. She had taken a bare half dozen steps when she saw the professor looming at the side of the road just ahead of her, the Rolls behind him. He took her arm without a word and marched her to the car, declaring coldly: 'You tiresome girl, as though I don't have enough to do without traipsing round the country looking for you!'

She couldn't see his face very clearly in the early dusk. 'I'm quite able to look after myself,' she pointed out reasonably. 'I didn't know what to do when the porter came to take the car away; he said you would be a long time and I thought that perhaps you intended remaining at the hospital. Is the child all right?'

'Yes.' He gave her arm a little shake. 'You imagined that I would do that without sending you a message? Don't be absurd!'

They were in the car now and she turned to look at him and observe in a kindly tone: 'Not absurd, you know. You had enough to think of without bothering your head about me.' She smiled at him. 'I can't think why you should.'

'I'll tell you why,' he ground out, and then in his usual cool voice: 'But not now.' He started the car without another word.

The Veskes had been very nice about it, Britannia decided as she got ready for bed that evening; they had asked the professor in for a drink, expressing discreet sympathy with her, murmuring comfortably about difficulties with language and misunderstandings. He had stayed for half an hour making polished conversation before making his farewells, not that he had bothered overmuch with his goodbyes to her; a nod, a casual *tot ziens* and her thanks shrugged off carelessly. And come to think of it, he hadn't bothered to thank her for the part she had played that morning. She tugged the covers up to her chin on a wave of indignation. He was arrogant and ill-tempered and just about the horridest man she had ever met, and she loved him with all her heart. All the same, she would cut him dead when she saw him again. She began to concoct episodes in which he was made to appear in a very poor light while she ignored him coolly, but presently she got a little muddled and before she could sort out the muddle, was asleep.

Chapter 4

The professor called the next afternoon and Britannia quite forgot to be cool and ignore him. Joan had gone off for the day directly after breakfast and now, after a morning shopping with Mevrouw Veske and a lunch à deux, she had got into slacks, a thick sweater and an old anorak of her hostess's and was on her way to fetch her bike. The weather was hardly promising, but Britannia was in no mood to bother about that; she was wondering how she could find out where the professor lived and if possible, despite her determination to ignore him, see him again, so that the sight of him striding towards her round the corner of the house sent her spirits soaring. She stood outside the garage, holding the bike, watching him coming towards her. Beautifully turned out, as always, assured, far too good-looking… She wished him a quiet good afternoon, and waited.

'I thought we might try again,' he said.

The urge to fling her machine to the ground and accept on the instant was very great. She clutched the handlebars with woolly gloved hands and said politely: 'How kind of you. But as you see, I'm just off for a ride.'

He didn't bother to answer her but took the bike from her, leaned it against the garage wall and took her arm. 'It's too cold to cycle. I've warned Zuster Vinke that you would be coming.'

Britannia stopped in her tracks to face him. 'That was a little high-handed of you,' she pointed out.

He grinned. 'I am high-handed, I shout, I'm nasty, ill-tempered, irritable… I forget the rest, although you have told me often enough.' He gave her a little shake. 'I have never been preached at so often in my life before.'

Britannia raised large, serious brown eyes to his. 'Oh, I don't mean to, really I don't; you're a splendid surgeon…'

'And so are thousands of others. Britannia, I'm sorry about yesterday. I was angry because I didn't know where you were, and I was angry with myself for not having done something about it. Forgive me and come with me now.'

'Well, I'm not dressed…' she began, already half won over.

'You look just the same as usual,' he assured her, and even while she was trying to decide if that was a compliment or not, he had her by the arm, walking her briskly along the drive to the waiting car.

There was nothing to interrupt their journey to Arnhem this time and the professor whiled away the short journey in light conversation, revealing a new facet of himself to Britannia. She had had no idea that he could be such an amusing and pleasant companion; it wouldn't last, of course; sooner or later he would get into a fine rage about something or other. It was extraordinary, she mused, that one could love someone so much even when they scowled and frowned and stared down with cold blue eyes...

'I was saying,' said her companion with exaggerated patience, 'that I hope to be finished by four o'clock. Zuster Vinke will be told when I am ready.'

Such arrogance, she thought lovingly, but she could alter that. Her 'Very well,' was meek.

Zuster Vinke turned out to be a big bony woman, with shrewd eyes behind thick glasses and a nice smile. And her English was more than adequate; she led Britannia from one ward to the next, finishing in the Children's Ward where Britannia was shown the small girl the professor had saved. She was sitting up in bed, playing quite happily with a doll. The pebble had been removed, she was told; as soon as the tracheotomy had healed the child would go to a convalescent home and then back to the isolated little cottage which was her home. It was while they were with her that they were joined by one of the doctors who had met them outside the hospital. Young and tall and nice-looking, he introduced himself as Tom van Essent. 'And of course I know who you are,' he told her eagerly. 'You were a great help to the professor, so he tells us; without your help the child would have died. It is a pleasure to meet you. You are staying long in Holland?'

'Under a week—not long enough.' Britannia smiled at him, quite ready to like him because he worked for the professor.

'Perhaps if you are not too occupied, I might take you out to dinner one evening?'

'Well, that would be nice, thank you, I'd like that. Could you telephone me some time?' She gave him Mevrouw Veske's number and then, because Zuster Vinke had been called to the telephone and came back with the news that the professor would be ready in five minutes, she went with him back to the entrance hall, with Zuster Vinke striding along on her other side. They were standing together, laughing and talking, when they were joined by the professor, who, making no effort to make a cheerful fourth, bade her two guides a curt goodbye, asked her grumpily if she was ready to leave, and walked out of the hospital at a great rate, with Britannia having to nip along smartly to keep up. In the car, sliding smoothly away from the hospital, he asked: 'You found your visit interesting? I see that young van Essent was with you.' It was coolly and carelessly said, but she thought she detected annoyance as well.

'Oh, he met us just before we returned to the entrance—in the Children's Ward—and he walked down with us. I liked Zuster Vinke and it's a splendid hospital. And how nice to see little Tinneke sitting up playing with a doll.' She turned to look at him. 'Doesn't it give you a nice feeling each time you see her?'

He shot the Rolls through a knot of traffic. His voice

was bland. 'Perhaps I haven't your youthful enthusiasm, Britannia.'

'Oh, stuff, of course you have, otherwise you wouldn't be a surgeon, you'd retire to your villa or whatever and mope and moulder away the rest of your days.'

A reluctant smile tugged at the corners of his mouth. 'Put like that I must admit your argument is a strong one. You liked van Essent?'

'Oh yes. He's young, though.'

'And what do you mean by that?'

'Just what I said—he made me think of my younger brother.'

'Ah—so you have brothers. And a sister perhaps?'

'No, only my brothers.'

'And parents?'

'Yes.' Really, he asked a lot of questions! 'And what about you…?'

'I am touched by your interest in me, but there is nothing of interest to tell you.'

'Unfair,' snapped Britannia. 'If you ask me any more questions I shall invent the answers.'

'And I shall know if you are fibbing, Britannia. Did Zuster Vinke give you tea?'

'No—at least she said we would have a cup of coffee when we had finished looking round, but there wasn't time—you sent a message.'

'Thoughtless of me.' They were clear of the town now, racing along the quiet road, passing the cottage where Tinneke lived and then the airfield; they would be at the villa in no time at all. But at the crossroads, instead of keeping straight on, the professor turned down the road Mijnheer Veske had taken when they had gone horse-riding.

'You're going the wrong way,' observed Britannia helpfully.

'I am going to my house. So that you may have that cup of coffee I so thoughtlessly deprived you of.' He slowed the car to turn between two stone pillars. 'Or tea, perhaps—you English drink gallons of tea.'

'That's why we're such nice people. I'd love to see your house.'

'So you have already said.' He didn't sound very enthusiastic, but she didn't care; she was going to have her wish after all, and he had been almost friendly... 'This is someone's park,' she pointed out. 'Should we be here?'

'Of course. It belongs to me.'

She hadn't thought of that; she peered out of the window, silent for once, her tongue held by surprise. The sanded drive wound through trees, swept round a high grass bank and then, with close-cut lawns on either side of it, made for the house. It was a grey, dull afternoon and would soon be dark, but Britannia could see it clearly enough; its gables and chimneys now wholly visible. And it was just as beautiful as she had imagined it to be when she had first glimpsed it from the other side of the park wall. It wasn't so very large as large houses go, but its windows were wide and high, giving a hint of the spacious rooms within, and although its front was flat, the windows arranged in neat rows on either side and above its imposing entrance, there were wings on either side, red brick and one storey high. There were trees grouped behind it and great sweeps of lawn on either side, and a little formal garden just visible beyond, a miniature of the large one in front of the house.

'Well,' said Britannia at length, 'you might have told me.'

'I can see no possible reason for doing so.'

'But I took you to see it the other day…you were there by the wall, you told me there was a better view…'

'I still can see no reason for telling you.' He added silkily: 'In any case, you being you, you would have discovered it for yourself.'

'Yes, of course I should, because I very much wanted to know who lived here. But it wasn't very nice of you—you've made me feel like a busybody poking her nose into other people's business.'

'If I thought that I shouldn't be bringing you here for tea, Britannia.'

They had reached the sweep before the house and he had stopped the car and turned to look at her. 'And what have you to say to that?'

She gave him a long candid look. 'I'm wondering why you have brought me here to tea,' she said soberly.

He leaned across her and undid her safety belt, then kissed her hard. 'Perhaps I want to get to know you better,' he told her blandly as he got out.

She got out too, trying to look as though she wasn't wildly happy, excited and completely at sea, and walked beside him to the door. By the time they had mounted the half-dozen shallow steps leading to it, it had been opened by a short stout man with a cheerful face, who answered the professor's greeting with a beaming smile, then turned the beam on Britannia, and she, still in a delightful haze, beamed back.

The glass-walled lobby gave on to a square hall with a branched staircase at its far end and a number of doors on either side. It was a handsome apartment with a tiled floor spread with fine rugs and furnished with massive side tables bearing great bowls of flowers. Britannia looked about her with frank, unselfconscious interest, wishing her father was with her to admire the fine ormolu clock on a marble-topped commode, the exquisite chandelier above her head, and the William and Mary armchairs set against the walls. She entered the room into which the professor was urging her with a lively anticipation of still more treasures, and she wasn't disappointed. It was large, lighted by great windows draped in claret-coloured velvet and with a polished floor adorned with still more silky rugs, but she had no time to examine her surroundings; there were two people there, sitting opposite each other beside the cheerful fire burning in the vast marble fireplace; a rather severe-looking lady who might have been in her sixties and the lovely girl who had been with the professor in church.

Britannia's pleasure ebbed away. Both ladies were eyeing her, the elder with a thoughtful expression, the younger with a smiling contempt, making her very aware of her slacks and anorak and sensible shoes, so that the pleasure was replaced by feminine rage at being caught at a disadvantage and an even greater rage towards the professor for allowing that to happen in the first place. She had time to wonder if he had done it deliberately before he said smoothly: 'Mama, this is Britannia Smith, without whose help I could not have saved the child I told you of. My mother, Britannia.'

Britannia shook hands and found that the severe features, relaxed in a smile, were rather charming after all; the blue eyes which looked at her so intently were very like the professor's and she found herself smiling back, conscious that she was approved of. It gave her a little added sparkle as she turned in obedience to the professor's suave: 'And this is Madeleine de Venz— you will have seen each other in church, I feel sure.'

They smiled brilliantly at each other; Madeleine's bright blue eyes were unfriendly as she looked Britannia slowly up and down. She said in a deliberate, sugary sweet voice: 'Of course, you were sitting with a pretty girl with curly hair.'

Britannia felt a surge of dislike. Several biting remarks crossed her mind and she longed to utter them. Her calm: 'Isn't she lovely? She's been a friend of mine for years,' was a masterpiece of forbearance. But the look she gave the professor was enough to freeze his bones, although he didn't appear to notice it.

His: 'We've come back for tea, Mama—I asked for it to be brought in here,' was uttered in exactly the right tones of a thoughtful host, as was his gentle urging that she should remove her anorak.

It was a pity that she happened to be wearing a blue guernsey, a garment which she had had for a number of years and wore solely for warmth during the winter at home. She had packed it at her mother's instigation and now silently blamed her parent for persuading her; it was a vast, loose sweater and seemed even bigger and looser than it was in contrast to Madeleine's slimly cut cashmere outfit, although, thought Britannia waspishly, the girl had a figure like a lead pencil, an opinion borne out when tea was brought in, for Madeleine drank only a small cup of milkless tea and ate nothing at all, while Britannia, telling herself sensibly that since she had been asked to tea she might as well enjoy it, ate the tiny sandwiches, the delicate cakes and the little sweet biscuits her host pressed upon her, carrying on a pleasant, desultory conversation with his mother while she did so, and when the professor chose to address her, answering him with cool politeness. Madeleine ignored her almost completely, addressing herself exclusively to the professor and speaking her own language until he interrupted her with a gentle: 'Should we not talk in English, Madeleine? You can hardly expect Britannia to understand Dutch after only a few days.'

Madeleine laughed, and she had a very pretty laugh.

'Darling Jake, I'm so sorry, you know I would do anything to please you.'

Britannia, watching him, couldn't see any change of expression in his face, but come to think of it, she seldom did. And she had learned one thing; he was called Jake, which was a name she entirely approved of. Quite pleased with this discovery, she plunged into a discussion about china. There was a handsome bowl on the table at her hostess's elbow—Weesp porcelain, she hazarded, and was pleased with herself when

Mevrouw Luitingh van Thien, seeing her glance at it, began to talk of it; the subject led to a discussion about antiques in general until Britannia glanced at her watch and said, with real regret, that she would have to return to the Veskes' villa, and when the professor, sitting by Madeleine and engrossed in some conversation of his own, was apprised of this, she added matter-of-factly: 'It's no distance, and I shall enjoy the walk.'

'It's dark,' the professor pointed out flatly.

'There's a moon.' She added defiantly, 'And I like the dark.'

He took no notice of this, however, but got to his feet, while Madeleine scowled at them all and then looked taken aback when Britannia went over to her. 'Forgive me, Juffrouw de Venz, for interrupting your talk with Professor Luitingh van Thien; it's only a few minutes' drive, though.' She added with sweet mendacity: 'I do hope that we meet again.'

But to her hostess she made no mention of hoping to see her again; she had been brought to the professor's home through some quirk of fancy on his part, she supposed, she wasn't likely to come again. She murmured all the right things and reflected wryly that at least she had had her wish; she had seen the house which had so taken her fancy and as an added bonus, she knew where the professor lived. She got into the anorak he was holding for her and accompanied him out to the car and got in without speaking when he opened the door. And she could think of nothing to say during the brief ride; it was all the more surprising, then, that when he stopped by the Veskes' front door and got out to open her door, instead of wishing him goodbye she should ask: 'Are you going to marry her?'

She wished she hadn't been so silly the moment the words were out; he would snub her coldly or not answer her at all.

He did neither. He said in a loud, forceful voice: 'No, I am not. Oh, at one time perhaps I considered it, but not any more—and do you know why, Miss Britannia Smith? Because of you, and God alone knows why; you preach at me, disapprove of me, constantly remind me that I am selfish and bad-tempered, and now you have seen my home, you will probably mount a campaign to persuade me to give away every penny I have…and yet I find that without you my life and my heart are empty.'

Her heart bounced into her throat, almost choking her. 'Well, you know,' she said soberly, 'you may say all these things—and you have surprised me very much— but you don't behave as though you mean any of them. No man with any regard for a girl would take her to his home to meet his mother and the girl who intends to marry him without giving her the chance of at least doing her hair.' She added severely: 'I looked a perfect fright, and you know it.'

He said quite seriously: 'I thought you looked beautiful, Britannia. And I have just told you that I am not going to marry Madeleine.'

'Yes, I know, but she doesn't agree with that.' She shivered a little in the cold early dark. 'You see, she's right for you, Professor. She comes from your background and probably you have known each other for years, she will run your great house for you and entertain your guests and wear all the right clothes. She's beautiful, you know; all willowy and graceful...'

The professor caught her by the arm. 'Bah—who wants willows and grace? I like women to look like women, and pray, what is to prevent you entertaining our guests and running our home and wearing what you call the right clothes?'

His hand was still on her arm and she was very aware of it. She shook her head slowly and began deliberately to tear her dreams to shreds in a quiet, steady voice.

'I hoped that I would meet you again, even though I thought that you didn't like me, but I wanted to be sure of it, if you can understand that. You had told me that you were rich, remember? But I didn't bother about that, not until just now, sitting in your lovely home. But now I can see that just being rich isn't at all the same...' She came to a stop, anxious to find the right words. 'You see, you aren't just rich, Professor, it's more than that—it's a way of life; you live in a magnificent house which I think must have been in your family for a very long time; you drink your tea from Sèvres china and the chairs you sit on are a kind which any self-respecting museum would jump at. But you've been born and brought up among them, you've eaten from porcelain with silver knives and forks since you can remember, and that's the difference; you take them for granted, just as your Madeleine does, that's why she'll be right for you. Don't you see?'

'No.'

'Don't say no in that fashion, Professor!'

She heard him sigh. 'Britannia, before we go any further with this singlarly futile conversation, may I beg you to stop calling me Professor in that severe fashion. My name is Jake.'

'Yes, I know. I like it—but if I call you Jake, that's how I shall remember you…if I call you Professor you'll always be just that.'

'My dear girl, let us get one thing clear. I have no wish to be just a professor dwindling away in your thoughts. I'm a man called Jake who has fallen more than a little in love with you.'

'But if you hadn't met me, you would have married Madeleine.'

He took her gently by the shoulders. 'I'll give you an honest answer, Britannia, because I can't be anything else with you, you have been honest with me. Probably I should, but not because I loved her; I'm almost forty and I must have a wife and children to live in my home after me, but having said that, I'll repeat that now I have met you, I shall never marry her.'

'Never's a long time. I think this happens all the time—people meet and—and fall in love, perhaps not very deeply, and when circumstances prevent them meeting again, in time they forget and take up their lives as they were before.'

Britannia spoke with quiet conviction, not believing a word of it.

'You don't want to see me again?' the professor spoke harshly.

She stirred a little and his hands tightened their grip. 'Well, I shall never see you once I've gone back to England at the end of the week. Would it matter very much if we saw each other just once more, to say goodbye?'

'It's your own fault that we do say goodbye, you silly, stubborn, high-minded girl—and don't expect sympathy from me, for you'll get none.' He caught her close and kissed her so hard that she rocked on her feet and then without another word, marched her to the door, opened it and then turning away with a brief goodnight, got into his car and drove away.

Britannia went indoors, shutting the door silently behind her. There was a good deal of laughing and talking in the sitting room so that no one would have heard her come in. Half an hour in her room would give her a chance to pull herself together; it had been harder than she could have imagined because she loved the professor so much; too much, she reminded herself, to let him make a mistake he might regret later on. He had said that he was more than a little in love with her, but she wasn't sure if that was quite enough. Infatuation seemed like love, but it didn't last, and they had only met a few weeks ago and then only briefly. For herself she was quite sure that she loved him, but that wasn't enough either, although it was tempting to pretend that it was. She crossed the hall silently and was on the stairs when the sitting room door burst open and Joan ran out.

'I saw the car lights,' she cried. 'Britannia, never mind about going to your room; come into the sitting room and drink our health—Dirk and I are engaged, isn't it wonderful? He's got to go back in a few days, but he'll get leave and come back in six weeks' time and we'll get married then.' She caught Britannia by the arm and danced her into the sitting room, which seemed full of people all talking at once. Britannia went around shaking hands, laughing and talking with an animation she didn't feel, although two glasses of champagne did help. It was late by the time she got to bed; she had changed quickly and there had been a long-drawn-out dinner party with more champagne, so that her slightly muddled wits had been unable to cope with her own problems. But in the morning, after breakfast, it was easy enough to make an excuse about buying stamps while Joan wrote letters and telephoned her family. She put on the anorak once more and went along to get her bike. She had the morning before her, she would take one of the narrow country lanes where there was no traffic to bother her, and sort out her problems.

She was standing outside the front door, pulling up her anorak hood against the cold wind, when a Mini estate car drove up and stopped beside her, and the short stout man who had opened the door of the professor's home got out. His 'good morning' was cheerful as he handed her an envelope and stood waiting. Her name was scrawled on it and she knew it was from the professor, so that her fingers shook a little as she opened it. The note inside was brief: 'Will you come out to dinner with me this evening? Half past seven.' It was signed J. L. T.

'You will be so good as to give me the answer?' asked the patient man beside her.

'Will you please tell Professor Luitingh van Thien that I shall be delighted to accept.' It would be their last meeting, she guessed, and she had no intention of refusing.

'I was to tell you also, miss, that it is hoped that you will have sufficient time in which to make yourself ready.'

Britannia chuckled; the prospect of seeing the professor again had quite cheered her up, even though it hadn't solved any problems. Let those wait, she told herself defiantly. 'That's very considerate of the professor. Will you thank him for me? I don't know your name...?'

'Marinus, miss.' His cheerful beam swept over her. 'Good day, miss.'

'Good day, Marinus.' She watched him get into the Mini and drive away and then went back to the house to tell Mevrouw Veske that she would be out that evening; she had to face a barrage of questions, of course; her hostess, with her goddaughter's future nicely settled, wasn't averse to her friend doing the same thing.

Britannia cycled a long way, trying to make herself think sensibly. She was aware that she was being foolish in seeing the professor again; a strong-minded girl would have said goodbye then and there... She sighed and got off her machine, leaned it against a gate and went to sit on a fallen tree. It was dim and damp along the lanes; the trees, their leafless branches arched above her head, shutting out what winter light there was. But it exactly suited her mood. Her impulse to refuse to see the professor again once she had returned home had been right, she felt sure; the reasons were good sound ones and sensible, but that didn't make them any easier to accept for herself. As for him, very likely he would thank her in years to come.

Presently she got up again and began her ride back to the villa; there was lunch to be eaten, and the afternoon to get through before she could get ready for her evening. The pink dress, she reflected, although she very much doubted if the professor would notice it, but it would give her low morale a much-needed boost; the evening, she had determined, was going to be a success, something happy to remember for always. It was to be hoped that he wouldn't lose his temper or raise his voice; his note had been a little terse. She patted the pocket where she had put it and started to sing cheerfully, keeping her thoughts on the evening ahead and no further than that.

Chapter 5

Britannia dressed with great care, with a meticulous attention to detail which would have done credit to an aristocrat on the way to the guillotine, and if truth were told, in very much the same mood. Fate and the kind fairies hadn't been so kind after all, or had they abandoned her because, with the professor in her hand, as it were, she had been too scrupulous?

She was ready far too soon and she went downstairs to sit with the Veskes, trying not to see Mevrouw Veske's coy glances while her host explained about the return trip he had booked for herself and Joan.

'Such a pity that you should have to return,' she observed, remorselessly interrupting her husband, 'but of course Joan will be with us again in a few weeks—

perhaps you will be coming too, Britannia?' She added guilelessly: 'You also have friends here.'

Britannia gave her a limpid look. 'Oh, yes, you've all been so super—but Joan's only having a quiet wedding, no bridesmaids and only family and you, of course— besides, I've no more holidays due.'

Mevrouw Veske knitted a bit of complicated pattern with effortless ease. 'You might like to come back on your own account, my dear.'

'Oh, you mean work here?' said Britannia, carefully misunderstanding. 'Well, it might be fun, but there's always the language difficulty, and…' She paused thankfully as Berthe bounced in to say that the gentleman had arrived.

'Then show him in,' Mevrouw Veske begged her in her own language, and got up as she spoke to greet her visitor.

The professor was at his most charming and very elegant, his dark overcoat open to reveal a dinner jacket and shirt of pristine whiteness. Britannia, returning his cool greeting with one equally cool, thanked heaven that she had put on the pink dress; it was a little late in the day to capture his fancy—she seemed to have done that with nothing more glamorous than slacks and a sweater—but she felt well dressed and that made her feel confident. Ten minutes were spent in polite conversation before the professor got to his feet, murmuring that they had better make a start if they wanted their dinner, and Britannia went thankfully to fetch her coat. The professor helped her into it and just for a moment she wished that it had been mink or chinchilla instead of sensible tweed. Well, it wouldn't have made much difference, anyway, she told herself sensibly. But it seemed that her companion wasn't quite so unobservant as she had imagined. He shut the front door behind them, kissed her with quite surprising force and remarked: 'Don't complain—if you will dress up in that pink thing, you must expect the consequences. You're beautiful, Britannia.'

It was a promising start to the evening; she got into the car determined to make the most of what she had. Surely Madeleine wouldn't grudge her a few hours of happiness when she had a whole lifetime before her, for despite the professor's protestations, Britannia thought the girl would somehow manage to marry him. She waited until he had got in beside her, then said: 'Thank you,' without either conceit or coyness.

'And thank God you don't simper,' observed her companion.

'And is that a compliment too?' she wanted to know severely.

He was taking the road south towards Arnhem. 'Ah, so my shortcomings are to be preached over, are they? My manners are at fault...'

'Don't be silly,' she begged him in a motherly voice. 'Your manners are very good indeed and you know that, and I'm not going to preach, truly I'm not.'

'Good. We're going to Scherpenzeel, just over twenty miles west of Arnhem. There's a delightful inn there. We can turn off the motorway just outside Arnhem and go through Ede. I know it's dark, but at least there are villages. Do you find the motorways rather bleak?'

'Those I've been on, yes—I expect they vary.'

He said silkily: 'Shall we discuss them in depth—so safe a conversation, don't you agree?—or may we talk about ourselves?'

'Well, I don't much care to talk about roads,' said Britannia reasonably. 'But there's nothing to say about us—we've said it all.'

'You're being a silly girl again. Why do you suppose I've brought you out this evening?'

She kept her voice very steady. 'A sort of goodbye dinner, I thought.'

He gave a great laugh. 'I shan't say goodbye until the very last minute, Britannia, and that is still two days away. I shall spend the evening persuading you to marry me.'

The pink dress must be doing its work very well. She said in her calm way: 'That will be a waste of time, and you know it.'

'I shall have you in the end.'

She allowed a few seconds of delight at the prospect and then damped it down with common sense. 'Perhaps we had better talk about roads,' she observed primly.

They had swung off the motorway on to the road to Ede, running through wooded country. 'We'll do no such thing. Tell me about your family.'

She began a little reluctantly, but he put skilful questions from time to time, so that she told him a good deal more than she had intended, although she stopped herself just in time from telling him just where her home was. She tried in her turn to ask questions too, without any success at all; his bland replies told her nothing; he had a mother, she knew that, but other than that she knew nothing about him and it was obvious that he had no intention of telling her; he kept the conversation strictly about herself and her own family until they arrived at Scherpenzeel.

De Witte Holevoet was an attractive inn, quite small but already almost full of people dining. The professor whisked Britannia inside, waited while she disposed of her coat before being shown to their table and then sat back in his chair to look at her. 'You're getting admiring glances from all the men in the room,' he assured her. 'It must be that pink thing—irresistible, isn't that the word?'

She answered him seriously, although her cheeks were as pink as her dress. 'That's what Mother always says.'

'And that is why you packed a pink dress to come to Holland?' His voice was bland, although she thought that he was amused.

She said defiantly: 'Yes.'

He smiled at her with a charm to melt her bones. 'I feel more hopeful. What would you like to drink?—we'll order presently.'

And from then on he kept the conversation light and impersonal, and she, cautious at first, presently realised that he wasn't going to talk about themselves at all—he had been joking about persuading her to marry him—she quenched quite unreasonable disappointment and followed his lead.

The meal was delicious; Britannia, who enjoyed her food, ate her way through lobster mousse, *Poulet au Champagne* and a lemon sorbet, helped along by a claret which even she, who knew very little about such things, realised was very fine. It was when they had finished their meal and she was pouring their coffee that she asked suddenly: 'Have you a dog?'

'Two—you didn't see them at my home because they were in the kitchen having their meal. Why do you ask?'

She handed him his coffee. 'Well, I just wanted to know something about you...'

'You will have every opportunity of knowing everything about me when we are married.' He was smiling at her and she didn't suppose that he was serious.

'What sort of dogs?' she persisted; anxious to seem as lighthearted as he, she smiled back at him.

'A Bouvier and a Corgi. They're the best of friends.' He added, still smiling: 'My housekeeper has a cat, and the gardener's children have rabbits and a tortoise.'

'Where does the gardener live? I saw a dear little house up against the wall when I cycled there...'

He nodded. 'That is his home. Marinus and Emmie— the housekeeper—and his wife, live in the house, so do a couple of maids. The laundrywoman lives in the other cottage.'

Her eyes were round. 'The laundrywoman—that sounds quite feudal! She surely doesn't do all the laundry for that great place.'

'Lord, no—just the personal things. I don't allow anyone else to iron my shirts.'

'Why, you are feudal!'

His smile mocked her. 'Disapproving? There are a great many things you don't approve of, aren't there, Britannia? But none of them matter, you know, and if you think about it, it's fair enough—old Celine does my shirts, and when she's ill, I look after her.'

She had to admit that that was true enough and he added in a wheedling tone: 'I'm quite a nice chap, really.'

'That isn't what you said in London. You told me that you were rich and something of a hermit and you didn't need to please anyone.'

'Ah, I wanted you to know the worst first.'

She laughed at that, but he didn't say any more, but began to tell her about the nearby castle of Scherpenzeel. 'It's owned by a family with the impressive name of van der Bosch-Royaards van Scherpenzeel, but no one lives there. It's neo-Gothic and I think rather nice.'

'Not as nice as your house. What is it called?'

'Huize van Thien.'

She asked meekly: 'May I know something about it?'

He passed his cup for more coffee. 'The oldest part is thirteenth-century, the whole of the front was added in the eighteenth century. The round tower at the back is fifteenth-century, its rooms are furnished, but we only use the sitting room on the ground floor.'

'Who's we?'

'You remind me of a schoolteacher examining her class! Myself, my mother when she is staying with me and my three sisters when they pay me a visit.'

'Three sisters?' repeated Britannia, much struck

with this homely piece of information. 'You're the eldest, of course.'

'Yes.' He went on blandly, 'I prefer the newest part of the house; they built roomily in the eighteenth century and their enormous windows let in the light. Tell me about your home, Britannia.'

She really had no choice after all her questions, and anyway, there would be thousands of small houses like her own home, there would be no fear of him discovering where it was. 'It's very small, a late Georgian cottage, built of stone with a slate roof. There's quite a big garden, though, with some rather ramshackle outbuildings. There are woods all round us and it's very peaceful, even in summer; the tourists don't come near us, only if they lose their way, and the village is so small there isn't even an hotel, just a pub.'

'I like your English pubs,' said the professor idly. 'What's this one called?'

'The Happy Return.' She hadn't meant to tell him that, she would have to guard her tongue, though it was a common enough name, and besides, why was she worrying? Once she had gone, he wouldn't come after her; he would see, as soon as they had parted, that the whole episode was just a pleasant little interlude. She had thought it so often that she almost believed it herself.

They lingered over their coffee and returned by a different road, across the Veluwe and a good deal further round, but as the professor pointed out, it was a charming route once they were through Barneveld, taking them through the National Park along a minor road which, he assured her, was quite delightful in daylight. So they didn't arrive back at the Veskes' villa until well after midnight, to find the house in darkness excepting for a welcoming light shining from the hall window. The professor got out and walked round the car to open her door. 'You have a key?'

'Yes.' She gave it to him and as he put it in the lock, said: 'Thank you for a lovely evening. I did enjoy it.'

He didn't open the door. 'We shall have many lovely evenings and enjoy them too, Britannia.'

She didn't know how beautiful she looked under the dim light streaming from the hall. She stared up at him and said earnestly: 'Please, Jake—I'm only a passing fancy.'

His face darkened. 'So I'm to be preached at again, am I? I don't know why I stand for it; how can you know what I want and what I think, and who are you to tell me what I must do and not do? I'll tell you: you're a sharp-tongued obstinate woman who thinks she knows best and spends her time poking her nose into my affairs so that I lose my temper.'

He opened the door and held it wide. 'In with you.' His voice was a muttered roar as she went past him and heard the door shut behind her. She had gone perhaps six paces when the door-knocker was thumped and she flew back to open the door before the whole house was roused.

'Such a noise!' she told him severely. 'You'll wake everyone, it's long past…'

'Not another word,' he said softly. 'I forgot something.'

He caught her close and kissed her slowly. Presently he loosened his hold a little. 'Will you come out to dinner with me tomorrow, Britannia?' And when she hesitated: 'You go home the day after. I'll behave exactly as I ought and we will say goodbye very correctly.' His voice was gentle, but she had the strange idea that he was laughing too, although when she looked up into his face it was serious enough. She found it quite impossible to say no, and indeed, she had no wish to say it. She nodded her head without speaking and he kissed her again, this time very gently, and pushed her just as gently into the hall and shut the door. She heard the car slide away a few seconds later.

Mevrouw Veske received the news that Britannia was going out again with the professor with delighted satisfaction. She didn't exactly say 'I told you so,' but Britannia could see her thinking it and the speculative look in her hostess's eye made her wonder if she was already envisaging a double wedding. She spent the day with her in Apeldoorn, shopping, arriving back at the same time as an excited Joan, who had spent the day with Dirk. She was flourishing her new engagement ring and teatime talk was almost exclusively of its unique beauty, the forthcoming wedding and the future bride's speculations as to what exactly she should wear for the occasion, so that when it was time for Britannia to go to her room and change for the evening, she was able to do so with only the smallest amount of interest from her companions.

The professor was in the hall, having just been admitted by Berthe, when she came downstairs, and as she went towards him she said with disarming frankness: 'I've only one dress with me, I hope you don't mind—you see, I didn't expect...' She paused, remembering why she had brought it with her in the first place, so that he looked enquiringly at her.

'Then why did you bring it?' he wanted to know. It didn't occur to her not to tell him the truth.

'It's a silly reason.' She was standing in front of him, looking up into his face. 'I thought—that is, I imagined that if I did meet you again, I'd like to be wearing something pretty, so that you would—would notice me.' She added seriously: 'Of course, I didn't know then about your house and your Madeleine...'

'Not my Madeleine. I think that I should have noticed you if you had been wearing an old sack, Britannia.'

She smiled a little shyly. 'Oh—well... I didn't know that, did I?'

'No. Are we really saying goodbye tomorrow, Britannia?'

'Yes.' She moved away and began to fasten her coat, and felt hurt when he said quite cheerfully:

'In that case, we'd better start our evening, hadn't we?'

They were seen off by a beaming Mevrouw Veske and a hasty wave and gabbled ''bye' from Joan, who was, as she so often was these days, on the telephone to her Dirk, and once in the car the professor observed dryly: 'What a pity it is that you don't share Mevrouw Veske's romantic outlook—now, if you did you might have come tearing down the stairs and flung yourself into my arms, instead of which you greet me with some matter-of-fact remark about your dress. What's wrong with it, anyway?'

Britannia was put out. 'There's nothing wrong with it—it's a copy of a model, a Jean Allen—but one doesn't usually wear the same dress on two successive evenings.'

He had turned the car in the direction of Apeldoorn. 'Why ever not? I wear my dinner jacket for several evenings in a row.'

She chuckled. 'Now you're being silly.' She didn't add that there was nothing she would have liked better than to have flung herself into his arms. 'But I was glad to see you.' And then, in case he had an answer to that, she asked quickly: 'Have you had a busy day?'

'Quite a list…' He began to tell her about the cases and it wasn't until they were through Hoenderloo that he paused to say: 'We're not going to Apeldoorn, by the way. There's a restaurant on the Amersfoort road that's quite good. I thought we had better not go too far this evening, I expect you have your packing to do.'

A damping remark which lowered her spirits considerably; she could pack, if necessary, in ten minutes and she would have all tomorrow in which to do it…

She thought his description of De Echoput was sadly understated when they reached it; it was a rather splendid place and the menu card quite baffling in its abundance. Over their drinks she studied it and presently asked the professor to choose for her. 'Because there's so much and I don't know the half of the dishes they offer,' she explained. 'You see now what I mean about our backgrounds—imagine having a wife who doesn't know what *Le Râble de Lièvre* is—it's hare, I know, but I don't know more than that.' She added thoughtfully: 'I don't like hare, anyway; I like to see them running in the fields.'

He smiled at her across the table. 'So do I, and would it really matter if you can't read the menu if I'm with you to help you choose?'

She shook her head. 'It wouldn't be as simple as that, and you know it.'

He didn't answer her, only smiled again and turned to the menu. 'They have delicious hors d'oeuvres here, shall we start with that—and what about trout? *Truite saumone au Champagne*. We'll drink champagne, too, since it's by way of being an occasion.'

The food was delicious, just as he had said, but Britannia hardly enjoyed it—he had called it an occasion, almost as though he was celebrating… It cost her quite an effort to join in his cheerful talk. Luckily the champagne helped, so that by the time the sweet trolley came round she was able to do full justice to the millefeuille recommended by the professor and, just for a little while, forget that she would never see him again.

Sitting over their coffee he brought the conversation round to her return.

'You'll be working next week?' he wanted to know, 'or do you go home for a few days?'

The champagne had made Britannia a little careless. 'I start work on Monday,' she told him. 'Even if I didn't, it would be too far to go home. I'll wait until I get my weekend.'

'You plan to stay at St Jude's?'

She stirred her coffee and didn't look at him. 'I haven't thought about it. Probably not.'

His voice was bland. 'Of course, the world is your oyster, isn't it, Britannia? A qualified nurse can go where she pleases.'

Put like that it sounded a lonely business; going from hospital to hospital, probably country to country, getting a little older with each move. She swallowed a great wave of self-pity and heard him say briskly: 'Well, you don't need to look so glum; think how fortunate you are compared with a girl who marries; a house to run, a husband to look after, children to bring up, never-ending chores—the poor girl has no life of her own.'

She didn't want a life of her own, but it wasn't much use saying so; hadn't she made it quite clear that she had no intention of marrying him? She asked in a rather high voice: 'Did you never want to travel?'

He seemed quite willing to follow her lead; they carried on a desultory conversation about nothing in particular until Britannia said that she thought she should return to the Veskes. 'They're so kind,' she spoke brightly. 'We've done exactly what we've wanted to do all the time we've been staying with them, it's been a wonderful holiday.'

He had opened the car door for her and paused to ask: 'And one to remember, Britannia?'

She would never forget it, however hard she tried. She babbled: 'Oh, rather, it's been lovely.' She went on babbling for the entire journey back and the professor tiresomely did nothing to stop her; by the time they had reached the villa she was worn out and so exasperated that she could have burst into tears, although why she wasn't quite sure. He had behaved exactly as he should have done; he hadn't mentioned seeing her again; he had accepted the fact that she was going back to England with no apparent disappointment. Either he was a man of iron with no feelings, or he hadn't meant a word…

Britannia slept badly and got up the next morning with a frayed temper and a pale face, and it didn't help when she found herself drawn into a cheerful discussion about Joan's wedding; indeed, a good deal of the morning was spent in reviewing the arrangements already made, re-making them, adding to them and speculating as to the weather, the number of guests and the names of those who just had to be invited, and when this serious business had been thoroughly talked out, there was always the more interesting one of clothes for the important occasion. By the time lunch was over Britannia, her nerves jangling like an ill-tuned piano and longing to be by herself, declared that she simply couldn't leave Holland without one more cycle ride, and since they weren't leaving until the evening and she was packed and ready, except for exchanging her slacks and sweater for her suit, she had ample time to indulge her fancy, and Joan and Mevrouw Veske, deep in the merits of various pastel shades, begged her kindly to do just as she wished. 'Only don't be late for tea,' counselled Joan. 'We shall be leaving round about six o'clock, love.'

Britannia promised, tugged on her hostess's anorak

and gloves and went round to fetch her bike. The day
had been overcast, but now it was clearing, to show a
cold blue sky turning grey at the edges, and the wind,
never absent for long, had gathered strength again. It
surprised her to find that it was icy underfoot, but going
cautiously down the drive she decided that she was safe
enough. The lanes she intended to take were sheltered
by the trees and thickets and their surfaces rough, and
she was a seasoned cyclist. She knew where she was
going, of course—to take one more look at the professor's home. She wouldn't be able to see much of it,
only its gables and chimney pots, but they were better
than nothing.

It would have helped, she reflected as she pedalled
down the deserted road, if he had wished her goodbye. But he hadn't. He had got out of his car and gone
to the Veskes' door with her and opened it, listened to
her over-bright thanks with a little smile, assured her
that he had enjoyed his evening just as much as she
had, wished her the most casual of goodnights without
once expressing a wish to see her again, and then stood
aside so that she might go in. She couldn't remember
what she had mumbled, certainly nothing of sufficient
interest to make him delay his departure. She had gone
past him into the hall, afraid that she might burst into
tears at any moment, and had heard the door close quietly behind her. There was no knock this time, either;
she had heard the soft purr of the Rolls almost immediately, and its almost soundless departure.

She reached the crossroads and turned down the
lane. There was still masses of time; she would be able

to go further along the wall where the view of the house was much clearer. The lane was a bit tricky, its surface slippery between the ruts, but she went slowly, putting out a leg from time to time to steady herself. She paused as she reached the first vantage point. There was smoke rising from some of the chimneys, blown wildly by the wind, and she wondered who was there. Not Jake, he had mentioned that he had a teaching round in the afternoon and some private patients to see, but his mother perhaps and possibly the beautiful Madeleine, invited there to spend the evening. She might even be staying there. Britannia shivered; the wind was really icy and a few drops of sleet from a sky which had suddenly turned grey again made her wonder if she wouldn't be wise to turn back. But the gap in the wall wasn't far, it was a pity to come that distance and give up within half a mile. She mounted her machine once more and pedalled on.

It was worth it, she told herself, when she stopped once more. The house, light shining from its windows in the gathering dusk, looked beautiful. She imagined the cheerful Marinus trotting to and fro about his stately business and Jake's mother sitting by the fire— she would be embroidering, something complicated and beautiful, to be handed down to other generations of the family in course of time. Britannia, deep in thought, mounted her bike once more, turned too sharply, skidded on an icy patch and fell off. She fell awkwardly and the machine fell on top of her, the handlebars catching her on the side of the head as she hit the ground, and knocking her out.

She came to quite quickly, feeling muzzy, and lay still for a minute, waiting for her head to clear before she attempted to get up. She was aware that she had a nasty headache, rapidly turning into an unpleasant throbbing, and she was also aware of the bitter cold.

'Well, it won't do to lie here, my girl,' she admonished herself in a heartening voice. 'Get to your feet, warm yourself up and get on your bike and go back as fast as you can.'

Sound advice, but not, she discovered, so easy to carry out. The cycle had fallen across her and she had to wriggle to one side to get free of it, and it was when she began to do this that she discovered that her left ankle was exquisitely painful. She essayed to move it cautiously, and a wave of nausea swept over her so that she was forced to keep still again.

'Clever girl,' said Britannia crossly, 'broken your ankle, have you, or sprained it? Well, you'll just have to roll yourself to one side.'

It took a few minutes, because the pain was bad and her headache was worsening, but she managed it at last and presently she essayed to sit up, but she jarred the ankle badly doing it and this time the pain made her do something she had never in her life done before—faint.

She came to presently and found herself wishing that she could have remained unconscious for a little longer, for her headache was steadily worsening and the pain in her ankle was making her feel sick. Nevertheless she tried to think what to do; she wouldn't be missed for a little while yet, and even when she was, no one would have the least idea where to start look-

ing for her. Somehow or other she would have to get
herself back to the road. She wasn't sure how she was
going to do it, because it was at least a mile and the
lane would be heavy going. She could try shouting,
she supposed, and remembered that the professor had
told her that there were no houses nearby. The gardener's cottage she had seen was, she judged, too far
off for anyone there to hear her, but it was worth a try.
She called 'Help!' several times, upsetting the birds in
the thicket around her and listening to her voice being
carried away on the wind before deciding that it was a
waste of time and breath. She would have to get moving and hope for the best.

She turned herself a little and looked at her ankle. It
was already swollen; to get her shoe off would lessen
the pain, on the other hand, she would need it for pro-
tection against the lane's deplorable surface, and not
only that, it was getting colder every minute and darker
too. She rolled over once more and edged herself forward. She had no idea how long she had been crawl-
ing along so painfully when her injured ankle brushed
against a sharp stone and she fainted again.

Tea was almost finished in the Veskes' household before Joan remarked: 'Britannia's awfully late—I wonder if she's in her room? I'll see.'

She came downstairs again looking faintly worried. 'She's not there. I wonder where she went? Not to
Hoenderloo, I remember she said she wouldn't be going
that way because I asked her to post a letter...' She

looked at her godmother. 'Where does she go when she goes off on the bike?'

Mevrouw Veske thought deeply. 'Well, dear, she has made a number of acquaintances, but not the sort who would go for a cycle ride with her. I daresay she goes on her own.' Her nice face cleared. 'How stupid of me—I expect she's gone to say goodbye to that nice Professor Luitingh van Thien. He's taken her out two evenings running, you know, and they seem to be getting on very well together,' and when Joan was about to interrupt her: 'Yes, dear, you're surprised, but I'm sure she's had very little time to tell you about that. You've been out a good deal yourself and there's been the wedding to talk of. Shall I telephone him? He'll be in the book and we have met, although we're hardly on calling terms, I suppose.'

'I'll go,' said Joan, and as she left the room: 'Will he be home?'

'I've no idea, but I believe it's a very large house, there's bound to be someone in it.' Mevrouw Veske got to her feet. 'I'll do it, Joan. If they don't understand English it will be a little difficult for you.'

A man answered her call, introduced himself as the house butler and told her that Miss Smith hadn't been to the house that afternoon. 'Although I will inform the professor when he returns; he may know something, *mevrouw*. If I might call you back?'

Marinus replaced the receiver, his cheerful face frowning in thought. The professor had returned home on the previous night in a towering rage all the more formida-

ble for being held in check. He had gone straight to his
room and that morning had left early for his consulting rooms in Arnhem, leaving no messages at all and
certainly none about Miss Smith. Marinus trod with
rather more speed than usual across the hall and down
the passage which led to the kitchens, where he found
Emmie busy at the kitchen table. He unburdened himself at some length and then asked her advice.

Emmie didn't pause in her folding of a soufflé mixture. 'Telephone him at once,' she suggested. 'He will
wish to know, I think, for he is very interested in this
English lady, is he not?'

Marinus looked at his old-fashioned pocket watch.
'He will be at his rooms, he will have patients…'

His wife began to pour her mixture into a buttered
and papered dish. 'Telephone him,' she repeated.

Marinus had to wait a moment or two before he
could speak to the professor; there was a patient with
him, explained his secretary, who would be gone in a
very short time; just time enough to give Marinus the
leisure to wonder if he was being needlessly foolish.
After all, Miss Smith was returning to England that
very evening and the professor hadn't even mentioned
the fact; perhaps dear Emmie was wrong.

But she wasn't, he could tell that by the sound of
the professor's voice when he started asking questions.
How long had Miss Smith been gone? Had Mevrouw
Veske said anything about searching for her? Had she
been warmly clad?

Marinus, being unable to answer any of these enquiries with any degree of accuracy, was told sharply

to see that the professor's horse was saddled and ready for him, together with a torch and blanket. 'I shall be home almost immediately, and I want the dogs as well.'

'You know where Miss Smith is?' asked Marinus.

'I believe so.' The professor's voice sounded harsh as he replaced the receiver.

He was as good as his word. Caesar, his great roan horse, was being led round to the front door as he got out of the Rolls and went indoors. Marinus, hovering in the hall, hurried to meet him. 'I've put out your riding things, Professor—' he began, to be cut short with: 'No time. I'll go as I am. Telephone Mevrouw Veske, will you, and see that there's a room ready just in case Miss Smith needs to stay the night.'

He had gone again, taking Caesar at a careful trot down the drive, the dogs at his heels.

It was a dark evening and the overhanging trees made it even darker. The professor kept the beam from his torch steady, not bothering to turn its light from side to side of the road, he was so sure where Britannia would be. He urged his horse along now, holding the reins with easy assurance, his face without expression, giving no hint of the mounting impatience he felt. At the crossroads he was forced to slow down, for the ground had become even more treacherous, but he whistled to the dogs and urged them on ahead, watching their progress. He paused for a moment where he and Britannia had first stopped, but there was no sign of her and he went on again, searching the thicket on either side of him until he heard Jason's deep bark and Willy's excited yap. He could just make them out by the torch's light, standing one each side of Britannia, sprawled across the lane.

The professor swung himself off his horse with the agility of a much younger man and knelt down beside her. Britannia was still unconscious. Her white face, with a nasty bruise down one side of it, looked quite alarming by the light of the torch, but the professor wasted no time in exclaiming over her appearance. He took her pulse, found it to be strong and regular, noted her grossly swollen ankle and said briskly: 'Wake up, Britannia, we have to get you home.'

He repeated himself several times, interlarded with several pungent remarks in his own language although Britannia, recalled to consciousness by the insistence of his voice, really had no idea of what he was saying. She opened her eyes to find him staring down at her, looking so formidable that she frowned and closed her eyes again. She opened them almost immediately though, because there were two dogs looking at her too. She said in a very small voice: 'The Bouvier and the Corgi,' and then: 'You're wearing a good suit…it'll be spoilt.'

The professor didn't smile. He said something forceful in his own language again and Britannia thought it prudent not to ask what it was. She said helpfully: 'I've hurt my ankle. I'm sorry I can't walk, I crawled for a while, but I don't think I got very far. If you wouldn't mind just helping me to the end of the lane, I'd be all right there while you go and telephone Mijnheer Veske. He'll take me to hospital and they can strap it…'

The professor was busy; he had cut the shoe lace of the sensible shoe she was wearing and was carefully slicing it open so that he could ease it off her injured ankle. He held her foot steady in one large gentle hand and worked with the other, and only when she stopped talking because the pain was so bad did he speak. 'Stop issuing instructions like a demented great-aunt, Britannia. You must know that I shan't listen to a word of them, nonsensical as they are. And now grit your teeth, my girl, this is going to hurt.'

It did, but she didn't utter a sound, only shivered and shook and felt sick, and then, when the shoe was off and she felt the warmth of the blanket about her, so relieved that the tears she had so sternly held in check escaped at last.

Her rescuer turned the torch on her face then and examined the bruise, muttering to himself so that she managed at last: 'Please don't be so angry, Jake, I know it's awkward—I mean meeting again after we've said goodbye.' Some of her spirit returned. 'And it's very rude to mutter and mumble so that no one knows what you're saying.'

'You want to know what I was saying?' He picked her up effortlessly, although she was a big girl. 'That if you had listened carefully, you would know that I didn't say goodbye.'

He strode over to where Caesar stood waiting and Britannia let out a squeak of surprise. 'A horse—he's huge!' She added apprehensively: 'I can't get up there...'

He didn't even bother to answer; she was lifted and laid across the great beast's neck and while she was still panicking about holding on, the professor had swung himself up behind her, picked up the reins, whistled to the dogs and had turned for home.

He went slowly and carefully, but all the same her ankle was agonisingly painful. It was quite dark now and the road when they reached it was deserted. She said suddenly: 'It's a good thing it's dark, we must look quite extraordinary.' She gave a tired little chuckle and when he didn't speak, she asked: 'Are you still angry?'

His voice came from the darkness above her. 'I am not angry.'

She drew a sharp breath as Caesar stumbled on a stone and she felt the professor's arm, holding her firmly round the shoulders, tighten. After a moment he said quietly: 'We're almost home.'

He hadn't once spoken a word of sympathy, she reflected in a rather woolly fashion. Any other man... but then any other man might have wasted time doing just that, while he had done everything possible with a swift efficiency and a minimum of talk, and he had known where to find her... She was framing a question about that when Caesar came to a halt and she was aware of lights and voices.

Being lifted down was a painful business; Britannia gritted her teeth and kept her eyes shut as the professor carried her indoors, suddenly too tired to mind about anything any more.

was to find that someone had got her out to her clothes and put her in a nightgown, she vaguely remembered lifting arms and raising her head and Hannie's voice

Chapter 6

Halfway up the staircase Britannia roused herself sufficiently to say: 'I'm too heavy,' but the professor didn't speak, keeping up a steady, unhurried pace until he reached the gallery above. Emmie was ahead of him, ready with the door open of a room at its end. She had the bed turned down too and a blanket spread on it on to which he laid Britannia, who, feeling its warm security and seeing Emmie's kind face peering at her, not surprisingly went immediately to sleep.

She didn't sleep for long, although when she woke it was to find that someone had got her out of her clothes and put her in a nightgown; she vaguely remembered lifting arms and raising her head and Emmie's voice murmuring comfortingly, and now she lay, nicely propped up with pillows, the bedcovers turned back, disclosing an ugly, swollen ankle. She was frowning at it when Emmie came back with the professor at her heels.

His 'Hullo, feeling better?' was laconic, but his examination of her foot was meticulous and very gentle. He hadn't quite finished when Britannia asked: 'Please will you telephone Mijnheer Veske? If someone could lend me a dressing gown he could take me to Arnhem...'

'And what do you propose to do in Arnhem?' the professor wanted to know without bothering to look at her.

'Well, get this strapped, then...'

'I believe that I am still capable of strapping an ankle.' His voice was silky.

'Oh, I'm sure you are,' soothed Britannia. 'What I mean is, I wanted to get away from here—at least, I don't want to, if you see what I mean, but it would be so much nicer for you.'

'You have a quite nasty contusion over your left eye, probably a little concussion as a consequence, which would account for your muddled conversation.'

Indeed her head did ache; she had done her best and she suspected that her ankle would become even more painful before it was strapped. 'I don't feel quite the thing,' she admitted.

'That is hardly surprising.' He sounded austere. 'I am going to strap that ankle. It is a sprain. I was able to take a look at it while you were in a faint. Tomorrow you will go to the hospital and have an X-ray of it, and also of your head.'

'But I'm going home—all the arrangements…' Her tired head whirled at the very thought.

'Leave the arrangements to me. You'll not be going home for a few days. And now let us attend to your ankle.'

Britannia lay still, willing herself not to let out so much as a squeak of pain. She clasped Emmie's kind hand and squeezed it hard, and when the professor had finally done, thanked him in a trembly voice.

She got a grunt in reply and an injunction to drink the tea which would be fetched to her and then to go to sleep. 'There's nothing much wrong with your head that a good sleep won't cure,' remarked the professor with impersonal kindness.

She opened her eyes to look at him, leaning over the end of the bed, staring at her. 'Then I don't need to have it X-rayed tomorrow—I've put you to enough trouble.'

'And probably will put me to a great deal more.' He nodded carelessly and went to the door, and Emmie drew up a chair and sat down by the bed. It didn't matter that she couldn't speak a word of English; she helped Britannia to drink her tea, shook up her pillows for her and then held her in a comfortable embrace while she cried her eyes out. She felt better after that and went to sleep almost at once, her head, very tousled, still against Emmie's plump shoulder.

She woke hours later to a darkened room lighted by a bedside lamp, by which the professor was reading. He looked up almost immediately and came to the bed, took her pulse, looked at her pupil reactions, turned her head gently to examine the great bruise colouring one side of it and asked: 'How do you feel, Britannia?'

She studied his face before she replied. His calm expression gave no hint as to his feelings. She sighed: 'Not at all bad, thank you. My head feels much better—my ankle's a bit painful but quite bearable. What's the time?'

'Two o'clock. Emmie has some soup for you, you will drink it and go to sleep again.'

'Two…but you ought to be in bed, you'll be tired out in the morning.'

There was the glimmer of a smile on his face. 'I shall go to bed very shortly. Here is Emmie.'

The housekeeper looked even cosier than she did by day, wrapped in a thick woollen dressing gown. She bore a small tray upon which was a pipkin of soup, a dazzling white napkin and a glass of lemonade. The soup smelled delicious and Britannia's pinched nose wrinkled in anticipation. The professor stood, book in hand, one long finger marking his place, while Emmie arranged Britannia's pillows, tucked the napkin under her chin, removed the pipkin's lid and offered her the soup. Only when Britannia had taken the first spoonful did he go to the door and with a quiet 'Goodnight, Britannia,' go out of the room. Undoubtedly he was annoyed at her having to be in his house at all. He was a good host and a good surgeon so she would receive nothing but courtesy and the best of attention while she was there, but that was all. Her lip quivered and tears filled her lovely eyes and she put the spoon down, to be at once comforted by Emmie's '*Nou, nou,*' and the offer of a clean handkerchief. 'Drink,' commanded Emmie with kindly firmness and Britannia picked up her spoon once more. She drank down the lemonade too because her attendant expected her to, but by then she was feeling tired again and her head was aching. She had barely thanked Emmie before she was asleep again.

It was daylight when she awoke for the second time, the curtains drawn to show a bright morning, a fire crackling in the steel grate. Britannia sat up cautiously and looked around her. She felt much better. There would be no need for her to be X-rayed and she would say so; she would also have to find out what had happened to Joan and whether she was to get back to the Veskes that morning…and when would she be able to go back to England? She closed her eyes and frowned, then opened them again to have a good look at the room she was in.

It was a large, airy room, with two tall windows draped in rose pink silk, a colour echoed in the bedcover of quilted chintz and the upholstered armchairs, the furniture was painted white picked out with gilt and the floor was carpeted in a soft misty blue, very restful to the eye. A charming room, and luxurious. Britannia closed her eyes once more and wondered what could be the time. She opened them almost at once, though, because someone was knocking at the door, and in answer to her 'Come in', Mevrouw Luitingh van Thien entered.

'Good morning, my dear,' she said, and smiled. 'Jake told me to wait until you were awake before giving you your breakfast. I'm glad to see that you have slept. Emmie is coming in a few minutes with tea and toast for you—he said to give you nothing more than that until you have been to hospital. He will be back for you at ten o'clock.'

'Oh—I was going to ask him if I need be X-rayed. I feel so much better.'

The professor's parent shook her elegant head. 'Oh, I shouldn't do that if I were you.' She sat herself down in a chair close by the bed. 'One must always do as one's doctor says.'

Britannia was on the point of saying that the professor wasn't her doctor anyway, but stopped herself in time because it might have sounded rude. Instead she thanked her companion for her kindness in offering her shelter for the night.

Mevrouw Luitingh van Thien looked surprised and then laughed. 'But, my dear child, it had nothing to do with me, this is Jake's house. I stay with him from time to time, that is all. When he left this morning he put you into my care and I am more than happy to do what I can for you. I have three daughters of my own, you know, they are all married and I can assure you that when they are all here with their husbands and children, it is indeed a houseful, something Jake enjoys very much.'

'Does he?' cried Britannia in surprise. 'I thought—that is, he never seems...'

Mevrouw Luitingh van Thien's features relaxed into a smile again. 'No, he doesn't does he?' she agreed. 'And yet he loves children and his home and family.'

'He told me that he was something of a hermit,' said Britannia indignantly.

'Well, so he is, if by that he means that he doesn't

have a busy social life or escort a variety of young women to some night club or other far too often.' The lady's tone made it plain what she thought of night clubs. 'He enjoys a pleasant life; he has a great many friends and he loves his work, as you have no doubt seen for yourself.' She broke off to say: 'Ah, here is Emmie, I will leave you to enjoy your breakfast. When you have finished, she will help you to dress.'

It was only when she was at the door that Britannia remembered to ask: 'I quite forgot to ask you. What did Mevrouw Veske say? And has Joan, my friend, you know—gone back?'

'Of course—I forgot too—I was to tell you that Mevrouw Veske will be over to see you this afternoon, and Joan has returned as it had been arranged. She will see the *Directrice* of your hospital and explain what happened. You may be sure that Jake has not over-looked anything.'

Britannia tackled her breakfast with a healthy appetite, her painful ankle notwithstanding, and when Emmie came back presently with her clothes, brushed and neat, she began the business of getting them on cheerfully enough. The problem of washing had been solved by Emmie bringing a basin to the bedside, but dressing didn't prove quite as easy as she had expected. But somehow she wriggled and twisted her way into her slacks and sweater, pausing for minutes at a time to allow the pain in her ankle to lessen, and the slacks had had to be cut in order to get her swollen foot into the leg. More or less dressed, she surveyed her person care-fully and deplored her appearance. Emmie had brushed

her hair and tied it back and then fetched a mirror reluctantly enough, and when Britannia saw her face in
it she quite understood why; she was a sorry sight, one
side of her face swollen and discoloured and a bump
on her forehead the size of a billiard ball. Even if the
professor had taken a fancy to her, which he hadn't, it
would have needed to have been a very strong fancy.
She was still staring at her reflection when he said from
the doorway: 'May I come in?' and then: 'You're going
to have a black eye.'

He said something to Emmie, asked: 'Are you
ready?' and scooped Britannia up and carried her
downstairs to the car. He had very much the manner,
she considered, of a man removing a misbehaving kit-
ten to the garden; kind, firm and faintly resigned that
he had had to do it in the first place.

He stowed her into the front seat beside him while
Emmie and Marinus proffered cushions with which to
protect her foot. This done to his satisfaction, he got
in, asked her in a rather perfunctory manner if she
were quite comfortable and drove to Arnhem, wasting no breath in conversation on the way and wasting
no time either. Britannia, seeking in vain for a topic of
conversation and unable to think of anything at all to
say, was relieved when they reached the hospital, where
he lifted her from the car and set her in the wheelchair
a porter was sent to fetch. She felt at a distinct disadvantage with no make-up, her hair austerely brushed
back by Emmie and Mevrouw Veske's amply cut anorak
dragged on anyhow; moreover, there was no vestige of
glamour about a wheelchair. Not that it mattered; the

professor muttered to the porter, said 'I'll see you in a minute,' and stalked away, leaving her to be trundled to X-ray, past a long line of fractured arms and legs, broken collarbones, barium meals and the like, all waiting patiently for their turn. Presumably this wasn't to be her lot; she was taken directly into the X-ray room where she was arranged on the table by a pretty nurse who nodded and smiled at her and then melted into the background as a thick-set bearded man and the professor ranged themselves beside her.

'That is indeed a splendid bruise,' observed the bearded man cheerfully. 'Let us hope that there is no hairline fracture beneath it.' He smiled broadly and held out a hand. 'Berens—Frans Berens.' He wrung her hand in a crushing grip and turned to the professor. 'The skull first, I think, Jake, and then the ankle.'

It was quickly done, but she was told to stay where she was while the plates were developed, and lay, cosily wrapped in a blanket in the half dark, half asleep until the professor's voice caused her to open her eyes.

'No bones broken,' he told her, 'just a nasty sprain. Bed for a few days and then massage and exercises.'

'But can't I go home?'

Doctor Berens rumbled disapprovingly. 'Indeed you cannot. You have had a nasty fall and you must have time to get over it; besides, that ankle must lose its swelling…'

'You will return with me, Britannia,' stated the professor in a no-nonsense voice, 'and when you are fit, you may return home.'

'To the Veskes?'

'I imagine not—they will be going away for St Niko-laas.'

'But I can't...'

The porter had returned with the wheelchair and Britannia was whisked into it, had her hand shaken once more by the genial Doctor Berens and was wheeled away while she was still gathering her wits. It wasn't until she had been settled in the car once more, and the professor was driving through the city, that she said again: 'I can't...'

Her companion's voice was silky. 'If you do not like the idea of staying under my roof, Britannia, I must point out that the house is large enough to shelter the pair of us with little risk of meeting.'

'Oh, no—it's not that at all. But if I stay with you I'm—I'm a continuing source of embarrassment to you.'

His surprise was quite genuine. 'Why on earth should you be?' he wanted to know. 'We shan't be on our own, you know. It is December—or had you overlooked that? My sisters, their husbands and children, not to mention nursemaids, my mother, an uncle or two and—er—Madeleine will be celebrating St Niko-laas with me.'

Put like that it made her feel lonely. 'You're very kind, but won't I be a nuisance?'

His careless: 'Lord, no—I'll get a nurse to look after you,' was really all she needed to round off a horrid morning, but she wasn't going to let it show. 'You will be good enough to let me have the bill for her fees,' she said haughtily, 'and I should like to be home—among my friends and family—for Christmas.'

'Long before that, I hope,' he assured her with off-hand cheerfulness, 'and it is your fault, if I may say so, Britannia, that you're not in the bosom of my family for St Nikolaas—but you turned me down, if you care to remember.'

Britannia's bosom heaved under the ample folds of Mevrouw Veske's anorak. 'You're quite awful!' she snapped. 'I didn't turn you down—at least, it was because...you know why it was.' She drew a deep breath. 'Couldn't I please go home?'

'No. Not unless you don't mind having giddy fits and falling down and spraining the other ankle.'

They had been travelling fast, now he slowed to turn into the drive. 'Mevrouw Veske is coming to see you this afternoon, she will bring your things with her. If you can bear to take my advice I suggest that you stay in bed for the rest of today. Emmie will look after you and I'll bring a nurse back with me this evening.'

Britannia bit her lip; she had no arguments left and now her head was beginning to ache. She said, 'Thank you, Professor,' in a meek voice, and when he reminded her: 'Jake,' repeated 'Jake,' just as meekly.

Mevrouw Veske came after lunch, escorted to Britannia's room by Mevrouw Luitingh van Thien. She was cosily sympathetic, and full of motherly advice and barely concealed excitement, because here was Britannia, as lovely and sweet a girl as she had ever set eyes on, and moreover, she felt sure, as lovely and sweet a girl as the professor had ever set eyes on too, actually guest in his house, and likely to stay for a few days at least.

She embraced Britannia gingerly with an anxious eye on the bruise, and began to voice her regrets about St Nikolaas: 'All arranged weeks ago, you understand, my dear,' she protested, 'otherwise we would have loved to have had you with us…'

'Your loss is our gain, *mevrouw*,' interposed Mevrouw Luitingh van Thien. 'We shall be delighted to have Britannia with us.'

'She will perhaps be confined to her room?'

'So I understand, but my son is bringing back a nurse this evening.'

Britannia, sitting up in her pretty bed between her two visitors, thought that it was very evident that however merry the celebrations were to be she was to have no part in them. She said a little desperately: 'Look, surely I could travel? If someone could take me to the plane…'

'Jake has said that you are to stay here, my dear.' The two ladies looked at her in a kindly fashion, each of them quite sure in her own way that Jake was right. Britannia gave up, for the time being at least; when the professor returned, she would have another go at him.

But he gave her no opportunity of doing this; indeed, thinking about it afterwards, she suspected that he had guessed her intention and made sure that she was unable to carry it out, for he had visited her on his return that evening but had stayed only long enough to introduce Zuster Hagenbroek, examine her bruises and ankle, assure her with cool sympathy that no great harm had been done to her person, and that she would be as right as a trivet in no time at all, before going away again, leaving her to the ministrations of Zuster Hagenbroek, a middle-aged, bustling person with a wide smile and kind eyes, who spoke surprisingly good English, assured Britannia that she was perfectly able to massage the offending ankle as well as exercise it, and that Britannia would be up and about before she knew where she was. Precisely the same sentiments as the professor had voiced, but with a great deal more warmth.

The next day or two passed pleasantly enough, the pain was less now and although her face was all colours of the rainbow down one side from eye to chin, Britannia's headache had gone. She sat out of bed on a chaise longue before the fire, playing endless games of cards with Zuster Hagenbroek, writing reassuring letters to her mother and father, and sustaining lengthy visits from the professor's mother, who, now that she had got to know her better, proved not to be in the least severe.

Of the professor she saw very little and never alone, either he came when Zuster Hagenbroek was on duty, or was accompanied by his mother or Emmie, and even then he didn't stop long, confining his conversation to her state of health, the weather, and any instructions he might have for Zuster Hagenbroek. Just as though, thought Britannia sadly, they were strangers.

It was on the following morning, after a particularly pointless conversation with him which had led to an almost sleepless night on her part, that the first of the visitors arrived for St Nikolaas—the professor's eldest sister, Emma, a young woman of thirty-five or so, accompanied by three daughters ranging from twelve years to six. There was a very small son, too, already whisked away to the nursery by his nanny: 'But you shall see him later,' said his proud mother, 'though you mustn't let the children bother you.'

She was very like her brother, tall and graceful and elegant, and, unlike him, warmly friendly. They were getting to know each other when another sister arrived, to be introduced as Francesca. She had two children, six- and seven-year-olds, who shook Britannia's hand and exhibited endearing gap-toothed grins before they were led away for their lunch. But the mothers remained until Marinus brought drinks upstairs, sitting around happily gossiping in their excellent English until Zuster Hagenbroek came in with Britannia's tray. Eating the delicious little meal, she reflected that perhaps St Nikolaas wasn't going to be so bad after all. And for the rest of that day it wasn't; the professor's youngest sister Corinne arrived before tea with a placid baby boy who slept through the not inconsiderable noise which his numerous cousins made. Dumped on Britannia's lap while his mother went on some errand, he tucked his head, with its wisps of pale hair, into her arm and closed his eyes. He had, she thought, the faintest resemblance to his uncle.

And presently the professor came home. Britannia, watching his sisters launch themselves at his vast person with cries of delight, wished with all her heart that he would look like that for her, laughing and relaxed and content, but when he broke loose at length and came across to where she lay on the chaise longue, and she looked hopefully up into his face, it was to meet cold eyes and an unsmiling mouth, although he asked her civilly enough if she had had a pleasant day and how she did. Conscious of three pairs of eyes upon them, she answered quietly that yes, her day had been pleasant, and she did very well, adding a conventional hope that he had had a good day at the hospital.

His 'So-so,' was laconic in the extreme.

She didn't see him for the rest of that evening, although his sisters poked their heads round the door from time to time, for there was a good deal of coming and going getting the children to bed, and when the various husbands arrived just before dinner, they were brought along to be introduced before everyone trooped downstairs to the dining room. But not Britannia; she thought wistfully of the family party downstairs and wished she were there too, but that of course was impossible; dressing would have been a bit of a problem, she reminded herself sensibly, and then there was the question of getting someone to carry her downstairs, and as no one had suggested it, presumably no one had thought of it, either. She ate her dinner in solitary state because Zuster Hagenbroek had the afternoon and evening free and wouldn't be back until bedtime.

Emmie came to take her tray and ask her if she wanted anything, but she had all she wanted; books, magazines, a book of crossword puzzles to solve, cards for Patience, all arranged on the little table beside her. She played a game of Patience, cheating so that it came out, and then lay back with her eyes closed. She kept them closed when the door opened and someone came in because if they thought she was asleep they wouldn't feel guilty about not entertaining her. No one else came, not until Zuster Hagenbroek returned and that astute lady, taking one look at Britannia's lonely face, embarked on a description of her visit to her family in Arnhem, which lasted through the preparations for bed and until she put out the light, saying firmly that Britannia was tired and must go to sleep immediately. She sounded so sure that she would do as she was told that Britannia did just that.

The professor came the next morning after breakfast, examined the ankle and pronounced it to be mending well. 'I will take the strapping off tomorrow,' he promised, 'put on an elastic stocking and you can try a little—a very little, weight on it. Exercises and massage as usual today, and see that you rest it.' He gave her a pleasant nod, added a few instructions to Zuster Hagenbroek, and went off, leaving Britannia with a number of questions she wanted answered and hadn't even had the chance to ask. To get away as quickly as possible was her one wish; whatever the professor had felt for her had obviously been transitory, for now he treated her with the scrupulous politeness of a good host entertaining a guest he didn't really want. And she must be a great embarrassment to him too, and hadn't he said that Madeleine de Venz would be there for St Nikolaas? Britannia pondered her problems until a headache threatened and then was fortunately prevented from worrying any more for the moment by the arrival of the professor's sisters, wandering in in ones and twos, some with their children, all talking cheerfully about the evening's festivities.

The morning passed pleasantly, and Britannia, with the prospect of an equally pleasant afternoon, ate her lunch with appetite, submitted to Zuster Hagenbroek's massage and exercises and then obliged Corinne by minding the baby for a while while his mother went off to help organise the evening with her mother. He lay in the crook of her arm, smiling windily at her from time to time and making tiny chirruping noises, and presently fell asleep, and because she was afraid to disturb him by reaching for her book, she closed her eyes too.

It was Madeleine's voice which roused her from her doze. 'What a picture!' declared her sweet, high voice from the doorway. 'Mother and child—only of course Britannia isn't a mother—in any case she looks quite unsuitable for the role with that bruise.'

Britannia turned her head. The professor was standing there and so was Madeleine, elegant—breathtakingly so—in a red fox jacket and a suede skirt. She said 'Good afternoon,' politely and hated the professor for not reproving the girl for her rudeness. She barely glanced at him, but fixed her eyes on his top waistcoat button and said quietly: 'Please don't wake the baby.'

The professor spoke softly to his companion and Madeleine gave him a surprised look which turned to ill-humour. Britannia had no idea what it was she snapped in answer, but she turned on her heel and went and he came into the room.

'Corinne seems to be making use of you,' he observed mildly.

'She had to do something or other, and the other children are out in the grounds with the two nannies.'

He sat down cautiously on the chaise longue beside her injured ankle, and said to surprise her: 'I'm sorry that Madeleine was rude—she's a highly strung girl and doesn't always choose her words. You didn't look very pleased to see us.' He grinned suddenly. 'Jealous of the fox jacket?'

Britannia wiped away a dribble on the baby's chin. 'What a silly question,' she said coldly. 'How could I be jealous of anyone who wears the skin of a trapped animal?' She added austerely: 'I hope you had a good day at the hospital.'

'You know, if you didn't ask me that each day when I get home, I should feel positively deprived. Yes, I had a good day. I'm home early because everyone in Holland who can get home does so on St Nikolaas. Zuster Hagenbroek will be going to the bosom of her family in half an hour or so; she will come back quite late, I expect.'

'I'm glad she can go home.' It was a pity she couldn't think of anything else to say; the conversation so far had hardly sparkled.

'And how will you manage?' he asked blandly.

'Very well. I'm perfectly able to look after myself.' She added with a rush: 'I'm well enough to go home, if you would be so kind as to arrange it.'

'All in good time, Britannia. You have enough to read? I daresay my sisters have called in on you...'

'Yes, thank you, and yes, they have. I enjoyed it.' She wouldn't look at him while she sought for something else to say. Since he appeared to have settled himself he could at least help the conversation along.

The little silence was broken by Corinne's whirlwind entry. 'You dear girl,' she exclaimed warmly, and: 'Hullo, Jake—here, take your nephew and give Britannia a rest.' She dumped her son in the professor's arms and sat down on a low chair by the fire. 'Well, we're all ready and the children are in such a state of excitement I should think they'll all be sick later on.' She glanced at them both. 'Having a nice chat, were you?' she asked. 'Did I interrupt something?'

The professor didn't bother to answer it, it was Britannia who said: 'No—we were only passing the time of day.'

'Oh, good. I told Emmie I'd have tea with you, Britannia, do you mind? I can't stand having to sit and listen to Madeleine dripping platitudes in that sugary voice.'

'I will not tolerate discourtesy towards my guests, Corinne,' observed the professor severely.

She made a face at him, got up and took her small son from him and tweaked her brother's imposing nose. 'You old humbug,' she said. 'I may be fifteen years younger than you, but I've got eyes in my head, you know. Are you going to the sitting room for tea?'

'You have never grown up, my dear, have you? No, I have some work to do.' He added with some force: 'And no remarks about that, if you please.'

He smiled at her, nodded to Britannia and went away, and Corinne, settling down in her chair again, remarked: 'He's an old dear, isn't he? Bad-tempered, of course, but then so was Father, and he hates to be bested, though I don't suppose anyone's ever succeeded in doing that; he's so clever, you see, and he knows just about everything, although he hasn't a clue how to manage his love life,' she added artlessly. Her blue eyes smiled into Britannia's. 'He's a super brother and he'll make a gorgeous husband to the right girl. Do you like Madeleine?'

'I don't know her.' Britannia had almost been caught off guard. 'She's very beautiful, isn't she?'

'So are you.'

Britannia pinkened a little. 'Thank you. Tell me, how is it that you all speak such wonderful English?'

'We had a nanny—a fierce old bird; and then we had a governess, and Father always made us speak English at meals, and Jake kept it up, and now we're all married and none of us have lost the habit. You don't speak any Dutch?'

Britannia shook her head. 'No—well, about six words, and if someone says something easy like "Are you cold?" very slowly, I can understand them. Otherwise it's hopeless.'

'You'll learn. Here's tea, and I'm famished.' Corinne handed Britannia the baby. 'Tuck him under your arm, will you, and I'll pour.'

Alone again after tea, Britannia lay listening to the distant small voices echoing up the staircase; there were a lot of children—she could imagine how excited they must be, although she was a little uncertain as to what exactly was to happen. She had been going to ask Zuster Hagenbroek, but that dear soul had already gone and although Emmie had been in once or twice to see if she wanted anything, her Dutch just wasn't up to asking; even if it had, she would never have understood.

But she was to find out. She was reading by the light of the table lamp beside her when the professor returned. 'The *Sint* arrives in ten minutes—do you want to comb your hair or anything before I take you downstairs?'

'Me? Downstairs? Why?'

'My dear good girl, you don't really imagine that I— or anyone else for that matter—would leave you sitting here alone when St Nikolaas comes to call?'

'I'm not dressed.'

His eyes swept over her pink woolly housecoat with its ruffled neck and velvet trimming. 'You are a good deal more dressed than most of the ladies downstairs.' He walked over to the dressing-table and came back with a hairbrush and a mirror. 'Here you are. Where do you keep the things you put on your face?'

She was studying her face, a normal size now but still blue and yellow all down one side. 'I'm a fright. They're in the bathroom, on the shelf.'

She brushed her hair and tied it back neatly, powdered her nose and applied lipstick. 'There, am I all right?'

He picked her up and started for the door. 'My darling girl, not only are you all right, you're quite breathtakingly beautiful.'

Chapter 7

The professor's remark, coming as it did after several days of coldness, so astonished Britannia that she stayed quiet as he took her downstairs and across the hall, this time not to the sitting room but down a wide passage at the side of the staircase, with doors on one side and a big arched door at its end. Outside this he paused, kissed her hard and swiftly and pushed the door open with his foot. The room was very large, with enormous windows with crimson curtains drawn across them to shut out the chilly dark evening. The floor was of polished wood with a great centre carpet and the furniture was satinwood, upholstered in shades of rose and cream and blue. Britannia, laid gently on to a sofa drawn up to one side of the great hearth, stared around her with great interest. It was a very grand room and the people in it looked grand too. The women had dressed for the occasion and she quite saw what Jake had meant when he said that she was more dressed than the other ladies present, for whereas she was muffled to the throat in cosy wool, they were in long evening gowns, beautiful garments such as she had often gazed at in Fortnum and Mason's windows or Harrods, and the men were in black ties to complement them. Very conscious of her prosaic appearance, she smiled rather shyly at Mevrouw Luitingh van Thien, who came across the room to sit beside her.

'My dear, how very nice that you can join us,' said that lady in a ringing voice. 'How pretty you look, and how I wish I had your lovely hair. You know everyone here, don't you? I must warn you that presently it will become very noisy and you are to say immediately if you get the headache.'

She patted Britannia's arm, her severe features lighted by a delightful smile. 'Jake's two uncles are here, you shall meet them presently, they are talking to Madeleine.'

Which gave Britannia the chance to look at her. Oyster crêpe, cut far too low for such a bony chest and too elaborate for the occasion. Quite unsuitable, almost as unsuitable as Britannia's own garment. She looked away quickly and met the smiling eyes of Corinne. 'We're going to sit near you, so that you will know what's happening. Jake has to be at the other end of the room to welcome the *Sint*. You see, we do it exactly the same every year, if we didn't the children would be disappointed. He's coming now.'

The big doors opened once more and the *Sint* entered, with Zwarte Piet behind him. The professor greeted him with a short speech and everybody clapped while he walked, with the professor showing him the way, down the centre of the room to where a space had been cleared for him and his attendant. He was an imposing figure in his crimson and purple robes and his mitre set on a head with a lavish display of white hair and beard. He carried a book which Corinne whispered held the names of all the children present. Provided they had been good throughout the year, each child would receive a present and an orange. Bad children were popped into Zwarte Piet's sack, but this, Corinne concluded, seldom happened.

Several of the children had come to sit on the sofa with Britannia; now they were called one by one and advanced to receive their gifts, so that there was a good deal of paper being rustled and whispered exclamations of delight going on around her. She nodded and smiled and admired the boxes of paints, dolls, clockwork engines and the like which quickly strewed the sofa, and was busy tying a doll's bonnet more securely when she became aware that the children had given way to the grown-ups. And certainly the good *Sint* had been generous; Corinne waltzed up to the good man, received her gift, kissed him for it amidst a good deal of laughter, and returned to the sofa to open it; earrings, quite beautiful ones of sapphires and pearls—antique and very valuable, thought Britannia, and then turned to admire Mevrouw Luitingh van Thien's gift, a thick gold chain with a locket and quite lovely. Everyone else had something similar too, although she was relieved to see that Madeleine's present—an evening bag—had a less personal flavour. She was quite taken by surprise when her own name was called and the professor said: 'I'll take it for you, Britannia. St Nikolaas has it from me that you have been a good girl and deserve your gift.'

He brought it over presently and she thanked him in a quiet little voice and undid the beribboned package. It was a headscarf, a Gucci, pink and brown and cream and a hint of green, a lovely thing. She wondered who had bought it and the professor, who hadn't gone away, bent and whispered in her ear just as though she had asked him. 'I hope you like it, the colours reminded me of you.'

She thanked him again and this time when she looked at him, his eyes were warm and he was smiling, so that she smiled too. She wasn't sure what she might have said next if Madeleine hadn't joined the little group round them, slipped a hand under the professor's arm and made some laughing remark about her present. 'And just the colour I wanted,' she went on. 'So clever of you, Jake dear, to choose it.' She smiled down at Britannia. 'That's a charming scarf—I don't suppose you have ever had a Gucci before.'

'No.' The sight of Madeleine's hand on Jake's arm, just as though it belonged there, made Britannia uncertain. 'I shall love wearing it.'

Emma had joined them too; she began to talk to Britannia almost immediately and Britannia didn't see Jake and Madeleine go away. The party began to split up into groups and the children made a dutiful round of goodnights. They had sung themselves hoarse as St Nikolaas had made his dignified way out of the room once more, they had drunk their lemonade and eaten their *speculaas* and as much of their chocolate letters as they had been allowed, now they were more than ready for bed. The room seemed larger than ever once they had gone, but very pleasant in the glow of the many rose-coloured lamps and the firelight. Presently Marinus came in with drinks and Britannia was just beginning to worry as to how she was to get back upstairs again when the professor returned, picked her up and carried her across the hall and into the dining room, where he sat her on a chair at one corner of the great rectangular table, her leg on a cushioned stool.

'Oh, but I can't,' she protested. 'It's a family dinner party—and I'm not dressed.'

'You've said that already. Here's Corinne's husband to sit beside you and Oom Jiers, and if you think that a strange name, he's from Friesland.'

He left her with her two table companions and went to the head of the table at the farther end so that she couldn't really see him very well unless she peered round Oom Jiers' considerable bulk. It was small comfort that Madeleine was seated quite close to him, near enough to talk to him if she wanted to. Britannia decided not to spoil her dinner by trying to see what he was doing and applied herself to Corinne's husband, Jan, and then to Oom Jiers, who proved to be a man of wit despite his elderly appearance.

They settled down to enjoy themselves. As Jan said, there was nothing like good conversation and good food to go with it, and it was certainly that; lobster soup, rich and creamy, followed by roast leg of pork with spiced peaches, served on a great silver dish and carved, suitably, by the professor amid a good deal of joking from his family, and as well as the peaches there were dishes of vegetables, handed round by Marinus and the two maids. Britannia, doing justice to her dinner, found it all the better by reason of the exquisite china upon which it was served and the rat-tailed silver spoons and forks, worn thin with use but as lovely as the day they had first been used some time in the seventeenth century.

The sweet was sheer luxury; mangoes in champagne, served in exquisite wine glasses, and they drank champagne too, so that by the end of the meal Britannia was feeling a good deal happier than she had done. All the same, as soon as they had had coffee she decided that she would make some excuse and go back to her room; it was, after all, a family gathering and although everyone—well, nearly everyone—had been very sweet to her, she was conscious of feeling an outsider. She had her opportunity quite soon, for the professor wandered round the table as they all got up to go back to the sitting room, with the obvious intention of carrying her there.

She didn't give him a chance to speak but said at once: 'I've had a simply lovely time, but I'd like to go upstairs now, if you wouldn't mind.'

'I mind very much, Britannia.' He made no attempt to lower his voice and she was painfully aware that Jan and Oom Jiers were both listening quite openly; not only that, Madeleine, from the other side of the table, was watching them.

'I think I'm tired,' she elaborated.

He smiled then, a tender little smile which was just for her but which must have been seen by anyone who happened to be looking. 'Shall we compromise? Don't go to your room just yet, we will go to the little sitting room my mother sometimes uses, and sit quietly and talk.'

She supposed that it was the champagne that made his suggestion sound so delightful, but all the same she asked: 'But your guests? You can't leave them.'

'Oom Jiers will fill in for me, won't you? And they're not guests—they're family.'

She eyed him steadily, not caring now that their two companions were drinking in every word. 'Madeleine isn't family—or is she, Jake?'

'You are a persistent young woman, Britannia. No, she isn't family, but I—we have all known her for a very long time, she has come to our St Nikolaas feast for years.' He added in a slightly louder voice: 'Of course, if you prefer, I'll take you to your room, we can talk there just as easily.'

It was the professor's mother who clinched the matter. 'Of course you can't leave us now, my dear. Why not let Jake take you to the little sitting room for a while? It will be quiet there and when you feel rested you can come back and join us.'

Britannia hadn't seen her join them, she had no idea how long the lady had been standing there but in any event, she didn't seem to mind. She looked across the table and saw Madeleine's face. If it had been unhappy she wouldn't have agreed, but it wasn't, it was furious, the lovely eyes narrowed, the mouth a thin line. 'All right,' she said, 'I think I should like to do that, if it's not being a nuisance.'

So she was carried once more across the hall and through a small arched door on the other side of it, to a much smaller room, but still large by her own home standards. She guessed that it was in the older part of the house, for the windows were narrow and latticed and the fireplace was an open one with a great copper hood above it. The professor set her down on a narrow Regency sofa drawn up to the hearth, turned off the wall sconces leaving only a couple of rose-shaded table lamps burning, and sat down in a winged armchair opposite her. 'We all love this room,' he remarked pleasantly. 'Mama used it a great deal when we were children, we used to come and talk to her here while she sat and sewed. When my father came home he would come straight here.'

'Was he a surgeon too?'

'Oh, yes, and his father before him. He died ten years ago, he was a good deal older than my mother.'

Britannia looked around her, more at ease now because the professor had apparently forgotten that he had called her his darling girl and kissed her into the bargain. The room was charming and she liked the furniture—applewood and walnut and a golden mahogany and some delicate pieces of marquetry, all welded into a charming whole by the deep red and blue patterned curtains and covers. 'It's delightful. You have a very beautiful house, Jake.' She sighed without knowing it. 'Sitting here and sewing...'

'I shall do exactly the same as my father.' She gave him an enquiring look, and he went on: 'Come straight to you here when I get home each evening.'

Britannia went pink; he was joking and it hurt, but she said austerely: 'If you brought me here to make jokes like that, then I'd like to go back to my room, please.'

'I brought you here to ask you, in peace and quiet, to marry me, Britannia.' He was still sitting back in his great chair, relaxed and calm and she jerked upright the better to stare at him. The sudden movement hurt her ankle and she winced, and he was at once beside her, rearranging the cushion.

'You seem surprised,' he observed mildly. 'Surely you must have expected me to do just that.'

Britannia said indignantly: 'Of course I'm surprised! If it hadn't been for this silly ankle I should have been back in England and how could you have—have asked me to marry you then?'

'Easily enough, although the journey would have been tiresome, my dear.'

'Yes, but I explained—I mean, about Madeleine... you said...'

'You said, darling Britannia—you had a good deal to say, I have never met such a girl for giving her opinion about this, that and the other.'

She kept doggedly to the point. 'But she's here, in your house, you—invited her.'

'To be honest, I did not. You must understand that

for a number of years Madeleine has been spending St Nikolaas with us, it has become a kind of habit, and one can hardly say: "Well, Madeleine, we don't want you to come any more," can one? She has, over the last year or so, taken it for granted just as, I'm afraid, it was taken for granted that sooner or later I should ask her to marry me.'

'She still takes it for granted.'

'Oh, I think not; I have never asked her to do so, you know, and she must surely realise by now that I have no intention of doing so.'

Britannia looked at him lovingly. Men were a bit foolish sometimes, even a man like Jake, self-assured and brilliantly clever and knowing what he wanted, casually taking it for granted that Madeleine would give way with good grace to a girl he hardly knew... 'You seem very certain of me,' she remarked with faint tartness.

He raised his eyebrows. 'But of course I am; you may preach at me and take me to task on every possible occasion, but you love me, don't you?'

'Yes,' said Britannia, baldly, and was instantly joined on her sofa by the professor, who put an arm around her and observed with satisfaction: 'That's better.' He kissed the top of her head. 'Now let us be sensible and assess the situation.' He paused: 'Well, let us be sensible presently.' He put the other arm around her and bent to kiss her, an exercise which took quite a time and which Britannia didn't attempt to interrupt. After a little while he said: 'How soon can you leave the hospital?'

Britannia lifted her head from his shoulder, the better to concentrate on her arithmetic. 'Well, let me see, today's the fifth of December, so a month away is the second of January, but I've got three weeks' holiday owing, so I'd have a week to do plus sick leave to make up...'

'Far too long—you'll allow me to deal with it for you. I think it would be nice if we got married before Christmas.'

She lifted her head once more to look at him. 'Jake—that's three weeks away!'

'Too long. Do you want to be married here or in England?'

She said instantly: 'At home, please. Jake, you're rushing me...'

His arm tightened. 'Yes, I know I am, but I won't if you don't want me to.'

She leaned up to kiss his chin. 'You're really very nice when one gets to know you. I want time to get used to it all, Jake. Would you mind very much if we don't make any plans for a few days—a week? Then I'll do anything you say, I promise you. I'd like to tell my parents, you see they know about you, I—I told them how we met...'

'Ah, so you knew, too.'

'Oh, yes, but I didn't think I'd see you again.'

The professor laughed gently. 'You forget that I knew where you were, my darling. I had every intention of seeing you again.'

'You said I had a sharp tongue.'

'And so you have on occasion, my love, but it doesn't worry me in the least, I quite enjoy it.' There was a pleasant little interlude while he proved this statement, but presently Britannia said: 'We ought to go back. I'd like to stay here with you for the rest of the evening, but it wouldn't do.'

The professor looked as though he was going to laugh, although he agreed quite seriously to this. 'But I shall carry you back to your room in half an hour or so. Emmie will help you get ready for bed. Is your ankle quite all right? We'll have that strapping off tomorrow—I'll come home after the morning list and see to it—you can try a little weight bearing once it's off and the stocking is on. You'll be walking quite soon provided you're sensible about resting it.'

He picked her up and carried her back to the sitting room, and just as he had done earlier in the evening, bent to kiss her before he opened the door.

She was settled on the sofa by the fire once more and Jake went away again, to reappear presently with Marinus bearing a large tray with glasses, and Emmie behind him with a magnum of champagne in a silver bucket. Marinus put the tray down and went back again for a second bottle and Emmie reappeared with another tray loaded with small dishes of petits fours and canapés. A toast was drunk to St Nikolaas, someone went over to the grand piano at one end of the room and began to play and presently everyone was singing the traditional songs of the Feast of St Nikolaas, and Britannia, unable to understand any of them, nonetheless picked up the tunes and joined in, greatly helped by the champagne. Not even the sight of Madeleine crossing the room to sit beside Jake could shake her happiness.

Poor Madeleine, imagining that she would marry him. Britannia, disliking the girl very much, all the same felt sorry for her.

The professor got up presently and came over to the sofa, reminded her that she was to go to bed, waited while she wished everyone a goodnight and carried her upstairs, calling to Corinne on his way to go with them, and once in her room he laid Britannia on her bed, kissed her gently on the cheek, wished her goodnight and went away immediately, leaving Corinne looking delighted and curious.

'I suppose it is one of those open secrets everyone knows,' she declared happily, 'you and Jake. When are you going to announce it?'

Britannia was wriggling out of her dressing gown. 'However did you know?'

Corinne giggled. 'I don't think I exactly knew, none of us did, but we guessed. Mother's so happy about it, so are we all.'

Britannia felt a delightful wave of happiness wash over her. 'How nice of you—only Madeleine...'

'She hasn't guessed. She's so conceited and sure of Jake that she can't imagine him falling in love with anyone but her.' Corinne sat down on the edge of the bed. 'None of us likes her, she wormed her way in and she was very clever, always good company for Jake and always at the same houses and parties and dinners...she was always there, you see, creeping into his life until he took her for granted.'

'Go on,' urged Britannia, and was disappointed when Emmie came in, taking charge with all the firmness of a trusted old servant, so that Corinne went obediently away and left her to help Britannia to bed.

But Britannia was too happy to lie awake worrying about Madeleine; she slept soundly on the thought that Jake loved her and they were going to marry very soon. This pleasant glow continued throughout the morning, and although no one actually asked her any questions, there was a good deal of family discussion in which she was included as though she were already one of them, and when after lunch Jake came home, he came straight to her room and with Zuster Hagenbroek's assistance, took the strapping off the ankle, examined it at length, encased it in an elastic stocking, pronounced it well on the way to recovery and declared that he would be back in half an hour, during which time she could dress. 'A stick and a strong arm is what you need now, we'll try them out presently.' He looked at Zuster Hagenbroek. 'I think we can manage without you after today—if you can be ready, I'll run you in after breakfast tomorrow.'

He went away, and Britannia got down to the business of dressing while Zuster Hagenbroek tidied the room and gossiped. She had heard about Britannia and the professor, she said happily, the whole household knew, and everyone was so pleased. She stopped to smile broadly at Britannia. Such a nice man he was too, very popular at the hospital and with an enormous private practice, but perhaps Britannia knew about that? And no puffed-up airs and graces, either, for all he was a wealthy man, but of course that wasn't news... And when, asked the dear soul, was the wedding to be?

Britannia said that she didn't know; nothing had

been decided, but it would be a very quiet one. 'And I hope that when I'm settled in you'll come and see me, for you've been so kind—I don't know what I should have done without you.'

Zuster Hagenbroek looked gratified. 'Well, you've been a model patient—and here's the professor back again.'

Britannia had done her face with extra care and brushed her hair until it shone. She had put on a tweed skirt and a pink woolly sweater which she knew suited her very well and now she turned to the door, her face alight with happiness as the professor came in. 'Are you home for the rest of the day?' she wanted to know.

'I must go back to my rooms for an hour this evening—I've a couple of patients I have to see, but I'll be back for dinner. How's the ankle?'

'Fine.' She felt a little shy of him because this was the Jake she didn't know very well, the calm, rather impersonal surgeon—not that she would have liked him to have been anything else while Zuster Hagenbroek was there.

He carried her downstairs, set her on a highbacked chair in the hall and fetched a stick from the wall cupboard. 'I thought you might like to see over some of the house, darling. We won't hurry and you can sit down every now and then. I know you've been in the sitting room and the big drawing room, but there are some quite interesting paintings and the silver is worth looking at too.'

He came over to her and pulled her gently to her feet

and stood looking down at her, laughing. 'Why do you look like that? Are you shy?'

She shook her head. 'No, at least, only a little. You see, I don't know you very well...'

'My darling, but you do. The number of times you have pointed out my faults and given me advice as to how to overcome them...'

She stood within the circle of his arm. 'I always thought you were such a bad-tempered man...'

'I am, but not at the moment.' He kissed her again. 'Let's start in the sitting room, shall we? We're bound to meet the family, but we won't let them hinder us.'

The afternoon was a delight to her; she had a natural flair for beautiful things and some of the portraits on the walls were beautiful, as were the silver and the porcelain in their great marquetry cabinets. They spent a long time in the sitting room before they inspected the dining room, the big drawing room, and a charming smaller room which was the little drawing room, with white-painted walls and soft pink and blue furnishings, little inlaid tables and a collection of watercolours hung on either side of the steel fireplace. Jake pointed out a Leickert, a van Schendel and a van der Stok which an ancestor had commissioned in the nineteenth century, and over and above those were a Carabain and two charming river scenes by van Deventer which he had bought during the last few years.

'We shall be able to search for treasures together,' he observed, and stopped to kiss her before picking her up and carrying her down a small staircase. 'This is the oldest part of the house and on a different level. There's

a games room and a garden room and here at the end
is the music room. Do you play the piano, Britannia?'

She hobbled to the baby grand piano in the big bay
window. 'A little.' She ran her fingers up and down the
yellowed keys and then sat down on the wide stool and
tried a little Chopin. She played with spirit if a bit in-
accurately, but she stopped when Jake sat down beside
her and took over the tune.

'No, go on, my love—I come here sometimes for
half an hour, now we can share an added pleasure!'

He played well and with no tiresome mannerisms;
they thundered through a mazurka and then skimmed
through a waltz, and when they stopped Britannia said:
'Jake, you play very well—I had no idea...'

He gave her a wicked glance. 'We shall probably
have a child prodigy.'

'Oh, no,' cried Britannia, 'not a musician, they'll all
be brilliant surgeons like their papa.'

'So I am to be rivalled in my old age?'

She answered him seriously. 'Not rivalled, for you
will have handed on your skill, just as your father did
to you. And you'll never be old.'

'My darling, there is fifteen years' difference between us.' He had closed the piano and was leaning on
it, looking at her with a little mocking smile.

'Pooh, what's fifteen years,' cried Britannia with
some asperity, and then suddenly: 'You don't think it's
too much? You don't think that I... Jake, perhaps after
we're married you'll wish we weren't. You don't know
much about me and nothing of my family, would it be
better if we waited?'

'You have second thoughts?' His voice was faintly cool and she hastened to protest.

'Of course I haven't, not for me.' She frowned a little. 'I think what it is, I wanted to marry you so much and now I'm going to and it doesn't seem possible. It's like a lovely dream and I'm afraid of waking up.'

'Then I must convince you that you are wrong.' Which he did to such good purpose that Britannia forgot all her doubts and kissed him back.

The garden room was full of colour even on the grey winter's afternoon; they wandered around while Britannia admired the chrysanthemums and the forced spring flowers and an enormous assortment of house plants.

'But it's one person's work,' observed Britannia.

'More or less—old Cor sees to this side of the greenhouses. When you can manage it, we'll go and look at the gardens and the hothouses. Shall we join the family for tea, or would you like it here?'

'They're all going tomorrow, aren't they? And they haven't seen much of you.' She would have liked to have stayed there alone with Jake, but it might look as though she wasn't prepared to share him with his family. They went slowly through the house again and into the sitting room, full of people. The children were there too, the little ones under the wing of the two nannies, the babies on any lap which came handy, while everyone talked their heads off. Britannia, settled on a sofa with her foot up once more, was instantly absorbed into the cheerful gathering and now they spoke quite openly about her joining the family, laughingly warning her that New Year would be a splendid opportunity for her to meet even more of them. 'You'll have to open up all the bedrooms, Britannia, there are hordes of us. Emmie cooks for days before and Jake gives a dance; it's tremendous fun.'

Britannia suppressed a tiny qualm; supposing she couldn't cope with entertaining on that scale? There would be any number of things she wouldn't know, and would Jake expect her to know them? Just for a moment she thought of Madeleine, who would know exactly what to do on such an occasion and be relied upon to be a perfect hostess. And supposing she did something silly and Jake felt ashamed of her? She looked up and found the professor's eye on her and he shook his head slightly at her and smiled, just as though he guessed what she was thinking.

He took her with him the next afternoon; he had patients to see at his consulting rooms and as he explained, it would be a good opportunity for her to see them and meet Mien, his secretary, and Willa, the receptionist and nurse. There were his two partners whom she must meet, too, he told her, but not just yet; one was on holiday, the other in Luxembourg. So Britannia, wrapped up against the cold wind and the fine powdering of snow which had begun to fall, was made comfortable beside him when he came to fetch her after lunch.

'Warm enough?' he wanted to know, sending the car towards Arnhem. And when she nodded, for who wouldn't be warm in such a magnificent car? he went on: 'I should like to wrap you in furs, my darling, but I think that you wouldn't like that—not just yet.'

He manoeuvred the car past a string of air force jeeps. 'I haven't given you a ring, have I? But a ring is binding.'

Britannia didn't know why his words should make her suddenly cold inside; after all, she had asked him to wait. She peeped sideways at him and saw that his profile was stern. She said meekly: 'Yes, it is, isn't it?' and when he didn't say anything else she forbore from further speech. But when he drew up before one of the tall, narrow houses in a quiet side street of the city, the face he turned to her was quite free from any sternness.

'Wait while I get you out,' he cautioned, 'and I shall have to carry you up the stairs—there's a lift, but it's out of order.'

His rooms were on the first floor, indeed they occupied the whole of it, three consulting rooms, a most comfortably furnished waiting room, a tiny office for Mien, a bespectacled, rather plain girl with a charming smile, and another small room used by Willa for any small treatment which might be necessary. Britannia was enchanted by it all and spent the ensuing hours sitting with Mien, whose English was really rather good, while Jake went away to see his patients.

'It is a large practice,' explained Mien, 'and as well as his work here, the professor has many beds in the hospitals. He operates several times a week and also goes to Utrecht and to London and sometimes Vienna.'

And Britannia, anxious to know all there was to know about Jake, listened to every word. There was still so much to discover about him and not a great deal of time before they married. With Mien on the telephone beside her, Britannia went into a pleasant daydream; being married to Jake was going to be fun.

Chapter 8

The old house seemed very quiet after everyone had gone the next day, leaving only Mevrouw Luitingh van Thien behind. The professor had left before breakfast and it was after that meal that his mother suggested that she might take Britannia over the rest of the house. 'That's if you can manage the stairs, my dear,' she added. 'Jake would not forgive me if I suggested anything which might harm your ankle.'

'I can hop,' declared Britannia cheerfully. 'It's much better, you know, and the elastic stocking supports it. I'd love to come with you.'

Their tour took most of the morning, there was so much to see: magnificent bedrooms furnished with what Britannia could see were valuable antiques, cunningly concealed bathrooms and clothes closets and a dear little room which had been called '*Mevrouw's ka-mertje*', a name which had been handed down from one generation to another without anyone really knowing why it should be so. It had a work table, its original silk lining still intact, though faded, and some small high-backed chairs which her guide assured her were most comfortable. There was a games table too, exquisitely inlaid with applewood, and a sofa table in the window, as well as an escritoire with its accompanying chair. The curtains were brocade in muted greens and blues and the highly polished wood floor had a scattering of fine rugs upon it. The only concession to modernity were the table lamps; little silver stands with peach shades which blended exactly with the room.

They sat there for a little while carrying on a placid conversation about nothing in particular until Mevrouw Luitingh van Thien remarked unexpectedly: 'I have said nothing to you as yet, my dear, for Jake has told me that you want a few days in which to think over his proposal—indeed, he tells me that nothing has actually been settled, but I hope very much that you will accept him. I do not mind telling you now that I—in fact, all of us, have been very much against him marrying Madeleine de Venz.' She sighed. 'Not that he would have taken any notice of anything we might have had to say. You can imagine my delight, Britannia, when after years of dreaded expectation that he would marry her, he should meet you and fall in love with you at your first meeting.'

'He intended to marry her.' Britannia wasn't asking a question but stating a fact.

Her companion corrected her, 'No, my dear, she intended to marry him.'

Which remark merely substantiated what Britannia herself already knew. She picked up a dainty little figurine, admiring its vivid blue glaze and then looked at its base. 'Longton Hall,' she said absent-mindedly, 'mid-eighteenth century and quite charming. Madeleine hates me.'

'Naturally, Britannia. You're not afraid of her?'

'Goodness me, no, *mevrouw*, not of her. She has become a habit with Jake—habits are hard to shake off. She has a lot that I haven't—breeding and knowing how to do things and what to say, she knows all his friends and, I daresay, how he likes his house run...'

Mevrouw Luitingh van Thien snorted elegantly. 'His servants dislike her, did you know that? Even the dogs avoid her.' She glanced round at the two faithful beasts who had accompanied them silently and were now sitting between them. 'And as for breeding, Britannia, I find your manners much more to my taste. She is sophisticated, certainly, and probably able to cope with any social occasion, but there is no warmth in her; her love for Jake, if one can call it love, is purely selfish; if he were to lose his possessions overnight or fall victim to some incurable illness, she would have no more to do with him. You, I know, would love Jake under any circumstance.'

'Yes, I would,' said Britannia baldly. 'I'd starve for him. And if I thought I wouldn't make him happy, then I'd go away.'

She frowned, for she hadn't meant to be quite so

dramatic about it; one's thoughts sometimes sounded silly spoken aloud. But apparently Mevrouw Luitingh van Thien didn't think so; she said approvingly, 'I have always been sure of that, my dear.'

They sat in a comfortable silence for a few minutes and then went on with their inspection: the remainder of the bedrooms on the first floor, and at the back of the house, in the older part, the large nursery, very much as it must have looked when the professor was a small boy; there was a night nursery too, and a bathroom and tiny kitchen and several smaller bedrooms. They inspected it in silence until Mevrouw Luitingh van Thien remarked softly: 'Jake's nanny married when Corinne left the nursery—she has a daughter who is also a nanny—a pleasant homely girl, like her mother.'

Britannia went a bright pink, but spoke up in her honest way. 'You mean she would come to us if we wanted her.'

'Yes, my dear, that is what I meant. We had better go back the way we came; there is a small staircase at the end of this passage, but it is too narrow for you. We will leave the top floor until you can walk in comfort. There is a wonderful view from the parapet and when the children were young, we turned one of the rooms into a games room where they could play those noisy games young people love. The other rooms are for the servants—they have a sitting room there too, and Emmie and Marinus have a small flat, and there are the attics, of course, full of the odds and ends families accumulate over the years.'

They were making their way back as she talked and

now Britannia was making her way clumsily down the staircase. At the bottom she said politely: 'Thank you for showing me round; it's quite beautiful. Would you mind if I put my leg up for half an hour before lunch? It's a little uncomfortable.'

Which it was, but she wanted a little time to think, too. At the back of her mind she was worrying about Madeleine. She couldn't believe that she wouldn't do all she could to get Jake back, if she had ever had him... Britannia lay back on the sofa, determined to be sensible about it, think the whole thing out in a rational manner and make up her mind what to do. She didn't get very far, of course; she knew what she wanted to do; she wanted to marry Jake and when he brought the subject up again, she would tell him that. Having settled everything in this simple fashion, she closed her eyes and went to sleep.

The professor came home after lunch, examined her ankle and pronounced it to be progressing splendidly, then suggested that they might drive to the outskirts of Hilversum and visit a friend of his, Reilof van Meerum. 'He has an English wife, Laura—I think you might like each other.'

'Don't you have any more patients today?'

'Lord, yes, but not until half past six at my rooms— I'll have to go on to the hospital after that to take a look at one of my patients there, but I'm free this afternoon. Like to come?'

Of course she liked to go with him. Madeleine was forgotten, she put on her outdoor things and limped downstairs under his watchful eye. 'You're making astounding progress,' he observed, 'but go easy on the stairs, my darling, and use a stick for another day or two.'

It was a cold, crisp day and the road to Apeldoorn was beautiful in the thin sunshine. Britannia occupied the few miles before they joined the motorway in telling Jake about her morning, and they passed the time pleasantly enough as they raced towards Amersfoort, and if she was a little disappointed because he had nothing to say concerning their future, she was careful not to let it spoil her happy mood. They left the motorway at Amersfoort and took the road to Baarn, and a mile or two beyond that pleasant town, along a fine avenue lined with great trees, he turned in between brick pillars and along a short drive, to stop before a large square house with a stone balustrade and a massive porch.

As Jake helped her out, Britannia asked: 'Are they expecting us?'

'I saw Reilof this morning and we are expected, my love.'

As if to substantiate his remark the door was flung open and a smallish girl with mousy hair and pretty eyes ran out. 'Reilof said you would be coming—what a lovely surprise.' She put up her face for Jake's kiss and turned to Britannia. 'I'm Laura,' she said. 'Reilof and Jake are old friends and I hope we'll be friends too.' She smiled and instantly looked pretty. 'Come in—Reilof's in the sitting room, guarding the twins— Nanny's got a day off.'

She led them indoors, where a white-haired man

took their coats and exchanged a few dignified remarks with Jake and was made known to Britannia as Piet, without whom, Laura declared, the house would fall apart. 'We're in the small sitting room.'

Reilof van Meerum was standing by the window, a very small baby over his shoulder. The baby was making a considerable noise, but his proud parent was quite unruffled by it. He came forward to meet his visitors, shook Jake's hand as though he hadn't seen him in weeks and then turned to Britannia. 'Jake and I are such old friends that I don't suppose he'll mind if I kiss you.' He grinned. 'He always kisses Laura.' He glanced at his small wife with such devotion that Britannia caught her breath and then smiled as he went on. 'We're fearful bores at present, you know—we've only had the twins a month, and our days revolve round them.'

Britannia took a look at the baby on his arm; dark like his father and at the moment, very ill-tempered. The other baby, sleeping peacefully in its cradle, was dark too. 'A girl?' essayed Britannia, and Laura nodded. 'Yes—isn't it nice having one of each? She's called Beatrix Laura, and he's Reilof, of course.'

Reilof junior stopped screaming presently and was put to sleep in his cradle and the two men wandered off to Reilof's study while the two girls settled down for a gossip. There was a lot to talk about, as they had much in common, for Laura had been a nurse before she married Reilof. It wasn't until Piet had been in with the tea tray and gone to fetch his master that Laura asked diffidently: 'I'm not being nosey, but are you and Jake going to get married?'

'Yes,' Britannia told her, 'I hope so. But there's nothing definite yet.'

There was no time to do more than exchange smiles, for the two men came into the room then and the rest of the visit was taken up with light-hearted conversation. They left presently and started their journey back to Hoenderloo, travelling fast because Jake hadn't much time; perhaps it was because of that he had little to say in answer to Britannia's cheerful remarks about their afternoon, and when she took a quick peep at him it was to see that he was deep in thought, his mouth set sternly, and a faint frown between his eyes, so that her efforts at conversation dwindled away into silence. Something was annoying him—was still annoying him. At last, unable to bear the silence any longer, she said forthrightly: 'You look vexed. Have I done something?'

They were travelling very fast and he didn't look at her. 'No.' And then: 'I'm glad you enjoyed your afternoon.' But it was uttered in such an absent-minded fashion that she knew that he wasn't really thinking about that at all.

She didn't say any more then until they had reached the house once more and he had helped her out of the car and they were indoors, and although he was as kind and considerate as he always was towards her she sensed his impatience. 'I've a mind to climb the staircase by myself,' she told him lightly, 'and it's a good chance, because you want to be off again, don't you?'

She didn't wait for his reply but started off across the hall, walking quite firmly with her stick so that he would be able to see that she was independent now. But when she heard his footsteps cross the hall towards his study she paused thankfully to lean on the carved banisters before mounting the wide stairs. Jake had forgotten to shut the study door, she thought idly, and then froze as she heard the faint tinkle of the telephone as he lifted the receiver and said: 'Madeleine? *Ik moet met je spreken—morgen middag—zal je thuis wezen?*'

He spoke clearly and Britannia, who had picked up a little Dutch by now, understood him very well. He wanted to speak to Madeleine the following afternoon and would she be home. She started up the staircase while she pondered the unwelcome thought that possibly it had something to do with his ill-humour in the car. It took her a few minutes to dismiss the idea as nonsense; he had every right to telephone whom he wished and just because it had been Madeleine there was no reason for her to feel as she did—coldly apprehensive. It hadn't been such a good day after all, she decided as she took off her outdoor things and did her hair and face. Perhaps he had had an extra busy day and hadn't really wanted to go to see his friends. She went downstairs again to find him gone and his mother sitting by the fire, looking so normal that Britannia called herself an imaginative fool and embarked on a cheerful account of the afternoon. Everything, she told herself, would be all right when Jake got home later on.

Only he didn't come. There was a message just before they sat down for dinner to say that he had an emergency operation that evening and would get something to eat in hospital, and although Britannia sat up long after Mevrouw Luitingh van Thien had gone to bed, he didn't come, so presently she too went to bed, to lie awake and listen for the car. She slept in the end without hearing its return in the early hours of the morning.

She was surprised and pleased to find him at the breakfast table the next morning, and then not quite so pleased to see that he was still in a thoughtful mood; something was on his mind and she longed to ask him what. Instead she wished him a cheerful good morning, hoped that he hadn't had too busy an evening and asked if he was going to the hospital that morning.

He glanced up from the letter he was reading. 'Yes, and I don't expect to be home until after tea. Have you any plans for today? Don't, I beg of you, over-exercise that ankle. It's made a very rapid recovery, it would be a shame to spoil it.'

She waited for him to say something else; something about their future. Perhaps that was why he was so preoccupied and it would be for her to say what she was going to do next. But how could she before he had asked her definitely to marry him? And would they marry soon, or was she to go back to the hospital for a while? When he didn't speak she said cheerfully: 'Oh, I'll take care—I'm going to have a lazy morning anyway, because your mother is going to visit a friend in Hoenderloo.'

'Oh, Jonkvrouwe de Tielle, they're great cronies.' He picked up his letters and stuffed them into his jacket pocket, came round the table to kiss her, said easily: 'I'll see you this evening then, Britannia,' and went away, leaving her determined to ask him what was the matter and what was more, to get an answer.

She frowned as she poured herself more coffee. He could have told her that he was visiting Madeleine that afternoon, he could have told her even why he wanted to see her in the first place. Surely two people who were going to marry didn't have secrets from each other—not that kind of secret, anyway. But perhaps, because she hadn't been quite definite about marrying him, he didn't feel bound to tell her such things. She told herself that she was being a little unreasonable and admitted that she was jealous.

And later that day, as she was getting ready for dinner in her room, she could see that it was she who had been at fault; Jake had come home, rather late it was true, but his usual charming self, and although his kiss had been a casual one, he had joined in the talk and when she had peeped at him, the frown had gone; he looked relieved…so it had been something to do with Madeleine, and whatever it was had been settled. Britannia, viewing herself in the green dress in the cheval mirror between the windows, decided that she didn't look at all bad; it was wonderful what relief did to one's face. She went carefully downstairs, with due regard to the ankle, and spent a pleasant evening. Mevrouw Luitingh van Thien had brought her friend back with her and after dinner the four of them played bridge—not a very serious rubber, which was a good thing, because Britannia was a more than indifferent player.

When she got down to breakfast the next morning it was to find Jake already gone. 'The professor was called out in the night, miss,' Marinus informed her, 'a nasty accident on the motorway. He came home to change and shower and eat his breakfast and was gone again by half past seven. A busy day ahead of him, I understand, miss.'

She agreed and thanked him, adding: 'Marinus, you speak such very good English—have you lived in England?'

He coughed in a gratified way. 'My family lived in Arnhem, miss. I had a good deal to do with the British soldiers at one time.'

'Underground?' asked Britannia, very interested.

'You might say so, miss. Everyone in these parts was more or less involved. I came here as a young man and the professor's father saw to it that I had English lessons; he found it a waste that I should have picked up so much of the language, and not always as correct as it should be.'

'Oh, Marinus, how nice—and isn't it fortunate for me and anyone else here who can't speak Dutch?'

'It has had its uses, miss. Can I fetch you some fresh coffee?'

'No, thanks. The professor suggested that I went to the library and had a good look at the books. I think I'll do that. Mevrouw Luitingh van Thien will be out, won't she?'

'Yes, miss. I will serve your coffee in the library presently, and I think that lunch in the little sitting room might be more comfortable for you.'

Britannia got up and went to the door. She wasn't using her stick any more now; her ankle was just about cured. 'Thank you, Marinus, that does sound nice.' She smiled at him as she went out and he beamed back. She was a nice young lady, he thought, and would make a good mistress to work for.

Britannia spent a pleasant morning; she had never seen so many books outside a public library before, not only rare first editions but a comprehensive collection of all the most readable books, and a reference section which had her absorbed until Marinus, coming quiet-footed to remove the coffee tray, told her that her lunch was about to be set on the table.

She had intended to go back to the library after the meal, but the sitting room was cosy and an armchair and a book by the fire was very appealing; she fetched an old crimson-bound volume of *Punch* and settled down happily for the afternoon. The house was quiet and already the winter dusk was creeping into the room. She switched on a reading lamp and opened the book. Perhaps Jake would be home in time for tea; he had had a long day, if he wasn't too tired she would ask him about the future. She hadn't done it yesterday; some-how there hadn't been the chance.

The doorbell rang almost before she had turned the first page and she looked up, wondering who it could be; Mevrouw Luitingh van Thien was still out and didn't intend to return until the early evening. If it was a visitor it would be awkward, for her few words of Dutch would prove quite inadequate when it came to conversation. Perhaps whoever it was would speak English or even go away.

She turned to look over her shoulder as the door

opened and Marinus came in, but before he could speak Madeleine had swept past him and shut the door in his face.

Britannia felt a quiver of rage which changed to amazement; this wasn't the Madeleine she knew, despite the tempestuous entry; this was a subdued, rather untidy girl who hadn't bothered much with her face or hair either. She stared at her, quite startled, hardly recognising her, and got out of her chair. 'You're ill!' she exclaimed.

Madeleine shook her head. 'No, I'm all right. I've been worried—I am worried now, for I have been trying to make up my mind to come and talk to you, but I think that you may not believe me, and why should you?' She shrugged her shoulders in a resigned way. 'Even now I do not think that it will be of any use, but I must try…'

'It's about Jake.' Britannia felt cold as she said it.

Madeleine nodded. 'Yes—you see, I wish to be honest with you—it's about Jake.'

'And this—whatever it is you want to tell me—is it important to you, or to him? And I'm not sure I want to hear it. And why can't you wait until he is here and tell him too?'

'He already knows.'

They were facing each other across the charming room. 'You want to make trouble,' declared Britannia, not mincing matters.

Madeleine came a step nearer. 'I don't like you, Britannia, why should I? But it is necessary that we talk; I do not wish to make trouble, but if I do not speak now, then there may be much unhappiness later on.'

Britannia was puzzled; Madeleine sounded sincere and she looked white and strained. Perhaps she had misjudged her after all. 'I'm listening,' she said steadily.

Madeleine didn't sit down. 'You must know that I expected to marry Jake, and I own that it was a shock when I heard that it was you whom he had chosen... You see, we have known each other for years.' She looked away for a moment. 'But there's more to it than that; are you quite sure that he wants to marry you? I mean, does he love you—a lasting love one needs for marriage?'

She looked briefly at Britannia, her face solemn. 'You are pretty and you amuse him because you speak your mind to him and he finds that diverting, but perhaps in a little while he will not be diverted any more, only irritated. You see, there is a gulf between you, Britannia. You do not come from his circle of friends. He met you in an unusual manner, did he not, so you are—how do you say?—attractive to him, but if that wears thin, what is there left? You do not know how to run a large house such as this one, nor how to entertain guests as he would want them entertained; you do not dress very well, you do not even speak his language. Even if he thinks that he loves you now, will there not come a day when these things will prove a barrier between you? Can you honestly tell me that this will not happen?'

Britannia got up and walked over to a window and looked out. The grey day outside reflected her feelings.

'I don't think that one can be certain of anything,' she said, and forced her voice to sound reasonable. Madeleine had touched unerringly on her own doubts, but she wasn't going to let her see that. And she hadn't said anything she hadn't herself already thought of.

Madeleine went on: 'I expect you thought that it was I who wanted to marry Jake, and that he has never loved me, but I can prove that he does—that his love for you isn't love at all, only infatuation, that he is already regretting...'

Britannia didn't look round, so that she didn't see Madeleine's quick glance, calculating and sly as she opened her bag and took out an envelope and crossed the room to give it to her. It was addressed to Madeleine in the professor's writing and it had been opened, and the letter she pulled out was in his writing too; Britannia would have recognised that atrocious scrawl anywhere.

'It's in Dutch,' said Madeleine, 'but I'll translate it and it will explain everything to you.' She held out the letter to Britannia with a sudden gesture which Britannia quite misinterpreted, and she saw the first words: '*Mijn lieveling...*' She couldn't see any more, because of the way the letter was folded, but she knew that it meant 'my darling', just as she knew that unlike the English word, the Dutch used it only as a term of real endearment between two people. And as though Madeleine had read her thoughts, she said quietly: 'You must know that we don't use the word *lieveling* in the social sense as the English do—it means much more to us than that.' She unfolded the letter and came a little nearer to show Jake's name at the end of the page, and Britannia, looking at it, thought dully that there must be a mistake. She drew a breath and said: 'I don't think I want to hear it, thank you.'

'But you must,' insisted Madeleine, 'otherwise you will never believe me. Why should you when you know that Jake and I...' She shot another look at Britannia, who had gone back to her chair, sitting there with her hands folded so quietly in her lap. 'I owe it to us all to be honest, and I am trying to be that.' She sounded very sincere.

She opened the letter and went to the window to read it. 'It begins: "My darling..."'

'No,' said Britannia sharply, but Madeleine took no notice. '"We see so little of each other and there is so much that I want to tell you—to explain how I could have imagined myself in love—but only a little—with someone else when you were there, waiting for me, for you knew it sooner than I. I intend to see her and tell her that it is you I will marry, and I think that she will understand, for her feeling for me cannot be deep. Perhaps you are wondering why I have not told you this instead of writing it, but somehow the time and place have never been right." It ends: "All my love, Jake."'

'When did you get this letter?' asked Britannia in a dry little voice.

'Marinus brought it round this morning.' Madeleine walked deliberately to the bell rope by the fireplace. 'I'll ring for Marinus to come here—you will believe him.' Her voice was so bitter that Britannia said at once:

'There's no need for that. I've seen the letter, haven't

I?' She stirred in her chair. 'Jake went to see you yesterday, didn't he?'

'Yes, and I had to see you first...'

Britannia glanced at the clock. Jake would be home soon and she wondered what he was going to say. Madeleine said quietly: 'Men like new faces even though they still love the old.' She was putting on her coat, ready to go, and Britannia got to her feet and said in a polite voice:

'Thank you for coming. I'm—I'm sure you have done what you think is right and at least I know what to do...' She drew a breath to steady her voice. 'I'm sure you'll be very happy together,' and then: 'I didn't know that you loved each other.'

Madeleine didn't answer her as she went.

The professor came into his house half an hour later, during which time Britannia had tried to sort out her thoughts and had failed lamentably. There was so much truth in what Madeleine had told her and she had sounded sincere; moreover, she had looked upset, not sure of herself, and the letter had been genuine...

So it was that when Jake entered the room she voiced her thoughts without allowing common sense to control them. 'You went to see Madeleine yesterday.'

He paused on his way across the room and gave her a long look. 'I did.' The smile on his lips had gone and his mouth had taken on a rather grim look. Britannia saw it and plunged still further.

'She told me you had—and it was in the letter, and although I believed her I thought there might be a mistake—that I hadn't understood...'

'Nor have I understood, Britannia. I take it that Madeleine has been here?' He frowned. 'And you speak of a letter?' His eyes had narrowed and Britannia said quickly before she lost her courage:

'The letter you wrote to her, of course. She showed it to me—well, the beginning and end with your name. I didn't want to see any more of it, I didn't want to hear it either, but she insisted on translating it, otherwise she said I wouldn't have believed her.'

'But you did believe her, my dear Britannia,' he observed blandly, 'without giving me the benefit of the doubt, too.' There was a nasty curl to his lip.

'Oh, dear,' cried Britannia in an exasperated voice, 'now you're in a fine temper...'

'Not yet, but I believe I shall be very shortly,' he agreed silkily. 'I thought that you trusted me, Britannia.'

She looked at him helplessly, aware that she had started all wrong and it was going to be difficult to put it right—indeed, she had the strongest suspicion that he wasn't going to listen to anything she said. 'Shall we talk about it later?' she asked quietly. 'It was my fault, jumping on you like that.'

'We will talk about it now.' He had become all at once arrogant as well as angry, and it was all so much worse because he was so coldly polite. 'If I am to be accused of—what shall we call it? Double dealing? Philandering?—then I would prefer to settle the matter now and not, as you had no doubt hoped, after I had been softened with a whisky and a good dinner.'

Britannia stamped her good foot, careless of what

she said now. 'You're impossible!' she told him bitterly. 'You won't listen—you don't want to. There must be some explanation, only you won't give it, only snarl at me. And you are bad-tempered and arrogant and now you won't listen…'

'Not listen?' his voice was all silk again. 'My dear girl, what else am I doing but listening, most unwillingly, to your tirade?'

'Oh, it's not—it's not, and I expected you to tell me,' she went on desperately.

He lifted his brows. 'I have no intention of telling you anything.' He smiled mockingly. 'Madeleine seems to have done that for me.' He added: 'And you believed her.'

Britannia regarded him with hopeless eyes. 'It's Madeleine you love and want to marry—she said so. I wouldn't have believed it, only there was the letter.'

'Ah, yes, this letter. And you imagined that I would—what is the old-fashioned term—trifle with your affections and then drop you when it suited me?'

'That's only one way of looking at it,' she pointed out fiercely.

'The only way, Britannia.' He wandered over to the fireplace and kicked a log into flames. 'And if that is how you feel about it, there is nothing more to be said.'

Britannia's insides went cold. 'Jake, please don't let's quarrel…'

He turned to look at her over his shoulder. 'I never quarrel, I say what I have to say and that is all.'

'It's not, you know,' cried Britannia in a high voice. 'You haven't said anything, only made nasty remarks.'

Her voice quavered for a moment, 'I thought we were honest with each other...'

His face was bland and expressionless. 'What would be the point of being honest with you, my dear girl? You have condemned me unheard and that, in my judgement at least, makes honesty between us quite pointless.' He added, 'I'm not sure what I should have explained to you, but nothing, and I mean nothing, would force me to do so now, even if I knew what it was.'

'But Jake, you do know.'

'Perhaps I can guess.' His smile mocked her again. 'But anything I had intended to tell you when I came into this room is quite purposeless now.'

Chapter 9

'I think I should go home,' said Britannia slowly.

'Of course you will go home.' The professor was in a towering rage, his eyes like blue ice, the nostrils of his magnificent nose flaring with his temper. 'I shall drive you there myself.' He glanced at his watch. 'We should be able to catch the night ferry from the Hoek. I imagine that half an hour is time enough in which to pack.'

Britannia goggled at him. 'Half an hour? The night ferry? Jake, you're in a most shocking rage and you don't know what you're saying.'

'Indeed I am in a rage, but I am quite aware of what I am saying. We should arrive at your home during to-morrow afternoon.'

'You're not coming with me.' She spoke defiantly.

'Yes, I am.' He glared quite ferociously at her. 'You wish to leave my house as soon as possible; the least I can do is to speed you on your way and make sure that you arrive home.'

She swallowed the great lump in her throat. 'Jake, please—you must try and understand. I can't hurt Madeleine—I hate her, you know that, and that's all the more reason…'

'I understand very well. I also understand that you have no compunction in hurting me.' His sneering voice made her shudder.

She was almost in tears now, but it would never do to cry. She said in a calm little voice which shook just a little, 'Jake, could we talk about it? You haven't given me a chance…and you haven't told me…'

His cold voice cut through her muddle. 'Why should I tell you anything? You already know.'

It was hopeless; he was angry because she had discovered that he really loved Madeleine before he had found a way to tell her himself. 'You'll forget me,' she told him miserably.

His smile was nasty. 'I have no intention of discussing the matter with you, Britannia. Like all women you have rushed into a situation without stopping to think.'

'I have thought!' snapped Britannia, stung by the memory of the last few hours. 'I've thought so much that I don't know my own mind any more.'

'So I perceive.' His voice was all silk. 'And now if you care to go and pack and say goodbye to my mother…?'

He held the door open and there was nothing else for her to do but to go through it.

A little over half an hour later, sitting beside the professor as he sent the Rolls racing down the motorway which would take them to the Hoek, Britannia reflected that it was like being in a nightmare where one wishes desperately to do something and is prevented by other people and circumstances. She had packed in a daze and then gone to wish Mevrouw Luitingh van Thien goodbye, and because there had been no time to explain, she had stated baldly that she wasn't going to marry Jake after all and that he was taking her home there and then.

His mother had said very little. 'A misunderstanding,' she had observed severely, 'and of course Jake is in one of his rages and won't allow anyone to say a word. I'm sorry, my dear—you were, still are, the right wife for him.'

Britannia let that pass even though she agreed with every word. 'He insists upon taking me all the way to Moreton,' she said helplessly.

'And quite right too. I hope you will have a good journey, Britannia.' She had offered a cheek and then added: 'It is Madeleine, of course.'

'Yes,' said Britannia, 'it is. Jake will forget me.'

'A pity that there is no time to tell me the whole. Jake has, of course, said nothing.'

Britannia had walked to the door and with her hand on the handle, had said miserably: 'He loves her,' and then gone out to where Jake waited for her.

The professor might be in a rage, but he had it under

control now; his flow of light conversation would have done credit to a seasoned diplomat making the best of a bad situation. Throughout the journey he was never at a loss for a topic; not that Britannia had much idea of what he was saying. Once she tried to stop him, but her desperate: 'Jake, please could we…?' was ignored as he went into a detailed account of the rulers of Holland. Britannia, bogged down in a succession of Willems and the Spanish Occupation, said 'Oh, really?' and 'Indeed,' every now and then while she tried to sort out her thoughts. But they were still only as far as Koningin Emma when they reached the Hoek and began the business of getting on board. Presumably the professor had found the time to telephone for tickets, for there was no delay in getting the car on board and after a polite goodnight, Britannia was led away to a comfortable cabin and presently a stewardess appeared with a tray of coffee and sandwiches, and the information that tea and toast would be brought in the morning.

Britannia drank all the coffee and nibbled at a sandwich and then, because there seemed nothing else to do, undressed and got into the narrow little bed. It was going to be a rough crossing judging by the way the boat was lurching out into the North Sea; not that that mattered. As far as she was concerned, it could sink with all hands and her with it for all she cared. But although she lay awake, she was quite unable to think sensibly. The arrival of her morning tea was a relief and she drank it thankfully, got up and dressed, made up her white face very carefully and then, uncertain as to what to do next, sat down on the stool by the bed and waited in a kind of daze, not thinking at all for by now she was too tired.

When a voice over the intercom told everyone to rejoin their car she picked up her bag and opened the door. The professor was outside, leaning against the wall. He gave her an icily courteous good morning, told her to follow him, took her bag and strode off. In the car presently, waiting to disembark, there was too much noise to talk, and presently going through the routine of landing there was no need to say more than a word or two, but once on the road to London the professor broke his silence.

'Rather a rough crossing,' he remarked pleasantly. 'I hope you weren't too disturbed?'

All she could think of to say was: 'Not at all, thank you,' but the baldness of this reply didn't deter him from keeping up a steady flow of small talk. It lasted right through Colchester and down the A12 and around the northern perimeter of London until they eventually joined the M3 at the Chertsey roundabout. Jake turned off again almost at once, remarking that she would probably like a cup of coffee, and drove the few miles to Chobham where he drew up before the Four Seasons restaurant and invited her to get out. Britannia shivered as she did so, for it was a chilly morning and she was tired and empty, but the coffee put new heart into her and she got into the car feeling more able to cope with the situation, until it struck her forcibly that very shortly she would be home now and her parents would expect some explanation. It was only too likely that they would dash forward with cries of welcome for their supposedly future son-in-law. Just as though he had read her mind, Jake said silkily: 'Have you got your speech ready? Do say anything you wish—don't mind me.' He added: 'I have broad shoulders.'

She blinked back tears, stupidly wanting to weep her eyes red because he had broad shoulders and large, clever hands and a handsome face, and very soon now she wouldn't see them again. She mumbled: 'I don't know what I'm going to say,' and cried pettishly: 'Oh, can't you see? I'm not doing or saying any of the things I want to…words are being put in my mouth. I'm forced to come home, there's so much I want to say and you haven't the patience to listen—what am I to do?'

'My dear girl, surely I am the last person to ask?'

She kept quiet after that while the Rolls swallowed the miles in its well-bred way until he turned off at Ringwood, went through the little town and travelled on to Ibsley where they lunched at The Old Beams. It was a well-known restaurant and the food was delicious, but Britannia ate what was put before her without noticing what it was, making a great effort to match her companion's relaxed manner and failing, did she but know it, miserably. They didn't linger over the meal, but drove on, back on to the A31, through Wimborne Minster and Bere Regis, to turn off on to a side road and then turn off again to Moreton. An early dusk was falling by now, and as they approached the cottage, Britannia could see that there were lights already shining cosily from its windows. 'It's here,' she said, and bade an unspoken goodbye to the Rolls as he opened her door and she got out.

Her mother answered the door and after a surprised moment cried: 'Darling—how lovely, and you've brought Jake with you...' She stopped there because she had seen Britannia's face, white and rigid, certainly not the look of a happy girl. 'Come in, both of you,' she continued, 'you must be cold.' She peered over the professor's broad shoulders and saw the Rolls. 'Well, probably not, in that car, but I'm sure you could do with a cup of tea.'

She submitted to Britannia's hug and held out her hand to Jake. 'I'm so glad to meet you,' she told him. 'Come and meet my husband.'

They were all in the sitting room, with Britannia taking off her coat while the two men shook hands and her father, rightly interpreting her mother's look, forbore from making any of the remarks fathers usually make on such occasions. Instead he asked about their journey, remarked upon the weather, begged his visitor to remove his coat and then embraced his daughter with a cheerful: 'How nice to have you home, Britannia—for Christmas, I hope?'

He didn't wait for her answer; even his loving but not very discerning eye could see that she was holding back tears, so he invited the professor to sit down and engaged him in conversation while tea was brought in and sandwiches eaten, and the professor, at his most charming, didn't look at Britannia at all but said presently: 'This has been delightful, but I must start back. I intend to catch the night boat.'

Britannia looked at the clock on the mantelpiece. 'It's almost five o'clock, you'll never do it in the time.'

He smiled at her quite nicely. 'What a pity that we can't bet on that,' he told her. 'As it is, I'm afraid you'll have to guess whether I do or not.'

He made his farewells quickly, including Britannia in them without actually speaking to her, and to her thanks for bringing her home he murmured: 'As I have already told you, Britannia, it was the least I could do.'

He didn't wish her goodbye, only smiled a little thinly at her. Her mother and father saw him to the door, but she stayed where she was, not moving until she heard the last murmur of the Rolls' engine die away.

Mr and Mrs Smith came back into the room together and Britannia said at once in a high voice: 'You must be wondering... I told you that I'd found the man I wanted to marry, didn't I, and it seemed as though I would; everything went right for me—well, most of the time. I—I thought he loved me even though there was this other girl.' She looked at her mother. '*Vogue* and *Harpers* and utterly beautiful—you know what I mean.' She lapsed into silence and her parents waited patiently, not saying a word. 'She was furious, of course, and she hated me—still does. We didn't see much of each other, and then the day before yesterday she came to Jake's house and showed me a letter from him; not all of it, but enough to make me see...'

'In Dutch or English?' asked her father quietly.

'Oh, Dutch, because it was to her, of course, but she translated it for me...'

'You are sure it was to her?'

Britannia nodded. 'It began "*Lieveling*", that's darling, and it was his writing and his name at the bottom, and the envelope was addressed to her. She offered to show me the whole letter, but she was so quiet and sad and she couldn't have invented all of it. She told me she hated me, but she thought that if I married Jake and he still loved her, I would be miserable if I found out, and he would be wretched as soon as he had recovered from his infatuation, tied to me and loving her...'

'He brought you home,' observed her mother softly.

'He's the kind of man who does his duty,' said Britannia bitterly.

Her mother asked: 'And did Jake mind very much when you told him you weren't going to marry him?'

'He wouldn't even discuss it, he—he was furiously angry; he has a very nasty temper.'

Her mother nodded. 'But I don't quite see why he should have been so angry. After all, if he loved this girl all the time and was only passing the time of day with you, he should have been glad that you had found out about it—it saved him having to tell you, didn't it?'

Britannia sniffed. 'He likes to do things his way—I expect he'd got it all planned how he wanted it. It's over now, anyway.' She began to collect the tea things on to the tray. 'May I use the telephone? I thought I'd ring the hospital and start straight away—I've ten days to work still, then if I may I'll come home for Christmas and find another job.'

'Of course, dear. Your father will help me with the washing-up; you telephone now and get it fixed up.' Her mother picked up the tray. 'Your ankle will stand up to it?'

'Well, I think so, I thought I'd ask if I could work somewhere where there's not such a rush.'

'Geriatrics,' she was told by the Senior Nursing Officer. The ward Sister there had gone off sick and Britannia's return was providential, and could she report for duty as soon as possible?

A day or two at home would have been nice; on the other hand, if she went back on the next day and saved her days off, she would be finished before Christmas; she agreed to report for duty the following afternoon, and went to tell her mother, and that astute woman said not another word about Jake but for the rest of the evening discussed plans for Christmas and sent Britannia early to bed. 'Father will drive you up,' she said comfortably. 'You can leave after breakfast and that will give you plenty of time.'

So Britannia retired to her room and unpacked and repacked a smaller case and went to bed, to lie awake and think of Jake and then force her thoughts to the future.

The geriatric wards of St Jude's weren't in the main hospital but five minutes' walk away, down a narrow street made gloomy by the blank walls of warehouses. There wasn't a tree in sight nor yet a blade of grass, and the annexe itself was an old workhouse, red brick and elaborate at that on the outside and a labyrinth of narrow passages, stone staircases and long wards into which the sun never seemed to shine. And yet the best had been made of a bad job; the walls were distempered in pastel colours, the counterpanes were gay patchwork, there were flowers here and there and sensible easy chairs grouped together round little tables so that those who were able could sit and gossip. To most of them, the place had been home for many months and probably would be for the rest of their lives, and Britannia, eyeing the female wards which were to be her especial care, supposed that it was probably a better home than the solitary bedsitter so many of them occupied. True, they hadn't their independence any more, and most of them set great store by that, but they had regular food, warmth, company and a little money each week which they could spend when the shop lady came round with her trolley, and some of them, though regrettably few, had families who came to see them.

Britannia took the report from the agency nurse who had been called in to plug the gap and settled down at her desk to read the patients' notes before she did a round. She had been a little surprised when she arrived at the hospital at lunch time to be asked if she would go on duty immediately, but she hadn't minded. Having something to do would get through the days and if she had enough work she would be tired enough to sleep. She had been given her old room in the nurses' home; she didn't bother to unpack but got straight into uniform, donned her cloak against the cold, and hurried along the miserable little street to the annexe. Sitting at the desk, it seemed to her that she had never been away from the hospital and yet so much had been crowded into those few weeks, and the whole telescoped into the quick journey home again. She thanked heaven silently for understanding parents; a pity she wouldn't be going home for her days off, but if she saved them up she would be able to leave two days sooner. Eight days, she told herself with false cheerfulness, and buried her pretty head in the pile of notes before her.

She went to see Joan when she got off duty that evening; a very excited Joan, her head full of plans for her wedding, but she paused presently to ask: 'Why Geriatrics, ducky? Isn't the ankle up to the rush and scurry of Men's Surgical? And I had a letter from Mevrouw Veske saying that you would have some wonderful news for me.' She paused to look at Britannia's face. 'But I can see that she's wrong. Do you want to talk about it?'

'No, not now, Joan. I'm only on Geriatrics for a week, then I'm leaving.'

'You're not getting…no, of course not. It's that professor, isn't it?'

'Yes. Now tell me more about your wedding…'

The geriatric wards might have been easy on her ankle, but their occupants made heavy demands on Britannia. They had taken to her at once and most of them saw in her a kind of daughter, there to fulfil their many and several wants; she was also Staff, someone who gave them their pills, saw that they had their treatments and got up in the morning and went to bed in the evening, ate their meals, and twice a day did a round of the wards, stopping to talk to each of them. The nursing was undemanding but heavy and Britannia had a staff of part-time nurses and auxiliaries, but still it was tiring and she was thankful for that; it meant that she slept for a good deal of the night. All the same, the first two days dragged even though she filled her off-duty with Christmas shopping, willing herself not to think of Jake at all. It didn't work, of course. She thought of him all the time—he was there beside her, behind every door she opened, round every corner, beneath her eyelids when she closed them at night.

On the third morning she went on duty with a headache and the nasty empty feeling induced by too little sleep and too many meals missed, and when she had taken the night nurse's report the Senior Nursing Officer telephoned to say that the part-time staff nurse who was to do the evening duty wouldn't be able to come in, and would Britannia mind very much filling in for her. 'You can save it up and leave half a day sooner,' said the voice cheerfully, 'and you should manage an hour's quiet this afternoon during visiting.'

Britannia thought that very unlikely; visitors liked to talk to Sister, the patients who hadn't anyone to see them tended to make little demands of her because they felt lonely and left out... She said she didn't mind and heard the Senior Nursing Officer's relieved sigh as she put down the receiver.

She realised as soon as she went into the first ward that the day had begun badly; for one thing, it was a grey, cold morning, and despite the gay counterpanes and bright walls, the grey had filtered in, making the patients morose and unwilling to stir from their nice warm beds. Britannia set about the patient task of cheering them up, an exercise which took a great deal of the morning. Luckily it was the consultant's weekly round, one of the highlights in the old ladies' week, and they had brightened up considerably by the time Doctor Payne and his houseman arrived. He was a good doctor, nearing retirement; Britannia had had her medical lectures from him when she was in training and he had always been pleasant to the nurses, even when those on night duty had fallen asleep under his very nose, or the brighter ones had asked obvious questions in order to show off. He remembered her at once and observed forthrightly: 'Staff Nurse Smith—I thought you were a surgical girl. Been ill? You look under the weather.'

'I'm fine, Doctor Payne, a bit tired, that's all. I'm filling in a few days before I leave.'

'Getting married?' he wanted to know. 'All the pretty girls get married just as they're getting useful. Who's the lucky man?'

'There isn't one. I—I just wanted a change of scene.'

Doctor Payne shot her a look, said 'Um,' and then: 'Well, well,' and coughed. 'And how are my old ladies?'

She gave him a brief report and they started off. The round took some time, for although most of the patients had nothing dramatic wrong with them they had a variety of tiresome complaints and aches and pains, all of which had to be discussed and if necessary treated. It was time to serve dinners when Doctor Payne had at last finished and after that there were the old ladies to settle for their afternoon rest and then the medicines to give out. Britannia went to her own dinner rather late and ate tepid beef and potatoes and carrots and remembered all the delicious food she had eaten in Jake's house, so that she rejected the milk pudding offered her and went with the other staff nurses at her table to drink the cup of tea they always managed to squeeze into their dinner break, however short. The talk was all of Christmas, so that she was able to parry the few questions she was asked about her trip to Holland and trail the red herring of Joan's approaching wedding across her listeners' path. They broke up presently to go back on duty and Britannia made her solitary way back to the annexe.

Her superior's hopeful suggestion that she should take an hour off during visiting hour came to nothing, of course; there were fewer visitors than usual, which meant that the old ladies made a continuous demand on her and the nurses on duty. It didn't seem worth going back to the hospital for tea; she had a tray in her office before getting on with the evening's work, and when it was time to go to supper, she decided not to go to that either; she wasn't hungry and she could make herself some toast later. The wards were quiet now, with all the patients back in bed, most of them already dozing lightly. Britannia sent her two nurses to supper, finished her report and then went softly round the wards, saying a quiet goodnight to each old lady. It was at the bottom of the second ward, when she was almost through, that she found Mrs Thorn out of bed.

'Now don't you be vexed,' said Mrs Thorn in a cheerful whisper. 'I just took a fancy to sit out for a bit longer and I got that nice little nurse to put me back in the chair for half an hour, and don't go blaming her, because I told her you'd said that I could.' She laughed gently. 'I'll go back now you're here.'

Britannia hid a smile. Mrs Thorn was the oldest inhabitant in the Geriatric Unit and was consequently a little spoilt. She said without meaning it: 'You're a naughty old thing, aren't you? But doing something different is fun sometimes, isn't it?'

Mrs Thorn was small and fragile and very old, with birdlike bones knotted and twisted by arthritis. Britannia lifted her out of the chair and popped her gently into her bed. It took a little time to get the old lady's dressing gown off, for Mrs Thorn liked things done just so and she enjoyed a chat too. Britannia was tucking in the patchwork quilt when she became aware that someone was walking down the ward, to stop at the foot of the bed. Jake, elegant and calm and self-assured as always. Mrs Thorn, with the childlike outspokenness of the old, broke a silence which for Britannia seemed to go on for ever and ever.

'And who are you?' she demanded in a piping voice. 'A handsome, well-set-up man like you shouldn't be here. You should be out with some pretty girl, or better still by your own fireside with a wife and children to share it.' She smiled suddenly and caught at Britannia's hand. 'Perhaps you've come to fetch our dear Staff Nurse away? She's a lovely young thing and she shouldn't be here—we're all so old...'

The professor was looking at her gravely, without even glancing at Britannia.

'I hope that when Britannia here is your age, my dear, she will be as charming as you, and yes, I have come to fetch her; she's my girl, you see, and although I haven't a wife and children I hope she will soon fill that gap for me.'

He spoke loudly so that several of the old ladies in nearby beds popped up from beneath their blankets, nodding and smiling their approval.

'Oh, hush,' begged Britannia, quite forgetting unhappiness and misery and tiredness in the delight of seeing him again. 'Everyone is listening.'

He looked at her then, his eyes very blue and bright. 'And I am glad of it, my darling. The more who hear me say that I love you, the better. Perhaps if I repeat it a sufficient number of times and in a loud enough voice before as many people as possible, you will bring yourself to believe that I mean it.'

Britannia still held Mrs Thorn's bony little claw in her own capable hand. 'Oh, Jake...but you must explain—Madeleine told me...'

The professor sat himself down on the end of Mrs Thorn's bed and stretched his long legs before him as though he intended to stay a long time. 'Ah, yes.' His voice was still much too loud and clear. 'Well, dearest girl, if you will hold that delightful tongue of yours for ten minutes I will endeavour to do that.'

'Not here, you don't,' declared Britannia, aware that old eyes and ears were tuned in all round them, 'and not now. I'm on duty until eight o'clock and then I should go to supper—I haven't been yet.'

She trembled as she said it in case he walked away in a temper because he wasn't getting his own way, but she wasn't going to give way easily. There was still Madeleine's shadow between them; she would have to be explained.

The professor spoke with such extreme mildness that

she cast him a suspicious look which he met with such tenderness that she had to look quickly away again in case she weakened.

'I've had no supper myself, perhaps we might have it together.'

Britannia tucked Mrs Thorn in carefully. 'Have you been here long?' she asked. A silly question really, but she had to say something ordinary; her head might be in the clouds, but she had to keep her feet on the ground.

'I landed at Dover three hours ago.'

She retied the ribbon at the end of Mrs Thorn's wispy pigtail.

'Oh?...'

'I knew you were here,' he supplied smoothly, 'because I telephoned your mother and asked before I left home.' He got up off the bed. 'How long will you be, Britannia?'

'Another ten minutes. But I have to go back to the Home and change...'

'I'll be outside.' He wished Mrs Thorn and the other eagerly listening ladies a good night and went away. Britannia, watching him go, wondered as she saw the ward doors swing gently after him, if she had had a dream, an idea Mrs Thorn quickly scotched.

'Now that's what I call an 'andsome man, Staff Nurse. He'll make you a fine husband.'

Oh, he would, agreed Britannia silently, but only if he made it very clear about Madeleine. She forced her mind to good sense, wished Mrs Thorn a good night, visited the remaining patients, answering a spate of excited questions as she did so, and went to give the report to the night nurses.

They were already in the office and the night staff nurse hardly waited for her to reach for the Kardex before she exclaimed: 'I say, Britannia, there's a Rolls at the door and the most super man in it.' She stared hard at Britannia as she said it; she had heard rumours in the hospital. 'Is he the boyfriend?'

Britannia said deliberately: 'Mrs Tweedy, bed one... He's the man I'm going to marry.' She hadn't really meant to say that, but as she did she knew without a doubt that was just what she intended doing, even if she never got to the bottom of the riddle of Madeleine. Before anyone could say a word, she went on: 'A good day, Mist.Mag.Tri. given TDS. She's to have physiotherapy by order of Doctor Payne. Mrs Scott, bed two...'

The report didn't take very long. She handed over the keys, wished the nurses goodnight and went down to the entrance, her cloak over her arm, the bits and pieces she had found necessary to have with her during the day in a tote bag. She had quite forgotten to do anything to her face or her hair, but it didn't matter. She was so happy that a shiny nose and hair all anyhow went unnoticed.

The professor was in the hall, a bleak dark brown place no one had had sufficient money to modernise. It had a centre light, a grim white glass globe which did nothing for the complexions for those beneath its cold rays. Britannia didn't notice it; she came to a halt before Jake and said a little shyly, 'I have to go to the main hospital and change.'

He took her bag from her and fastened the cloak carefully. 'No, there's no need. We'll go to Ned's Café, where we first met. I suspect, dear heart, that I have a romantic nature.'

'It'll be full...'

'No matter, the more people there the better. If necessary I shall go down on my knees.'

Britannia choked on a laugh. 'You can't—you simply can't...'

'I simply can.' He swooped suddenly and kissed her. 'That's better—let's go.'

The Rolls looked a little out of place parked outside Ned's place, and one or two people turned to stare at them as they went inside. There was an empty table in the middle of the room and the professor led the way to it, wishing those around him a courteous good evening as he went, and when Ned came over with a pleased: 'Well, I never, Staff—I 'aven't seen you for weeks, nor you neither, sir. What's it to be?' He ordered bacon sandwiches and toasted cheese and a pot of tea, and when Ned had gone again: 'You're pale, my darling, and there are shadows under your eyes...'

'Well, of course there are! I've been... Jake, you must explain.'

'Of course. Here is our tea.'

Ned lingered for a few minutes and Britannia's hand shook a little with impatience as she poured the strong brew. But Jake didn't seem impatient at all; indeed, he entered into quite a conversation about the hospital rugger team so that when Ned at last took himself off,

Britannia said quite fiercely: 'I want to know…and all you can do is talk about rugger!'

'My darling, I was a rugger player myself—besides, I have a soft spot for Ned. He is, as it were, our fairy godfather.'

The bacon sandwiches arrived then and a moment later the cheese and then Ned went away to serve a party of six who had just come in. The professor passed the sandwiches and only after Britannia had eaten almost a whole one did he say: 'Before I say anything, I want you to read this.' He took a folded letter from his pocket and handed it across the table to her.

She saw what it was immediately. 'But why should I? I mean, it was written to Madeleine.'

He gave her a quizzical look. 'Was it? My dear Britannia, all at sea, aren't you? Read it.'

She read it silently, pausing once to look at him. He was sitting back watching her with a tender smile. She finished it and then read it for a second time, more slowly.

'It was for me,' she whispered. 'She found it… Marinus didn't take it.'

'Yes, love.'

'But the envelope—she showed it to me…'

'And if you had looked carefully you would have seen that it was in Madeleine's own hand. You see, my darling, you expected to see my writing on the envelope, didn't you, and so you did.'

She folded the letter carefully and held it in her hand. 'What a fool,' she said, 'but you could have told me,' she began, and then: 'No, of course you wouldn't have done that—you thought that I didn't believe you.'

'I see that you have a tremendous insight into my failings, dearest, so useful in a wife.'

She poured more strong tea for them both and the professor asked quietly: 'Will you marry me, Britannia?'

She put her cup down. 'Oh, Jake, yes—you know I will!'

'I have a special licence with me, we can marry tomorrow at your home.'

For a moment Britannia had no words. The thought that there could be nothing nicer than to get up from the rickety little table and just go home without more ado and marry Jake in the morning lingered for a few seconds in her head before she said: 'But I can't, Jake. I've another four days—I should have to pack and...'

'You can if you want to. I've dealt with all that. I don't know how important the packing is—half an hour? Your mother said she would leave the door for us and something on the stove.'

'Mother? How does she know?'

'I telephoned yesterday to say that we would be coming. Your father was kind enough to advise me about the licence.'

'I thought it took days...'

'A day or so, yes. I telephoned him when I got back to Holland and found out about Madeleine.'

Britannia bit into a sandwich. 'How did you do that?' she wanted to know.

'I asked her what she had done. Will you mind very

much if we go straight back to Hoenderloo tomorrow, my darling? I have a list for the following day, but after that I'm free until after Christmas. We shall have the house to ourselves, Mama is going to Emma's and we are invited there for Christmas Day, so we shall have a day or so together, and at New Year, the whole family will come to us again, and I thought we might ask your mother and father as well...'

Britannia's eyes filled with tears. 'Oh, Jake, I'd love to go back to Hoenderloo—your mother doesn't mind?'

'She loves you, dearest, they all do.' He smiled at her. 'Are you going to cry? Do you want my handkerchief?'

She shook her head. 'I'm not crying, truly I'm not. Must I see anyone before I go?'

'Your Principal Nursing Officer said that she would be in her office until ten o'clock. What about your friends?'

'They'll be together in someone's room, having tea,' said Britannia. 'I can see them all at once and pack in ten minutes.'

'Then eat some of that cheese, my darling, and have another cup of this extremely strong tea and I'll take you back.'

The café had thinned of customers by now, the last of them had gone by the time Britannia had obediently gobbled down the toasted cheese. Ned came over with the bill and the professor paid with a handsome tip, and Ned, who was no fool, melted through the little door behind the counter and left them alone.

'Ready?' asked the professor, and came round to button her into her cape once more.

She looked up at him and smiled. 'We'll have to hurry.'

'You are quite right, my darling, as you so often are, but no one is going to hurry me for a moment.'

He put his arms round her and bent to kiss her, and no one, least of all Britannia, hurried him.

* * * * *

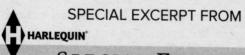
After the walk on the beach, she'd become overly polite
and distant. Knowing he wasn't going to sleep, Noah sat
up and tossed back the sheets. He found a pair of shorts
and slipped them on. Barefoot, he unlocked the screen
door and walked out into the night. He saw something
out of the corner of his eye and spied someone sitting on
the beach. A full moon lit up the night, and as he made
his way down to the water, he couldn't stop smiling.

She glanced up at him and smiled. "It looks as if I'm
not the only one who couldn't sleep."

Noah sank down next to her on the damp sand. Even in
the eerie light, he could discern that the sun had darkened
her skin to a deep mahogany. "I was never much of an
insomniac before meeting you."

Viviana pulled her legs up to her chest and wrapped her arms around her knees. "I'm not going to accept blame for that."

"Can you accept that I'm falling in love with you?"

Her head turned toward him slowly, and she looked as if she was going to jump up and run away. "Please don't say that, Noah."

"And why shouldn't I say it, Viviana?"

"Because you don't know what you're saying. You don't know me, and I certainly don't know you."

Don't miss
Dealmaker, Heartbreaker *by Rochelle Alers,*
available May 2019 wherever
Harlequin® Special Edition books and ebooks are sold.

www.Harlequin.com

HSEEXP0419R

Looking for more satisfying love stories
with community and family at their core?

Check out **Harlequin® Special Edition**
and **Love Inspired®** books!

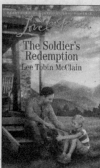

New books available every month!

CONNECT WITH US AT:

Facebook.com/groups/HarlequinConnection

 Facebook.com/HarlequinBooks

 Twitter.com/HarlequinBooks

 Instagram.com/HarlequinBooks

 Pinterest.com/HarlequinBooks

ReaderService.com

**ROMANCE WHEN
YOU NEED IT**

HFGENRE2018

Need an adrenaline rush from nail-biting tales
(and irresistible males)?

Check out **Harlequin Intrigue**®
and **Harlequin**® **Romantic Suspense** books!

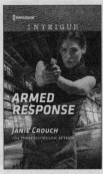 

New books available every month!

CONNECT WITH US AT:

Facebook.com/groups/HarlequinConnection

 Facebook.com/HarlequinBooks

 Twitter.com/HarlequinBooks

 Instagram.com/HarlequinBooks

 Pinterest.com/HarlequinBooks

ReaderService.com

**ROMANCE WHEN
YOU NEED IT**

SGENRE2018

Looking for inspiration in tales
of hope, faith and heartfelt romance?

Check out **Love Inspired**® and
Love Inspired® **Suspense** books!

New books available every month!

CONNECT WITH US AT:

Facebook.com/groups/HarlequinConnection

Facebook.com/HarlequinBooks

Twitter.com/HarlequinBooks

Instagram.com/HarlequinBooks

Pinterest.com/HarlequinBooks

ReaderService.com

Love Harlequin romance?

DISCOVER.

Be the first to find out about promotions,
news and exclusive content!

Facebook.com/HarlequinBooks

Twitter.com/HarlequinBooks

Instagram.com/HarlequinBooks

Pinterest.com/HarlequinBooks

ReaderService.com

EXPLORE.

Sign up for the Harlequin e-newsletter and
download a free book from any series at
TryHarlequin.com.

CONNECT.

Join our Harlequin community to share
your thoughts and connect with other
romance readers!
Facebook.com/groups/HarlequinConnection

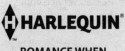